Journey of the Hidden

D. L. Crager

ISBN 978-1-0980-5702-2 (paperback)
ISBN 978-1-0980-5703-9 (hardcover)
ISBN 978-1-0980-5704-6 (digital)

Christian Faith Publishing, Inc.
832 Park Avenue
Meadville, PA 16335
www.christianfaithpublishing.com

Printed in the United States of America

CHAPTER 1

"Toca, wake up!" his father, Jucawa, yelled as he pulled up on the edge of the hammock, flipping him out onto the floor of the hut. While still asleep, Toca hit the ground hard. "Get ready for your ceremony! The chief will be waiting at the tribal hut for you when the sun rises over the mountaintops. Your mother is fixing your last meal before you finally leave us," Jucawa said with an eager smirk, looking down at him.

As he walked outside, Jucawa turned around, looking at the hut, saying, "Hurry and take your cleansing bath in the river. You're filthy and you stink!" Now scowling at Toca in disgust. "I'm going to talk with the chief." He continued down the path while putting on his prized black jaguar skin. The legs flapped with the long sharp claws draped over his shoulders, dangling the rest down his back, draping to the ground. He filled the empty skull mask of fur from the beast by pulling it down over his head so his eyes could bring it to life, peering through the hollow holes of the dead cat's eyes.

Toca's mother had just stepped into their home a few moments earlier from gathering fresh food from the forest as Jucawa was leaving. She heard him giving Toca orders as the boy rose up, rubbing the sore spots from his fall. With her warm comforting smile, she said with enthusiasm, "Good morning, son, today is your big day. Are you excited?"

He quickly responded with a frown, "I'm torn, Mother. I can't wait to leave Father's rule as I have dreamed of this moment for a long time. The other men don't treat their families the way he does. I am excited to go on my Katata but I'm more anxious to leave Jucawa!"

he stated while gritting his teeth, looking in the direction Jucawa walked. He turned back to his mother. "But I don't want to leave you alone, he hurts you too." His expression toward her was soft and compassionate. "I'm afraid when I leave, he will hurt you more and I will not be there to stop him. One of these days, I will disrespect him and protect you!" Toca insisted as he stood up as tall as he could, sticking his chest out to show his courage, although still shorter than his mother.

"Oh, my fearless Black Ghost, you are a wonderful son. But don't worry, Jucawa won't hurt me more than he has," Layana said, putting her arms around him. "You must go on your journey, and when you come back as a man, you will have fulfilled my heart's dreams more than you know." His mother stepped back and took ahold of his shoulders, saying with excitement, "You want to protect me"—pausing to make a statement—"not only complete the Katata but go and accomplish the Katata Ado! You come back with a shell from the faraway place." She hesitated again to make sure she had his attention, looking directly into his eyes. "You can change our lives and the lives of everyone in our tribe." Her eyes went back and forth, staring into Toca's, then continued, "Now go, do what your father told you for your time is coming."

He walked out of the hut toward the river, trying to fully understand what Mother was telling him, but his mind kept thinking about his father instead. He never understood why Jucawa was so mean to his mother and him. More times than he can count, Jucawa hurt them, not only with his words but also with his hands. It didn't bother Toca as much when he was mean to him, but when he would hurt his mother, he would get very angry and want to protect her. Since he was younger and smaller, there was nothing much Toca could do about it.

Jucawa was the man of the family, even though he wasn't Toca's real father. He was told his real father, Tundra, was killed by a rare black jaguar when he was born. Tundra and Jucawa were on their manhood journey together since they were the same age. Toca was given his shadow name Black Ghost, from Chief Acuta, out of respect and in memory of Tundra.

Layana and Tundra were in love as old children and, against tribal laws, secretly slept together before they accomplished their manhood and womanhood journeys, and she became pregnant with Toca just before Tundra and Jucawa left on their journey. Then hid it physically for four moons until it couldn't be hidden any longer.

When Jucawa returned before the thirteenth full moon rose, he told everyone the story of what happened to Tundra and the attack of the black jaguar. There was incredible sadness because everyone loved Tundra. He was a special old child gentle, kind, and helpful to everyone.

At the same time, there was great excitement because of the mighty journey Jucawa had survived while completing the full Katata Ado. He was the only old child in the tribe to complete this great journey since the present Chief Acuta did many, many sun seasons ago to become a man.

Layana was the next young adult female available to have a man, so Chief Acuta rewarded Jucawa with Layana and baby Toca. The new baby needed a father as much as Layana needed a new companion.

Besides being the man of the family, he was also the only one next in line in the tribe to be chief for accomplishing the Katata Ado. These two things gave him authority to do what he pleased with his family, even though everyone in the village quietly disapproved of how he was mistreating them.

Often times, Toca would overhear Chief Acuta speaking to him about being kinder to his family but Jucawa would ignore him. He gave the chief honor only when it benefited him in front of the tribe.

Jucawa's manhood journey gave him great respect from all the people because the jaguar that killed Tundra also attacked him at the same time. He was severely injured with four long slashing gouges on his leg and deep bite marks and scratches on his neck and shoulders. The scars are still easily seen today. Even though he was hurt, he was able to kill the fierce cat and fully complete the Ado despite his bad injures. It was a big victory, killing a rare black ghost, one of which no one in the tribe had ever done before. Surviving such an attack with terrible wounds and still finishing the Ado was a feat more honorable and respected than what any chief before him had ever done.

Even though Jucawa was immensely respected by the tribe, the respect was turning into fear as the sun seasons continued. He made everyone uneasy by continuously boosting about his triumph and always talking down to the people as if they were not worthy to be in his presence. He wanted everyone to know and believe that he was the greatest Nashua.

Chief Acuta frequently attempted to guide him on how to treat his family but tried even harder at teaching him what it takes to be a chief and how to lead a tribe. But again, Jucawa would not listen. There was a dark and prideful selfishness about him and it was staining the tribe while controlling the atmosphere.

Chief Acuta was the oldest in the tribe and it showed. He had long grayish-white hair loosely hanging down past his bony shoulders. His weathered face had many deep wrinkles, matching the dangling skin on the rest of his thin shrinking body. Both eyelids drooped over his worn-out hazy eyes which he could barely peek through. Most of his teeth had fallen out except for a few worn-out dark-stained nubs. When he talked, all you saw was a gaping black hole with his tongue doing its best to pronounce each word.

His waist wrap covered his manhood with two large weathered flaps of old, dried, scaled caiman skins going down to his knees. One in the front and one covering his backside. No other man in the tribe wore this. The edges of the flaps had the claws and teeth of the caiman sewn on it all the way around. It was not clearly known why he wore the bulky flaps except to give him a larger strong appearance while helping to hide his frail bony frame. Additionally it was the skin of the caiman that killed his wife many years ago.

Around his thin neck was displayed the cherished thin spiral-pointed shell the length of a man's finger attached to a necklace of sinew from his Katata Ado, dangling down to the middle of his bare chest. Colorful feathers were attached to the string as well by their roots, going all the way around and sticking out wide over his chest, shoulders, and back. Once again, giving him a larger and brighter appearance.

His original anklet that was put on him by his chief at his Katata ceremony was still tied to his ankle. The three small talisman carvings attached to it included the tribe's sun symbol, his father's shadow image, and his own shadow image of the monkey. His knife, which had his shadow image carved in the handle, was strapped to the inside of his forearm, the image barely noticeable from the many years of use.

His bare feet were wide with a thick layer of callus on the bottom, built up over the many long years.

Finally you never saw the chief without his walking stick. It was more than a walking stick. It was a long spear, twice his height, with a sharp pointed rock blade at the top. It was decorated with feathers where the rock was embedded and strapped to it. Down the long shaft were detailed designs of animals and plants carved and painted, except where the chief would hold onto it. This spot was smooth and darker than the rest of the stick because of the sweat and oils from his hands, over time, had built up and stained while the wood was worn down.

The spear was lightweight but very solid and was used for more than walking. Once in a while, he would throw it at a prey. Also it was a communication tool. When Chief Acuta wanted to get someone's attention, he would stomp the end of the stick down on the ground, making a thumping sound. Everyone knew this sound, and if anyone heard it three times in a row, they would immediately go to the chief. If he needed to get everyone's attention in the village and the surrounding area, he would hit it down on an old log and the sound would powerfully echo through the valley and the whole tribe would go to him.

He was always kind to his people, especially Toca. Throughout his childhood, they spent many days and nights together in the forest. He taught Toca everything about living and surviving away from the village. Everything Toca know about hunting, fishing, and shadowing, he owed to the chief. He would always tell Toca there are no limits to who he could be and what he could do. Always saying, "If you want to climb higher in the trees, do it. If you want to jump farther to other trees, like monkeys, do it. If you want to run as fast as the deer on the ground, do it. If you want to swim as fast as fish, do it."

The chief instructed Toca not to believe anyone if they said he couldn't do something but believe he could do anything he dreams. "Don't allow anyone or anything to keep you closed in like a turtle in its shell. Being afraid and hiding will never help you grow, it only helps you die." This was Chief Acuta's favorite saying to Toca.

Jucawa never lifted a finger to teach Toca anything, except how to do his work for him. Rarely did he do his manly responsibilities around the village but instead spent his time in everyone else's business, trying to influence them and telling them what to do. Toca even hunted for him which was fine because it meant time away from Jucawa and he loved hunting and was good at it.

*****

Earlier in the morning, the chief gave instructions to Toca about what was going to happen these special days in his young life. It was later in the evening and the village had just finished their sendoff celebration for Toca. Arriving at the tribal hut, he was wide-eyed and full of excitement and anticipation. Stepping inside, he saw Chief Acuta in the middle of the room, seated on one edge of the ceremony mat. Toca was waiting at the entrance for the chief's hand signal to come forward. It was only a few moments but felt like a day to Toca before the signal came. Trying not to run, he quickly got to the chief and respectfully greeted him, slowly bending over and softly touching their foreheads together. He stepped around items that were lying in the middle of the mat and sat down facing him on the other side.

Silence echoed through the room as Toca waited as patiently as he could, as an old child, for the chief to begin his Katata ceremony. Breaking through the thick air of expectation, Chief Acuta said slowly, with his quiet raspy voice, "Nashua is the name of our people which means 'new beginnings.' We get this name from our old ancestors that found the hidden valley we live in. They came from a faraway land to start a new life here, a new beginning. Every day since, the sun has given us a new beginning so our tribe's talisman is the shadow image of the sun. Under the sun, each one of us is given a shadow image and yours, old child, is 'Black Ghost.'"

Toca sat up straight, proud of his new name, and hung on to every word that was spoken. "Toca, you are here to begin what every man of the Nashua have done since the first chief was chosen to lead our people. Before he was made chief, as an old child like yourself, he had a special gift of knowledge regarding the ways of hunting, fishing, and surviving in the forest. He and a group of men and women were journeying from the faraway land in search of a safe place to live. On this journey, he taught them the secrets he had, saving their lives."

He continued, "Once they found this wonderful safe hidden valley, the old child, now thirteen sun seasons old, decided to go on another journey by himself. He wanted to be wise and understand everything about this new place they called home. Returning thirteen full moons later, one complete sun season, everyone thought he was dead for being gone so long. But he had journeyed in the direction where the sun rises, until he ran out of land, to a place what we chiefs now call 'the endless water.'"

Toca was enthralled as the chief went on. "When this old child came back, he no longer looked like a child or acted like a child. He had become strong because of the tough journey and was wiser beyond his years. Already having the people's respect for teaching them the secrets to live in the deep forest, now they had a mature young man with much experience to go with his knowledge. This is how the Katatas started and why we do them. They make you a man!" the chief stated proudly while sitting up high as best as he could.

Continuing on, "Not every old child is meant to be chief. Very, very few can accomplish the journey it takes, but every old child is meant to become a man. That is why there are two Katata journeys in front of you tonight, you must choose one.

"For both, you must leave the hidden valley, living on your own to grow and prove you can survive becoming a man. You have to be away for twelve moons, returning before the thirteenth full moon fully shines in the night sky. When you return your first night, you will enter this hut, leaving your anklet that I will be giving you during this ceremony on the mat. This will tell me you have returned and I will expect you the next night, shadowed, just as you will leave tonight, sitting right where you are now.

"On your return from one of these Katatas, I will grant you man status. This means you have earned the right to be mated with a female, to care for and have children. Also you will be able to hold important positions with our people, except for *chief.* The only way for you to ever become chief, you have to achieve the Katata Ado journey. This journey, you must travel far away and back from the endless water where all rivers flow, just as our first chief did. When you get there, you must find a shell in the endless water like this." He held up his that was hanging from his neck. "And bring it back. Then and only then will you be able to become chief when it's your time."

Pausing while motioning Toca to stand in front of him, he looked down at the items in the middle of the ceremony mat. "These are the only things you may take with you." Reaching down, the chief picked up one of them, Toca's first male member cover. Putting it on Toca's naked young body, he tied the heavy main strap of leather around his waist, then positioned the small pouch made from monkey skin, sewn to the main strap, fully covering his manhood parts. The final string, tied to the bottom of the pouch, went between his buttock cheeks and tied to the main strap at his waist in the back.

Finishing, he said, "From now on, your manhood member will be hidden from all to see when you come back as a man. Only your mate-to-be is allowed to see and have your maker of life."

Picking up the next item from the mat, Chief Acuta revealed an anklet that had three talisman carvings, made out of monkey teeth, and attached to it to one of Toca's ankles. "There are three talisman shadow images on your anklet." Pointing to the first one, he said, "This one is the shadow image of our tribe, the sun." It was small, round, and stained yellow. "This will remind you on your long hard journey that the sun will rise each day, giving you a new beginning. The next one is the shadow image of your father." He paused, knowing it would come as a surprise to Toca what talisman he carved. He looked up into Toca's eyes, wanting to make a new and different connection with him, and said, "I decided to carve the shadow image of me, the monkey."

Completely surprised, Toca's eyes and smile couldn't have gotten any larger.

"You lost your father as a baby, and Jucawa has not been a good father to you, please forgive me. You and I have spent much time together over your young years like a real father and son should. So with your permission, I want to give you this talisman, my shadow image, believing it will help remind you of our good times spent together."

Toca was speechless. The chief, the most powerful one of his people, wanted to give him this gift, an amazing gift. It was a gift that touched him deep, filling a part of his life he desperately longed for—to have a father that cared and loved him. "I don't know what to say," Toca slurred out. "This is a great thing!" Hesitating as he stared at the prized talisman, he then looked back up. "Yes, Chief Acuta, I accept your shadow image as my father's!" He looked back down at his ankle, staring at the small carving again and couldn't stop smiling.

The chief returned with his old smile as his lips sank back into his mouth from the lack of teeth and said, "Good...good." They momentarily locked eyes, confirming there was much more to their relationship than simply a chief and an old child from his tribe of thirteen-sun-seasons-old.

Looking back down to the final talisman, the chief said, "The last one here is your shadow image, the Black Ghost. I gave you this name in respect of your real father and you have grown to resemble it. You have learned to be the great cat, shadowing through the forest, not being seen or heard. Hunting with instincts beyond your age." The chief smiled, showing he was proud of the old child but also happily, within himself, acknowledging the name he gave Toca was perfect.

Continuing on, he looked away to the next thing on the mat and asked Toca to stretch out his weaker arm. Doing so, he strapped onto the inside of the forearm a sheath that had a knife in it, facing the handle toward his wrist. Withdrawing the knife, it had a strong sharp rock blade with a deer bone handle that had the carving of

Toca's shadow image on it. He held it out for him to see. "This is the only weapon you can take from the valley. Protect it and care for it and it will do the same for you."

Gently sliding the knife back into the sheath attached to Toca's inner forearm, he gestured for Toca to sit down and remain silent. Patiently waiting, Toca could tell his chief, his newfound father, was thinking deep, as though struggling with something, then nodded his head, making a decision.

Straining to get up, the chief walked slowly with a slight limp to the back corner of the hut, kneeling down to move a pile of furs. He lifted up a small piece of the bamboo floor, exposing a hiding spot. Reaching down, he picked up a small colorful decorated wooden bowl with a lid on it. Taking the lid off, Chief Acuta took a small object out, then set the bowl down on top of the pile of furs, and walked back. He sat down in the same painful manner in which he got up, holding the object in his hand. Stretching out his arm toward Toca, he opened his hand and exposed what he had uncovered. It was a small pouch made of spider monkey skin with sinew strapped around it in several different directions, making sure what was in it could not be seen or fall out.

It was now completely dark outside, except for the bright full moonlight shining through the thin bamboo walls. He lowered the volume of his voice to a soft whisper, taking on a serious tone, leaning forward, saying, "What I hold in my hand, Toca, only chiefs may see what's inside and know what it is." He looked at it with fear in his eyes, as his hand slightly shook, as he peered into Toca's eyes without moving his head.

"The story I told you earlier about the first chief and the rest of the ones that started the Nashua tribe is true but only a small piece of the truth. It's the piece of the story and only one I've shared, and the chiefs before me have shared, with our tribe and all the old male children that leave on their Katatas since the first ones here in the hidden valley."

Chief Acuta looked back down at the pouch in his hand. "This came with the original people that started our tribe here, many, many generations ago. The whole truth of our past and where we came from purposely has been keep secret and hidden from our people. What's inside this pouch is the last piece of history that represents where we originally came from." Chief paused, drawing his arm back, quickly dropping the small pouch on the mat between them as if it was hot.

For a moment, he collected his thoughts, then with reservation, but great urgency, quickly grabbed Toca by the arm with his bony fingers, blurting out in a whisper, "Toca, our tribe is in great danger, it is dying! If we don't change what we do and who we are, this slow and unforeseen reality soon will have us all!" he stated with a terrifying look in his eyes. Toca flinched back and then relaxed as the chief let go of his arm.

He thought to himself, *Why would he say this to me? Dying, no one is dying in our tribe, what is he talking about?*

Chief Acuta settled in closer to Toca, almost touching their bent knees together, making sure their conversation was only theirs as he began to explain. "I've decided to tell you the truth and the complete story of our people's past so you will understand what life-ending journey is ahead of us. But most importantly, that I need your help." The chief breathed deeply, relaxing himself to tell a story that no one else in the hidden valley has ever heard except for him and the chiefs before him.

"The first people of our tribe in this valley came from a terrible place far, far in the northern direction. We belonged to a mighty people, numbering more than one can count. They built tall rock structures that stairstepped their way higher than the trees so the chiefs could touch the sky. The tribal chiefs back then were called priests who wore big headdresses imitating animals on their heads and permanently marked their skin and faces with pictures and symbols. They looked fierce and larger than the normal people.

"The people worshipped powerful gods that demanded human sacrifices." Then Chief Acuta began motioning with his hands the actions of his words as he explained, "These mighty priests would lay a person across a large smooth slab of rock called an altar. With a large knife, they cut open the stomach of the person lying on the rock while they were alive and reached in, grasping the heart, tearing it out as it was still beating, giving it to the gods as a gift."

The chief was holding his hand in the air as if he was the one giving the heart up. His eyes were the widest opened Toca ever saw as they were glowing from the reflection of the moon shining through the gaps in the bamboo walls of the hut. It caught his breath and he wanted to turn his head away. The more the chief talked, the more terrified he was getting and more frightened the old child was becoming.

He continued his story. "The blood of the dead was then poured over the priests to cleanse them to be worthy to talk and walk with the gods. The heads of the people killed were cut off and used by the warriors or hunters to play with by kicking it around in open fields. After that, the heads were placed up high on sticks for the gods as decoration. Finally the rest of the body would be burned in giant rock firepits inside of the tall buildings where they were killed. Smoke of burning bodies never stopped coming out of the top of these mighty rock buildings, day or night. The smoke pleased the gods, and if the smoke of the dead stopped rising, the gods would come and severely punish everyone."

Toca gasped for air in the surprising horror he was hearing, his heart was pounding in his chest. He felt sick to his stomach as his head started swirling around with confusion.

The chief never stopped talking. "The more sacrifices, killing people, the stronger the gods made the mighty tribe. Daily screaming of pain, death, and sorrow continued on and on.

"The warriors of the priests were brutal and treated everyone as slaves. You did what they told you or you would be punished. Warriors were trained by the priests. They were taken from their mothers when they were very young and served the priests. Everyone that wasn't a warrior was a rock-building maker for the gods, or a dirt worker to grow food out of the ground to feed the vast amount of people. Only the warriors could train to hunt and fight and were the only ones allowed to have weapons. Remember when I said our first chief had the secrets to hunt, fish, and survive in the forest?"

Toca nodded.

"That is true, his older parents had this secret handed down from their parents but were caught training him these secrets and were sacrificed for it."

Sitting there, not knowing what to say, Toca just stared, slightly shaking while soaking in all this unbelievable and shocking history.

Chief Acuta continued, "No one was allowed to grow old, except the priests. When you grew to the age of not having babies anymore, both men and women were sacrificed. No one of knowledge or wisdom was allowed to live, except for the priests."

Pausing while bowing his head in shame, he said, "These stories, handed down from only chief to chief, about our old ones are repulsive and hard to comprehend but they are true."

Chief Acuta adjusted himself on the mat with a grimace of pain on his face. His old body has been failing him for a long time. Taking in a few more deep breaths, lifted his head, and looked at Toca with a refreshing smile of hope as though a heavy burden had been lifted from his shoulders and mind then continued, "There were a large handful of brave people that secretly came together and decided to escape this terrifying life. They wanted to live somewhere they could be free to grow old not having to worship and be sacrificed to the powerful gods. This group of people left in the dark of the night and ran for their lives.

"Soon warriors found out that they had left and went to hunt them down. The warriors were getting close so the group decided to split up to confuse them. Half the people went north, the other half went south. They agreed to meet back the next full moon where they split up, then continue their escape together. The group that went south returned at the appointed site but the northern group never showed up and were presumed killed by the warriors.

"Reluctantly leaving their friends and families behind, these courageous people left and decided to go south as far as they could until they were safe from these gods. It took more than a sun season of journeying until they found this hidden valley where we now live. After being here for thirteen full moons, the first chief was named which we discussed earlier about how the Katata's started."

Chief Acuta hesitated again, deeply considering what he was going to say next. Toca sat there, staring at him, still trying to take this story in, overwhelmed with shock of what people did to one other or what these gods made people do.

The chief continued, "When our founding people believed this valley could hide them from the gods, they made it their home and decided to make drastic changes about themselves. Changes in how they lived, but most of all, what they believed. They did not want their people to fear anything or anyone and felt the need to protect the generations to come from the terrors they experienced and their families before them. They decided to let their history die with them and not pass on any of the knowledge of their past and of the horrifying gods, except from chief to chief.

"A decree was made that no gods exist or the knowledge of gods and they would not worship anything from that point on. Because the only gods they knew of were terrible—bad gods that did horrible things to people."

He stopped the story and asked Toca to get him some water. Getting up, Toca went next to the entrance of the hut where the watering bowl was and scooped some water up with the bamboo drinking cup. Arriving back, he gently poured some water into the chief's mouth and sat back down as the chief asked if he had any questions.

Looking up, Toca stared out the window across the hut, into faint light of the night, and silently went through all the things that had been talked about. There was one thing he didn't understand throughout the whole story so he innocently asked, "Chief Acuta… what is a god?"

He smiled for a second, then responded, "Toca, I've told you things that are not supposed to be talked about or even known by our people. A history that was to have died long ago. I'm telling you these things, as I mentioned earlier, because our people are now in trouble and they don't know it. We are slowly dying as a tribe because our people have nothing to do but survive. We breathe, eat, drink, and sleep, day in and day out. We have lived in this valley for so long, in the same area, and nothing has changed since our ancient fathers first found it. We shadow in our world, hiding in silence, and we are suffocating because of that. Only the ones that have completed the Ado have dreams of other places and things. I have fought over the years within myself of this tragic ending that is to come in the next few generations, unless we change. We have not grown in numbers, we have less people in our tribe now than we did when I became chief. And my memories show me it was the same for the chief before me.

"Toca, our people have no encouragement for life, but most of all, we live for nothing. Nothing else but only to breathe, eat, drink, and sleep, just like all the animals in the forest. There has to be more to life than what we know and have here. I have come to the conclusion we are on the path of destroying ourselves because we have no purpose. We have no purpose for living, we just exist only to die so the ground can swallow up our lifeless bodies, just like everything else in the forest. With no purpose, there is no ambition to do anything but just exist. Do you know why we don't have purpose?"

Chief Acuta questioned as he looked at him, knowing he didn't have an answer, then immediately gave it to Toca. "Because we have nothing to inspire us. I have concluded at my old age that inspiration is the key to life. Without it, nothing changes. When nothing changes, it begins to decay which is the pathway to death and that's the path the Nashua tribe is on—death. There is nothing to give our people meaning or reason to grow. If we don't change who we are and what we do soon, we will no longer exist. The name of our tribe is the Nashua which means 'new beginnings.' The originals named us that because that's why they took the great risk of escaping for and was the hope for the generations to come. But as time has gone by, it has become the beginning of the end for their people.

"There are only two people in our tribe alive that know of the original decree, me and, now, you, Toca." The chief paused, looking deep into Toca, trying to get his point across, then continued, "And because of that decree is why you have asked the question they wanted their people not to have or knowledge of...what is a god? Proving why I had to bring the whole true story of our people to you. I have shared all this with you because I believe in you, trust you, and you are possibly our only hope. We have spent a lot of time together through your young years and I consider you as my own child."

Toca's eyes opened wide again and his heart jumped for joy when he said that because he felt the same way about him. Toca replied quickly, "Chief Acuta, you have been much more of a father to me than Jucawa ever has. I wish you were!"

He smiled. "I understand, young one." Then his facial expression instantly changed to disappointment. "Jucawa has not been good to you or your mother and I blame myself for that. But we must stay focused on this moment and your Katata."

The chief stretched his legs out and moved them back, adjusting how he was sitting to get more comfortable, then picked up the small pouch of the tribe's history. He looked at it in his hand then continued as he stared back at Toca, sitting across from him in the night's dark light of the tribal hut.

"You asked the question, 'what is a god?' I have asked that same question many times and have come up with more questions than answers. But what I know from the ancient stories, a god must be mystical, like morning fog, and very big and powerful if the people built large and high buildings for them out of rock, not bamboo. They must need man's heart to live and grow strong. They reward for the things done for them, that's why I believe the priests continually sacrificed people—the more hearts the gods received, the greater in number and stronger the people became. This must have been the inspiration for the priests to continue to do what they did. Which could be an answer for my concern for our tribe's future."

Being silent for a few moments and taking a few more deep breaths, the chief was getting very nervous for what he was about to say. "I said we have no inspiration to live but…" He stopped himself, knowing he was about to break their forefathers' decree, the evil secret the original tribe had and everything they risked their lives to get away from. But he knew if he didn't do anything, his people were doomed. He boldly continued, looking into Toca's eyes with encouragement.

"But…if we had a god…it could inspire our people and we could grow and be strong like the people we ran from."

Toca jumped back on the mat, gasping as fear swept through his whole body at what the chief said. All he saw in his mind was their people being cut open and blood going every direction. Seeing the expression of horror on his face, the chief put a hand on his shoulder to calm him down.

"Listen to me before you start thinking of the past. What I'm envisioning, I don't have an answer so let me explain myself." He paused with a grimace on his face, trying to find the right words. "Our old people before the hidden valley had fearful, cruel, and bad gods that demanded and treated their people the way they did to make them strong. My question is, are there different gods that do good things to their people and treat their people in different ways to make them strong?" Gazing past Toca, thinking his idea through, he continued, "You have experienced a good person, someone that treats you well and cares for you, right?"

Shaking his head slowly, putting on a smile, Toca replied, "Yes, you."

"Now do you know someone that is bad and hurts you and seems to not care for you?"

He was understanding what the chief was getting at and harshly responded, "Yes, the man my mother and I live with!"

"So what I'm asking you to do, Toca, on your manhood journey is to search for a good god, if there is one? A good god that could inspire our people and make us strong so we can grow again.

"I have felt deep inside for a long time"—the chief put both of his hands, making fists, up against his chest—"my spirit image telling me there is a good god but I must go look for it and I will find what we are needing."

Giving Toca a confirming and confident look, that what his spirit image has been telling him is true, he continued, "You will encounter many things and other people on your Ado."

Surprised, Toca looked at the chief, confused at the thought of seeing other tribes. No one ever mentioned or talked about other people. He always believed the Nashua were the only descendants of the ancestors.

"Yes, other people, Toca, I saw them when I was on my Katata Ado but they didn't see me. We are shadow people and I went by all of them without being seen. They live in small villages, like we do, along the mighty rivers on the way to the endless water. At the endless water, there are big villages with strange-looking huts. When I got back to the hidden valley before the thirteenth full moon and told my chief about my Ado journey and of the others, he told me like his chief told him, 'never mention anything about others to our people. They must not know of others because they may go looking for them and our people will be in great danger.'

"I didn't know about our tribe's past and about gods when I went on my Katata Ado. Only when I was made chief, the old chief, before he died, did he tell me about everything I have told you tonight. I was not looking for a god at the time, and if I saw one, I didn't know it. We live by not being seen so I believe their gods didn't see me. I have shared all this knowledge with you so you can do this great thing for our people and what my spirit image is telling me."

The chief took him by both shoulders, gripping firmly, slightly digging in his jagged nails, and stated, "Toca, find a good god and bring it to our village to inspire us so we can be saved from our certain death. But if there are only bad gods from our past, run from them and let this be our destiny. Better a quiet death than have our hearts cut out of our bodies while we're alive," the chief stated, then smiled, while letting go of Toca's shoulders and sitting back.

Toca was trying to take in what he was being asked to do. He could have never dreamed this is what was going to take place during his Katata ceremony. The pressure of doing a Katata is big and the Katata Ado giant. It is one thing for the old male children that actually accomplish the Ado, but now, the chief is asking him to find a god, which he has no idea what it is, what it looks like, and then bring it back.

Thinking about all this, Toca started giggling to himself then it came out as he smiled big to Chief Acuta, trying to keep silent.

The chief looked at him, puzzled, then asked, "What are you laughing at?"

"Do you hear what you're asking of me? Bring back a god? If I found a god, how am I to bring it back? It's big and I am only an old child. Also how do you know I will go all the way to the endless water and back, finishing the Ado?"

Chief Acuta instantly changed his demeanor and sternly looked at him. Toca thought he was in trouble, *What did I say wrong?* thinking to himself.

Slowly leaning forward, close to Toca's face, firmly and almost angrily, he stated. "You have no choice, you will finish the Ado!" He stared at him for a moment, letting him know how important this was.

Now whispering, he wanted to imprint every word onto Toca's mind. "Toca, if you do not accomplish the Ado, Jucawa will be chief." He hesitated again. "If you come back with a shell, I have the right to choose who will be the next chief."

Toca's mouth dropped open at what he said. He had no idea that could be done; Toca thought that who was next in line was the one to became the next chief.

It made sense now what his mother said earlier in the morning. "If you bring back a shell, you can change our lives and the lives of everyone in our tribe."

The chief leaned back slightly where he sat and peered around the room and out the openings of the tribal hut. He was making sure no one was listening in on their conversation, then continued whispering, "Toca, I need you to do these two things for our tribe. You must bring back a good god and you must complete the Katata Ado!" He looked again into his eyes with great encouragement. "If you don't, Jucawa is the only one to take over the tribe. I feel…no!" The chief corrected himself, shaking his head. "I know he will do great damage and bring pain to our people as chief, just like those bad gods I told you about. I don't understand why he acts the way he does with his arrogant, mean, dark behavior. The Ado has proven to bring back only strong honorable men. Ones that look out for the people, not men that are only concerned about themselves. He approaches me all the time, as he did this morning, asking me to step down and honor him by giving the chief position to him. He tells me I'm weak and cannot lead anymore."

The chief looked down at the mat where they sat and started looking defeated, then looked up at Toca again. "I am physically weak at my old age but my mind is very strong. I sense the others in our tribe appreciate me as their chief. I am also aware they look at Jucawa with great respect for what he accomplished on his Ado. But they are confused and don't know how to respond to him. A chief leads his people with peace, wisdom, and a vision for strength, safety, and prosperity. I believe as a chief, Jucawa will lead by force and fear, only doing what is good for himself, hurting our people and any chance for a growing future for our tribe."

Taking Toca's hands in both of his, a big toothless smile came across his face. "You, Toca, you can accomplish the Ado. I have seen your strength and endurance. I have taught you everything I know about surviving, and you have a great shadow connection to everything in the forest." The chief started squeezing Toca's hands so hard, he began to shake. "I have seen a great man waiting to come out of you. Not only can you accomplish the Ado—you must! You must accomplish it and bring back a good god for your people, if you don't..." He paused and began to relax his grip on Toca's hands. "I only see, in time, a village empty of its people and the forest growing over everything to the point you would never know that a tribe ever existed here. That is our future if you don't do what I have burdened you with, my old child. The great risk our old ones took escaping their home to have a better future will only end up all for nothing."

He stopped talking and an uncomfortable long silence entered the hut. Toca suddenly realized the chief was waiting for him to answer his challenge. Standing up, he walked around to the backside of the chief and kneeled behind him as he put a hand on each of his shoulders.

"My father, Chief Acuta...," he said, making the bond in their relationship they both longed for. "You have shared visions and one of them must not come true. I relieve you of the burden you carry and take the responsibility to fulfill the other. The next time you see me, I will be a man worthy of becoming the next chief of the Nashua tribe. I will not only return with a shell from the endless water but with a god. A good god to inspire our tribe, giving us a new beginning our forefathers started. All that we may prosper and grow as a people that will now have purpose for living."

He stood up and walked around in front as the chief slowly raised himself, facing Toca. He had grabbed the last item on the mat, a piece of blackened charcoal wood and started drawing shadow lines on his own body. When he completed his body, he started covering Toca's while speaking to him.

"My son, Toca, your shadow image is the Black Ghost. There is nothing this powerful cat fears because it sees before it is seen. You must journey as the Black Ghost if you are to be successful." Chief Acuta change his tone. "One more thing...I almost forgot. Protect the songbird and bring it to the valley. I know this sounds strange but I had a strong stirring dream last night that a songbird was in trouble and a Black Ghost protected it and brought it back home gently in its mouth. I don't understand the meaning but my mind was very strong in telling me this and my chest is heavy for you to do this important thing."

The chief stopped talking and motioned him to sit down as he himself continued to stand. He covered Toca's eyes with his hand so he would close them, then let go.

"Your time is here, Toca, before the thirteenth full moon rises from now, return to this spot with a shell, a good god, and a songbird and you will become the greatest chief the Nashua will have ever known."

He sat there with his eyes closed in the dark of the tribal hut. His mind was trying to sort out all the overwhelming things talked about. Moments went by and the chief had said nothing so he opened his eyes and looked around into the empty darkness. He was gone; Toca's time had come to leave and start his manhood journey.

CHAPTER 2

Two full moons have passed since Toca left his tribe in the hidden valley. Swiftly and silently, he's been racing through the forest toward the endless water, just as Chief Acuta taught him. He has come a long distance for the short time he's been traveling. Courage and confidence grew, stretching their boundaries daily within him, just as the sun would rise effortlessly, pushing the darkness of the night to another place.

Waking up in his temporary nests, safely in the trees every morning, Toca would grasp the talisman on his anklet, reminding himself what each of them meant. The yellow round one was the sun representing a new beginning every day, reminding him to look forward to new things to come that day. The monkey was his father's spirit image which, to him, was Chief Acuta. This reminded Toca of all the training given to him, plus the close relationship that awaited him when he got back home. Finally the carving of the Black Ghost. He would tightly hold it in his hand, close his eyes, and see his own image in his mind. Drinking in a refreshing and energizing mental picture of himself as the silent and powerful animal flowed through the thick rain forest smoothly as the mist of the morning fog. Speed and agility moved him, being smart and experiencing new things was maturing him. Toca was growing daily while becoming a man.

There wasn't anything truly hindering his journey, except for the night and the frequent downpour of rain. But even so, he was adapting to this new life moving forward and not settling in one place for more than finding a meal and resting.

Quickly running on the forest floor, gliding over and around the vegetation or swinging through the trees, leaping from limb to limb was mesmerizing for him. Once he got into a rhythm, with his legs and arms working together, he virtually wasn't thinking, just doing.

His eyes, ears, and nose became sharper in their abilities. When a leaf fell from a tree, Toca was able to see it as if he had eyes of an eagle. He could hear it quietly drifting through the air, like ears of a deer, and smell it settling to the ground, equal to that of the nose of an anteater.

This day was hot; as he journeyed, the sky was clear but a nice breeze was whisking through the forest, cooling things down. Toca had briefly stopped at an old fallen tree to peel back its decaying bark to find white juicy grubs to eat. He was getting hungry, and usually, this was an easy meal to find. As he was working the log, his nose caught an unfamiliar odor. He twisted his head around, deeply smelling, trying to locate the direction from which it was coming.

Finally catching the breeze that brought the odor to him, he headed directly in that path. With curiosity, Toca made his way, looking past the vegetation into the unknown.

After slithering through undergrowth of the tall trees for a while, he froze midstride when his eyes caught movement in the distance. Waiting for another glimpse of what he saw, Toca took a step back behind a large fern and knelt down. All of his instincts were telling him something was different here. He didn't know what, but for the first time since he left home, he was uneasy.

Looking down at his body, he noticed his markings were gone and he hadn't shadowed himself the last few days. For a moment, he was upset for not being prepared; but slowly backing away, he headed to a muddy pond near the log where he was eating.

Squatting down at the edge of the muck, Toca scooped up a handful of the dark mud and striped his body with it. Once done, he headed back, with knife in hand, weaving smoothly back and forth through the vegetation, staying unseen in the shadows. Toca's eyes and ears, anxiously wanting to be satisfied, were absorbing everything they could so he would know what was in front of him.

Finally he heard something sounding like shallow banging on a hollow log or a low grunt of an animal. It came and went with no distinct pattern. Slowly drifting closer, from shadow to shadow from the trees, to see what was making the noise, his heart started to beat faster as his breathing quickened with each step. The smell that first alerted him became very potent. His hand that had the knife began to sweat. Catching his breath, his eyes stopped moving and narrowed their focus on something in the distance through the dense vertical lines of thin tree trunks, pointing up as their vines dangled down to the ground.

Unable to figure out what he was looking at, Toca moved closer. It was the color of clouds and slowly waved in the breeze but stayed in one spot. When he got close enough, still peering through the vegetation at a distance, Toca was able to see the whole thing as it was in a rare open clearing. It was about the size and shape of the huts in his village. He decided to go around the clearing and see this thing from a different direction.

With stealth, Toca was around to the other side and sat halfway up a tree on a small limb, just inside the forest, without disturbing anything. From this vantage, he could see the whitish object and everything else in the clearing.

What is this place? Toca thought to himself as he peered across the small open area. The big thing, still waving with the breeze, was in the middle with a firepit next to it, slightly smoking.

The choppy vocal noise suddenly came from it again. *There's that sound again*, he thought to himself as his head slanted side to side as an eagle trying to focus in on its target. "It sounds like choking or coughing," he softly whispered to himself as curiosity was consuming his caution.

Suddenly the thin branch he was crouched on snapped and he dropped a short distance to the ground. Just like a cat, Toca landed on his feet but the sound of the breaking branch and the grunting of hitting the ground gave away his concealment.

Quickly he stepped a short distance further away from the clearing to hide and regain his concealment. Stopping behind a large tree trunk, he slowly peered around, just exposing enough of his face that an eye could look back and see if he had attracted attention.

Looking on, suddenly the side of the whitish structure facing the fire opened and a person quickly stepped out. His eyes went wide as it caught his breath.

Other people! Toca asserted in his head. *But what is he wearing?* The person had a long light-bluish body covering with markings or decorations on it that went from his neck to his feet. It was puffed out at the shoulders then traveled down the arms to his elbows. Over that was another covering extending only over the chest down to his knees, carefully held up with a strap around the neck and strapped again around his waist. It looked like some type of body protection, the color of brown caiman skin, like Chief Acuta wears but much longer. Something was covering his head, puffed back like it was holding all his hair, then it came out in front over his eyes, shadowing his face.

"This must be the chief!" Toca whispered to himself.

Standing in front of the fire, the person raised his arm to the sky. Something thin and long appeared in his hand as he waved it back and forth in the direction of Toca. A squawking scream of noise came from his mouth that Toca couldn't understand.

Stunned, Toca thought to himself, *He sees me. He knows I'm here, even back inside the forest!*

As the person waved the long object in the air, it exploded with flashes of bright light.

Toca's body began to quiver; fear was taking over him as he watched in amazement.

This isn't a man, it must be what Chief Acuta was talking about...a god. He slowly rolled his face away, putting his back fully against the tree, attempting to disappear. Building up the courage to look back at the god, Toca closed his eyes and grasped at anything that would help him. In his mind, he heard his mom's voice say, *You can save our tribe.* Then Chief Acuta, saying, *Bring back a good god and you will save our people.*

Toca opened his eyes, while taking a deep breath, as he cautiously looked around the tree again.

He stared straight forward toward the god, for a moment not knowing what to expect. Then his eyes worked the clearing while he moved his head from one side of the tree trunk to the other. The god was not there—it vanished. Toca didn't know what to do but just stand there. The entrance of the big white thing flew open again and Toca flinched back as the god walked out with something bulky in its arms, not acknowledging him at all.

The god laid the things in his arms on the ground. Toca noticed the long shiny light thing wasn't there. Kneeling down and picking up one of the items, the god raised it up, looking close at it for a moment. Toca noticed it seemed to have arms as the god tossed it into the smoldering fire.

Toca gasped out loud for air then turned quickly, pressing his back to the tree again, trying to blend into the bark. What he saw scared him more than anything he had ever seen. Memories of the conversation with Chief Acuta about the ancient ones and the old tribe they ran from flooded through his mind.

Fear-stricken, he thought, *This is not a god but a priest! He just threw in the fire the top half of a man with no head and hands.* Toca peered around to look again. This time, the god held up the lower body part of a person with two legs but no feet and threw it in the fire that was beginning to grow and smoke profusely.

He's burning dead people! Chief Acuta was right about his story of the old ones and what their priests do. Then it occurred to Toca about the odor. *That's what I'm smelling, burning bodies and the sound was of a choking person dying as his heart is being ripped out.* Toca couldn't take it anymore; shocked with horror and getting sick to his stomach, he ran away from the clearing as fast as he could.

I've got to hide from this priest before he comes after me and rips my heart out and burns my body! Toca cried out in his head as he dove deep into the thick dark unknown forest, away from the clearing.

*****

Shana, kneeling inside the canvas tent next to her father, was getting frustrated with the mosquitoes as she swatted at them in the air. "These things are horrible, they never quit and they are all over the place."

"I know, honey." Her father, John, coughed again as he was lying down on his bedroll. John has been sick the past month and was getting worse every day.

John finished coughing, saying, "Shana, why don't you—" He coughed a couple more times then said, "Put more wood on the fire and get it smoking again? That will help keep them away." John struggled to get words out. Breathing was difficult and he had a fever.

"We've burned up all the dry wood. I need to go out into the forest and find more but I don't want to leave you alone," she said as she wiped away the sweat from his face with her handkerchief.

"I'll be fine but I do worry about you being out there by yourself. I'm sorry—" He coughed again then continued, "That I don't have the strength to help, sweetheart."

"Father, I'm not scared, you've taught me how to take care of myself," Shana calmly said with a smile, looking down at the only family she had left.

"You look so much like your mother when you smile," John said, squinting and blinking rapidly, trying to keep the sweat from his fever out of his eyes. "She would be"—weakly coughing several times more then finished—"so proud of you." He closed his eyes and tried to find some comfort from this illness that inflicted him. He started getting sick when they first headed up the Amazon River, inland, going deep into the rain forest from the city on the coast.

"Get some..." Shana paused for a second and twisted her head so she could hear clearer. She thought she heard something in the distance like a tree limb breaking and falling to the ground with a thump. After a moment of silence, she turned her face back to her dad and finished. "Get some rest, I'll find some wood to smoke up the area."

*****

For years, John had been a missionary on an Indian reservation in the southern part of the New Mexico territory in the United States.

His Indian wife, who was from the tribe he was a missionary of, had passed away from cholera over a year ago. He was heartbroken and left with their twelve-year-old daughter to raise. A few months later, God gave him new direction in his life. "Go to a faraway forest in South America and travel up the giant river, telling the Indians there about me."

Crossing over land and sea had taken them almost a year to get to the mouth of the Amazon River. When they arrived, they met up with local people in the towns and learned about hidden tribes in the interior forest of the Amazon. They told them some tribes were easy to get along with while others would try to kill outsiders.

John would smile and tell them, "It sounds like the Indian tribes of North America, up until they were all overtaken and given reservations to live on by the government."

Every person warned them this wasn't a place for outsiders and how dangerous it was. "If you didn't grow up in this forest, have someone teach you the ways to survive or you will die. Finding food was difficult and keeping dry was almost impossible. The amount of poisonous and dangerous plants, animals, fish, and insects were too many to count. If they didn't kill you, losing your sanity will."

John's response was always the same. "God has sent me to witness to the South American Indians in the forest. As his servant, I must go."

John met a shipping merchant from Portugal who was one of the few outsiders he ran into that had actually gone far up the river and into the forest for any amount of time. This sea traveler had a handful of shipmates looking for gold or any other treasures that could be found.

The Portuguese seaman told him they found nothing and lost every one of his shipmates. Either killed along the way by Indians, animals, or snakes or died when they got back to civilization from sickness. Very few Europeans ever come back out of the big forest alive and he's never seen an American go up the river.

John wasn't sure if he was being told the truth or if these were attempts to scare him to keep him from going upriver to find their treasures. Bound and determined to obey what God had told him to do, nothing was going to intimidate him. Before he became a missionary, he escaped death many times, fighting in the Civil War from start to finish.

Over the past year, his selfless obedience to God was subconsciously a smoke screen. The bitterness of losing his wife was what pressed him forward out of spite to God. He walked boldly, almost without caution, to a point that he didn't care if he got hurt.

But now in his present condition, his body was filled with the deadly malaria illness as his heart and mind were being set free from being hardened against his Creator. Having refreshed his relationship with God, he knew he wasn't being punished for the person he has been. John was too spiritually mature to believe that but was sorry he had demonstrated this behavior to his precious daughter. A daughter he knew would soon be without both her parents in the middle of nowhere.

Right now, John and Shana are lost. They had traveled by steamboat from the ocean up the Amazon River to the heart of this great forest to the city of Manaus. It was a short distance north up the Rio Negro, one of the main rivers that forms the Amazon.

Once there, they bought a canoe big enough to carry them and all their belongings—tent, bedrolls, clothes, cooking supplies, extra food, Bibles, and many gifts to bring to the Indians.

They were headed to a tribe they were told by the locals was upriver but would take over a week to reach by canoe. After ten days of rowing upriver, it began raining hard and they went up a wrong tributary that flowed into the Rio Negro. They had been turned around for a couple of weeks since trying to find were this tribe lived.

*****

Shana stood up in the tent, grabbed the machete for protection and to chop wood, then turned and flung open the entrance of the tent and stepped outside. She looked around to see where there might be any dry wood and was veraciously swarmed again by mosquitoes. In frustration, she swung the machete in the air desperately trying to shoo them away. The sun reflected off the long shiny metal knife, shooting blasts of light into the forest. Not making any progress, she screamed at the buzzing insects to leave her alone.

Stomping back into the tent, she suggested to John, flabbergasted, "Father, you told me earlier to bury your old clothes because they have your sickness on them. How about if I burn them to smoke up the area to get rid of these terrible bugs?" she said, waving her hand by her head to swat at the mosquitoes.

"That's a good idea, sweetheart," John said groggily.

Shana walked out to the smoldering firepit with a couple of pieces of his dirty clothes and dropped them on the ground. Picking up one of his long-sleeve shirts, she held it up to make sure it didn't have anything in the pockets then threw it into the pit. She did the same thing with a pair of his pants.

Satisfied that what she did would work, she looked up across the small clearing, scanning her eyes into the forest, trying to figure out what direction to go for wood. For a moment, she thought she saw movement but it disappeared like it was never there.

*****

After quickly making some distance from the clearing, Toca finally stopped running because he thought he heard someone calling his name. Bending over with his hands on his knees, breathing heavily, he twisted around, looking for someone chasing him.

This time, he heard it clearer. "Toca, go back and you will find what you are looking for."

Standing up, he slowly shadowed himself with his back up against a tree and pulled his knife out from the arm sheath. His eyes frantically moved all around, trying to locate who was talking to him. Not seeing anything, he carefully and slowly swayed his head, looking back and forth, but no one was there.

Just then, he heard something close in front of him on the other side of some thick bushes. As he narrowed in on the sound, stretching his head forward, movement in the dark shadows shocked fear through his whole body that he definitely wasn't alone. Frozen where he stood against the tree, he couldn't move. Slowly one of the shadows came alive as it smoothly and gently walked directly to him with an amazing and powerful presence. Stopping ever so close, he could feel the breath of the shadow on his face. Fully exposed, Toca realized his was literally face-to-face for the first time with his spirit image, a Black Ghost. Everything stopped—he couldn't think, breathe, or move. All he could do was look into the hypnotizing gaze of the large black jaguar.

Staring at each other, it was a first for both of them as the rare big cat had never seen or smelled man before. It slowly sniffed up and down Toca's body then, with the side of its head, softly nudged Toca's shoulder. Their thoughts were the same, *This thing is real.*

Satisfied and not intimidated, the jaguar slowly turned and began to walk away. When Toca realized he wasn't in danger when the cat turned, a shower of questions flooded in and he asked out loud, "Why do you want me to go back?"

The jaguar stopped and swung his head back to the strange animal making noise.

"How do you know what I'm looking for?" Toca asked.

The cat just stood there, staring.

"Is it because you're my spirit image?"

A soft deep hair-raising growl came out of the jaguar as if it was answering him. Before Toca knew it, the cat mystically disappeared into the black shadows of the forest.

Standing against the tree, Toca closed his eyes and sighed with relief. Soaking in what just happened, peace and confidence was winning the battle, conquering any fear he had with his spirit image, but most of all, what he was running from.

Eyes still closed, his vision of the clearing instantly changed. A boldness was brewing inside him and what he saw didn't seem so scary or overwhelming anymore. Purpose and duty was rising within him as the echo of Chief Acuta's plea to save their people was building a mountain of courage within him.

Turning around, he headed back to the clearing, understanding his journey was maturing. He began to sense everything would be different from now on.

Once back to the open area, he decided to go around to where he first saw the back of the white waving hut. Peering carefully through the foliage, shadowing himself with every move, Toca eased closer. Every so often, he could hear someone coughing then voices coming from the inside. He couldn't understand a word; it was all scrambled noise to him. Curiosity was drawing him near to the point he would have to go into the open where there was nowhere to hide.

It went silent for a while. Toca looked around but nothing was moving except for the vertical rising smoke from the firepit which, he assumed, was a burning body. Even the breeze had stopped. It was later in the day and the clouds were slowly making their way, floating over the forest, hiding the blue sky. "It's going to rain soon," Toca said to himself as he scanned the area, deeply inhaling and looking around, trying to sense any other dangers. Then he bobbed his head slightly back as the stench of the area bit his nose. *It must be the burning body*, he thought to himself again.

Looking at the details of the hut from where the person emerged, Toca saw it was staked to the ground along the bottom. What looked like tree vines were attached to it on its top edges and corners stretched outward to other stakes.

He wanted to see inside. No, he needed to see inside. Trying to figure out how he was going to do this but stay unseen was going to be hard or impossible once he stepped out of the forest. He was at a moment of indecision, everything he was taught about staying alive was telling him don't go out there. But he knew inside himself this had to be done. He had to be seen if he was going to meet a god.

Toca looked down at his anklet to see Chief Acuta's talisman. He thought to himself, *What do I do, Father? What would you do*?

There was no response. Still looking down, his eyes went to his talisman and he stared at it for a moment. Just then, it came to him loud and clear like a flash of lighting piercing the dark of the night. The vision of the black jaguar, with grace and power, walking out to greet him, completely exposing itself to smell and touch him to see what Toca really was.

Toca pulled back his shoulders while taking in another deep breath. Without caution but with a renewed confidence of who he was, he stepped out from the shadows into the open, toward the unknown, as his shadow image demonstrated. With the same boldness, grace, and magnificence, he approached the large challenger, walking around to where the priest had come out.

He was Toca the Black Ghost, son of Chief Acuta of the Nashua people, and he was not afraid.

Black Ghost leaned close to the structure and smelled, as he closely examined it, looking all around the outside. Then he lifted his hand up to touch the thing, then suddenly the flappy door of the hut opened, almost hitting him in the face as he flinched back. He was staring eye to eye with the priest he saw earlier. Horror reached out to him through his eyes; they were brightly colored as the blue sky and appeared to dance like flames as they flashed back and forth, looking into his eyes. The priest began screaming so loud that when the vibrations of his breath reached Toca, in his mind's eye, it appeared as if a ferocious beast was coming out of it to devour him.

*****

Shana had quietly gotten up after her father finally fell asleep and was going out to the forest to get some wood for the fire. She picked up the machete and tiptoed to the door of the tent and opened it. Standing less than an arm's length in front of her was a person with his hand up, appearing to be reaching out at her. He was skinny and no taller than herself with long scraggly black hair and brown skin with wide slashes of dark dirt racking his whole body. The only clothing he had was a small piece of ragged animal hide covering his private parts.

It took her a few seconds to get her lungs to work so she could scream for her life. Remembering she had the machete in her hand, she raised it while she was screaming.

Toca, terrified and numb with fright, couldn't move until he saw the priest raise his hand, holding the long shiny weapon. His eyes went even wider and his feet finally moved as his body followed. He turned and ran across the clearing but the screeching sound of the priest wasn't getting farther away. Toca looked back as it was running after him, slashing the long thing in the air at him. So he ran faster than he ever had before, dashing into the forest.

Instantly the screeching stopped then the sound of a thud, followed by an *oof* finalized the noise in the clearing.

Shana had tripped over her blue dress and hit the ground hard, knocking the air out of her. She looked up to see the man but he had disappeared. She sat up, looking all around then back to where she last saw him running, and he was gone like he was never there.

Once in cover of the forest, Toca shadow-jumped, blending into the forest to lose the one chasing him. Feeling confident he lost him, he quickly climbed a tree and swung over to a couple more, then knelt down on a strong limb and turned toward the clearing to see where the priest was.

The white hut caught his eyes first, in the distance through the trees, then glanced around until he finally saw the one chasing him. The priest was getting up from the ground, wiping dirt off its body covering, then looked around on the ground and picked up the long lightning thing. *He tripped and fell,* Toca thought to himself as the frightening moment began to transform into shallow confidence as a partial smile came to his face and whispered to himself, "He cannot catch the Black Ghost!"

*****

Shana was heading back to the tent as her father was just walking out of the opening to see what the bloodcurdling screaming was about. But he collapsed to his knees then fell forward, passing out from exerting himself. Shana ran to his side but didn't get there in time before he hit the ground.

"Father, you needed to stay in bed," she scolded him as she knelt down next to him. He was unconscious. "Father! Father!" She tried to wake him, shaking his body, but he didn't move. She strained to roll him over onto his back, then put her ear to his chest. "Thank you, Lord," she said out loud, lifting her head up with relief as she heard his heart beating.

Looking at her father, she started to get anxious as reality was setting in that he was only getting worse. Looking around, trying to figure out what to do, her emotions started crashing. Not finding any answers, she laid her head back down on his chest and started to cry.

After a few moments, Shana sat up and bowed her head and began to pray. "God, I'm so scared. I don't know what to do. Could you please heal my father? He's here for you, you told him to come here and tell these Indians about you. Why is this happening? Please help him get better." She was now raising her arms and face to heaven, pleading with God. "Jesus, we need your help, please tell me now what I'm supposed to do."

Shana's heart was beginning to recognize feelings she had over a year ago when her mother was sick then passed away—empty, lonely, and heavy with sadness. "No, Jesus, I don't want to feel that again, please make my father well, take the sickness away. Please! Please!" She laid her head back down on his chest and quietly cried. A breeze gradually swept into the clearing from the forest. The thick dark clouds that had been floating in thinned out in a small spot, exposing blue sky. A few rays of sunlight softly beamed down to the clearing.

"Shana, do not be afraid, I am always with you." She slowly opened her eyes while keeping her head still on her father's chest. She didn't want to move. The voice was very clear and calming but startling. *Who was that?* she thought to herself.

"Surrender to him and I will guide you." Her eyes went even wider. Slowly lifting her head, she looked around but no one was there. With apprehension, she spoke out, "Who's there?"

John answered with a moan, "Mmm...what did you say?"

"Oh, Papa, you're awake! Thank you, Jesus!" She leaned into him and gave him a big hug.

John barked out several coughs as she told her father, "I was so scared."

John slowly opened his eyes, moving them around, and asked, "Where am I?"

"You're outside the tent."

"What...what am I doing here?" he said, trying to lift his head up.

"I don't know, maybe you came out to look for me. I screamed and chased an Indian man away." Shana had forgotten about that then, with excitement, exclaimed, "Oh, Papa, I found a person! Well, actually a man or boy, I'm not sure." She shrugged her shoulders and shook her head. "He was trying to get into our tent"—talking faster the more words she said—"I didn't know he was there, and when I opened the door to the tent to go get firewood, he was standing right in front of me."

"Shana—" John coughed again and tried to lift his arm to grab hold of hers. "Where is he?" He asked, gasping for air.

"I chased him into the forest..." It just hit her that the people they were looking for she scared away. "Oh no, what did I do, Papa?"

Finally grasping Shana's arm, he weakly squeezed to get her attention. "Go find him."

"But he scared me...I'm scared."

"He ran..." John paused, trying not to cough. "From you. He's more scared of you than you are of him."

"I don't know where to find him." Then stating with surprise, "He vanished, Papa, right before my eyes, into the forest."

"He'll come back—be nice next time. Sing out to him, sweetheart, that will attract him back." John was having a difficult time breathing or even staying conscious. He didn't want to alarm his daughter but he knew deep inside he wasn't going to live much longer.

Shana looked back to the forest and peered around, it was different. Before she was looking out at a thick maze of green plants making strange noises with birds and monkeys in the trees. Now it became a dwelling with human eyes looking straight at her. She was beginning to feel exposed and very vulnerable.

Looking back to her father, she said, "Let's get you back into the tent, it's getting late." She lifted with all she had as John wobbly got to his feet and they both stumbled back into the tent, holding each other tight.

*****

Toca watched on as the priest was walking back to the hut holding the light-flasher. Suddenly a giant man came out of the hut then fell dead, directly facedown to the ground. He was wearing different body coverings than the priest, ones like the dead body thrown into the fire earlier and had white skin and short hair. The priest ran to him, knelt down, and rolled him over, laid his head on his chest, then sat up and raised his arms to the sky, saying something.

A stream of light shone through a hole in the dark rain clouds directly onto the people. "He's calling out to a god in the sky!" Toca said under his breath, looking on with amazement as the powerful light beamed down, responding to him raising his arms.

The next thing that happened shocked Toca while taking his breath away as he stared in disbelief. The dead man came back to life after the sky's light touched him. Then the smaller priest helped the big man up as they went into their white hut.

Toca watched on as many thoughts were running wild through his mind. Was the light from the sky a good god because it gave the dead man life instead of having the priest cut his heart out? Why, earlier, was a dead person burned in the fire and what did he do with the head, feet, and hands? The giant man wearing different body coverings than the priest must be a rock-building worker or field worker growing food as Chief Acuta told him. But why was his skin the color of white clouds?

Now with the people in the hut, Toca peered around, noticing other things like the birds had begun their evening calls. Thinking to himself, *It will be dark soon and probably rain, I need to gather bedding and make a nest.* He looked hard one more time at the hut then, without hesitating, took off into the forest, knowing he would be back here when the sun rises, chasing the darkness away.

CHAPTER 3

As usual, the birds were the first to greet the new day, waking up everything in the forest, except for the animals that came alive and hunted at night. It was music to their ears, letting them know it was time to go to sleep for another day in their comfortable hiding places in trees or holes in the ground.

Toca was already awake. He had a hard time sleeping after the most unbelievable and exciting day of his life. His mind wouldn't stop racing through all the things that happened. So when the soft glow of sunlight finally began to show itself, he was out of his bed and on the ground quickly to find some water and food. Once satisfied with a few deep swallows of water from a stream, he ate some sweet roots of the nyhali plant he dug up next to the stream. While still kneeling next to the water's edge, he shadow-striped himself from head to toe with fresh mud then was on his way back to the clearing.

*****

Shana was up, anxious for the new day, when the harmony of a few birds turned into a full orchestra of dozens and dozens of feathered creatures attempting to outsing one another.

She had gotten up several times in the night to check on her father. His breathing consisted of a continual wheezing inhale, followed by a coughing exhale. She knew he needed help and he needed it now. However, her determination in finding the person she chased off was the only thing on her mind.

Stepping out of the tent with renewed purpose and drive, Shana walked around the firepit, trying to figure out what exactly she was going to do to find this person in this giant maze of vegetation. Then she remembered what her father said, "Sing to him." She looked up through the fog, into the trees, trying to see the birds singing as though telling her, "We want to hear your beautiful voice, Shana, join us."

There was nothing moving in the clearing except for the morning fog gently rising as Shana slowly walked around. Her mind drifted off into her morning prayer time with God and found herself humming a song. Finally reaching her favorite part of the chorus, she began to softly sing. Singing came naturally to her and was her strongest gift, and everyone in her tribe back home enjoyed it because it was soothing and invigorating.

Her voice carried through the forest and all the birds stopped singing. Almost as though they were listening to a master at work, bringing colorful sounds to brighten the dark interior of the forest.

*****

Toca shadowed perfectly, hiding against the side of a large tightly woven group of vines and branches. His arms and legs vanished as they appeared to be a natural part of the growth positioned just inside the forest, a few steps from the edge of the clearing. He had no idea what he was going to do but knew he had to confront the priest and ask him about the god in the sky. As he was peering into the fog, waiting for it to lift, he softly heard something new to his ears. Listening intently, cocking his head back and forth, trying to see and hear clearer of what was making the peaceful sounds, a person slowly and mystically appeared through the fog. It was the priest, a short distance away, walking directly to him with a glow of peacefulness on his face as gentle and soothing sounds were coming out of his mouth. As Toca watched the priest's mouth, he was being hypnotized by the aroma of sounds flowing into his ears, holding him motionless were he hid.

Suddenly realizing the priest was upon him, he instinctively stopped breathing and moving his eyes. Perfectly shadowed against the branches and vines, the priest walked past him, less than an arm's length away. He continued in the forest a few more steps then slowly turned and looked in Toca's direction, never stopping in making the wonderful sounds, which now had reached down into Toca's heart. The priest turned back and continued walking around the clearing just inside the forest.

The fog finally lifted enough that Toca could see him coming out of the plant life across the open area, walking to the hut. The priest stopped making the gentle sounds that were controlling the rhythm of Toca's heart, then briefly looked in Toca's direction before disappearing through the entrance.

Sighing out heavily with relief, then drawing in fresh air, Toca shook his head to wake himself as though he had been dreaming. *What just happened?* he thought to himself. Then without thinking, he opened his mouth like the priest's and tried to quietly make the sounds he heard. All that came out was choppy twisted grunts that made his tongue move into awkward positions. He fumbled while making agonizing noises, then went silent to refocus on his purpose. Shortly movement caught his eyes as the hut entrance opened and the priest walked out holding the long light-maker.

*****

Shana got back to the tent after a soul-refreshing time with God and singing into the forest, as though calling for the Indian to come back. Hesitating before she went inside, she looked toward the forest where she had entered, wondering why she had the feeling someone was watching her. But when she turned, no one was there.

"Father, how are you?" she asked as she walked into the tent and knelt to where he was resting.

"My beautiful daughter..." John coughed as he opened his eyes to see her face as she approached. "I could hear you singing the whole time." He painfully took in a deep breath then continued, "You always make me feel good when you sing, Shana. Especially that song, 'How Great Thou Art.' It rejuvenates my spirit every time, thank you."

"I did what you said and I sang to him. I hope it works, Papa. Wonder if I scared him too far away to hear me sing?"

"He'll come back. We're in his home. It's human nature—" John softly coughed with the lack of energy. "To be curious. How they are going to react to our presence is my concern. Are they going to be friendly or not?"

"I know, I'm sorry I chased him away but he scared me and I didn't know what else to do."

"It's okay, don't worry," John said as he shivered in his blanket. It wasn't cold, he was reacting to his fever.

Shana picked up the towel next to John she had been using and wiped down his forehead and neck that had a buildup of sweat.

"Shana, I need to have a serious talk with you." Pausing, letting her finish wiping his face, he then started. "What I'm going to say are not new things to you but very important for all people." John tried to raise himself in a better position to talk but was too weak to make any major adjustment. "I haven't been a good example for you since your mother passed away." He closed his eyes as tears formed and began to flow. John was getting emotional, not only reflecting from the loss of her but mainly from how his heart has been ever since.

Blinking his eyes open, looking into his young daughter's face, he said, "I've been very upset with God for taking her away from us. And now I see what a fool I've been. I don't want you to follow in my steps when I…" John hesitated to tell Shana the reality of what will happen to him soon, knowing he needed to prepare her for it. He needed to give her final instructions, guiding her to live free from the disastrous attitudes and emotions man puts himself through. Like those he did to himself—anger and self-pity. The two things that have violently anchored him down from his relationship with God the past year. Voiding out love and joy, resulting in the decay of his spirit.

Deep inside, John was screaming out regret; he was the one to let go of the hand that would comfort him with the death of his wife.

John finished the sentence. "When I'm gone."

"Father, don't talk that way, you're going to get well. I'll find the Indian and he'll get help." She was attempting to avoid what she knew could be inevitable.

"Shana, listen to me..." John tried to raise his voice to get her attention and shallowly coughed. "You need to see clearly what life is about. It's not about who we are, what we have, what we do, or what we've done that is important. But rather who Jesus is and what he has done for us." Painfully swallowing to clear his throat and give him a second to think, he continued, "When you sing to God, how does that make you feel?"

"It calms me down and my heart feels...I don't know?" Shana looked to the side, shrugging her shoulders.

"Your heart feels free, filled with peace and joy?"

"Yes, that's it!" She excitedly agreed, looking back at him.

John took her hand in his as she sat beside him, lying on his back, saying with as much meaning and passion as he could with tears softly streaming down his face. "Your life has just begun, sweetheart. God opens his hands and lets us freely choose how we want to live, that's one of his greatest gifts. What we need to remember is that he never closes his hands for us to hold. They are always open. We are the ones that lets go of his and closes our hands.

"He allows us to plan our ways through life and that's exciting. But he wants to direct our steps through our lives to guide us to grow in our relationship with him while we get to wonderful destinations around and through things that always appear to be impossible mountains to climb.

"If we don't follow in his steps..." Narrowing his gaze deeply while attempting to embed the importance of what he was saying, he said, "Be afraid, Shana, be very afraid!" His eyes widened. "If you don't, your world will get very small and dark and you will only see and believe what is in front of your eyes. Completely missing out on the majestic wonderful blessings God has waiting for you when you faithfully step forward, hand in hand with him!

"Always take his hand and follow in the footsteps he's laid out for you to walk with him. Even if the journey ahead looks difficult, painful, and scary or you don't understand it and you want to take control, don't let go and take control. If you have faith and follow him, I guarantee he will give you peace, rest, and comfort along with more blessings than you can imagine. And you will have complete meaning and purpose, and you will never get lost in the dark valleys of life."

John paused, grimacing as he again swallowed, taking in a deep breath. In his mind, he was giving thanks to God he was able to speak this whole time without coughing, then asked, "Could I have some water?"

Shana grabbed the canteen and gently tipped it over as John lifted his head as the water slowly poured into his mouth. Tipping up his chin to tell her that was enough, he then dropped his head back down on the blanket, exhausted, but continued talking as she put the canteen away.

"Shana, promise me you will follow in the footsteps of Jesus. If you do, then you will never, never have anything to be afraid of. He will always have a way to help you through what you don't understand."

Shana interrupted John as she took one of his hands, telling him, "Father, you don't need to be preaching to me right now, you need to rest."

John raised his voice again. "Shana, please—" The sudden exertion caused him to cough a few times. "Please listen to what I'm telling you! You're still young and I know many times, things will not make sense. That's why I'm telling you all this to say this very, very important thing." John paused, catching his breath, closing his eyes, trying to keep his mind clear. His head was starting to cloud up and it was getting hard to concentrate, but he was able to continue, opening his eyes again. "Everything in life comes down to believing Jesus is your Lord and Savior and loving him and everyone else. This is his greatest desire and will for us.

"My little one who's not so little anymore, hear me clearly. Without love and having faith and trusting in God with our life journey, we have nothing to hold onto. There's nothing there, just human clutter filled with fear, worry, and selfish wants and desires. Life is totally worthless without our faith in the one who made us, sweetheart."

Smiling, John let go of Shana's hand and lifted it to her face, gently stroking his daughter's cheek with his fingers, showing his love for her. "Who you are, Shana, is a child of God. Always have a child-like faith. Trust him like you have always trusted me but more—much more—with your whole heart to provide, protect, and love you. Read his living words in the Bible and talk with him daily. Most times, you will not hear from him when you want him to talk to you so be patient. He knows exactly when you need to hear from him. Do you understand, Shana?" She nodded her head in agreement.

John, knowing the importance of what he was saying at this moment, repeated it in deeper terms. "When you pray to God, you need to believe he hears you and he will answer you. But here's what is hard for us, sweetheart. He will always answer in his time. God knows the perfect time to talk to you, the perfect time to have the greatest impact on you, and the perfect time that will prove he is the all-knowing God."

John nodded his head, emphasizing he agreed with himself so she would know he believed what he was saying. Shana then lifted her hand to the back of his that was softly at the side of her face and tilted her head into his palm, touching it with her cheek as warmth and compassion flowed to each other. She was beginning to understand what he was doing. Giving her what he worked so hard for most of his life, all wrapped up into a few moments—his last sermon of his life.

She closed her eyes as if she was absorbing his love and words of wisdom through his hand and was locking them up safe within her heart. They shared this peaceful moment of love between a father and daughter until John fell asleep.

She bent over, kissing him on the cheek, and said, "I love you, Papa." Then she laid his hand down on his chest and adjusted the blanket behind his head. She stood up, whispering to him, not expecting a reply. "I'm going to look for the Indian and see if I can find some food." Picking up the machete, Shana walked out of the tent into the direction of the river.

*****

Toca watched, from the safety of being shadowed within the vegetation, as the priest came out of the white hut and disappeared into the forest on the other side of the clearing. Hesitant of his next move, he thought, *Do I go into the white hut or follow the priest?* Figuring in the forest he had the advantage, he quickly ran around the clearing after him. With what was becoming a natural body motion, Toca was swift, silent, and powerful in every stride. His movements were precise, working together in harmony. He was the Black Ghost on two legs.

Very quickly, he was around on the other side, following in the direction the priest traveled. It wasn't difficult to locate him because he was leaving a trail of broken branches and prints in the ground behind. Even the small children back in his village could easily find and follow them. He knelt down to look closer at the strange footprints. Each print representing a foot, at the heel, there was a deeper impression in the dirt with straight sides all around with a much larger pattern shaped like an egg in front of that. *This man must have no toes*, he thought. Toca looked up and could hear the priest way ahead, thrashing through the brush, like he wanted to make noise, and said softly, "He is scaring all the animals he's hunting." He got up and shadowed his way forward. Soon the noisy thrashing stopped and he began hearing the beautiful sounds he heard earlier. It was like a pure misty fog slithering through the forest, captivating him with arms of wonderful and colorful sounds, drawing him in closer and closer. Almost bumping into the priest standing at the edge of a sandy beach next to the big moving black water, he stopped perfectly in the shadows as the priest was in the sunlight on the sand, squinting his eyes, making the beautiful sounds louder, out toward the open flowing river.

Just then, something struck Toca in the eyes, flinching his head back. It hurt and took him off guard; he breathed in quickly, making a noise from the shock. The priest didn't hear him and kept making the peaceful loud flowing sounds.

Recovering from whatever hit his eyes, Toca thought to himself, *He didn't hear me because he's too loud.* Then he was looking closely for hunting weapons the priest had—and there it was, the lighting thing.

It was the only thing in his hands. Again he was painfully hit in the eyes, then realized it had come from the long thing in the priest's hand. *What was he doing with that thing and why*? Toca thought. Suddenly his eyes caught movement of something in the river and it was the same bright shine that kept hitting him in the face, moving around. Keeping his head still, he only moved his eyes up into the sky at the sun.

It has to do with the sun shining off it. It's the same type of light that's on the water. And the same light that came out of the sky the day before when the two people were on the ground and when I first saw the priest waving the thing in the air, he thought to himself as he started putting everything together.

The priest stopped making the wonderful sounds and stood there for a while, looking and listening. He took a few steps closer to the water's edge and looked up and down the moving water.

Toca took a few steps back to a more secluded position and began to think how he was going to engage the priest. He looked around the open sandy area. It didn't feel right, his senses were telling him there was something wrong and it wasn't the priest himself. Being uncomfortable, Toca looked up to the trees where he always felt safe. Dropping back farther into the thick vegetation, quickly without making a sound, he went around to one end of the open beach where it met the water and was up high in a tree before the priest looked back upriver his way. Kneeling on a branch, he carefully peered around the wide trunk, just enough to see with a part of his eye. The priest never left his spot but was now looking into the water then at his body covering and began to wipe it with his hand.

*****

Shana was looking at her dress and brushing off dirt. It was filthy from her fall while chasing the Indian. *When was the last time I washed it? I want to look my best. How am I going to attract anyone if I'm this dirty*? She thought to herself while deciding it was time to clean up, especially if the Indian came around.

By habit, she looked around to make sure no one was watching, then stood up straight and untied her hair bonnet then took it off. Her beautiful black hair dropped down to the middle of her back as she tilted her head backward, swinging it from side to side, letting it breathe and fluff itself out. She bent over, lifting her dress, then unstrapped her shin-high boots and pulled them off. Next she untied the brown apron from the back and slid the neck loop over her head, tossing it to the ground. Reaching back, she untied the bowknot of the dress and unbuttoned the collar behind her neck. The dress dropped to the ground. As she stepped out of the dress, she pulled off her undergarments, completely exposing her naked body. The only thing left on was her necklace that had a grayish rock-carved pendant dangling down her chest.

Bending down, she picked up the dirty clothes and stepped into the water a few feet and began to soak them, then rubbed them together, washing and rinsing each piece. After finishing the wash, she gathered up the clothing and walked across the warming sand to the edge of the forest where she had left the machete and hung them to dry. Turning around, Shana went back to the water to take a bath herself. Once to the edge, she investigated the water and saw movement. "Fish!" she whispered. Then she saw more and more of them swimming around. *I'm going to bring Papa fish for dinner,* she thought to herself. She went back to where the machete laid and picked it up while looking around for the right stick or tree limb. Finding an old dried-up skinny lengthy limb, she chopped it to perfect spear-length and began to sharpen it at one end, poking it with her finger off and on until she was satisfied it was sharp enough. Then gently, she carved a backward notch close to the point so the fish won't slide off once stabbed.

Shana slowly approached the water, attempting not to scare any of the small fish. They were out a little beyond her reach so she gently stepped into the water, barely making waves, inching her way deeper and closer. Finally in perfect position, she lifted the spear high and back, throwing it hard into the school of fish. It stuck firm into the ground under the water. Anxious she waded out to it and slowly brought it to the surface. Nothing, just a glob of mud dripping off the end.

*****

Toca watched intently as the priest finished wiping his body covering off then stood straight up, raising his hands to his head. He took off the headdress as his hair uncoiled itself, falling down, then bent over and took off strange foot coverings.

"Oh, that's what made those prints in the dirt. Why would he cover his feet?" he said to himself.

Straightening back up, the priest worked at getting the rest of his body covering off. *What's he doing? Maybe he is going to swim across the river?* Then an idea came to him. *He's been calling for his people, just like birds and animals do. That's what the sounds coming out of his mouth are for. Now he's going to swim across to find them.*

Just then, as the last piece of strange body covering came off, Toca almost fell from the tree. Shocked, he momentarily lost his balance because of what he saw. He didn't know what to think as his mouth dropped open and his eyes grew wide. *It's a woman!* he shouted in his head. At first, he thought he said it aloud as he moved completely behind the tree to hide. "It's a woman. I can't believe it?" he whispered under his breath. He slowly peered back around to take another look. "It is a woman," he repeated to himself. Toca tilted his head and squinted his eyes to get a sharper look. *No... no it's not. It's an old female child.* Recovering from the shock, he was now more confused. *What is a female child doing by herself, especially in the big water?* His eyes moved to the river, glancing around the area. Instinctively his mind and body were overwhelmed for the safety of this child.

Toca straightened his posture while taking in a deep recovering breath. Perched up high, looking down, his demeanor completely changed. No longer were there any questions about this mysterious person or hesitation on how he was going to talk with whom he thought was a priest. Now he was all about protecting this female child from all the dangers seeking her out.

"Black Ghost will keep you safe, old female child," he silently whispered down to her as he crouched and assumed an attack position. On the tree limb, he was silently ready to pounce at anything that would hurt this one now under his protection.

As he watched over her, he realized why she took off her strange body coverings when she washed them and hung them to dry as dirty water came out of them. "She has to be hot and sweaty all the time with all that on her body, that's why she needs a cool cleansing bath," he said to himself.

His attention for protection was distracted when she ran back to the forest edge after seeing something in the water. She picked up a long stick and began using the thin light reflector to sharpen the end of the stick. *It's sharp like my knife.* He understood this use of the thing which became more interesting and meaningful.

When the girl went back to the water, Toca figured out what she was going to do with the stick and smiled, thinking to himself, *Child, you are not in the shadows, the fish see you.*

She threw the stick and pulled it out of the water—empty. He watched on as she slowly waded in the water, looking for more. Soon she had slowly wandered almost directly underneath the branch he was on that stretched out over the water's edge.

Toca began to get nervous because beneath him, in the water, was a large collection of lilies and other water plants appearing to have gathered around a very large log. Knowing areas like this, danger hides underneath the vegetation, shadowing themselves, waiting to attack helpless prey—giant anaconda's, big predator fish with long teeth, or worse—a caiman.

Toca began to fiercely examine the grove of plants from his perch. The female stopped short of walking into the lilies. She peered into the patch of water flowers, admiring their beauty; suddenly she fletched back slightly as a frog jumped away, startling her.

Toca was looking at the details of the area when two small flickers of light reflected back to him from near the end of the log closest to the girl. *What is that?* he thought to himself while cocking his head back and forth, much like an eagle focusing. Just then, an explosion of terror shot through him as one of the shining spots slowly moved.

He pulled his head back, widening his view of the area, and realized he wasn't looking at a log but at a huge black caiman.

Glancing back at the female child, only a step away from the beast, Toca pulled his knife out of his forearm sheath. Without thinking, he leaped into the air from high in the tree, yelling at the old child to get away. The caiman reacted at the same time, bursting out of the water toward its next meal. With great force, his body hit the animal, embedding his knife deep behind the head. Then bounced off the giant animal, splashing into the water.

*****

After flinching back from the frog, Shana relaxed, smiling at her fright. Suddenly the floating garden burst open in front of her. She was staring in a mouth of teeth, open as wide as she was tall. Her speechless breath—taken away—was replaced be the sounds of what she thought was an angel yelling as he flew from the sky to save her. Everything happened so fast all she could do was shut her eyes, tensing up her body, waiting for the worst as she was splashed with water.

After a few moments, shrunken in a defensive posture, there was complete silence. Shana built up the courage to peek open one eye to see if she was dead or if the animal was there waiting to see her eyes only to devour her but nothing was there. Slowly she opened both eyes, straightening her body back up, astonished at what was in front of her. A giant alligator, five times the length of her body, floating motionless upside down with its lighter-colored belly reflecting the sunlight. The thought of an alligator this close—dead or not—was horrifying.

Calming down with a sigh of relief, her ease instantly vanished when the water erupted again as a man shot straight out of the river, gasping for air. He ended up standing in front of her, a couple of arms' lengths away. Frozen, she couldn't speak but thought, *Was this the angel I heard? What else is going to jump out of the water*? Thoughts were mixed up in her head.

Shana stared at the one standing in front of her, staring back, catching his breath. Looking at each other in the eyes, she was wondering what to do. It suddenly struck her this was the Indian she chased away. *He's an angel? I scared away an angel?* Then she looked down his wet body and noticed he was naked.

"You're not wearing clothes!" she said aloud, turning her head. Her head still turned, she asked, "Are you an angel?" There was no reply. She glimpsed back with her head held up to keep from seeing his private body parts. His head was slightly tilted, as if trying to understand what she was saying. Slowly it was coming to her that this wasn't an angel, further confirmed when he began to speak, pointing to the top of the tree then to the alligator. It was gibberish with choppy words but there were parts she thought she recognized; but he was talking too fast.

*****

Toca's body flopped hard on the caiman, knocking the air out of him, but his knife hit its target all the way to the handle. Bouncing off the giant beast into the water, he struggled for a few moments, tangled in the vegetation as the flow of the river slightly drifted him under the dead animal. Freeing himself, he pushed off hard from the shallow river bottom, shooting into the air, filling his lungs back up with life.

There he was, face-to-face with the old female child he just saved. She looked at him briefly, then turned away, saying something. She looked back at him, and he noticed she was wearing a talisman around her neck like Chief Acuta. But it wasn't a shell from the endless water, it looked like a grayish white rock carved into some shape. Excited, he began to explain how he saved her by jumping from the tree then landing on the caiman. This time, looking into her eyes, it didn't frighten him as the calming blue color held his attention.

Toca knew this was his moment to meet others. He was the Black Ghost and he just had a great victory saving her. His confidence was as high as ever. He continued to talk, explaining that he's been watching over her this whole time when she took off her body coverings and washed them, pointing in their direction, drying in the sun across the beach.

Suddenly the girl looked down at her body and covered her female parts with her hands. She said something then ran to the body coverings, picking them up and dashed into the forest.

He stood there alone, motionless. "What did I say, where is she going?" he asked himself. Looking to the caiman, it had started to drift downriver. He dove in, swimming a short distance, grabbed the fat heavy tail, and began pulling it to shore as the body floated. Struggling, he finally got back to the beach, only able to get the tail and a small portion of the body on land before the dead weight of the beast was too much for him to pull.

Toca walked back into the water, submerging himself under the head of the black caiman to get his knife. He pulled and wiggled it back and forth, still wedged along the side of the back of the skull. Underwater, holding his breath, he put his back to the shallow river bottom while placing both of his feet on each side of the knife and pulled. One of his feet slipped off the head, shooting out of the water. Pulling his leg back in, he worked more on the knife, then turned right side up, slowly poking his head out of the water on the other side of the head of the caiman, taking in a deep breath. Back under with his lungs refreshed, he fought to get his knife out. He pushed and pulled, upside down, again placing one foot on the long nose and finally jerked the killing weapon out of the dead animal.

Toca slowly rose, standing out of the water, at the nose end only to see the female doing some frantic ritual to the caiman. With most of her body covering back on, she was screaming, hitting, and poking the belly of the caiman with all her might. The stick she used to throw at the fish earlier was bouncing off the stomach as fast as she was hitting it, making drum-like sounds. Toca stood there silently for a moment, observing as the female stopped beating the dead animal while bending over, breathing hard. When she looked up, she was startled as the Indian was standing there, watching her. She threw the stick down, ran, and splashed into the water, diving open-armed into him, almost knocking him down as she held him tight.

Toca's first natural reaction was to flinch back to protect himself, but when he saw she threw down the stick, he let her embrace him.

Realizing she was hugging him for saving her, rejoicing in his victory, he confidently thought to himself, *I am Toca, killer of the giant caiman, you are now safe, female.*

Then just as fast as she dove into him, she pulled away, stepping back and looking at his body, then down to his man-member area. She pointed while turning her head, saying something.

She kept pointing so he looked down, finally understanding what she was saying and why she kept hiding her face. He realized his waist wrap that covered him was missing. *She must know I'm on my manhood journey.* Thinking deeper about this, he thought, *She must be on her female journey, preparing to be given to a man. That's why she's hiding her lower female parts.*

He twisted his head around, looking in the water and on the sand for the wrap. Not seeing it, he went to the original spot where he stabbed the caiman. Peering down and around, he reached into the undergrowth of the water lilies and pulled it out, raising it in the air, looking back at her. "I found it!" he said with a smile as he strapped it back on.

*****

Shana was frantically putting on her clothes just inside the forest's edge. Embarrassed, no one has ever seen her body except her mother and father. Also she had never seen a man naked except for babies and young children back with her people.

After putting her clothes on, Shana looked toward the river but no longer could see him. Stepping out on the beach, the large alligator was partially onshore. *It moved...was it still alive? But it's on its back?* she thought to herself. Carefully looking up and down the river for the Indian, then back at the animal, suddenly a leg came thrashing out of the water next to its mouth. She screamed in horror, "It's got him in its mouth." Without hesitating, she ran toward it, picking up the stick she used earlier, and began to stab at it and hitting it, trying to kill it. The alligator lifted and shook its head around while upside down. Movement caught her eye on the other side; this time, she saw the Indian's head appear then disappear. She began beating the animal faster now, yelling at it to let him go. Terrified, she thought to herself, *I found the Indian, now he's going to die because of me!* Then she prayed out loud, repeating it over and over. "Please, God…let him live, let him live!"

After beating the animal for a while, she noticed its head wasn't moving anymore so she stopped, bent over, exhausted. Looking up, there, watching her was the Indian, standing in the water. At first, she was stunned but recovered quickly, jumping up to him, dropping the stick, and hugged him, giving thanks to God. She stepped back to see the damage the alligator did and saw nothing until her eyes got to his waist, and once again, there was his private parts, exposed again. Turning her head quickly, she pointed to his waist and told him to get his clothes on.

As if the Indian understood her this time, he walked around in the water, looking for his clothes, and pulled up a small piece of animal hide with strings dangling from it. He held it in the air to show her he found it then put it back on.

CHAPTER 4

Toca walked back to Shana on the beach next to the dead black caiman. Standing there, looking at each other, they both were oddly relaxed. Having shared a life-changing moment, they instantly had a mental connection of trust. Understanding each other would protect the other even when they didn't know who the other was and didn't understand what the other said.

Shana attempted a conversation, telling him he needed to come to the tent and look at her sick father. She talked slowly and loudly, thinking it would help him understand as she pointed back in the direction of the clearing with a motion of her hand to follow.

Toca understood she wanted him to go to her hut but he had a lot of work to do. He spoke verbally and, with hand gestures, pointing to the caiman, explained they needed to cut it up and start drying the meat. He went as far as to touch her dress then pointed to the area she had hung it to dry, trying to get her to understand. He glanced up into the sun and looked back down, telling her it was getting hot and they needed to hurry.

Shana had no interest in what he was talking about; the only thing on her mind was her father and this new Indian who could help. Finally she impatiently grabbed his hand and started to walk away, pulling him along the sand.

Toca stopped, jerked his hand back, and raised his voice, slowly stating, "Female! I am in charge here. You will do as I say! I saved your life by killing the giant caiman, now we need to dry the meat."

Stunned, Shana quickly turned and looked straight at him with wide eyes and a serious look. Toca stepped back; it wasn't the reaction he was expecting.

Out of place in the moment, a smile came to her face as she asked very slowly, not in English this time but in her mother's native Indian language, which she spoke fluently, "Did you call me a female?"

With surprise, Toca bobbed his head forward, smiling, and said, "Female." And he pointed to her.

Shana figured out if the young man talked slowly, she might be able to understand what he was saying, and vice versa, in her tribal tongue from the United States. It wasn't exactly the same language as her but very similar.

"You talk slow then I can understand," she told him slowly while pointing to his mouth and her ears.

"I talk, you work," Toca answered deliberately, glad they were understanding each other as he pointed to her then to the dead caiman.

Her smiled vanished and the serious face was back but not for the same reason. "We go back to my papa!"

Toca cocked his head, not understanding what papa meant and tried to repeat it. "Paapa?"

Shana quickly replied, "Father, Father."

Understanding, shaking his head, he replied, "Father." Then it came to him, the tall white man was her father. He repeated father again as he gestured with his hand high above his head that he was tall. Then pointed to his face, looking around for something that was the same color, and there was the whitish belly of the caiman. Pointing back and forth to the caiman's stomach and his face, saying, "Father."

She smiled and said, "Yes, he's tall and his skin is white. We need to go to Father, he is sick and needs help."

Toca looked at the dead animal and repeated they needed to work on it. Frustration was setting in between them both and neither one was going to give in. For Shana, her emotions began to swirl. She didn't know if she was getting angry or if she wanted to cry.

Toca wasn't sure how to handle this disobedient female. He knew this was her tribe's area but there were priorities and the one right now was taking care of the kill.

He was done with the arguing. He turned to the caiman and started to cut it apart. While slowly cutting the tough skin, he thought how much time it was going to take.

Then it came to him like a slap in the face—he has spent two days in one spot. He began to cut faster and harder to get back on his journey to the endless water and start back to the hidden valley. Only eleven moons remained and he still doesn't know how far it is to get his shell for the Katata Ado status.

Forgetting about the female while concentrating on the work, suddenly she knelt next to him with the long light reflector in her hands. Shana saw he was using a stone knife to work on the alligator. Knowing from experience with her tribe back home, seeing stone knives and tools and listening to the elders of the old ways, the machete would be much faster so she handed it to him.

It startled him at first, seeing it, then curiosity set in, especially when the female tried to give it to him then demonstrated what it can do. She cut the hide where he was working, easily slicing through the tough armor. His eyes went wide, catching his breath with excitement. She handed it to him, almost pushing it into his hands. Putting his knife away in the sheath on the inner side of his forearm, he slowly grasped the machete. Examining it closely and touching it with great care, he was amazed. It was smooth, hard, and very sharp, as he found out sliding a finger down the blade. He sliced his skin with ease, jerking back from pain as blood appeared from the small cut. Toca laughed but Shana gasped at what he did. What he had in his hands was life-changing to him. His head was spinning with all the things he could do with it. The mystical light reflector faded away now as this long knife was introduced.

"Chief Acuta would be very excited to have this," he stated rapidly, looking back at the young female as though she knew who he was he was referring.

Shana looked on as this young man was in awe of such a simple thing. She was clearly beginning to comprehend who this person truly was. A young man of the forest, barely clothed, using tools of the past. Fearless with the abilities to kill big animals. Yet completely naive to the outside world. He isn't aware of all the wonderful things that could make his life easier. But he is hidden from all the bad and evil things of this world where the wonderful items easily can turn into horrible things.

A rush of stories started coming to her that the elders would talk about back home. Great adventures of the past filled with mighty warriors, exciting hunts, and the freedom to live and be who they were—a proud strong people.

Then the white man came, bringing gifts of new things. Things that helped them work and live easier. Changing the way they have been doing things for thousands of years. Slowly tearing their world and identity apart. Eventually treating them as a lower form of human, mocking their lifestyle and beliefs. What the Indian nations had to say meant nothing and their way of life and heritage brought forth by their ancestors was worthless.

Through this invasion, the outsiders began taking land that didn't belong to them, destroying ancient hunting grounds, and bringing to a pure race of people diseases that easily killed the Indians. "Like my Indian mother," Shana whispered out loud, thinking through this process of this innocent Indian and herself, a half-breed.

A person of both worlds trying to figure out what is truly the right way to live. For the most part, she was socially rejected by her own tribe and the same with the white people. It was difficult and confusing, finding her identity and a place of belonging even at her young age of thirteen.

Suddenly she wasn't feeling good inside and her enthusiasm flattened. It struck her she was one of those her mother's people talked about, and at this moment, right in front of her eyes, it just happened. *I'm an outsider going into someone else's land. And I just showed him his first new thing,* she thought to herself. *What are we doing here? God, is this right for us to be here? Showing innocent people a different way of life*? Still kneeling next to the Indian, watching in a daze as he was having a great time working on the beast. Her mind was swirling on the thought of what was happening. *I don't understand, God, my people don't mind the comforts that make their life easier. But all the old ones talk about the great days of the past. Was it a good thing for our people to change their lives and live like the white man? But without my father coming to my mother's nation, you and I wouldn't be talking.* Shana smiled on that final thought.

A slight breeze came off the river, bringing cooler air while refreshing her skin.

"Shana, follow him and you will see clearly what I have for you." A soft voice quietly spoke to her. She looked at the Indian, concentrating on his work, then looked around for someone else talking but no one was there. She realized it was the same voice from yesterday, saying, 'Surrender to him and I will guide you.' Peace began soaking into her heart and she instantly stopped worrying. The things her father said this morning about holding God's hand and he will guide her by directing her steps were beginning to make sense in the midst of this confusing situation.

Thank you, Holy Spirit, for speaking to me, she thought and smiled just in time; the Indian handed her a long thin slice of meat, pointing to the area she hung her clothes to dry. Without words being said, she knew what he wanted. They continued this arrangement for a long time. He kept cutting the meat and she, hanging it to dry. She was beginning to run out of room because there was so much meat. Walking up and down the edge of the forest, she was figuring out more area to hang meat so it would be in the sunlight.

The bugs had been flying around since they started, but now, the air was getting thick with them and Shana wasn't liking the insects attacking her or the meat. She broke the silence between her and this new person in her life by swatting the bugs away with her hands and voice.

Toca looked around at her to see what was happening. He stared at her, perplexed, thinking to himself, *Why is she just standing, slapping at the insects*? He got up as he walked to her, looking at all the meat hanging, and gave it a gratifying grin. Then he stepped up to her and said, "Why do you not have juja oil on?"

Shana looked at him, not understanding the word and repeated it. "Jajo?"

"Juja oil."

"Juja oil?" She shrugged her shoulders, not having a clue what he was talking about.

"Juja oil, keeps the insects away," he stated as though everyone knew what it was.

"I do not know what it is?" Shana had a blank look on her face, holding her palms up. Toca looked around into the forest, focusing on something deeper in, and darted toward what he was looking at. Moments later, he was back with a long branch of a bush that had many green leaves, shaped like a star, with reddish dots in the center of the leaf.

"Juja plant," Toca stated, holding the branch toward her. He ran his hand down the branch, sliding off most of the leaves and rolled them up in a large ball, grinding them together over and over. Once the leaves were crumbled to the point she could no longer recognize it as leaves, he handed a dark green oily ball to her gesturing with his hand to rub it on her skin. She took the slithery ball and held it to her nose. It didn't smell bad but had a very distinctive strong odor, not bitter or sweet but one she never smelled before.

Looking hesitantly at the ball, she looked up at the Indian as he was smiling, nudging with his head to put it in on her arms. She went ahead and began lightly dabbing it on, and when finished, she handed it to the Indian. In his hands, he turned and walked up and down the rows of meat and, every so often, dropped pieces of crumbled leaves next to the meat until the whole ball was gone.

Shana looked around in the air and there wasn't a bug in sight. "Wow, they're gone!"

"Gone insects," Toca repeated, nodding his head with confidence and walked back to the remaining part of the caiman that needed to be finished. All the meat was cut up but now the armor hide required some attention in order to be dried for use at a later time.

As he was stretching it out and scraping off the unwanted internal parts, an idea came to him with what he wanted to do with a portion of it. Chief Acuta needed a new front and back flap cover around his waist. The one he has is very old and not black anymore but brownish gray from all the use. Toca looked up with excitement at the female and said quickly, "This will make Chief Acuta very happy."

Shana replied, "Slow down, I cannot understand when you talk fast."

Nodding his head yes, he said, "Chief Acuta will be happy."

"You are a chief?" Shana jerked her head back, surprised as she pointed to him.

"No, no!" Toca waved his hands. "Chief Acuta is a *great* man of my people," he exclaimed boldly with arms out and hands made into fists to show strength.

She nodded her head, understanding, then asked, "Where are your people?"

Toca started to explain, then something the chief told him came to his mind. *Protect our people.* Suddenly he closed up, looked away, and continued to finish the hide.

Shana looked on, bewildered. "What is wrong? Where are your people?" He didn't look at her and began to get nervous.

"Do you have any people?" she asked again as he looked back at her, nodding his head yes. "Where are they?" Then he shook his head no. *Why won't he say where his people are?* she thought to herself.

Then he turned and asked her the same question. "Where are your people?" She put her hands on her hips and said sarcastically, "You want me to tell you where my people are but you won't say where your people are?"

He ignored her, then asked, "Your father is in the clearing. Where is everyone else?"

"We are here by ourselves," she divulged. Then it struck her—her father has been by himself this whole time. Frantic, she turned and ran into the forest to the clearing, yelling, "Father, I'm coming, I'm coming, Father!"

Toca watched as this old female child ran away to her hut, calling for her father. He thought to himself, *Did I say or do something wrong*? Not thinking too much of it, he finished the preparations for the drying of the hide. He cut up a handful of short sticks lying around and sharpened them at one end. Then he hauled the hide higher up on the beach on its backside with the open stomach side cut wide open during the butchering process. He struggled, pushing the sticks through the edge of the tough skin and into the ground. Walking to the opposite side, he stretched the hide tight, repeatedly putting in stakes until the whole hide was stretched out tight, anchored to the ground. Going to the bone pile, Toca worked on the skull, digging out all the teeth, some the length of his fingers. Holding them in the air, as the sun glistened off them, he smiled, looking at his trophies and placing them on the hide.

To finish off the drying process, he went into the forest and got more juja leaves, rolled them around his hand for a moment, then sprinkled the pieces all around the hide and some on the hide itself to keep the insects and most smaller animals away.

Pacing around the area to make sure all the work was done, he carefully went to the river's edge, looking intently throughout the water, making sure no other predator had quietly eased in for a meal. Feeling it was safe, he squatted down in the water and washed the long knife as he admired it for the quick work it did and for all the things it could do. He began thinking how he could get one. *Maybe this one. The female did put it in my hands to use. Maybe she gave it to me?* Twisting it back and forth, looking it over, it instantly flashed in his eyes, causing him to squint. He held it out from his body to keep it from doing it again, but it was no use, it poked a beam of light at him again. "It's like the sun," he said as he looked up into the sky.

Slowly it was coming to him what was happening and he giggled at himself. This time, he purposely twisted the long knife to make the flash of light and it worked. After a few moments, he was learning to direct the flash of light all over the place; it became a game.

Soon bored, he laid it on the sand and got his knife out to clean. A much smaller stone knife, it wasn't smooth or shiny; but when he looked at the handle that had his spirit image carved on it, he smiled. Then he said aloud, "Thank you for making this for me, my new father. I will make you proud, I will finish my Katata Ado by bringing back a shell, and I will find a good god to save our people."

Getting out of the water from washing the knives and himself, he walked to the forest's edge. With the long knife in one hand

and picking up a medium-size piece of meat that was drying with his other hand, Toca started walking back to the clearing. An overwhelming feeling of satisfaction welled up in him from the great accomplishments of the morning. His body language was shouting out to the world, "I am Black Ghost! Protector, killer, and provider, soon to be honored as a man that will be the next chief of the Nashua people."

Just inside the forest, he heard screaming coming from the direction of the clearing. "Female child!" he exclaimed and ran toward her voice. He ran with all he had, slithering between the trees and vines, leaping over bushes as he gripped the long knife harder, ready to defend her.

He got to the clearing quickly and the female was standing next to the hut, crying. Once upon her, he looked around to see what the danger was but there was nothing. He looked at her body covering and it was okay, *No blood,* he acknowledged to himself.

"Why do you scream?" he asked, trying to see in her face that was covered by her hands.

Sniffling with tears flowing, she tried very hard to clearly get out words. "My father won't wake up. I think he's dying." She twisted her head in the direction of the tent.

Toca remembered the man falling down out of the hut yesterday, lying there motionless, when the female pointed to the sky and her father came back to life.

Toca stepped back, dropping the long knife and meat on the ground, lifting his hands up in the air and said, "Call the light."

Pulling herself together, she asked, "What are you talking about?"

"Your father fell down yesterday. You lifted your hands to the sky and the sun came through the clouds, shining on you and your father, and he woke up."

"You saw that?" she asked while calming down, then stated, "God answered my prayers."

Toca stood motionless, any confidence of control just fled his body; he was right. There is a god here! His eyes began to wander around, looking for it. Then he twisted his head, rotating his body slowly to see this god she just mentioned. Instantly feeling small in the open clearing, he knew he couldn't see into the forest but what was in the forest could see him.

Toca kept stepping backward in circular rotation looking for something to come out after him from the forest or the sky.

Shana, still standing next to him, reached out and grabbed his hand. Toca's whole body flinched and he gasped, inhaling and making noise.

"What is wrong?"

Saying with his eyes, working the forest edge. "You do have a god."

"Yes, that is why we are here."

Toca pulled his hand away from her and slowly bent down, picking up the long knife with both hands, grasping it in front of him, and asked, "Where is your god? I don't see it?"

"God is everywhere." She reached out and touched his arm again to change the subject, stating, "But right now, I need you to look at my father. He is very sick and he will not wake up." She let go of his arm and collapsed her face into her hands and began crying again. Her heart was breaking before his eyes. To her, reality was setting in; she was losing her father, the only family she had left.

Toca looked at her and tried to reason the situation, thinking to himself, *She wasn't scared of the god she spoke about so why should I? If this god was a good god and friendly to the young female, maybe if I am friendly to her, this god would be friendly to me.*

Toca slowly dropped his guard but kept the long knife in one of his hands and said, "Take me to him." He held out his other hand for hers. She opened her eyes to see his invitation, then took his hand.

They walked into the tent, cautiously stepping inside, as Toca's eyes quickly looked at all the details, then saw the man lying on the ground at the other end. His nose recognized the smell that first drew him to the clearing in the first place and it definitely came from this hut. As she pulled him to her father, Toca continued to gaze at all the things lying around. Objects with different shapes and sizes, some colorful, others plain. He was in awe; there were so many things he had never seen before.

"This is my father. His name is John. He started getting sick when we first started to travel up the big river," she explained as she knelt next to him, letting go of Toca's hand to grasp one of her father's hands.

He stared at the man lying down with his eyes closed, barely breathing. *His face is white like the clouds, why would someone's skin be this color*? he thought to himself. Then he saw that the man had been sweating profusely as his body coverings were wet as well as the strange bedding he was lying on.

Toca cautiously touched John's cheek with his finger. First to see what white skin felt like, then to check if he was hot. He was, and when he let go of his face, his finger left a temporary depression. Looking closer to the side of his cheek, next to his ear, Toca noticed John had a very large dark odd-shaped growth.

Still looking at the growth, he asked, "What is that?"

Shana replied, "It is a mole. He has had it all his life."

Toca had never seen anything like it on a person's face before, then told her, "Your father is hot and needs water in him."

"Yes, I know but he will not wake up to drink?"

With the same hand, Toca nudged John's shoulder to wake him but he didn't move.

Toca sat there for a moment, thinking, then an idea came to him. He stood up and told the female child he would be right back.

He ran out of the tent into the forest, looking up into the trees. It took a little while but he finally spotted what he was looking for. Up on a big branch, where it came out of the trunk, was a clump of multicolored flowers with petals so large they grew over the mound of moss from which it was growing. The whole head of flowers was resting on the mound which appeared not to have stems. He climbed the tree, grabbed the whole mound of moss, flowers and all, and went back to the hut.

Back inside, he knelt beside the female's father as she was wiping his face with a wet towel, trying to cool him down.

Shana looked at what the Indian had in his hands. "Flowers? What are you going to do with flowers?"

"Not flowers. Flower roots," Toca said as he pulled the flower heads off and dug into the mound of moss, pulling worm-like roots from it. Once he had them all pulled out, he laid them out on top of one another, going the same direction to make a neat small lengthy pile. He held them in his hand, looking around for a water bowl. Not seeing one, he asked, "I need water." Still looking around, the female handed him a canteen. He grabbed hold, trying to figure out what she just gave him. He looked up at her with a questionable frown.

"Oh, sorry." She quickly retrieved it from him and took the cap off then tipped it over enough so he could see a few drops of water coming out. "Water," she stated.

Amazed with where the water came from, he held his hand out with the roots and motioned for her to pour water on it. She filled his cupped hand that had the roots, then he gently rubbed the roots together and let it sit for a moment. Then he brought it to his nose and slowly took in a deep breath, enjoying the aroma with a smile.

He held it to the young female's nose and she breathed in deep, like he did, then quickly shook her head as if it was burning her nostrils and lungs. After the initial shock from the different sensation than she was expecting, she closed her eyes as the aroma took effect. It was awakening everything within her body. Her air passages were clearer than she ever felt, followed by her lungs which opened deeply, and eventually gave her tongue a refreshing minty flavor. She opened her eyes and everything appeared to glow with newness.

Toca rubbed the roots softly one more time then placed the string of thin roots on top of the tall white man's upper lip, just below his nose, so every time he inhaled, his body would begin to fill with the inspiring scent.

"We wait."

They both sat there, watching, as the young female did not know what was going to happen.

After a while, Toca broke the silence this time, still watching the man's face.

"Is your god a good or bad god?"

It was such an odd question that came out of nowhere, Shana was taken back for a moment before she could answer.

"God is a good god," she answered while turning to him.

He looked at her and asked, "Does your god make you kill people for it?"

Stunned again, with such a horrible thought, she began to think if she should have looked for this Indian. *Why is he asking this? Does this have anything to do with him not telling me where his people are?*

Taking a few moments to continue, she said, "We do not kill for God. Our God loves everyone," she said, putting on a smile, hoping it would tell him they were good people.

"I am looking for a good god to bring to my people," he said boldly, acting as if he knew what he was talking about.

She couldn't believe what she was hearing. He was asking about the very reason they were there in this place. *But why is he asking specifically for a good god? Did something bad happen to him and his people to ask such a thing*? she wondered. Different questions kept coming to her mind.

She pointed to her father and to herself and said, "My father and I are here to tell the Indians of the forest about God."

"What are Indians?"

"You are an Indian."

"I am not, I am Nashua!" Toca said with pride.

"Naachuu?"

"Nashua," he said slowly, correcting her.

"Nashuua must be the name of your tribe."

"Nashua is my people. Who is your people?"

Shana suddenly was without words. Who was her people? She was born part American Indian and part white man. And with her mother gone and her dad now dying, who was she going to be? She didn't know how to answer him without confusing him. She was confused herself.

She remarked, "I…I…don't know exactly."

Toca looked at her with a bewildered expression on his face and asked, "You don't know who you are?"

"I know who I am. It's hard to explain," she replied.

"Where are your people? Are they near the endless water?"

"What's the endless water?" Shana questioned.

"It's where I have to go to get a shell," he said, motioning with his hands the size and shape of it. Shana thought for a moment, trying to figure out what he was talking about, then exclaimed.

"The ocean? Are you talking about the ocean?"

"I don't know 'oshuun.' Chief Acuta said it's where all the rivers flow to."

"Yes, it's called the ocean," she said proudly.

"Are your people there?"

"No, but I've been there."

"Chief Acuta said that's where others are."

"Yes, there are others, as you put it, but they are not my people."

Toca was getting confused. His face was showing frustration, trying to find out who this old female child and her father with white skin were. He shook his head to clear the cluster of their conversation.

"Who are you? Where are you and your father from?" he stated, raising his voice slightly.

"She is a child of God," John answered calmly in his dead wife's language, with his deep voice, scaring both Shana and Toca. Toca quickly squirmed back away from the big man, not knowing what to expect next.

"Father!" Shana shouted as she draped herself over him, hugging him tight while taking the roots off his face. The flower root did its job and gently woke John up. He had been quietly listening to the conversation going on in his tent as he lay there peacefully. At first, he thought he was somewhere else, in a different place and time; but when he slowly opened his eyes, he realized he wasn't dreaming. He was looking at his daughter talking in a mixture of her native tongue and something else with a young man doing the same thing. He was able to make out words here and there, knowing her native language as well as Spanish and English.

Quickly understanding the dilemma she was having, telling this new person who she was, he had the answer. Reiterating what he told his daughter earlier to give her a foundation for her life as well as meaning and purpose.

"Who is our new friend, Shana?" John coughed out, asking in English, barely having enough energy to speak.

She looked back at the young man, who was still in a defensive posture, holding the handle of his knife still in its sheath, and asked, a little embarrassed, they hadn't told each other their names. "What is your name?"

Toca hesitated, looking back and forth between these new people. He was outnumbered and the man lying down was very big. Shana softly put her hand on the Indian's hand, grasping the knife handle, smiled and asked again, "It is okay. What is your name?"

Her touch was reassuring and put him instantly at ease. The young Indian looked at John and answered, "Toca."

John, trying to stay awake, strained with all he had and lifted his hand up and held it out. Toca looked at the man's hand then looked back to the female. Shana said, "Father wants to shake your hand."

Not really understanding what that meant, he went ahead and put his hand in John's. When John's large hand swallowed Toca's, as he gently clasped around it, Toca almost jerked his back. But there was a brief moment when Toca looked into John's peaceful face and, for some reason, knew there wasn't anything to be afraid of so he left his hand there.

"Toca, listen to me carefully." John struggled to do his best, not to speak the Indian language but to come up with energy to speak at all. Still holding on to the boy's hand with his head lying down on the blanket, facing Toca, he looked deep into his eyes and said, "Take my daughter with you to your people and make her one of your own, keeping her safe," John asked, knowing indigenous people are very good at taking care of their own people. His final moments of his life, he had to do what he could to care for Shana.

"What are you saying, Father?" Shana shouted out in English. "I'm not going with him and living with his people. I'm staying with you." She grabbed John's other hand as she stepped over his body, kneeling down on the other side of him, facing him and Toca.

Toca, completely overwhelmed with what her father asked, looked on with a shocked expression, not knowing what to say or do. He didn't know who these people were and they didn't know him. Where is their tribe? Why would this man ask him to take his daughter? He did sense, however, that this giant white-skinned man was about to die.

Toca has only known a few of his people that have died, a couple were really old and one was a baby.

John closed his eyes for a second, opened them, looking at her, and replied in their Indian language so Toca would be a part of his last breaths. "I will not be here for you anymore…" He was inhaling as much as he could. "We are lost in the middle of the forest and you have no one else to keep you alive." John rolled his head back to face Toca and smiled, letting him know he had confidence in him. Then pleading with his eyes, he mouthed. "Please, take her with you and care for her."

"No, no, you're not going to die, Father! He knows medicines—he will make you better!" Trying to hold back tears and give encouragement, she pleaded with him, grasping tightly his hand in both of hers.

Still slowly talking in Indian, John continued, "Sweetheart, I am completely at peace to go home now. I know Jesus is reaching out to me and I want to reach out to him. Your mother went to be with Jesus this same way. I now understand what she was saying."

Shana couldn't hold back anymore and began crying. The thought of her father not being here with her was the loneliest feeling in the world. The only person left in her life that she knew, trusted, and loved was hollowing out her heart.

"Do something! Don't let him die!" she pleaded over and over to Toca as tears streamed down her face.

Squeezing her hand to get her attention, she quieted down as John continued, "You are a young woman now, Shana, you must live as one. Remember what I said earlier, that God gives us the gift to choose where we go in life. Choose wisely and take his hand and follow in the footsteps he lays out for you on your journey. Then you will always have a life of hope, peace, and joy in your heart."

Struggling, John turned his head and looked at Toca. "Take care of my daughter. She knows the God you're looking for."

Toca's eyes went wide; it just came to him. Now he had true purpose to take this old female child with him.

John centered his head on the blanket, looking up to the ceiling of the tent, and slowly closed his eyes. He weakly drew his hands together with both of the old children's hands still in his, placing them on top of his chest. He let go of their hands, putting them together, covering them with both of his. Taking in a shallow breath and exhaling for the last time, he said, "I love you."

Without struggle or pain, John's body went silent. Then as though he was taking a shallow breath, his chest ever-so slightly raised then collapsed, empty, as his soul left his body.

CHAPTER 5

Toca watched on as the female's head laid atop of their hands on her father's chest. She had been crying for a while, heart-broken over losing him. He could tell she was slowly falling asleep, calming down, drawing in choppy breaths from crying so long.

He reflected this whole time, while she was grieving, trying to put the pieces together since the day before. The person he thought was a priest was actually an old female child with strange body coverings. The burning of body parts were only extra body coverings of her father. But why would she burn them and why did he have so many coverings? He recognized now that the long mystical light reflector was a long sharp knife, not something coming out of it.

The one thing he couldn't figure out was who was talking to him when he ran from the clearing and just before the black jaguar walked up to him, saying, "Toca, go back, you will find what you are looking for." And how would anyone or anything know what he was looking for? Only Chief Acuta knew he was looking for a good god.

He sat quietly, letting all these thoughts settle to only hear the female's father's voice repeat over and over, telling him, "Take care of my daughter, she knows the God you are looking for."

How am I supposed to take care of her? I have to move fast on my manhood journey to complete the Katata Ado. She can't move through the forest as I do, she will only slow me down. Then what will my people think of me bringing a person into the hidden valley, especially a female? he thought to himself.

It was late in the day and he was getting hungry. He remembered that he had brought a piece of the caiman meat from the river and left it outside. All their hands were still together so he slowly pulled his hand away, not to disturb Shana, and quietly went outside.

Stepping into the open clearing, he instantly felt free and refreshed. Inside that hut was confining with walls he couldn't see through and it smelled. Looking around for the meat on the ground, he picked it up and went to the firepit. The pit was piled high with ash and clumps of burned pieces of wood spread out in it.

These people are strange. They don't know how to use fire and why is the pit so big for only two people? he thought, shaking his head.

Toca knelt to the side of the firepit and gently put his hand on the charred logs. They were cool to the touch so he slowly poked his finger down into the ash. He kept going down until his whole hand was almost swallowed up and then he smiled.

Not to disturb the ashes, he slowly lifted his hand out and sat the meat down at the end of one of the logs in the pit then cautiously ran into the forest, looking up to the trees again.

Soon finding what he needed for the fire, Toca climbed up and pulled off a large piece of a termite nest. When he did that, termites fell all over the place, squirming to recover from the destruction of their home. His eyes lit up and began picking them up as fast as they were running and popping them into his mouth.

After the hordes of the miniature appetizers finally disappeared, he dropped down from the tree and started back to get the fire going. Suddenly, as if he was reliving a moment earlier, he heard the old female yelling from the direction of the hut. This time, he heard his name over and over again. Running toward her, he made out the words she was yelling, "Toca, where are you, come back! Please, don't leave me!"

Running back into the clearing, she spotted him and began to run to him as fast as she could. He slowed down, and when they got to each other, she threw herself on him, wrapping her arms tight.

"Why did you leave me?" When Shana awoke, he was not there. When she stepped out of the tent and didn't see him, panic set in.

Thinking Toca had left her, she felt as if she was the only human left in this unfamiliar world with strange plants, animals, and weather.

"I didn't leave you. I needed to get the fire going to cook us the caiman," Toca said calmly, understanding she was an old female child that needed protecting.

"Don't ever leave me, you are the only person I know," she said, holding on to him.

He gently pulled himself from her and, with a concerned look, asked, "Where are your people?"

"I don't have any," Shana said as she began to cry again. The influence of her father passing pried open her heart where loneliness had been building ever since she was a little girl. Finally it was all coming out from its hiding place where she had locked it up subconsciously in order to not feel the pain.

She was alienated equally from her Indian family and white people because she was a mix of both. Continuously being called half-breed and many other hateful names that beat her down inside, to the point she was numb and didn't feel anymore. The truth of who she was had been in hiding for so long, she didn't know who she really was or who she should be.

"Please, don't leave me, Toca. I have nobody," she said, pressing herself again to his bare body. She didn't know who this young man was but she was comfortable and felt safe. Most importantly, her heart was at peace being with him.

"Old female child, I will honor your father's request. I will take care of you and take you to my people," he stated as he put his arms around her. The feeling he had at the river when she was hugging him was sweeping through him once more, growing in his mind. He was the protector, and the man within him slowly began to show its maturity. Responsibility and courage were swelling up and he liked it.

She stopped crying, as her head was laying on his shoulder, and said, "My name is Shana."

"Shana, old female child with no people, I am Toca, the Black Ghost, son of Chief Acuta of the Nashua people." They remained in each other's arms for a while as their hearts felt warm with comfort, seemingly beating the same rhythm.

After lingering together for a while, Toca finally separated himself from her and said, "I am hungry, you must be too."

Once at the firepit, he gently whisked away the top layer of ash and slowly blew deep into that spot. Repeating this for a while, it started to smoke and he saw a glimpse of an orange spark down inside. He lightly crumbled the extremely dry and flaky termite nest onto the smoking area. Blowing again, it began to smoke more and more until finally, a flame instantly appeared, engulfing the whole broken nest.

He then took a couple pieces of charred sticks in the pit, breaking them apart to expose unburned cores, slowly adding them to the small flame. Soon the flame was strong and alive, worthy for cooking. He cleaned off the meat and stabbed it with a long thin stick then held it over the flames.

After eating, it was getting dark and the birds began singing their goodbye songs to the sun, reminding Toca he needed to find them a place to sleep. Peering to the forest edge, he let his eyes adjust to the darkness but let his ears and nose do most of the work locating any danger that might be near. Sensing none, he walked into the trees and found a big spot where two large branches crossed each other next to one of the trunks, making a secure area to nest.

Quickly finding a juja plant, he broke off a branch and grabbed an armful of large broad leaves from various plants. He scaled the tree to his spot then rolled the juja leaves then wiped its oil all around the trunk and branches, making a protective barrier while they slept. Neatly he laid out the broad leaves to lay on and to cover up if they got cold or it rained.

Climbing back down, Shana met him at the base of the tree and asked, "What are you doing?"

"Our nest is ready when we sleep," he said, smiling.

"I'm not sleeping up there," she stated sarcastically while pointing to the nest.

"Where are you sleeping?" he asked, thinking he might have missed another bedding area.

She replied, "In the tent."

"What is a tent?"

She turned and pointed to what he called the hut.

"You can't sleep there," he replied, looking at her with a frown.

"Why not?"

"Your father is dead. We don't sleep near dead people."

Shana paused for a moment, realizing she hadn't thought about that. *He's right, I can't sleep in there. But I'm not sleeping up in a tree like a monkey.* Looking up into the tree, she was contemplating where she was going to sleep.

"I'll just sleep out on the ground next to the fire," she answered, then turned and headed back to the tent to get some blankets out and made a bed.

Toca caught up with her as she walked, saying, "You can't sleep on the ground out in the open."

"Why not?"

"Night creatures are everywhere. And if it rains, you will get wet."

"I'll take my chances," Shana said, stating her intentions.

"What is 'chances?'" Toca asked as they got to the tent.

"A chance is when you don't know the outcome and you hope for the best to happen."

"Why would you do something like that?" He looked at Shana with a confused expression.

"Everyone takes chances."

"I don't chance, everything I do has purpose," Toca stated then continued, "You take chance. I will sleep in the tree." Toca was grinning inside, knowing for some reason she didn't know the forest like he does, she needed a lesson about being safe. He quickly understood if he was going to take care of her, she needed to learn how to be smart to survive in his forest.

He planned on letting her sleep out in the open but he would be right by her side without her knowing it, to protect her. Chief Acuta would do this all the time with him when he was growing up. Letting him do what he thought was best during hunts and exploring, but if it got too dangerous, the chief would come out of the shadows, saving or protecting him.

Shana went into the tent and got out her things for the night. Toca watched as she laid everything out for her bed, then she asked, "Where is the machete?"

"What is 'machete?'"

"You know, the long sharp thing I gave you to cut up the alligator."

"Oh, what is 'alligator?'"

She stared at him, for a moment thinking he was playing with her. But as he stared back, expressionless, she could tell he was being honest. They were beginning to talk more fluently so she was forgetting his innocence and that they come from totally different worlds.

"An alligator is what you killed at the river."

"You mean a caiman."

"Okay, if that's what you call it," she said.

Toca pointed across the dying small flickering fire toward the tent. "The long knife is in there."

In the near distance of the forest, a troop of monkeys sounded off, whooping over and over, telling the world good night.

Startled, Shana quickly went into the tent and got the machete and came back to her bed and stuck it into the ground with a smile. "I'll be just fine."

Toca grinned back then bent down and reached into the firepit on one side where it had burned out. He picked up a couple of the larger pieces of remaining semiburnt logs that were warm and stashed them deep, hiding them in the warm blanket of ash, nestling them on the hot ground. Next he picked up several smaller pieces of charred wood and some thin sticks lying around outside of the pit and stood them up, touching one another at their peak. The fire mystically reappeared with strength as Toca replied, facing her, "Okay, but if you need anything, you know where to find me." He walked away in the direction of his nest.

Shana stood there, watching him vanish into the night of the forest. The monkeys had stopped whooping, and besides the few small flames of the fire flickering, the clearing was silent. Alone, the darkness crept in all around her as her confidence seemed to have followed the Indian boy. Once she couldn't see or hear anything, loneliness and fear began whispering to her. She looked around the clearing and beyond but nothing was there, everything was black. Shana didn't want to move. It felt like if she did, the darkness would awaken and begin to strangle her and she wouldn't be able to find her way out. Transfixed by the moment, all she wanted to do was hide. But from what? She didn't know, except from the darkness. Shana's mind was running wild with crazy images. Tightly closing her eyes, she began to pray.

It did help her feel some comfort, grasping out to God; although she heard words echoing back from yesterday, *Surrender to him and I will guide you.* She contemplated if it was God speaking to her. And if so, was he talking about surrendering to this Indian of the Amazon?

She knelt down, feeling around for her pile of blankets and slid in between them. Feeling a little secure with a protective covering, she gazed up into the sky, lying on her back. Slowly the stars were coming into focus, waking up to a new night. There were so many of the tiny dots glowing it was difficult to find the ones she was looking for.

The chief of her tribe where she grew up always told stories, bringing them to life, pointing at specific stars, connecting them together to form different animals and mighty hunters. The stories were handed down from generation to generation and no one ever got tired of these magnificent tales of the past.

Shana found herself finally at peace as her eyes closed from being heavy. She began to hum as her mind drifted to her father's body lying still in the tent text to her. Opening her eyes again, focusing deep into the night lights, trying to peer inside heaven, she asked aloud, "How is mother doing, Father?" Closing them for the night and humming herself to sleep, she dreamed of her parents walking hand in hand, smiling at each other as they always did when they were both alive.

*****

Once Toca got into the forest, he quickly gathered a lot of juja leaves then stealthily worked his way around the clearing, coming in on Shana from the opposite side of the tent. Sitting on the ground, just behind one of the corners, he watched on as she fell asleep. He had shadowed himself with a charred piece of wood he got from the fire earlier to be invisible to her in the shadows as well as large animals that would happen to come in the area.

Once asleep, he silently moved in on her and sprinkled an excessive amount of crushed leaves around her bedding, making an unbroken circle. He made it as potent as he could to distract any insect, snake, or animal, no matter how big they were.

He then looked up into the starry night and saw faint clouds slowly sneaking their way over the clearing. *Rain,* he thought. To the forest he went again, coming back with an armload of large broad leaves, half the size of his body length. Gently he positioned many of the light leaves over her bedding, in angles to capture any water and drain it away to the sides off to the ground. Then he leaned together, at the stems, several leaves, forming a miniature teepee. After tying the stems together with tree vine, he fit it slowly over her head, leaving plenty of room for her to move around inside the cone. Confident she was fairly protected, he turned and went back to his spot hiding around the corner of the tent. With leftover foliage, he spread juja leaves around where he sat then tied together at the stems the rest of the large fern leaves. Spreading them apart, he fit it over his head and let it drape over the rest of his body, touching the ground around him. He looked like a broad-leaf bush tipped upside down.

It rained lightly off and on through the night as both of them slept deeply. Morning came as usual with the birds welcoming the new day. Toca was already up and on the other side of the tent, hidden from Shana near the forest's edge, digging a large hole. After the hole was to his satisfaction, he glanced around the tent to see if she was still asleep. Still not moving, he decided to go the river and check on the drying meat and stretched-out hide.

Soon at the beach, he saw the meat was doing well even with the soft rain through the night. He knelt next to the hide, about to scoop up a handful of sand to spread over it. But instead, he exploded up to his feet, jumping away from the water, drawing his knife, frantically looking to each side of him. All around the hide in the sand were large fresh wet prints of another caiman that had a deep drag mark from its tail between the prints. He followed the prints with his eyes and saw, with relief, they went back into the water.

"Stupid, you know better. Always be aware," he said aloud. Letting his guard down was something he should never do, especially now that he has to take care of an old female child. Looking from where he stood into the water, he was trying to find the beast but didn't see it. He went back into the green vegetation and got a long stick then cautiously made his way to the water. Still searching but not finding anything, he patted the top of the water as far out as the stick would reach. After several moments, concluding it was safe, he knelt and warily put his lips to the water and drank until he was full. Then he filled his mouth as full as he could with water and went back to the hide and blew the water all over it. He did this two more times until he thought he had enough water on it then knelt again, scooping up a large handful of sand. Mixing up the water and sand, Toca began working the hide by rubbing his mixture in swirling motions. It was gently scraping off unwanted muscle and fat he didn't get off yesterday as well as softening the leathery hide interior.

When finished working on it, he went and got a strong branch full of bristly leaves from one of the trees and began sweeping the sandy water off the hide. Looking back at the meat, he admired all the food they had, thinking how long it would last. Then a frown came to his face as he began to think of how they were going to carry it all and how it was going to slow them down. Contemplating this, he headed back to the clearing.

On the way, he picked a few different pieces of fruit, one of which was his mother's favorite. Thinking about her drew in the rest of his people and he smiled, thinking of them one by one until he finally came to Jucawa. The smile quickly vanished as he thought of the horrible ways his mother and he had been treated, imagining how she was being treated while he was gone. His good mood of the morning was nowhere to be found. Now he was focused on getting back to the hidden valley in order to get in the way of Jucawa becoming chief.

Toca knew he was going to change things for his people. He would be a great chief like Chief Acuta and save them with a new god. A good god that would give them purpose and make them strong so his people would live forever, not disappearing without their existence ever being known, as his old wise chief told him.

Shortly to the edge of the clearing, he waited before going in to see where Shana was. Everything was the same. Her bedding and rain protector were in the same place. *Is she still sleeping?* he asked himself while looking toward the sun on the horizon as it was rising slowly to show its full splendor to all the living things in the forest.

He quietly walked up to her head that had the large green leaves tied together above her and waited for a moment. *She's still under there,* he thought, hearing her breath and watching the bedding slowly rise and fall with each breath.

"We have to go," he whispered to himself. Gently he lifted the head covering, exposing her face to a new day. The light got her attention as she slowly moved, wincing, her eyes still shut. "Shana, wake up," Toca said calmly. "We have to go."

"I want to sleep some more," she grunted out in English. Her mind still attached to a dream she was having, not realizing where she was physically.

"You need to get up," he said, staring down at her.

"Father, please let me sleep some more, I'm tired," she said, rolling over on her side.

Toca stepped over to where she rolled away from him and squatted down, facing her, giving her a hard nudge on the shoulder. "Shana, get up, we must get ready to go."

"Why are you talking Indian, *Father*!" She screamed the word *father* as she opened her eyes to see someone with a scary mask on. Scrambling out of her bedding, she turned away from the person to where the machete was sticking out of the ground and picked it up, facing him, ready to swing.

Toca didn't move as he watched the female burst up frantically.

"Who are you?" she shouted in English.

Toca realized he was still shadowed, smiled as his white teeth almost glowed inside the mask of dark designs, slowly stood up, and said, "Shana, it's me, Toca."

It took her a moment to completely come back from where she was in a dream and clear her mind to whom this person was with black striping all over his body and face. Relaxed and putting the long knife down, she said, "You scared me. What do you have all over yourself?"

"I didn't mean to scare you. I shadowed myself so you and the animals couldn't see me last night."

"Why would you do that?"

"So you couldn't see me taking care of you while you slept." He smiled again.

She looked down at the blankets with large leaves spread over them. "Why are these all over my blankets?" she asked.

"Before it rained, I covered you so you would stay dry."

"And this?" She pointed to the tied-up leaves off to the side of the blankets.

"I made that to cover your head."

"That was over my head?"

He nodded his head yes.

"Wow, I guess it worked. I'm dry," she complimented him as she looked around at the wet ground to the sides of the blankets. "Plus, I don't remember waking up from bugs landing or crawling all over me. This cover must have kept them away?" she stated as she picked it up.

He pointed to the thick circle of juja leaves.

"Oh, jahja oil."

"Juja," he corrected her kindly.

"Here, you need to eat." Handing her a piece of fruit, he continued, "Do you have water in that thing you had yesterday? Drink a lot," he told her, pointing to the tent.

"Yes, there is water in the canteen."

"Catein?"

"Canteen," she corrected him this time with a smile then continued, "Thank you, Toca, for taking care of me last night. And I'm sorry, I was rude to you by not sleeping where you made a bed for me. It's just that I've never slept in a tree before."

His mouth dropped open and was speechless for moment. "You have never slept in a tree?"

"No...Why would I?" she asked as if he should know.

"To stay alive!" he stated, looking at her, puzzled.

"What are you talking about, to stay alive?"

Asking himself, *Why wouldn't she know this*, then staring at each other, it came to him, *She mentioned her father got sick when they started downriver at the endless water but they were not from there. Where is she from and how long have they been traveling up the river?* Toca was thinking he needed answers. He has saved this female's life and now is going to take care of her. He needed to know who she was and where she was from. Especially if she has a god he needed to bring back to his people.

"Where are you from? You have different words I don't understand. What is this different body coverings?" He touched her dress. "All these things I've never seen." He pointed to the tent and then to the machete. "Why is your father's skin white like clouds? Chana, you are not from here. Where are you from?"

"Sha, Sha, Shana, not Chana. Let's sit down, this will take a while." Toca sat straight down to the ground as Shana pulled up her blankets, making a fat comfortable seat, gently sitting down on it. She took a bite of the fruit he gave her and Shana's face gave off a sour frown as she verbally commented with a *blahhh*.

Toca laughed then said, "You have to take the outside off and eat the inside."

"Oh!" She peeled off the outside then cautiously took a small bite. "Wow, that is really sweet!"

"It's my mother's favorite," he replied as they both smiled.

Shana began to explain her story. "My father and I are from a place far, far away called North America. It is a big land, very different than this." She looked around, pointing to the forest. "There is no forest like this."

"I don't understand—no forest, what can it be?"

"All these types of plants and animals, raining all the time, and every day, it's hot. We don't have this," she explained.

Toca sat there, almost in shock. "What is there?"

"Many different types of landscapes, there are mountains—"

He interrupted with excitement. "We have mountains. My people live between mountains."

"Does it snow and get really cold?" she continued.

"What is snow?"

"Instead of rain coming from the sky, soft white flakes, ice pieces come down." She did a floating motion coming down with her hands and her fingers wiggled.

"What is ice?"

"Frozen water."

"Frozen water, what does that mean?"

"Okay, we can't go through everything now." Shana was getting a little frustrated. She just wanted to get their story out so they could move on. "This will take forever for me to explain everything. Toca, let me give you an overall picture of where my father and I came from and how we got here. Then later we can go through the details. Is that all right?"

"That will be good. We have a very long journey until we get to my people. We have a lot of moons."

Shana answered, not comprehending what Toca fully meant by the length of their journey. "Good, so we have mountains with snow, then there is the flatland with only grass and small brush. Next, desert, where I am from. It only rains a few times a year. There are hardly any trees or a lot of plants except for cactus. It's mainly dirt and sand everywhere." She took another bite of the fruit as he looked on, envisioning the story she was telling.

"There are many colors of people. The white man, like my father, black people, then there are the Indians with brown skin. The Indians like you." She pointed to him. "The Indians have many tribes all over this land. My mother is from one of the smaller Indian tribes named Manso. Much like you are from a tribe called Nochuo?"

"Nashua," he said, correcting her proudly.

"Nashua," she repeated. "The Manso live in the desert area of North America. My father came to the Manso tribe to bring God to them." Toca's eyes lit up at the word *god*. "My father married my mother and they had me." Pointing to herself, at first smiling then turned into the sad face he saw yesterday.

"My mother died over a year ago. God told my father to leave the Manso Indians and go to the forest of South America to tell the Indians, far deep in the forest, about him."

Sitting there, lowering her eyes, she started to draw randomly on the ground with her finger. "We got to the Amazon River about two months ago and paid someone with a big boat to take us up the river. That's when my father started getting sick.

"More than four weeks of traveling deeper into the Amazon, we came to a city along this river." Shana pointed toward the beach where Toca killed the caiman. "The boat people wouldn't go any further up the black river so we bought a canoe. From there, Father wanted to keep going upriver so we canoed about another week, looking for a tribe he was told was in this area, but we got lost. We found this clearing by accident. By then, my father became too weak to travel any more so we stayed here and have been here for over a week. Then you found us." Shana looked back up and put on a smile, reaching out, touching Toca's arm to silently say, "Thank you."

There was silence for a while. It didn't bother Toca as he was reliving the story in his head, trying to understand words, places, and things she talked about. The quietness was irritating to Shana and couldn't take it anymore.

"So tell me about you, Toca, man of the forest!" She was anxious to hear his story.

"Did you say, Shana, you were looking for a tribe around here?" Toca suddenly felt very uneasy.

"Yes, we were told there was a tribe this way from the small city. Some of the local Indians there said other Indians were far deeper in the forest than these we were looking for, that no one had ever seen but only heard about."

Nervously Toca slowly got up, looking into the forest, telling Shana to get up and follow him. "Why? What's wrong, Toca?"

"Just come." He took her hand and grabbed the long knife and, in a crouched run, went into the protection of the green dense maze.

Once in, they stopped and knelt between two large thick ferns.

Toca whispered, "You said you have been here in the clearing for over a week. What does that mean? How many days is that?"

Shana hesitate for a second, not sure what was going on, then replied, "Um…maybe ten days and nights." She was holding up both her hands, showing ten fingers.

"I don't like this, Shana, we need to start journeying."

"Why?"

"I don't know these others, I have never met other people before." He looked hard at her and said, "You are the first other I have seen or met."

She stared at him in unbelief. She once again reached for him, this time with both hands grasping his shoulders, and slowly asked, "Where are you from, Toca?"

"I am on my manhood journey and I have been running through the forest toward the endless water for two moons until I smelled you and your father."

"Two moons…" She closed her eyes and shook her head, thinking what that meant, then exploded open, saying loudly, "You have been traveling for two months?"

"Sshhh!" Toca scolded her.

She continued quietly, "By two moons, you mean when the moon is full again?" Shana raised her hands in the air, putting her fingers together, making a circle and rotated it around two times.

He nodded his head yes, peering through the ferns, looking at the detail of everything in the clearing.

"By yourself?"

Again, nodding his head.

"How old are you?"

"Thirteen sun seasons."

"Sun season, sun season…oh! You are thirteen years old."

He nodded, hoping they were saying and thinking the same thing. His mind was on something else and his age wasn't important right now.

"Shana, we need to journey and leave this place. But first, we need to bury your father. I have dug a hole on the other side of the hut. We will work around the clearing in the forest and stay shadowed."

He began to stand, then she again grabbed his arm, pulling him back down, and asked, "What is wrong? Why are we hiding?"

"Others, I don't know who they are. We must stay shadowed so they don't see us."

"Is that what's on your face and body? Markings to hide with?"

He nodded.

"Toca, if there are others around here, we can't hide from them, maybe they could help us."

"We don't need help and I don't have to meet others now."

"Why not?"

"You have a good god. Chief Acuta said to bring back a good god to save our people from dying away. Your father said to take care of you. I am taking care of you now. You will come back to my people and save them with your good god."

"You think I'm going to live with your people?" Shana replied, stunned by the idea.

"Yes," he factually stated.

She hesitated, sitting back down hard on her heels. It just occurred to her, she hadn't thought through what she was actually going to do now and what it meant when her father asked Toca to take care of her. Reality was setting in as things were instantly getting clearer of her situation and what the meaning of the words from the Holy Spirit about Toca, *Surrender to him and I will guide you. Follow him and you will see clearly what I have for you.*

Then she saw her father's face in her mind when he was talking about Jesus, *Always take his hand and follow in the footsteps he's laid out for you to walk with him. He will give you peace, rest, and comfort along with more blessings than you can imagine. Then you will have meaning and purpose, never getting lost in the dark valleys of life.*

A moment of awe showered Shana as peace and understanding washed through her as she thought, *How perfect was the timing for all this to happen and these words from God and my father to be said to me.* The last of her family just died, she wasn't wanted where she was born, and now a total stranger needs what she has and she needs what he has—family.

She lifted her hand to Toca's face and gently directed it to hers and said, "I will follow you."

CHAPTER 6

The two old children worked quietly, burying John. Toca couldn't stop gazing around anxiously, watching for signs of the others Shana said lived in the area. She was very solemn and didn't show much emotion.

When they were finally done patting the last pile of dirt mound on John's body, Shana kneeled and bowed her head to pray. She first started praying by habit in English then moved to her native language. In her mind, while praying, she recalled her father making that mistake all the time with the Manso Indians. It put a smile on her face while her eyes were closed because she understood why he did it.

Toca, glancing back and forth, was trying to figure out what she was doing. He heard her say God several times, thinking that might be who she was talking to; but why were her eyes closed and facing the ground? The last time he thought she was talking to her God, she was looking to the sky.

When she finished, she looked to Toca and said, "Thank you for helping me with my father and thank you for taking care of me."

Toca gave her a slight nod of his head and kept looking around.

"So what do we do now?" she asked.

"We need to hide all these things you have and leave, shadowing into the forest and journey fast."

"You want me to leave all my things?" she stated more than asked, eyeing him as if he was crazy.

He faced her straight on, understanding she didn't like his idea and said, "Yes, we do not need anything, only some of the drying caiman. Then we'll pick the rest of it up on the way back to my people."

"What about all my clothes and bedding to sleep on?"

"What are clothes?"

"It's what I wear." She touched her dress and pulled on it.

"Body coverings," he answered. "Adult females of the Nashua wear monkey skin flaps over their lower front." He gestured to the middle part of her female area. "Adult males wear this." And he pointed to his manhood wrap. "Our old children, like us, start wearing body coverings when we leave on our journeys to become adults."

She stared at him, speechless at the idea of not bringing extra clothes, even though her father and she had seen most of the Indians on their short trip hardly wearing anything. It was a shock to both how anyone could live without wearing clothes and not be bothered that they were naked.

"How many sun seasons are you?" he questioned.

"I am your age, thirteen." She smiled, realizing they had something in common.

"Oh, have you gone on your female journey?" Toca asked innocently.

She thought for a moment how to answer, then smartly said, "I started my female journey when my father and I left our home. It will not be finished until we get to your tribe."

Toca popped his head back and smiled. "So we're on our adult journeys together!" Excited he added, "Sorry you have to wear body coverings. It must be hot and uncomfortable." He adjusted the position of the waist strap holding the small piece of hide to his body. "I will make you a female flap before we journey. I can make it out of the caiman skin!" Again, showing excitement, he was beginning to like the thought of her going with him and him taking care of her.

"But I like my clothes, Toca. My people cover their whole bodies."

"But why wear body coverings? It has no purpose. We wear these only to show the people in our tribe that our male and female parts are only for our mate to see and have."

That makes total sense, she thought to herself then said, "We wear body coverings to keep us warm, hide our private parts, and to look nice."

"Keep warm? It's always hot. The only other things we put on our bodies are paint and feathers when we have celebrations."

Thinking this through to herself, *That sounds just like my people back home, wearing headdresses and painting their faces and horses during special times.* Speaking back to Toca, she said, "Here in the Amazon, it is hot. But as I mentioned before, it gets cold where I'm from." She was attempting not to insult him for not wearing clothes but, at the same time, he was making sense.

Contemplating what she was saying, he responded, "But you live here now and you have no people. The Nashua will be your new people. You will be like Nashua, no longer a white Manso Indian."

Her eyes glazed over from the truth of her reality. She didn't know if she wanted to cry or be excited from his comment. But he was right; Shana Mathews, daughter of John and Wohani Mathews, the half-breed from North America, was going to live in the middle of the Amazon Forest with a tribe nobody knows exists. "I am now absolutely a nobody," she said aloud and then dropped her head into her hands, distraught.

"You are a child of God."

She looked up at Toca. "What?"

"Your father said you are a child of God. I don't understand, but that's what he said."

She grinned, looking into his eyes, and replied, "Yes, that's what my father said." Pondering that thought gave her comfort and some meaning to her life. Then Shana started to think about this issue with the clothes. It is hot here and this heavy dress is very uncomfortable. Most of the people around here, except for the civilized people in the cities, look at her strangely.

Then it struck her, she was treating these native people just like the American Indians talked about the white people treating them. Calling them savages and uncivilized. *How could I do that, I'm one of them. Just like I'm going to be one of these here.* She thought while getting confused with her identity.

"Toca, I will wear this dress for now. I have to think about what to do. But in the meantime, if we could hide everything really well, just in case I change my mind on the way back, are you fine with that?"

He hesitated for a moment, then nodded as he was still peering around the clearing.

"Great," she responded with relief, then continued, "Where are you going again? To the ocean…or endless water…for a seashell?"

"Yes."

Toca couldn't stand being out in the open anymore. He stood and said, "We will shadow into the forest and talk." They went a distance in until he felt safe, hiding in the thick plant life and began to explain as they sat back down.

"I must return to my people with a shell to accomplish the Katata Ado."

"What is that?"

"For my people, all old male children, when they become thirteen sun seasons old, must do the Katata. Which means they have to live away from the hidden valley for thirteen moons by themselves. This proves they are worthy to be a man. If they return, they come back as a man and are given a female. If you choose to do the Katata Ado, you must journey far and fast to the endless water and come back with a shell like the first chief of our people did long ago. The Ado proves you are not only a man but have experienced and learned what it takes to lead and protect a tribe.

"When an old male child accomplishes the Ado, he will be chief when his time comes. Very few have ever completed the Ado." With great confidence, Toca slowly stood with his skinny framed body, pulling his shoulders back and expanding his chest out, looking down at Shana, not whispering anymore, and stated, "I will accomplish the Ado and be chief of the Nashua people."

This time, it was Shana's turn to think about what was being explained. A few moments later, she asked, "So we are going to the ocean so you can get a seashell. Then we're going to come all the way back, continuing on for about two or more months deeper into the forest, until we get back to your people?"

Still standing tall, he put on that big bright smile, letting her know she was understanding correctly.

Then she asked, "You said my father and I were the only others you have ever seen. Is that the case for everyone in your tribe?"

Nodding, he sat down. "Yes, except Chief Acuta. He said when he was on his Katata Ado many, many sun seasons ago, he saw people near the big rivers and by the endless water."

"So when you say others, does that mean other Indians in the forest as well?"

Toca shrugged his shoulders and said, "Everyone not Nashua is other to my people. Only Chief Acuta and I know others exist."

"How is that possible?"

"The ancient ones who started our tribe found the hidden valley and we have safely lived there ever since." Toca stopped his story there, protecting the whole truth of which only chiefs are to have knowledge.

She was blown away by this incredible story of his people. But what amazed her even more was the whole reason why her father was told by God to come here. And that his exact instructions were to go deep into the forest to tell those Indians about him.

This was more than a coincidence but a miracle. She now was completely convinced she and her father were supposed to be here. *But why did he have to die*? she thought while thinking about him.

"Shana, follow him and you will see clearly what I have for you." This time, she didn't look around for who was talking to her; she knew, smiling to herself.

Toca quickly grabbed her arm with one hand, making her jump. With the other hand, he put his finger to her mouth to tell her not to make a sound. Lifting his nose up into the air, smelling deeply, he slowly rotated his head to look around. Something was wrong. He thought he heard a different sound in the distance earlier and now the birds in the trees around the clearing had stopped singing. His gaze came back to her, looking up and down Shana's body. *She can be seen,* he thought.

Leaning to her ear, he whispered, "Something big or others are in the clearing."

She popped her head back and mouthed, "How do you know?"

He pointed to his ears and nose. Leaning into her ear again, he said, "I am shadowed but you can be seen with your body coverings. Take it off, your brown skin color can hide better in the shadows."

Backing away, she quickly said in a loud whisper, "I'm not taking my clothes off!"

He pressed his finger to her mouth and opened his eyes wide, scowling at her, then jerked his head toward her, telling her to take it off.

She grimaced back at him, shaking her head no.

He spun his head around, looking toward the clearing. He definitely heard something this time. He turned back, looking around the spot they were in, and motioned for her to go deeper into the large bush she was sitting against. Reaching to the inside of the fern next to him, he quietly broke off several large leaves and leaned them against her. He then took her hand to instruct her to hold on to them to shadow her. Looking into her eyes, he whispered, "Do not move or make a sound. I will be back for you."

Her eyes went wide with fright. "Don't leave me," she mouthed. Before she could say another word, he went the opposite direction from the clearing behind her. She turned to see where he went but he disappeared. Instantly he was gone. She couldn't believe he left her there by herself, still looking around then turned back, facing the clearing.

Toca stealthily went back into the forest, a little deeper, then turned to circle around to the other side of the clearing. He stopped and shadowed behind a tree when he was to the opposite side and listened. He peered slightly around the trunk so one of his eyes could see what he was hearing.

Looking into the clearing through the vegetation, he didn't see anything so he decided to go quickly up the tree to perch above everything. About halfway up, he settled on a large limb, peering around the trunk again as his eyes caught movement that just went into the forest toward the beach where the caiman was drying.

Quickly dropping to the ground, he went in pursuit around the clearing, staying hidden. Once at the spot where he saw the movement, he looked for signs of what it was. There in the soft dirt was several normal footprints. *Others,* he thought, slowly looking around, squatting over his find. His senses reached out for any information, his ears were the first to get a response. They heard, in the short distance, most likely on the beach, soft talking of several people. Toca couldn't make out any of the words but he was guessing they were what Shana called Indians.

Needing to see these people, his curiosity was too great to ignore. Looking back down at the prints, he put his foot into one of them and concluded these were bigger grown men. Thinking through his strategy, he decided to come in at the end of the beach, where he jumped off the tree to kill the caiman, and go up the same tree. He worked his way out and around until he was to the backside of the tree. Out of sight, he effortlessly climbed to the limb he was familiar with and blended into the bark. Before looking around the trunk, he let his ears and nose do what they were very good at doing. Besides the smell of drying caiman meat, there were other things he sensed: a little bit of smoke odor from a fire, salty man sweat with a hint of fruit mixed in. *Bananas,* Toca thought, *They have been eating bananas.* Then there was something strange, still thinking to himself, *Seeds of the achiote tree. Why would they have a powerful odor of the seeds on them? It stains everything.*

Suddenly his ears found what they've been waiting for. He couldn't understand anything from their slurred grunting speech, talking very softly and quickly. Nothing like the language Shana and her father had talked to each other with.

Curiosity climaxing, it was time to see these others. With sloth movement, he peered around the tree, looking down at the beach. It was nothing he expected but answered his questions. Three men, with red and black painted designs all over their bodies, caught his eyes first. *Achiote seed paint!* He stated in his mind, smiling inside, answering his own question. They were wearing no body coverings except for large flat round things hanging from or in their ears and something that looked like little sticks going sideways through their noses. Their hair was cut short above their ears in a straight line around their heads. One was carrying a spear and the other two had long sticks, twice their body length, that seemed to be hollow like bamboo. They were standing around his stretched-out caiman skin as they talked, pointing to it and all the meat hanging up.

Once done with their conversation, they went to the meat, each grabbing several large pieces. Then they walked to the far side of the beach where they got into a long narrow canoe then smoothly and silently paddled downstream, disappearing into the distance.

He sat there for a while, reviewing in his mind the details of the men. *They are like me. Not like Shana and her father,* he thought to himself. *How they moved and gestured with their hands was familiar but what was all the stuff they were wearing on their bodies and what did it mean? Why would you cut your hair like that?* He smiled a little then frowned, thinking it looked silly but, at the same time, scary with the achiote seed paint all over them.

What did they use the long hollow sticks for? Their canoe did look similar to the small ones his people build for the smaller river that flows out of their valley. Many things were going through his head but there was a difference seeing these others from when he saw Shana for the first time. Maybe because the shock of seeing others has worn off but he definitely wasn't intimidated with these Indians as he was with Shana and her father.

He slithered down the tree, staying in the forest, and decided everything was all right for the moment. But it did confirm to him they needed to get going on their journey—now. He ran quickly out and around the clearing, coming in on Shana as he left—from behind her. He squatted down, less than an arm's length, and whispered, "Shana, it's time we prepare to leave." There was no response. He whispered again, this time, looking deeper into the fern, then realized she wasn't there. His heart began to race as worry set in. He looked around the area; then in the direction of the clearing, he heard something.

Quickly he shadowed to the edge, she wasn't in sight. He waited for a second, with his senses reaching for anything to locate her, then his eyes caught movement on the side wall of the hut, pushing outward. Focusing in, he began to hear loud rustling inside. "She's in the hut. I told her to stay, why would she—" Suddenly he saw movement, now outside the hut, in the air on the opposite side where the entrance was. It looked like the tip of the long knife glistening but he wasn't sure. "There are definitely two different things moving, one inside, one outside," he said, talking to himself as he decided to sneak in on what was going on. He darted to the backside of the hut as the rustling inside got louder.

Instantly he started smiling as he recognized the sounds of the thing moving inside. Slowly he crouched, stepping around to the side wall, peering around the corner to the entrance; he was relieved to see Shana standing, holding the long knife high, opening the flap entrance. *What is she doing? She's only going to make it mad*, he pondered to himself.

Just then, Shana broke the silence, shouting something loud inside the hut, he jerked his body with surprise, then she quickly turned, dropping the flap, running away and yelling, "Toca, Toca, help!"

He began giggling, saying aloud, "She definitely isn't from the forest," watching her run away, screaming. Just as fast as she turned to run so did the animal inside as it ripped open the entrance flap, taking off after her. Once he saw the boar catching up to her, he began to run as fast as he could, still laughing about the moment, yelling out to Shana, "Jump up into a tree! Jump into a tree!"

As he ran, Toca swiftly scooped up a rock and, with all his might, threw it at the wild pig, hitting its mark on the rear end. The boar turned; seeing something running after it, it instantly stopped and faced the new opponent.

Shana made it to the forest edge, hearing Toca's instructions, and jumped up to the first tree limb she could reach and pulled herself up. She turned around just in time to see Toca changing directions and running from the fierce squealing wild animal with huge fangs protruding up from its lower jaw. Amazed at how fast and smooth Toca darted, and before she knew it, he and the animal disappeared into the forest and it went silent.

Sitting on the limb for a while, waiting, she softly began to call out, "Toca, Toca." Then terrible thoughts ran through her head of him being torn up or killed. She got louder, "Toca, Toca. Oh, what did I do?"

"You did not listen to me."

Startled she looked around and he was sitting on the tree with her. Relieved she dropped her head and said, "I heard something making noise in the tent, you went the other way and I decided I had to do something."

"You do not know the forest, I do. You will do what I say or you will die." Completely changing his demeanor about the situation, he wasn't being soft on her. His memories reflected back how Chief Acuta taught him; sometimes he was hard, other times soft. This new person from far away needed to learn fast to obey so he was hard, even when he saw tears start to flow down her face.

"I'm sorry, Toca. I was scared and I needed to protect my things."

"Why do you need things? The forest is everywhere and has everything we need. My people do not need things, only a god which we do not have. You bring your God and we will provide everything else you need."

Then it hit her so hard she almost fell off the tree, saying to herself, *They have what I need on the outside and I have what they need on the inside.* Everything was becoming clearer and clearer to Shana as purpose and direction were being magnified. What she would bring to his people will change their lives and what they would give her will change the person she longed to be. Free with a family that would treat her equally.

She blinked her tears away, replying, "I understand more now, Toca. I will listen to you and I will leave my things here." She wanted to hug him but didn't want to let go of her tight grip on the tree. She smiled and apologized again, slowly working her way off the tree, but her dress got caught. After pulling to try and free it, the dress ripped, letting go of the tree, dropping her a little ways to the ground onto her buttocks. Recovering from the minor fall, she leaned over, lifting the torn part of her dress, examining the damage. She gave out a loud sigh then said, looking up at Toca who effortlessly dropped to the ground next to her, "Well, you're right, the dress isn't for the forest, especially when it comes to climbing trees."

They stood up and she grabbed the long knife she dropped to climb the tree then started to walk out into the clearing. He took her hand to stop her. "Be aware, Shana!" he stated quietly.

"What?"

"Be aware of everything around you." He pointed to his eyes, ears, and nose, then with the same finger, pointed all over. "You must learn to stay alive in the forest, and if you are going to be Nashua, you must not be seen, heard, or smelled. You must do all these things before you move or go anywhere, then you will live."

She took his instructions to heart and did all three things, at the same time, exaggerating each of the senses. Stretching an ear way out to the side as her nostrils widened, inhaling deeply, along with her eyes protruding out, trying to look far away. Toca looked on and wanted to laugh again at her young childlike innocence. Watching her, he realized he needed to train her, just as the mothers begin to train the little ones, how to live life. They have no idea why they are doing things until they experience the reason. And right now, watching Shana, she has no idea what she's looking, listening, or smelling for. How would she know if what she's sensing is good or bad unless she's told or experienced it?

As Chief Acuta treated him when he was young and didn't know what he was doing, he still encouraged him after he went through the motions. So Toca did the same after she used her senses then walked them forward to the hut.

Once at the hut, Shana looked inside and said, "What a mess," then entered as Toca followed. She looked around and began to think of the things she really needed then looked back to Toca and concluded with a half-grin. "I guess I don't need anything as you said, Toca. Oh, wait, there is one very important thing." Quickly Shana scrambled around the littered tent until she found what she was looking for.

Holding it up, she turned to him and said, "This is all we need to live."

He focused in on the black thing and asked, "What is it?"

"It's my Bible."

"What's bibbl?"

"Bible, the Bible is God's holy Word." Toca somewhat understood the word *God*.

Gazing at it, he asked, "Is that your god?"

Now the tables turned and she became the teacher. "No, this is his words and one of the ways he speaks to us." It wasn't clicking in Toca's mind what she was saying. He leaned forward toward the Bible with his ear and listened.

"I do not hear anything."

Almost stunned, she realized how childlike he was. "No, no, we don't hear with this, we read this." She opened the Bible, exposing pages so he could see the words written on the paper.

Toca looked at her as if she was crazy or if she was trying to trick him, then he asked, "What is read?"

How stupid can you be? she thought to herself. Then moments of her past came flashing to her when the old ones in her tribe didn't know how or what it was to read.

"Reading is hearing in your mind what you see." She pointed to her eyes, then to the side of her head.

Toca looked closely at the pages, intently listening. "I still do not see or hear your God."

Again, Shana realized this was going to take a while, like everything else, to explain so she changed the subject while closing the Bible. "I must take this with us, I don't need anything else."

"We need this!" Toca lifted the long knife with a confident expression.

She smiled and replied, "Yes, that is a good thing to take with us also."

They stepped out of the tent and Toca intently listened. The birds were singing, and he heard monkeys making noise far away in the forest. He didn't see anything moving except for whispers of clouds above as birds darted here and there. Inhaling to fill his head with scents, too many rushed through his nose. Multiple foreign odors from inside the tent confused the natural fragrances he was used to smelling. Even though John was buried and covered with dirt, he smelled death. This made Toca anxious to get away from the clearing. He began to give directions to Shana in more of a demanding tone.

"Shana, we need to make carrying pouches to bring the caiman meat with us as well as something to hold the long knife and your God thing," he said, pointing to the Bible she was holding. "Our hands must always be free. These pouches our females make out of monkey, deer, or pig hide. And they use them to hold food when collecting in the forest. Also to hold babies close and tight." He gestured, with his hands, something going around their shoulders, holding out in front of his body as well as his back area.

She smiled and understood what he was needing. Her people had the same thing to carry things and their babies so she quickly answered what he was asking for. "We will use this." She reached out and touched the side of the tent.

He touched it with her, running his hands over it, and said, "It is too big."

"No, I'll cut it up in pieces to make caring pouches. My people have them too. I'll need my sewing bag, it has strong thread and needles in it!" She was getting excited then peered into the damaged tent, looking around for the sewing bag. He looked at her with surprise. Still touching the canvas tent, an idea came to him as he started to pat really hard on the foreign material.

"This is strong?" he asked.

She responded, coming out of the tent with the bag in hand. "Yes, very strong."

"It can hold weight?" He gestured something heavy.

"Yes," she answered, wondering what he was thinking.

He stepped to the long thin things he thought were tree vines that kept the top corners stretched out and anchored to the ground, realizing it was something else. "What's this?"

"Rope, it's very strong too."

He nodded his head with a confident smile. "We make hanging beds. My people sleep in hanging beds. It keeps us safe off the ground and is comfortable. Better than sleeping on hard tree limbs," Toca said, smiling at her, knowing this would make her happy.

She was trying to envision what he was saying, but whatever it was, if she didn't have to sleep in a tree, that was definitely a good thing.

She smiled back and said, "That sounds good, Toca, but I don't know how to make one."

He knelt on the ground next to the firepit and drew a picture of a hanging bed attached to trees with the ropes. Then he laid down on her blankets, wrapping them around his body, demonstrating what it was like being in a hanging bed.

She nodded her head rapidly, understanding what he wanted, and agreed she liked the idea. "I understand now, they are called hammocks. I can make those." Looking back at the tent, thinking this through, she blurted out, "Toca, how about if the hammocks and carrying pouches are the same thing?"

He tried to imagine what she was talking about. Excited, she bent down to his drawing, and with hand gestures and drawing over his, she showed him how they could fold and roll the hanging beds up using the end ropes to go around their shoulders and hold it tight, keeping everything together inside.

Calmly he looked up into her eyes and said, "You are a smart female, that will work."

She contained herself from laughing at his comment and replied, "You are such a romantic gentleman."

"What is romantic?"

A slight giggle leaked out, answering him, "That's what I thought."

He frowned at her, understanding she was making fun of him, then said, standing up, "You start making hanging beds, I will take care of the caiman meat and the hide." He turned around, peering at the forest edge, and started to run off.

"Wait, Toca"—reaching out with her voice to stop him—"you never told me where you went when you left me alone." She pointed in the direction of the forest behind the tent.

"I followed others to the river until they went away."

"What, you saw others?" She stood up, looking into his eyes, shocked.

"Yes, three men with painted bodies and big spears. They took some of our meat." Toca turned and ran toward the beach, instantly vanishing into the vegetation.

Watching him disappear before her eyes, she held back panic. This new information ignited the same drive as Toca to leave the clearing and start their journey.

CHAPTER 7

Toca was back to the edge of the open area from the river, dragging as much meat as he could on the hide of the caiman. Before leaving the beach, it took him a while to naturally erase the evidence on the sand they had been there. He carefully whisked away, with fern leaves and dried up tree branches, footprints, drag marks, anything that would show a caiman was cut up and spread around to dry. The last thing he wanted to do was attract more others because they left something behind to follow.

Before stepping out into the clearing, he looked to see what Shana had done. To his amazement, the hut was completely down and cut up as she diligently worked on the hanging beds. Finally getting to her, he was tired. The amount of meat on the large hide was almost too much to drag through the thick vegetation. Also it had not completely dried out so the weight of it made a deep drag mark through the forest which Toca had to continually rearrange into a natural appearance.

"You have done a lot of work," he commented between breaths, bending over with his hands on his knees.

"You too," she said, seeing the sweat pouring down his face as she handed him the canteen. "Isn't that more meat than we need? Why are you worried about it?"

Looking at the strange round thing she handed to him with two flat sides, it took a moment to remember how to get the water out, then he drank down a couple of big swallows. Still catching his breath, he answered, "Nashua do not waste anything. When we kill an animal, we use all of it we can." That sounded familiar; the older people of her tribe talked about using every part of the animals they killed, not only for food, clothing, and tools but also out of respect for giving up its life so they could live.

Shana stood as Toca commented with surprise, looking down at her legs, "Your body coverings, you cut it off!" When she was sitting down, he couldn't see she cut the majority of her dress off and undergarments from her knees down, still wearing her boots.

"Do you like it?" she asked, smiling as she tasseled it around, swaying her hips.

"That will work," he stated with confidence.

It wasn't the answer this young thirteen-year-old girl was looking for but at least she knew he approved.

"You take your top covering off and you will be good. You will be Nashua then."

She stared at him. *Couldn't he just be happy with what I did?* she thought. "Toca, I will not take my upper clothes off."

"It is too...bright. You can be seen through the forest. You will not be able to shadow and hide," he stated.

She thought for a moment, realizing his true motive again for her not wearing clothes. It had nothing to do with her being female and him being male. His motive had true purpose—a purpose for surviving in the forest. Then she remembered he told her that yesterday, *Everything he does has a purpose.* Figuring this out, she looked around in the open area of the tent and spotted something that could work. Picking it up, she put on one of her father's button up long-sleeve shirts he had not worn yet. It was brown with large black patches on the elbows. It was big on her, hanging low over her new short skirt as the sleeves draped past her hands.

Toca raised his eyes, admiring it. "That will hide your body coverings, but when we need to shadow, you have to take everything off so I can mark your body to disappear into the dark light." He pointed to the remaining black charred ash on his body that hadn't worn off from sweating.

"I'm not willing to take all my clothes off, and especially, I will not allow you to touch me," she boldly stated, having a stare down with him.

He stood there for a moment, reflecting her gaze, then his train of thought went to more important things. He looked down at the fire and said, "I need to get a fire going. The meat isn't dry yet so we are going to have to smoke it tonight and leave when the sun comes up."

Not resolving the body covering issue, she went along with the change of subject, saying, "You go get wood and I'll find the fire starter in this mess." She turned and looked around on the open tent floor.

He looked up, surprised. She went along with his idea quickly, but more than that, she told him what to do. Replying firmly, he said, "Females get firewood."

Oh no, he didn't just say that, did he? she thought, then remarked, "I'm not your female. You know the forest and you move fast in it. You will find the wood better than I will," she told him, standing her ground as she put her hands on her hips.

He knew she was right about everything said. Toca turned, not showing emotion, and ran into the forest. Shortly he came back with an armload of dried tree branches and withered up leaves and moss. Dropping them into a pile next to the firepit, he went back again and was gone a little longer. This time, he had to cut down a lot of bamboo; returning with the long stems, he stopped short of the clearing, stunned at what he saw—a large fire burning in the pit. *How did she get a fire going so fast?* he thought.

Peering about the edge of the forest, around the open area, he looked for detailed things that didn't belong. But everything seemed to be all right as Shana sat next to the fire, working on something. Still uneasy about the clearing, he exposed himself and walked to the firepit, dropping the bamboo, then looked around the ground for her fire bow stick or rubbing stick. Not seeing it, he asked, "How did you get the fire going so fast?"

"We have these to start fire with." She dug into a small leather pouch, bringing out, what appeared to him, two different rocks.

Looking at the rocks then at her, then to the rocks again, he shrugged his shoulders.

"This is how we start fire." She demonstrated, striking the two rocks together at an angle, shooting a large spark into the fire.

Completely unexpected, he jumped back. "What just happened?" he said, then asking her, "Do that again." She struck the two rocks and a few sparks flew into the fire once more.

"How did you do that?"

"These are special rocks that start fire." He squatted down next to her and observed the two rocks. *They do look a little different than any rock I've seen, but how do they make fire*? thinking to himself.

Curious, he slowly lifted his hand and hesitantly touched one of the rocks with the end of his finger and jerked back. "It's not hot," he said aloud. So he touched the other one. "It's not hot either." He cautiously took the two rocks from Shana, warily looking at them, then clanked them directly together but nothing happened.

She instantly replied verbally and, with hand motions, said, "You have to hit them hard sideways. Like scraping and bouncing them off each other."

He nodded then tried it again, and this time, it sparked and he jumped away from the surprise. "Oh...this is good," he said, still uneasy about it.

The firepit popped, getting their attention and sending sparks of miniature pieces of flaming wood around. He handed the rocks back to her and watched as she put them back into the pouch. "Shana can bring her fire rocks," he said with confidence, knowing she would be happy to bring more of her things. Also Chief Acuta would like to see these, just like the long knife. *The long knife,* coming to mind while looking on the ground for it, he asked, "Where is the long knife? I can cut bamboo faster to make a drying rack."

She put the small rock pouch down and picked up one of the finished hammocks that was rolled up, ready to use, and handed it to him. "I hope you like this?" He took it from her, examining the new addition to his Katata Ado journey. It was tight and compact with the rope loops hanging out. She noticed he didn't know how it went on, so taking the pack from him, she gestured for him to turn around. Spreading the rope loops apart, Shana told him to put one arm through one loop and the other arm through the next loop. Once it was strapped to his shoulders, she turned him around, facing her, and asked, "What do you think?"

Toca wasn't sure if he liked something on his body. He twisted and swayed his body back and forth as it stayed on. Then he jumped and the back pouch flipped up and something hard hit his head from inside the pack. "Ouch, what was that?" he asked, rubbing the back of his head.

"I'm going to have to put a strap around the waist to hold the bottom section down, I guess." She paused, thinking how she was going to do that, then added, "But let me show you where the long knife is. Its handle hit you in the head." He turned to her with a questioned look on his face. "Turn back around and lift up your hand, reaching back to the pouch behind your head." She guided his hand to the top of the pack, reaching just inside, and he felt what she was doing. He grasped the handle and slowly lifted it out.

He turned to her with a big smile. "This is good, Shana!" She was excited at first from his response but the look in his eyes were that of a child.

She began to ask herself if showing this Indian all these new things was right, reflecting back to the sadness on the elder's faces and heaviness of their aching hearts about their people. A proud nation, free to hunt and go where they wanted for generations, are now caged up in reservations, being told what they can and cannot do by someone that is an outsider. Who at first brought gifts, new things to make peace, then civilize them, only destroying their way of life. She is that outsider right now.

Still watching him play with the simple canvas pack, she asked silently from her heart, *God, are you sure this is right? I don't want to destroy Toca's way of life and be responsible for the change of an innocent people.* There was no response. Shana watched on as Toca set the pack down and began chopping the bamboo into the same lengths.

He turned to her and said, "I need tree vines." Without hesitating, he ran into the forest, soon returning with several long vines dragging behind him.

She continued to finish the second pack as Toca quickly built two tall drying walls with the bamboo sticks. Kneeling on the ground, he placed the bamboo in rows, spacing them parallel a hand-length apart one way. Then on top of those, he placed other bamboo sticks, going parallel the other direction, the same distance apart. This made big square openings throughout the walls then tied the sticks together where they crisscrossed with the vines. Once done making the two walls, he stood them up, each one on opposite sides of the pit, leaning them until they touched directly over the fire several feet, then tied them together.

After putting more wood and leaves onto the flames, smoking the area up, he began layering rows of caiman meat, draping them over the open squares. Getting a large portion of the meat on the racks, he wrestled the rest of it, still on the hide, to the edge of the clearing, hanging it on limbs sticking out in the hot sunlight. With the hide empty of meat, he bent down and scooped up a handful of dirt, tossing it into the interior of the hardening skin.

He ran back to the fire, checked on the meat, then grabbed the canteen. Back to the hide, he poured some water on it, he mixed the dirt and water then began scrubbing the bright-colored interior part of the skin over and over. Soon it softened up then tipped out the muddy water.

Disappearing back into his source of where everything he needed to live, looked for a specific tree. Finding it, he climbed to one of its fat vines growing out of a large limb. Slowly he cut it off with his stone knife, holding the open end of the vine up, not to spill out what was inside the center of the hollow core. Carefully climbing down, he went to the other end of the vine growing into the ground. He put the open end of the vine into his mouth, clogging the center of it with his tongue. Swiftly he cut the vine on the ground, tipping it up quickly in order not to lose a drop of the precious liquid inside. Back to the hide with the vine ends in each hand, holding them upward with his thumbs corking the cut ends, he called to Shana to come to him.

When she arrived, he held out one of the vine ends and said, "Here, drink some of this."

Shana took ahold of the fat vine and asked, "What is it?"

"Laminia tree milk."

She lifted it to her nose. *There isn't much of a smell,* she thought then slowly tilted the vine above her head and poured a few drops of the whitish clear liquid onto her tongue. Hesitating with unknown anticipation, she quickly opened her eyes wide and said, "Mmm…it has a bland milky taste." Then she decided to take a real swallow of the tree milk. "Wow, Toca, it tastes good! Do you drink this all the time?"

He nodded and said, "All the time but not a lot at once. It makes you…" He was looking for the right words. "It makes you go really bad." He was pointing to his buttocks and gesturing something coming out.

"You mean it makes you have…stinky mud?" she said, wrinkling her nose.

He thought about her words then added, nodded his head yes, "Stinky watery mud."

They embarrassingly giggled at the same time.

"Drink one more, then put some on your head," he said, pointing to her hair.

"You want me to put this in my hair?" She pulled on her long black hair.

"Yes, it makes it shiny and soft."

"Okay," she said, answering his challenge. She took another drink of the tree milk then poured some over her head and handed the vine end to him. Then she worked the milky water through her full head of hair.

"Now what?"

"Let it dry then take bath in the river," he instructed her as he took a long drink then began emptying out the rest of the liquid in the long vine onto the caiman hide where he rubbed earlier.

"What are you doing?" she asked, astonished he would waste the white liquid.

"Just like your hair, it makes the hide soft." Finishing the last drop, he threw the vine into the jungle then knelt, rubbing the skin again over and over. After a few moments, he stood up and said, "It is finished, when you take a bath, I will wash this off and both of you will be soft and shiny." He smiled as she smiled back, amazed at how quickly they have built a friendship in two short days.

"Toca." Keeping her smile, she got serious. "Thank you for being here and becoming my friend."

She glanced over to her father's grave across the clearing and began to tear up as her face formed a mushy impression. Through the emotional surge, she fumbled out, "I didn't want to leave my home, even though my people treated me badly. I couldn't understand why God would send me and my father so far away. Then for him to die when we got here. I don't know what I would have done if you didn't find me, Toca." She looked back to him and helplessly cried.

Even though it was foreign to him, he knew deep inside what he needed to do. He stepped forward and put his arms around her as she flung hers around him. Shana began to pour out all the pain bottled up inside from her past and the agony of the fresh wound of losing he father. Her knees buckled and they both went straight down sitting, holding each other.

After a while, she quieted down, resting, feeling safe and secure. Toca wasn't used to any close contact with females, especially old female children; it was against their village rules. This was a unique and different situation but he couldn't do it much longer, making him uneasy, so he said, "Let's go back to the fire and finish our work."

Back at the remaining pieces of the tent, she continued what she was working on. Both hammock packs were completed with Toca's having the machete holder made from her father's leather belt and tent canvas. She put the leather along the side where the blade would rest so it wouldn't cut up the canvas, keeping it safe in case someone fell on it. She also fixed the flopping issue by threading a wide strap through the pack that went around their waists to hold them tight.

Now she was working on a special pouch for the Bible using the canvas tent material which had an oily wax coating to help it be waterproof. She double layered the pouch to make sure the paper of the Bible never got wet when it rained.

Toca stood and walked away a short distance, looking in the direction of the river. Then he looked up at the thick smoke in the air then back down toward the beach.

"What's wrong, Toca?"

"I do not like this."

"Why?"

"Others."

"You see others again?"

With a concerned look, he answered, "No, but they can see the smoke and know we are here."

"Are you sure we cannot meet these others? Maybe they are friendly."

"No, we cannot meet them, they must not know about the Nashua people. I have to protect my people like I must protect you." He looked back at her in a way, letting her know he was very serious. Then he looked around at the opened tent and everything in it. "We must hide all this now, it will be getting dark soon. I will shadow you in the forest while you sleep in your hanging bed, and I will work the meat all night, keeping watch for others. When the birds wake up early morning, we will pack the dried meat in our carrying pouches and bury the rest. Then we will start journeying to the endless water." He slowly nodded his head, taking a deep breath of relief that they will finally be leaving.

"Are you planning on walking through the forest to the ocean?"

"No, most of the time we will be running."

"What, are you crazy? I can't run through that stuff!" She pointed toward the thick green maze of foliage.

"You will have to learn quickly. I must be back to Chief Acuta's ceremony hut before the thirteenth full moon rises. I only have eleven moons left."

"Why are you not floating on the river? Wouldn't that be faster?"

"It takes a long time to make a canoe, we have no time. Also Chief Acuta did not say I could use one."

"Did he say you could not use one?"

Hesitating for a moment, thinking about all their conversations on journeying, he couldn't remember the chief saying he could not use one. Probably because he knew it would take too long to make one after the old male children left the valley, so why bring it up?

"I don't remember him saying I could not."

"Good because I have a canoe, remember?" she said proudly.

Toca answered, "You said your father bought one from a village? I didn't see it on the edge of the river."

"It's near the beach. I pulled it into the forest, hidden away from the water when we first got here. It was raining so hard the river was rising fast and the beach was disappearing. That's how I found this clearing. We needed an open area for the tent. My father was too weak to walk around so I went into the forest, looking for a spot and this was here."

Toca didn't know what to think. This was totally unexpected.

"So what do you think?" she asked.

He didn't answer, he was too deep in thought.

Pressing her idea to him, she said, "Canoeing downriver is easy and fast. We could be to the ocean maybe in three months. I mean, three moons. You said that you have been traveling for two moons?"

He nodded yes.

"We can cut that time in half with the canoe. You should be back in plenty of time." She was doing everything to convince him, not looking forward to a full dense-forest experience.

As Toca pondered the idea, one thing he or Chief Acuta didn't plan on was him bringing back an old female child. Especially one that knew nothing about the forest and how to live in it. He thought, *I was to bring back a god but what does a god look like? I still haven't seen Shana's God. So how much room is it going to take up in a canoe and is her God like her? Doesn't know anything about the forest?* It was getting confusing.

Looking to her, he asked, "Shana, I haven't seen your God. Is it going to take up too much room in a canoe?"

She didn't know how to respond. Once again, it was a reminder of how innocent he was. "Well, I'll try to explain God. He is everywhere," she said, motioning with her hands all around. He looked into the sky and toward the forest, not as skittish this time because before he hadn't seen anything and nothing happened.

"There is plenty of room in the canoe for him because he doesn't take up any space." She fumbled, finding the right words so he would understand.

He looked puzzled and asked, "Is it heavy?"

"No, God doesn't weigh anything."

"Shana, you make no sense. Where is your God?" Raising his voice, he was beginning to get upset.

"Toca, it might take a long time to explain who God is. Let me tell you during our journey. But I need you to trust me like I trust you with taking care of me." She paused, taking charge of the conversation and making sure he was listening closely. "He is a good God as you asked. He's more than that—he is a great God! Bigger than any other god out there. But the most important thing to know is, he is a God that loves you, me, and all others." She put her hands over her heart and gave him a gentle and kind expression. "He will love the Nashua people, give them purpose, and they will be strong."

She said everything he needed and wanted to hear. Still looking at each other, he responded, "I will trust you." He waited a moment then gave her what she wanted to hear. "We will use the canoe to journey."

"Yes! Thank you, thank you, Toca." She danced around, raising her arms in the air, then gave him a hug. He stood there, letting her do what she seems to always want to do and thought to himself. *Happy and sad, happy and sad, she is always changing.*

They spent the rest of the evening gathering the items in the tent. Blankets, clothes, utensils, and all the other things John brought to live and give the Indians as gifts, wrapping them up in the remaining water-resistant canvas tent.

In the center of the large protective bundle, Shana securely put the batch of Bibles they brought. Then inside the forest, they dug a deep hole under a large fallen log that had many overhanging tree limbs, attempting to keep the buried items dry and secretly hidden away.

Toca found a good spot not far into the forest and hung Shana's hammock. He was very impressed with what she made and how it worked, giving her compliments. He showed her where to find the juja plant and had her work it on the trunk of the trees and cover the rope ends of the hammock with its oil to keep things from crawling along the ropes and onto where she would be sleeping.

The night went well as Shana was feeling good and at peace with everything which helped her sleep. Toca worked the meat all night, rotating it then changing the finished meat with the meat hanging on the clearing's edge where the caiman hide was drying. He had not heard or seen any evidence of others.

Morning finally came, finding Toca sleeping hard, shadowed as he leaned against a tree. It was a long night for him but he had no problem waking up, the excitement of journeying energized him.

Quickly moving, he gathered many large broad leaves and thin tree vines, making a pile next to all the finished dried smoked meat. He lined the leaves out in groups of three and piled dried meat on each of them. Then he rolled the leaves around the piles of meat tightly and wrapped vines in all directions around the packages, securing them so the food would be protected and wouldn't fall out.

Near where Shana was still sleeping, he found a small open area within the vegetation, between fallen logs and large ferns, and began digging. He dug as deep and wide as he could with many roots in the way. Finally getting it to the depth and width he wanted, he swiftly darted through the forest, looking on the ground for as many small rocks as he could find. After two armloads piled next to the hole, he then went looking for a chuacha tree.

Taking a while to go deeper into the forest, he found what he was looking for. Taking out his stone knife, he climbed the tree halfway up then stabbed the tip of it into the bark and slid down the trunk, slicing the thin smooth soft bark all the way down. He went back up to where he started the cut down and cut all the way around the tree this time. Once that was done, he put the knife back into its sheath and began peeling the pliable bark away from the trunk, all the way down. At the bottom, near the ground, he made a cut around the tree and the long piece of bark was freed.

Toca dragged it, picking up many juja branches along the way. Back to the hole, he strategically placed all the rocks at the bottom, making two layers. He then worked half the juja leaves, sprinkling them all over the rocks. Satisfied with his work thus far, he went back to the clearing, making several trips with the leaf-wrapped packages of meat until he had it all, except for what they were taking downriver with them.

Placing the meat on top of the rocks, weaving them through the roots, he was able to get it all in. Grabbing the chuacha tree bark, he cut large pieces of this waterproof bark and wrapped the sides, covering the top of the packages. Again he worked the rest on the juja leaves, sprinkling them all around and on top of the layer of waterproof bark. Quickly putting the final touch of filling back in the dirt over his treasure, he stomped hard to pack the dirt. Having sizeable pieces of the chuacha bark left over, he spread the wide strips on top of the ground where he buried the meat and back over the area they buried the other big bundle of items John had brought. This would help run off rain to the edges and seep into the ground, away from the buried treasures.

It was time to get the old female child up. Watching her sleep in the hanging bed, he couldn't believe she could sleep with all the birds singing, monkeys whooping, and the sunlight getting brighter every moment.

"Shana, it's time to get up." He gently swung the bed like his mother would do to him. It made him think about how he missed her and the kind soft voice waking him up, always encouraging him. He wondered what she would be doing right now, then Jucawa showed up. Immediately his mood changed as he reflected how Jucawa would wake him, pulling the bed up, dropping him to the floor of the hut and laugh.

"Toca, what are you doing?" Shana said aloud. He realized that his gentle swinging turned into a hard pushing motion, jerking her back and forth.

"Oh, sorry, Shana. My vision in my head was somewhere else." He let go of the hammock, and as soon as she got out, he untied the ropes and gave the bed for her to roll up.

They went to the packaged meat left in the clearing and ate a few pieces that were left out. Going over to the firepit, Toca attempted to make the area look natural and undisturbed as Shana went through the other things they were taking. The pouch with the Bible, the leather sack with the fire rocks, her small sewing bag, the long knife and its sheath. Finally she had made, without Toca knowing, many short strips of soft cloth, cut from her father's clothes, for her monthly female blood visits began when they first left North America. She secured the Bible, fire rocks, sewing bag, and her private things in her pack and the long knife in his with both having two heavy packages of meat each.

Toca, watching on after he finished, said, "It will be best you take the long knife pack and I take the other."

With a questionable look, she responded, "Why? You like the long knife."

"That is true but I have my knife to protect me and you will have nothing."

"I don't need anything to protect me, I'm with the alligator killer."

Cocking his head, Toca knew she was complimenting him but he couldn't remember what alligator was.

Then she said, "I mean, giant caiman killer."

The words made him stand tall with confidence, mostly because she thought of him that way. It was the best most meaningful comment she has given him in their short friendship.

"That's true but remember the caiman killer first ran from a screaming old female child waving the long knife."

She smiled back as they both laughed at their first meeting.

"You need to be able to protect yourself. There are too many things that will kill you in the forest and on the rivers. Also I don't know how the others will treat us if we run into them so we need to always be prepared."

"I see your point but that doesn't mean you will not protect me, right?"

He lifted her hammock pack as she turned around and put it on her, saying, "I will honor your father's request and take care of you, child of God."

His response was not what she expected. It wasn't personal but true and to the point.

I need to work on his communication skills, she thought to herself.

With the packs on and Toca doing his best to hold the large heavy caiman skin, rolled up tight with leftover rope in both arms, they looked around the clearing. It was cleaned up of anything, proving they were never there, until her father's grave caught both their eyes. They walked over to it and Shana remembered something she forgot to do. "Toca, can you get me two strong sticks, the length of your arms, and some of the tree vine you used to wrap the big leaves around the meat?"

Setting down the caiman hide, he quickly ran in and out of the forest, handing her what she asked for. Taking one of the sticks, breaking it in two, she crisscrossed the longer one two-thirds the way up, tying them together by wrapping the vine around and around where they intersected.

When finished, she knelt at the head of the grave and stuck the cross deep into the ground firmly, then stood up. "You were a wonderful father, husband, and preacher." She didn't know what else to say as soft tears fell from her face, except for, "I will hold God's hand tightly, following where he leads me. I love you, Papa. Goodbye."

CHAPTER 8

Finding the canoe well-hidden under the different vegetation among trees near the beach, they pulled it out to the sand. Toca looked in the river and across it, slowly searching for anything not wanted, especially others. The only things he saw on the beach different than what he left were fresh prints of birds and where a medium-size snake had slithered across the open sand he had smoothed out the day before.

"Shana, take a bath," he said, not taking his eyes off his detailed search.

"What?"

Turning to her, he repeated bluntly, "Take a bath."

"Okay…," Shana replied with a scowling look on her face. "We need to work on how you talk to me because that came out wrong," she told him as she took off her hammock pack and her dad's brown shirt while leaving on the trimmed-up dress.

"What was wrong?" he asked.

"The way it was said, it sounded like you were bossing me around and that I was dirty and smelled."

"You are dirty and you do smell, that's how I found you, remember?"

"Yes, but you don't have to be so rude about it."

"What is 'woowd?'"

"Rude…it's when you say something not in a nice way."

He looked at her without an expression, not understanding how he was not nice to her. "I said, take a bath so you would be clean and to wash off the chuacha tree milk to smell good and be refreshed before we journey. The Nashua females take a bath one, two, sometimes three times every day, mainly to cool off."

"Just forget it, you were helping me." Disgruntled, she apprehensively stepped near the water's edge.

He watched her as she took precaution, glad she was beginning to start being aware of things.

She turned to him to see if he was looking on, then with confidence, she started to step into the water.

"Stop!" Toca said.

She turned back, seeing he had picked up a long stick and was handing it to her. "Slap the top of the water with this before getting in. It will help you know if there is something close you can't see looking to eat you."

She widely opened her eyes taking the stick, understanding his caution from when they first met. Shana extended the stick out and slapped the water several times then jumped back, waiting for something to happen. When nothing did, she looked back at him as he gave her a nod that it was okay to get into the river.

She slowly walked in then submerged her whole body. Coming up out of the refreshing water, she flipped her hair back and forth then dunked her head, scrubbing her hair, then rinsed it. Once done, she stood, flipping her head up, tossing all her hair to her back, and turned around, stroking the water out of her long black shining crown. She walked up onto the beach and stood in front of the old Indian boy. Not blinking an eye, he stared at Shana, seeing her in a totally different way.

She is beautiful, why haven't I seen her this way before? he asked himself as his mouth dropped open.

"You are right, Toca, I do feel refreshed and look at my hair." She had it swung around her shoulder, closely looking at it while running her fingers through it. "It's so soft. You have a lot of knowledge about the forest. Thank you."

He hadn't taken his eyes off her. This was the first time he looked at a female in this manner and didn't know how to react.

"Toca." She bumped his arm. "Are you okay? What are you looking at?" She turned to look behind her, thinking he might be staring at something. Then she looked back, and he finally came to his senses, like he just woke up from a nap, and replied, "Oh, nothing, your hair does look shiny."

She picked up her pack and shirt then walked back to the canoe. His eyes followed her and noticed the rolled-up caiman skin next to it. "Oh, I need to wash that," he said aloud.

As he untied it and rolled it out, Shana said, "That is longer than the canoe. He was a big one, right?"

"Yes, it was, but there are bigger ones out there," he said, again admiring his kill.

He washed it over several times, then laid it out flat on the sand, belly-up. Stepping up to their new form of journeying, he examined the canoe and admired the skilled craftsmanship and well-made paddles. He pulled it out into the water and washed it clean of leaves and bugs crawling around in it. Jumping in, he checked how it balanced and got out, telling Shana it was time to go.

Putting the packs in the center of the canoe, Toca then laid the hide wide open on the floor with the legs draping over the sides as the tail and head were over the back and front, barely off the water. "We'll sit on the hide until it dries, then I will roll it up again," Toca said.

"Before we leave, we need to pray," Shana said, looking at Toca. Closing her eyes and bowing her head, she thanked God for blessing her with Toca coming into her life and asked for protection along the journey.

Again Toca watched her bow her head and close her eyes, talking to her God. He looked around, trying to see this God to whom she was talking. Still questioning, *Why does she close her eyes? And why doesn't her God talk back and show himself?* He glanced to the canoe as she was finishing, attempting to comprehend how the God of hers is going to come with them but take up no room in the canoe.

When she was done, he asked, "So how is your God coming with us?"

Shana swung her arms out, looking all around, and said, "He is everywhere and doesn't need to sit in the canoe with us, even though he will be there all the time."

Toca just stared at her with a blank face. *That still doesn't explain it,* he thought to himself.

"I will explain God along the way, let's go." She was now excited to start the journey.

Heading out onto the water, Shana had to work on her balance, sitting up front, finding a sweet spot, then began to row. Looking back to make sure Toca was there, she said, "You are good at this, Toca. I never heard or felt you get in."

He gave her a nudging smile then looked downriver once they were in the middle of it. Staring there for a while, he didn't find what he was looking for—the others. He asked Shana, "How far is it to the village you said your father got the canoe?"

"It took us about ten days to come upriver. Father was given instructions of a smaller river up here somewhere to go up where the Indians would be. We got lost going back and forth up several of the smaller ones that flowed into this big black river. When it started raining hard for several days, that's when we barely found the beach."

He thought of that amount of time and considered the speed of the current, then said, "If we row hard, we should come to that village in maybe four days or less," he said, raising his hand with four fingers held up.

"Yes, I agree. You are better at this than my father and me. Plus you weigh a lot less than he did. It's easier to maneuver the canoe because it's not so low in the water," she stated as she looked over the side.

"Toca, what are we going to do when we get to the others in the village?"

He went into his silent mode to think this through, then said, "We will stop before we go past them and wait for the darkness. Then in the darkness, we will go past them on the river."

"Wow, you are quick with good ideas," she answered, smiling back, then said, "But it's not a village, it is a city called Manaus. It is where this river flows into a larger river."

"What is city?"

"It's a very, very big village with many people."

He didn't like the sound of that, then asked another question, "Is the other water of the larger river milky-brown color?"

"Yes, how did you know?"

"Chief Acuta told me about the different color of rivers that follow into the endless water. The white river is upriver from here. I crossed it about twelve sunrises ago. We will pass it on our way back."

"I should have known, your chief is a very wise man."

He nodded with pride then replied, "I will be just like him when I get back."

Shana began getting concerned as she thought through their experience with people in the city and on the boat docks where they bought the canoe. She said to Toca, "We need to make sure we don't run into the others at this city. It will not be safe."

"Yes, stay away from others," he answered back in agreement, pleased she was thinking as he was about others.

As they rowed, Shana drifted off to past conversations and remembered her dad being very uneasy with the people and the whole place. The men there looked at her oddly. She was brown-skinned, dressed like a white woman with a white man, and she couldn't speak their language. It was scary at moments because John spoke very little Spanish. If he said something wrong because of translation or said something they didn't like, they would raise their voices and begin to point and look at her. Later her father told her most of the European people there forced the local natives to be their slaves to work the rubber tree plantations that were growing in large numbers. All while paying the stronger Indian tribes to find and imprison other native Amazon Indians to be slaves. They thought she was an Amazon Indian and his slave and they wanted to buy her off him because young girls were valuable to them and it wasn't for working in the plantations. Also when he explained he was a Christian missionary from the United States, they didn't want to have anything to do with him because they were Catholic and they acted as if they didn't want any English-speaking American in the Amazon.

*****

Several days went by gliding easily down the black river with no signs of others. Casual conversation continued with the two getting to know each other better, as speaking became very fluid the more they talked. Shana was still trying to figure out how they could understand each other so well. When she and her father got to South America, they couldn't understand any of the local Indians they came in contact with along the way. Only some Spanish or Portuguese spoken by the Europeans. They found out traveling up the river from the ocean, from the steamboat people, there were hundreds—if not thousands—of different Indian languages in the Amazon.

Shana's father said, when he first became a missionary to the Manos Indians, he had to learn their language. So his intentions were to do the same here, once he found a tribe that would let them live with them, learning their language.

But still the question was, "How could they have so many similarities in their languages that within a week, they were talking to each other as though there were no differences at all?" They blended her Manos and Toca's language, the Nashua people spoke, developing their own dialect. They were now speaking without thinking of the words to say except for the detailed words of references they couldn't understand.

Toca taught her about the different animals and plants they were seeing and their names as they drifted. Shana spent many hours talking about her trip to the forest and where she was born back in the desert on the reservation. She told him stories of them traveling across North America to the Atlantic Ocean, then being on a large ship that went from port to port until they finally got to a city where the Amazon River flowed into the ocean.

Toca's imagination was running rampant. There were so many things she was explaining to him that he had to tell her to stop talking so frequently because he couldn't keep up with everything she was talking about. Many of which he questioned her because it was so far for him to believe that he started telling her she was making things up.

It was getting late in the evening and they decided to go to shore for the night. It took a while to find a small opening to land through the thick overhanging vegetation that grew out into the river, hiding the shoreline. They coasted in until the canoe was abruptly stopped by the muddy bank. Shana began to stand, then Toca quickly stated with a whisper, "Shana, be aware!"

She immediately sat down, whispering back, "Sorry."

They waited, listening, looking, and smelling. She was doing better but Toca still had to remind her to be patient and watch before doing.

He whispered again but in an urgent tone, "Shana, stay seated, slowly take your paddle and push us back off the ground."

She looked around, asking, "Why?"

"Just do it and do it now! Push off hard and now!" he said, gritting his teeth, trying to stay quiet.

She turned and did what he said. Once the boat was free, floating slowly backward, he added, "Don't move and keep your paddle out in front of you for protection."

She turned, looking toward the shore that was gently distancing itself as she frantically moved her eyes back and forth, trying to see what Toca saw. Once the canoe caught the current and began drifting downriver, Toca slowly put his paddle in the water. Using it as a rudder, he turned the canoe facing downriver and whispered, "Quietly start paddling."

She did what he said, then softly asked, "Toca, what was wrong?"

"Nothing, it just didn't feel right," he said calmly.

"What?" she said loudly. "You scared me!"

Suddenly a burst of loud splashing came from the shore as the water exploded where they were just at as two large black caimans jumped into the water, torpedoing toward them.

"Paddle, paddle, faster, faster they're catching up!" Toca yelled. Both of them dug deep and fast as water splashed all over the canoe and out into the river as the paddles did their job. The canoe quickly picked up speed. Toca glanced back and, out of the corner of his eye, watched both the huge reptiles' bodies slowly disappear with only the front of their faces exposed, watching their meals frantically getting away.

"We can slow down, Shana, they stopped chasing us." The screaming in her head from the terrifying moment was so loud her ears didn't hear him.

"Shana...Shana," he said without a reaction from her. He lifted his paddle and reached forward, tapping her back with the wet piece of wood.

"*Aaahhh*," she yelled, as she paddled harder, splashing him. Toca started to laugh as he had never seen someone so scared. He kept laughing and finally got her attention when she glanced back to see when the caiman was going to bite her. All she saw was Toca with his bright white teeth, glowing with laughter and not rowing anymore.

Moving her eyes back and forth in the water, assessing what was actually happening, she asked, "What are you laughing at, are they gone?" she asked, out of breath.

It took him a moment to calm down then said, still chuckling, "Yes, they're gone."

She swallowed hard and began inhaling deep breaths, realizing she stopped breathing during the rush of panic. "Why...why are you laughing, what was funny about that?"

Still amused, he answered, "You should have seen yourself. You were so scared I couldn't get your attention no matter what I did."

"Stop it! Just stop it, Toca. That wasn't funny—we almost died!" By her facial expression, it looked like she was going to cry.

Taking some time, he settled down and got serious and calmly stated, "We almost die every day, Shana. Be aware every moment or you will die!" He pointed back upriver as his eyes stayed on their target, looking into hers. He was trying to imprint that fact into her mind.

She turned around, embarrassed. It was quiet as they slowly floated, looking for another opening in the tangled branches, reaching out into the water. Toca saw ahead a space they could fit and guided in the canoe.

Shana's heart began to race and her breathing quickened. She started scooting backward in the canoe, causing the front to lift.

"Shana," he whispered. "Move forward and put your paddle in front of you."

She hesitated, then slowly went forward, but she didn't grab her paddle. She reached back in her pack and slowly retrieved the long knife with both hands, spearing it out in front of her.

Toca's eyes went wide with excitement to see her do that. The boat softly touched ground and both of them didn't move. Toca went through his routine—breathing deep to smell danger, looking into the shadows for crouched killers, and listening for the silence before the attack. Shana sat still, listening and looking for anything moving, more focused than she had ever been.

Birds were singing their normal late evening songs, frogs were calling out for a mate, no disturbing odors in the air, and nothing appeared visually wrong. Toca told Shana she could get up and out of the canoe. Hesitant, she tossed the paddle out onto the ground to see if anything would attack it. Seeing no movement, she slowly stepped out and quickly pulled the boat up, putting the paddle back in.

A little way into the forest, they found a set of trees that worked well to hang their hammocks. Shana hung them up as Toca looked for some juja plants. He noticed it wasn't as plentiful around this area but, after a while, found some and started stripping the leaves off a branch then suddenly stopped. Noticing something that made him uneasy, he lifted his head and looked through the forest, slowly examining every detail around him. Not seeing anything, he looked back down at the plant where it had already been stripped in areas. On the ground around the plant, he spotted what he suspected—a set of footprints in the dirt.

Once back to Shana with the leaves rolled, he swiped the tree and the ropes. He got out a couple of small strips of meat and they ate as they climbed into their beds.

"Be aware, we are close to others, Shana," he said calmly, not wanting to alarm her.

"How do you know?"

"I found footprints at the juja plant. They were old so was the woman they were from."

"How would you know the footprints were old and it was an old woman?"

"They were shorter and not as wide as a man's with wrinkles and scarred marks here and there. In the prints were a few dried raindrops and a leaf had fallen in one, telling me the woman picked juja leaves about ten sunrises ago."

"Toca, now you are sounding like you are making things up," she said softly as she ate.

He asked her, "When did it rain last, Shana?"

Thinking before she answered, she said, "The night you covered me up with the large leaves."

"Good. When did it rain before that?"

Lying comfortably, looking up into the darkening night sky through the high tree branches, she said, "Maybe three or four days before that?"

"It was five days before that. So sometime the following day of that rain, the old female picked the leaves, ten sunrises ago."

"You amaze me, Toca, how do you know all this and you are only thirteen years old?"

"Years old?

"Umm..." She tried to remember what he uses in its place. "You call it sun seasons."

"We will use sun seasons," he stated then continued proudly, pointing to his chest, "This is where I live. You have to use our words and have our knowledge to live here."

Answering her question, he said, "My mother and Chief Acuta trained me since I started walking."

She asked, "Didn't your father teach you things?"

Toca snapped back, "We do not talk about him!"

"Sorry, did he die or something?" she asked gently with concern.

"I said, we do not talk about Jucawa." Then he mumbled to himself, "I wish he was."

Shana was taken aback by his sudden harsh response about his father. It went silent for a while as Shana found out they will not be talking about his father but curiosity kept her mind wondering about it.

Both still awake and listening to the night, another question came to her. "How did you know we needed to leave the first spot where the caiman attacked us?"

"It was too quiet and I smelled rotten meat and caiman stinky mud."

"I didn't smell anything?"

"You will learn, you have to keep practicing to be aware."

"So you didn't see anything?"

"Every animal and fish smell their meals first. Smell the air right now, what do you smell?"

She inhaled with her nostrils flared out. "I smell this canvas we are sleeping in from the tent."

"What do you hear?"

"The canvas material when I move my arms and head and some frogs along the river's edge."

Toca slithered out of his bed quietly without her knowing and asked, "What do you see?"

"Nothing, it's dark."

It went completely silent. She waited for him to respond but there was nothing.

"Toca…Toca, are you there, are you asleep?" she asked softly into the night.

She listened and lifted her head toward his hammock but it was pitch-dark because of the full canopy of the trees above, hiding the stars in the sky. She laid her head back down and tried to sink in protectively. Her mind began to imagine but before it got too far—

"*Roar!*" Toca silently blurted out, jumping up from his crawling position, wrapping his arms around her hammock, squeezing her.

Shana flinched then started to scream and Toca quickly covered her mouth. "Shh, it's just me." He didn't laugh this time at her being scared, he was teaching her a lesson. The same one Chief Acuta taught him about depending on your other senses besides your eyes.

He let go of her mouth when she stopped struggling. "I teach you the same lesson I learned."

"That wasn't nice, you scared me."

He stood next to her, talking in the dark. "You need to learn to trust more than your eyes. I couldn't see the caiman but I smelled everything about them. The forest was also telling me there was something there because it was too quiet. But most of all, it felt wrong. My head didn't like it and my chest was uneasy." He pointed to his heart, even though she couldn't see.

"You could have just said that, you didn't have to scare me."

Toca replied, "Now you will remember to think of all these things, right?"

"Maybe so but don't scare me anymore. I've been scared enough by the things in this forest," she sarcastically answered.

"You have no idea of all the other things that will scare you and will kill you if it has a chance. Shana, you must always be aware!" He went back to his hammock and they quietly fell asleep, thinking of the day's events.

Halfway through the next day on the river, Toca started to faintly smell something different. "We are on our fourth day on the river, we should be getting close to the big village. I think that is what I am smelling."

"You do?" She turned back, then put her nose to the air, smelling for all she was worth. "I don't smell it?"

"What do you smell?" he asked, going into teaching mode.

"The water, the dried caiman skin, my body odor. I seem to be the only one sweating. I hardly see you sweat, why?"

"You are wearing too many body coverings. You have on your father's brown covering, then you have the covering under that, then I think you have another under that. Of course you are sweating all the time, you're hot."

"Why are you always talking about my clothes?"

He frowned, stating, "Because they are most of your problems and you will not listen to me."

"I like my clothes and I like having them on. You and your people might be fine with being naked all the time, but where I come from, we wear body coverings all the time."

"What is naked?"

Shana was stunned. Again how stupid has she been about this, thinking to herself. It didn't matter to him that she was female, he had made that clear. Everything had to do with her or their protection. Her clothes could be seen in the forest and she was always hot and sweating. She did notice that she drinks three or four times as much water as he does, probably because she was always sweating it out.

"I tell you what, Toca, later I will take off both layers of clothes under my father's shirt. But I will keep that on to keep my body covered. You also said it will be harder to be seen or shadowed as you say all the time."

She stopped paddling and turned back again to get his response.

"That will help you be cooler but I still don't understand what the purpose is for the upper covering?"

Thinking to herself, *Is he serious*? She got flushed and answered, "To hide my breasts."

He asked, "Why would you hide those?"

"Because they are private?"

"Private?"

"It means they are for no one else to see."

"I know what private is but you make no sense again, Shana. Why private and hide them? It is part of you as a female, they give your baby's food. Is that bad where you come from?"

"No, no it's not—"

Toca quickly interrupted, looking way ahead, "What side of the river is this village on?"

"Why, what do you—"

"Now, Shana! What side are the people on?" he demanded her to answer.

"They are on that side." She pointed to their left side.

"Paddle hard, we go to the other side and shadow," he stated as he directed the canoe to their right then added, "Can you see the smoke way ahead of us up in the sky?"

"Oh, yes," she answered, looking downriver.

"I also think I see something in the river far ahead."

The river was getting very wide and their canoe was close to the middle so it took them a while to finally reach the river's edge. After searching for an open spot, Toca got impatient because they were getting closer to what he saw. He back rowed, slowing the canoe down, and grabbed ahold of several long thick branches hanging over the water, then pulled them to him, gliding the canoe into the thick cover of vegetation. They disappeared from the open river but couldn't hit ground because the brush and winding tree limbs surrounding them held them tight.

"Others can't see us now," he said, sighing with relief.

"What are we going to do?" Shana asked, when just moments ago, they were in the wide open and now they could barely move with the branches reaching out poking everything. She was suddenly getting claustrophobic.

Looking through the tangles of leaves, vines, and branches toward the shore, he said, "We can get out and wade in the water, climbing through this stuff, then when it gets dark, wade back. Or we can stay in the canoe and sleep until it gets dark and push out of this shadowing spot?"

"We can stay in the canoe!" she said quickly, looking disgusted at the situation. Not wanting to step in the water and climb over and around a jumbled mess of vegetation with spiders, ants, and other crawly creatures working their way around, looking for their next meals.

Toca picked up his hammock pack, sitting in front of him next to the large rolled-up caiman skin, and laid it behind him, propping his head up as he got comfortable. Shana did the same but turned around toward him, using the upward slanted front part of the boat to help prop her up as well. Facing each other, it was hard for them to just fall asleep when the sun had a distance to go until it relieved itself, letting the partial moon take over, lighting up the world.

"It is always hot here," she commented, grasping her top and puffing it in and out, trying to get cooler air underneath the layers she had on. "I've had enough of this. Toca, I'm going to take off the other layers of clothes I have on under my father's shirt and hopefully it will work. You're going to have to turn around while I do this."

"Why? I have already seen you with no body coverings."

She frowned at him, telling him through her stare down she wasn't going to go over this again.

"Okay, I will give you your…privacy…"—still bewildered with what the big deal was—"and go to land and look around. You stay in the canoe and I will be back in a while."

"Thank you," she stated in a manner to show she was the sophisticated person here.

Toca was out of the canoe and through the vegetation, barely touching the water, and out of sight on land before Shana made her next move. "He is incredible, how he can work his way through this stuff?" she commented to herself.

Toca had long been back before nightfall finally arrived. He had gathered several long straight bamboo poles, a rolled-up ball of very thin tree vine, and a handful of different-colored bird feathers he found along the ground. Shana asked what they were for, and he said he was going to teach her how to catch fish, teasing her that she didn't know what she was doing when he saved her from the caiman when they first met.

Shana had her clothes packed away in her pack which she had taken off; all her undergarments except her bottom underwear, the apron, and the top half of her dress. The bottom half of her dress now looked like a short skirt. She kept her boots off as well but didn't pack them away. Shana wasn't happy the way she looked, wearing her dad's oversized shirt and the ragged bottom half of what was left of her pretty dress. But she felt much better and wished she had done this days ago.

Ready to move through the night, he grabbed ahold of one of the bigger limbs dangling over them and pulled, moving them out of their hideout, then pushed away, shooting them into the current. Fortunately the sky was clear as it had been over the past few days. The stars were out and the moon was beginning to claim its right to the night, peeking its glow over the horizon. The light reflected off the smooth water which guided the two old children in the thin, long, and shallow canoe which was just a faint splinter in the massive flowing body of water.

CHAPTER 9

Drifting in the dark in the large river was a nervous experience. Shana and her father came up the river to the city of Manaus almost nonstop day and night, taking approximately five weeks from the ocean. But they were on a large steamboat, hundreds of times larger than the small hollowed-out log she and Toca were traveling on.

Occasionally a splash of a fish surfacing on top of the water would break the eerie silence and their imaginations would go wild with nightmarish thoughts of something coming after them, feeling defenseless.

The moonlight exposed ripples in the water from current variations and the aftereffects of what seized their attention from the splashing going on around them. Even Toca's heart beat a little faster, uneasy from what they were hearing but more from the unknown of where the river was taking them, having no point of reference of exactly how far they were from shore as the darkness swallowed everything except the moonlit path in front of them.

In the distance, a shallow glow of light shining into the sky from the river's edge, going inland, became more visible the closer they got to the deep forest city in the Amazon. Shana explained to Toca that others had different ways of lighting the darkness of the night besides firepits. She talked about wax candles and lanterns fueled by a liquid that burned. Again something difficult for him to understand but it was evident because he had never seen such lighting at night except for the blasts of lightning bolts that would flicker across the sky and to the ground.

Toca whispered, "Shana, we need to paddle to the opposite side along the shore to stay out of their light." She didn't verbally answer but nodded her head which, from the moon's glow, he had no problem seeing her.

As he navigated, he tried to keep the moonlight in front of the canoe downriver as much as he could so they would be slowly drifting straight but to the right, toward the river's edge. After a while, without warning, the moonlight suddenly disappeared, going black. They were closer to the bank than he thought. Invisible in the darkness, the high-canopy tree line was walling the moonlight. The shoreline had curved out in front of them from the right to their left, into the river, forming a slight bay area.

Shana blurted out in fear, "Toca, what happened? I can't see anything!"

Trying to focus his eyes to the darkness, not knowing what to expect, he said, "Don't paddle and hold on to the sides."

She dropped the paddle to the bottom of the canoe, echoing out a clanking sound. Immediately to their right, they heard a couple of voices react from the shore that was quickly approaching.

He whispered out, "Keep quiet, Shana, lie down at the bottom of the canoe!" She leaned all the way back, bringing her hands to her face attempting to hide. Toca instantly wanted complete control of the canoe and its balance, putting her at the bottom toward the center would greatly help.

One person shouted out to them but both Shana and Toca did not recognize a word. Shana knew it was a native language, not Spanish or Portuguese, so she whispered to Toca, "It is Indian from the forest."

Still not able to see anything, Toca quietly stroked the water with his paddle directing their canoe to his left, away from land, using the darkness and silence to hide.

The same person repeated what he said and added a few more words.

Not responding, Toca kept going.

Suddenly the male voice screamed, then many voices joined him, spreading along the shoreline. Soon Toca heard light splashes in the water dotted around them, then a loud *thunk*. Something hit the side of the canoe, vibrating it. Toca leaned forward, still unable to see in the dark and felt where he heard the sound.

Now realizing what was making the dotted plops in the water, he whispered, "Shana, stay down." He quickened his paddling, now directly facing the middle of the river. The dotted plops stopped and was replaced with yelling and the sounds of hurried splashing along the shore.

Toca stopped rowing to listen carefully to confirm what he suspected, then told Shana, "Sit up and paddle like you did when the caiman chased us. Hurry, they are coming after us in canoes!"

"What? Why would they come after us? We didn't do anything." Her voice crackled, becoming more scared with every moment.

"Shana, if we paddle at the same time, we will go faster. Stop… now go, go, go," he repeated, getting them into a rhythm. They increased their speed significantly. Once back into the moonlight, he slowly turned the canoe downriver with the current and they began to feel a faint breeze with the speed they were going.

Toca looked back now that he had the night light reflecting off the water and saw several canoes with three bodies in each and they were gaining on them quickly. Being in the open water, there was nowhere to hide. He was thinking what he could do but there was nothing besides jumping into the water, diving deep and swimming away. But that was too dangerous, especially for Shana. He thought, *She might not be able to hold her breath long enough or swim fast.* Looking toward the land, he estimated its distance. It would be a very long swim, and by the time they got there, something in the water could probably have attacked them. Frantically trying to figure out what to do, his eyes glanced to the side of the boat at what he had felt hit their canoe moments ago. In the moonlight, he fully saw the long shaft of a spear sticking outward with its sharp tip embedded in the wooden wall of the canoe.

Looking back, the others were catching up. Without thinking, just reacting, he laid his paddle down, leaning forward on his knee and worked the spear back and forth, trying to get it free.

The canoe began rocking and Shana looked back to see what was happening and screeched out, "What are you doing?"

"I must save you. They threw spears and I don't know what they will do if they catch us. I will stop them with their own weapon!" Toca, the old male child, stated.

He worked the spear loose and told her, "Shana, stop paddling." She stopped and turned around, watching Toca stand and steady himself planting one foot forward, balancing the long spear in his hand, facing toward the onrushing enemy.

"No, Toca, don't do this!" she blurted out.

Toca hesitated, waiting for the front canoe to get in his range, then with precision and speed, he let the spear fly with all his might.

Instantly the wooden missile hit its mark in the center of the man's chest sitting in front of the canoe. But with the power Toca put on the projectile, combined with the target quickly moving toward them, the spear had enough energy to go through him and stab the man in the middle of the canoe in the leg.

The second man began screaming in pain as the man in front of him sat there, gasping for air, looking down at what was in him. Slowly he leaned to the side of the boat, falling in the river as the spear slid the rest of the way out of his body. All the men in the oncoming canoes saw the whole thing, given the moonlight was at the right angle in the sky, shining their direction.

The man that threw the spear at them was only a black silhouette figure, illuminated with the moon to his back. His shadow was cast long down in front of them in the water which made the young Nashua appear to be a giant.

Toca bent over toward Shana's back pouch and took out the machete, swinging it around in the air, screaming for all he was worth, ready to fight to the death.

They were stunned what this shadow giant did. Powerfully killing one of their own and badly hurting another with one spear. But when they saw him swinging a long knife, glistening in the moonlight, facing them to fight, they started yelling at each other to paddle backward and escape as fast as they could. The well-organized rowing crews suddenly were fumbling with their boats sideways, splashing water everywhere, trying to get away from this monster.

Shana sat frozen, watching this unbelievable moment. Then her eyes caught the body of the man in the river floating by, dead.

"Shana, start paddling," Toca said out the side of his mouth.

"But, Toca, there is a body, what are we going to do?"

"Do what I say, female!" he yelled at her between his screaming at the others.

The others were working their way back to where they came from and finally disappeared into the darkness along the shoreline.

Lowering his arm and sighing with relief, he inhaled deeply and yelled out one last time, "I am Toca, Black Ghost of the Nashua. Do not follow or you will die!" He stood there for a moment as Shana, looking downriver, slowly began paddling.

*****

Calming himself down from the sudden and unexpected events he never dreamed himself doing, he heard Shana sniffling and knew she was crying quietly. This was a reaction from being scared or that someone just died—maybe both—Toca wasn't sure but softly told her, "I had to protect you. You are safe now, daughter of John and child of God."

Having long passed the city of Manaus, silence between them paralleled the quietness of the night in the middle of the soft flowing river. Not wanting to repeat what just happened, Toca kept them as close to the center of the river as he could and planned on staying on it until the sun rose enough to see land clearly.

*****

The sun began to give its morning glow on the horizon, and slowly, the lost world was coming back. Shana had fallen asleep sitting up and was awakened by the light. She looked ahead and saw what Toca had been staring at—wide open water on all sides of them.

The river had widened so much the shorelines were but only dark even thin lines in the distance.

Shana broke the silence and said calmly, "This looks like where the two big rivers come together. We should be seeing the milky-brown water soon, Toca."

Toca was in awe at the massive amount of water. "It looks like endless water. I can barely see land."

"It looks that way but there is land over there." Shana was pointing in front of her. "It's where all this water comes together from the different directions." Shana started to get excited, pointing in front of her "Look! Look, Toca! The milky-brown water!"

It was another incredible sight for him to see. The two rivers came together, forming a line, separating two different colors where they met. As the two old children in the small canoe floated over the line, the water became mildly turbulent, swaying the dugout log softly this way and that.

They had been traveling on the black water river long enough that when they started to float on this new brighter-colored water, it took a while for their eyes to adjust. Toca felt the direction change in the current and said to Shana, "We are now going into the way of the rising sun."

"The river flows this direction all the way to the ocean," she added.

"Tell me again, how long it took you to journey upriver from the endless water?"

"A little more than a month."

"How many sunrises or days as you say it?"

She looked back to him and held up one finger. "You count by moons so it took just over one moon."

Working his paddle to keep the canoe balanced from the continued turbulence, Toca was trying to calculate their journey down to the endless water and back to the black river. He asked, "The canoe you were on, you only journeyed when the sun was shining?"

Shana smiled to herself, looking forward, answered back, "The canoe we were on was the size of the boats I told you we traveled on in the ocean. I mean, the endless water. Picture in your mind a hundred of these canoes put together."

"How many is a hundred?"

She turned back around and opened both hands with all ten fingers spread out. "Do you know this number?" Counting aloud, she drew in each finger for every number until all that was left was two fists. "Ten, this is ten."

"Yes, I know that number," he replied sarcastically, defending his pride. It was starting to bother him that she talked to him sometimes like his people talked to little children.

"Okay, so picturing that number, now add this many to it." She opened her hands, spreading out the fingers, then retracting them nine times. By the time she finished, he was astounded at the number.

"That is how big your boats are?" he replied with wide eyes.

"Yes, they hold many people and things and they are faster than canoes."

Toca sat there for the longest time, picturing what the boats that big must have looked like.

Back in a location she's been before, Shana was feeling enlightened, even with the nightmare from last night being very vivid. As they quietly floated, Shana started to hum. After a while, the humming turned to soft whispered words; then as her energy and excitement grew with the song so did the volume of her voice. Singing came so natural to her and it always put her mind and spirit at ease.

She was attempting to wash away the pictures going over and over in her head. Those of Toca boldly standing up in the canoe, throwing the spear, killing a man as another screamed out in excruciating pain. Then her eyes following a dead person floating by in the river.

The singing was helping her feel better, moving her mind forward to more peaceful thoughts as Toca was in a trance with what he heard. What came out of Shana was so beautiful, even though he couldn't understand what she was saying. It was in the language her and her father spoke to each other.

Shana finished singing and it was like something instantly weighed him down to the bottom of the river and he desperately needed to come up for air. "Shana, don't stop, that what you do makes me feel I am floating like a cloud in the sky."

She looked back at him and absorbed the expression on his face then turned back. "Toca, don't tell me you never heard singing before?"

"I've never heard sounds come out of a person like that. Except the first time when you walked past me, just outside the clearing, the day after you chased me."

Quickly turning her body completely around, facing him, she exclaimed, "So you were there! I knew I felt something, but when I turned around, I couldn't see anything or anyone."

Toca proudly smiled. "Because I was shadowed. I could have reached out and touched you. That's how close you were to me."

Shana thought the scenario through and finally realized the value of what Toca had been trying to teach her—shadow and not be seen in the forest.

Toca went back to her singing. "We sing or chant our life stories but it doesn't sound anything like you. Your voice is so soft and gentle and powerfully flows that it captures my mind and takes it to another place. I can't think about anything else in those moments."

She was the one smiling proudly now, having heard statements like that many times from her people back home. Then her smile turned downward as she also remembered most everyone in the tribe would add, "But she is still a half-breed, she will never be anything else."

Toca saw the sad look come upon her face and thought she was thinking about last night when she was crying. "Shana, you know I had to do what I did. The others were coming after us and I had to protect you."

She looked up and slowly gave him a grin of appreciation and said, "I know, Toca…Black Ghost of the Nashua." Knowing that statement would be more profound to him than anything else she could say, feeling the way she did at this moment.

She turned back around, facing the front of the canoe, picking up her paddle, and began rowing forward to start what she thought would be the longest part of their journey.

*****

Seven moons have passed and the two old children finally found themselves back to the black water of the Rio Negro from the endless water in their thin well-worn canoe. Being on the milky-brown Amazon River for so long, they couldn't wait for a change and signs of getting closer to the end of this exhausting journey.

About a half-year has passed and they have done and gone through many, many things. The rainy season hit and lasted a long time but they were able to make a waterproof roof with the large caiman hide. Assembling a bamboo frame within the inside part of the hide, stretching it out to its original shape, giving the appearance it was full and alive. Then attaching bamboo legs to the frame, just long enough so it slightly hovered over the old children's heads, it was then secured to the bottom of the canoe. The caiman hide was wider and longer than the small boat so all the rainwater drained off into the river, keeping the two dry as they journeyed.

Unexpectedly it came in handy as a deterrent and camouflage. Several times in the middle of the river, during daylight hours, Toca was able to see the giant boats Shana had told him about floating up and down the river. They were not fast enough to paddle to shore to be out of sight so Toca would quickly collapse the bamboo legs, dropping the framed caiman hide straight down on top of them, resting on the sides of the canoe. This gave the effect that a large caiman was swimming in the river. Toca was so proud of himself with the idea he became giddy every time they did it. Other times, they had to lower the caiman roof when they spotted other small canoes with Indians fishing or traveling to other villages in them. The Indians would paddle away as fast as they could, screaming when they saw the huge killer floating by high in the water.

When they finally got to the endless water, Toca was amazed at this new place. Everything was different; the smell of the air, the feel and taste of the deep clear blue water. The plants, animals, and fish were different but what caught his attention more than anything was the number of others and what their homes and villages looked like. They were very careful to stay a far distance from everyone and anything that didn't look natural. Toca had been teaching Shana how to shadow, and more than once, it came into play where they had to become invisible.

Shana had slowly changed her clothing again. With her dad's shirt, she removed the sleeves to her shoulders and cut off the long bottom hanging portion up to her belly button. Her previous cut-down dress had easily been wearing holes in it. Toca was able to kill a good-size monkey and made oversized front and back flaps with its skin, tying it around her waist. She was going to make it with the upper dress material she had left over but Toca convinced her it wouldn't last as long as the monkey hide. Shana wasn't pleased wearing something that was not completely secure or pretty but what was she to do?

After getting to the endless water, it took a couple of days to finally find what Toca's journey was all about and what consumed his life existence. In the shallows of the blue water, not far off one of the beaches, he stood up out of the water, waist-deep. The sand sifting between his toes as the small waves went back and forth, the moment of transformation had begun. He stared, in his hand, at the small object that held immense power. With this in his possession, it now will change his destiny and the destiny of his people.

Instantly Toca felt an eruption of joy, strength, and wisdom bursting out from within him. Shana, watching on from shore, keeping a lookout for others, saw him standing there in the water, motionless, with his hand held up out from his chest and his head looking down to what was in it. After some time of not moving, she yelled out to him softly, "Toca, are you all right?"

Shaken from his trance, Toca slowly raised his head and lifted his hand into the air, the trophy that would be the giver of a different life, and yelled out to the world without holding anything back, "I, Toca, the Black Ghost of the Nashua tribe, will be chief and I will save my people!"

From this moment on, the transformation was continually taking place within him. First the reality of his dream was coming true that he could actually accomplish the Katata Ado. Next was the thought of the responsibilities of what that reality could bring. Taking over for Chief Acuta, leading his tribe and with Shana's God, he would change the destiny of his people. But hidden deep in his soul, he was jumping for joy, most of all, for the day he would be telling Jucawa, "Never will you be chief as long as the Black Ghost is alive!"

With all this wrapped up inside him mentally, outwardly the transformation was taking place as well. He was having a big growth spurt, becoming stronger from the long hard work of journeying. The gangly thin body of a boy was slowly giving way to mounding firm muscles, evolving all over him as he grew taller.

Mentally everything he did was now being performed methodically. He was thinking things through instead of just doing it or being reactive. He had to see the outcome in his mind first instead of relying on guessing and hoping things would work out.

Shana was changing as well. Physically her body was taking on more of the profound shapes of a grown woman, keeping up with Toca's height. Adapting well to life on the big rivers and forest, she was a quick learner of all that Toca taught her and began enjoying the elusive and unrestricted lifestyle. She asked herself many times what was attractive being away from people. All she could come up with was that there was no one making fun of her and no one telling her what to do.

When they did reach the endless water, it surprised her how she felt with seeing all the people and the buildings. She thought that once they were near civilization, with all the conveniences of city life—marketplaces, traveling by horse and buggy, going to church, singing hymns with other people, new clothes, etc.—it would change her mind. She even thought to leave Toca and try to get back to her home on the reservation. But to her surprise, it did not; it did the opposite. It brought back feelings of bondage, human selfishness, competitiveness, and judgment. She did not want anything to do with any of that. So she never had to tell Toca or God of her new plans.

A strong relationship was being slowly molded into a very close bond of friendship. They began to know each other well enough that one was able to predict what the other was thinking or was going to do in different situations.

Their days and nights were, for the most part on the river, routine—boring and extremely tiring, canoeing upriver all day and most of the nights when the moon was out to light their way. They would rest here and there, hidden just inside the forest from the river, hanging in their hammocks. This was going on for most of seven moons, day in and day out.

Conversation began to minimize after the first moon or so. It didn't take long for them to divulge all the information about their young lives and where they grew up. Shana talked about God and attempted to explain who he was. But Toca was continuously discouraged because he wanted to see and touch this God she talked about and said was always with them.

Many times, she showed him her Bible and explained how God speaks to them through it. Not understanding what reading was or how to do it, it was meaningless to him. He would put the Bible to his ears, trying to listen for this God, and get frustrated, accusing Shana of not having a god. She would pray and Toca would ask many questions of what she was doing and her answers would never satisfy him. This was becoming a bigger deal the more they journeyed, building the only wall between them.

She herself was getting discouraged as well and with God himself, thinking, *Where are you, why aren't you revealing yourself to him, God? He wants to see you, he needs to know you are real.*

She had seen the good works of Jesus in her short life but the moments of doubt in her faith were growing and sneaking in without her knowing it. She was missing the times when her father would preach from the Bible, pray and worship in song and the world would come alive with the holy spirit.

She kept with her prayers somewhat and would read occasionally from her Bible and do it aloud so Toca could hear, but it seemed to be repetitive nonsense. He was only interested in seeing this God of hers, not trying to understand about having a relationship with something he couldn't see as she did.

Again and again, listening and waiting, but God never showed up. Silence from her God is all that Toca heard and now Shana was hearing the silence as well.

Isolation and silence were finding their way into her heart and mind. She was putting less effort or heart into her relationship with God. Was it because it seemed to be only a one-way relationship? Hers only? Nevertheless, she was bewildered.

Toca's frustration about her God was beginning to show an ugly face, once in a while, with threats. He would get angry but he didn't know if his anger was at Shana or at her God hiding from them. He told her many times that when they get to the big village on the black river, they will go into it and find a different god that will show itself.

This churned her stomach and she wanted to be sick every time he mentioned it. She would respond to him, just as her father would tell everyone during his days of preaching back home, "God reveals himself at the right place and time. He is with us always, drawing us to him through life's circumstances so have faith and believe he is with us now."

This was the first time in her young life that there was not an adult hovering over her and giving her these instructions. She was starting to understand the value of her father's experience, encouragement, and guidance for her with things in her life. And now with this problem with God, she didn't know what to do or think. She thought she was doing what her father told her by holding on to God's hand and never letting go. But in her mind's eye, it felt like she was always reaching into empty air. How could she be holding on if it seemed there was nothing to grasp onto?

*****

Finally reaching the black river, there was excitement and relief but both of the old children were wrestling with what they were going to do with this God thing when they got here.

Toca turned the canoe up the black water and began journeying in a different direction for the first time in moons. The color of the water quickly reminded them of what happened when they were here last. Shana turned back and looked at Toca with a sorrowful expression. Guilt was running through her mind but Toca sat up a little more erect, inhaling deeply, puffing his chest out, never changing the look of confidence as he stared back at her. Killing a person or an enemy wasn't what made him proud, it was that he was able to protect Shana. Not only was he fulfilling the instructions of her father but it was the first time he challenged another person—a full-grown man—and he won. Not only did he protect her from one man but three canoes full of men. As he ran the scenario over and over again in his head, the more he thought of himself, *I'm only an old child. Just think what I can do when I become a man*!

It was the middle of the day and knowing they were getting close to the big village of Manaus, where many others and obviously other Indians were in the area, Toca didn't want to take a chance of being seen. He decided to drift to the shoreline, hugging close to be able to vanish instantly into the thick vegetation that was hanging over the banks into the river.

Shana questioned having an idea of his intentions. "Where are you going, Toca? We need to go to the other side of the river, away from the big village."

"We're going to the village!" he said firmly.

"Why, we need to stay away and hidden? We don't need anything from there."

"Yes, we do and you know it. Seven moons have passed since I found you and never have I seen this God of yours. Maybe it left you when your father died!"

Her voice began to shake. "Toca, I have told you many times, my God, your God, the one that made everything is alive. He's here right now—everywhere—and he will save your people."

Just then, lightning flashed and loud echoes of booming thunder was heard from the dark massive storm clouds that had been drifting their direction. The timing couldn't have been more perfect as it all fully hit her with what he just said. *He must have left you when your father died.* Stunned at such a statement, she had no words. Shana just sat there, looking at Toca with her jaw dropped open as her eyes seemed to sink back into her head because her mind went hollow of thought.

She slowly turned around, facing upriver. Not looking at anything specific but saw in her mind the imagery of God leaving with her father's spirit in his arms going to heaven. Not looking back down because all that was left was a half-breed. And who wanted that?

Toca understood the expression on her face and knew he had just hurt her. He didn't mean to but there was no other explanation. It was the first time either of them inflicted pain on the other. Taking them both off guard, Shana wanted to be invisible and Toca was lost for words after he thought through his last statement. He didn't know how or what to say to make her feel better, especially when he knew what he had to do.

He began looking for an opening in the limbs hanging over the river's edge to slip the canoe onto the bank. They made it a habit to rest during the hottest part of the day. By doing this, they were able to last longer on the river, rowing from sunup to sundown, continuing through the night if the moon was bright enough.

Finding a landing spot, they got out of the water and unrolled their hammock packs and found a couple of trees to hang them up. The distraction of this new blank painful wall between them made things awkward. Toca was so focused on this new emotional experience, he slacked on his routine awareness for safety of the area; and Shana was in a fog of despair that she didn't even wipe down the trees and hammock rope with juja oil. They both wanted to roll up into their beds and hide from each another.

Fast asleep, Toca began dreaming. Not long into his dream, there was a snap of a twig. It was loud enough his dream stopped and he opened his eyes. Moving nothing except his eyes going back and forth, trying to locate where the sound came from, he soon concluded it was actually in his dream as everything was quiet. His heavy eyes began to close and his mind continued with the motion of life that was going on in his head.

Suddenly the silence split open. "Toca! Toca!" Shana screamed at the top of her lungs. It was so loud and close that when it jarred him hard from his dream, it blew him out of his hammock straight to the forest floor. It was a good thing because two native Indian men were just about to grab him out of his hammock while he was sleeping.

Shana was not as fortunate. She was the alarm as other Indians grabbed her sleeping and started to tie her up, gagging her mouth.

For a spilt moment, Toca could not figure out what was going on. He was looking up from the ground at brown-skinned men that had red-and-black-colored faces. Their arms and legs had bands around them with things sticking out of their noses, lips, and ears.

They had not been this close to other people since her father, and he thought maybe he was still dreaming. Then his attention went to the wrestling that was going on next to him on the ground as Shana tried again to scream with something covering her mouth.

Others! echoed in his head and terror struck his heart. One of the Indians grabbed his arm and started dragging him out into an open spot, yelling at another Indian to help. The second Indian bent down and grabbed one of his feet, stretching Toca in two different directions.

Thinking quickly, his free hand grasped ahold of his knife in the forearm sheath. Withdrawing it in one smooth motion, Toca swung the blade deep across the man's arm holding his foot which he instantly let go. Then without hesitating, leaped high in the air as a monkey flipping backward, landing on his feet behind the man holding his hand. This caused the Indian's hand to be twisted backward in a painful position, forcing him to let go just as Toca buried the knife blade deep in the back of his attacker's neck, dropping his lifeless body straight to the ground.

The man with the deep cut on his arm, bleeding, yelled to someone in the forest behind Toca. Hearing several voices in the distance yelling back, Toca could tell they were running in to help. Not knowing what to expect, he jumped up into the air at the man, planting both of his feet in the center of his chest, kicking him hard back into the forest vegetation. Toca had again flipped backward in the air, pushing off the man, landing on his feet, staring at his next kill, growling with gritted teeth.

The men that were called for help came running in and saw the two young Indians. One tied up with two of their guys holding her down and, the other, a young man standing wild-eyed with a knife in his hand and blood dripping from it.

Toca looked like a trapped animal when the group appeared. Two of the men had spears and the other had a long knife. For a split moment, seeing the spears, Toca and Shana's thoughts went to the Indian he killed in the canoe and something like a puzzle was trying to come together with who these men were. They were the same people that came after them before on the other side of the river.

Rushing in with their weapons raised, Toca knew their intentions. Fast as a hummingbird, he shot up to a lower limb of a tree and swung over to another tree and another. As he gained momentum, he catapulted out into the air, leaping as a cat, disappearing into the shadows of the forest.

CHAPTER 10

"Look toward the water, a canoe is coming," Donta stated quietly, pointing out to the group of men in the forest, not far from the river's edge.

"Any young females? They've been hard to find," one of the other men questioned as they all grunted in agreement.

Donta replied, "I can't tell. Can you see any tribal markings on them or the canoe?"

The many eyes peered through the camouflage of vegetation as the two floating in the open water were getting closer.

One of the other men answered, "I don't see anything on them except for the one in front has some type of body covering like what the foreigners wear."

"They're coming to shore, let's step back into the forest and quietly wait for them to get out," Donta instructed.

With no more words, the hunting party slithered back into their hiding positions. This was not a normal group of natives hunting for food. These are the Rohunga Indians, helpers or employees of the foreigners that built the city of Manaus, deep in the Amazon, along the black river years ago. The foreigners came to their land in giant boats in search of treasure and found a great one—the rubber tree. The rubber trees were on the land of the Rohunga Indians and, with powerful weapons, took over the land of this strong tribe. These foreigners told the Rohungas they would give them food and shelter and they could stay in this part of the forest if they helped them with the rubber trees.

Large plantations were set up around the town of Manaus that quickly grew into a large city. The foreigners continually needed more and more workers because the demand for rubber around the world grew as did the plantations. There were not enough Indians in the immediate area to help so the foreigners made a profitable deal with the Rohunga people. Search out other Indians tribes in the vast forest and make them slaves to work the rubber tree plantations and be greatly rewarded.

This was an ongoing job for the Rohungans. Not only were the plantations always growing but the slaves were continually escaping and running away. The other demand from the foreigners were older girls and young women. Very few of the foreigners brought their own women to the great Amazon and the need for females was always there. When the Rohunga brought in new females, they were given bonuses because they were in such high demand.

"Why are they hanging hammocks and going to sleep, it's the middle of the day?" This was murmured among the men, watching the two younger people.

Donta, the leadman, whispered, "This is going to be easy, and the one wearing the top covering is a girl and she is very pretty."

All the men nodded their heads in agreement.

Pointing to two men, Donta whispered instructions, "When they are asleep, you two get the girl and Mundi and I will get the boy. The rest of you continue on to the Vaz Dias plantation and let them know we will be coming back with two and one is a girl of age." He was eyeing the young female that seemed to have slightly lighter shade of brown skin covering her breasts with some type of top covering.

Soon the two were asleep and the men started their capture. As they got close one of them stepped on a small stick snapping loudly. Their stealth approach vanished as they stopped, waiting for a reaction from the hammocks, but there was none. Donta waved them on to continue. When at the sleeping young ones, Donta and Mundi stood over the male, trying to find any identifying markings on him but only saw an ankle bracelet with three small bone carvings attached to it.

Suddenly a horrifying scream came from the young woman as the other two men grabbed her and quickly began tying her up. Still staring down at the male, they watched as he jolted awake so hard he fell out of his hammock. Donta reached down and quickly grabbed one of the young man's arms, dragging him a few steps into an open area while he told Mundi to grab hold of his feet. Mundi was only able to grasp one foot and pulled away from Donta, stringing him parallel to the ground in the air.

Out of nowhere, the young man drew a knife hidden on the inside of his forearm with his free hand and swiftly slashed deep across the meaty part of Mundi's arm, letting go of the foot as blood began gushing everywhere. Pain-stricken, Mundi glared in disbelief, holding his arm at the innocent-looking young male.

Moving with lightning speed, the young man flipped backward up in the air, like a monkey, over Donta's head. He landed behind Donta, impaling him at the base of his skull with the knife as the male's feet touched the ground. Donta's body instantly went lifeless, dropping to the forest floor. Mundi loudly yelled for help. The men heading to the plantation heard the cry and shouted back they were coming. Mundi looked up from seeing Donta's body into intense eyes of something not human but rather an awakened killer and he was its next prey.

Before Mundi took his next breath, the nightmare was at him, airborne, embedding his feet in the middle of his chest, bolting him like lightning, backward into the thick vegetation, painfully knocking all the air out of him. Mundi looked up, anticipating his life-ending blow, but as fast as the attack happened, it ended. The storm of terror vanished and all he heard was the squirming of the young woman and his brother tribe's men coming to his rescue.

*****

After some time, Toca stopped running between the narrow trees and ferns, leaping again high up in a tree and pressed his back up against the trunk, squatting on a large limb. With eyes closed and panting hard, trying to catch his breath, he just realized how out of shape he was from sitting in a canoe for months and not running daily through the forest. His arms and upper body had grown greatly from rowing but being able to run far had weakened.

"What just happened?" he whispered out loud between the frantic breaths. *Who were those others? What did they want, and why did they grab me*? A confusing shower of questions were going through his mind then, "Shana!" he shouted aloud, twisting his head around the tree, looking back.

Turning back, he closed his eyes again to think, *What do I do*? Toca's chest was beating hard but now it wasn't from lack of air, it was panic striking.

Why did they tie her up and put something in her mouth? What are they going to do with her? He sat there, trying to think but nothing was coming to him except, *Why do others always want to hurt us? They are all bad people. Just like the ones Chief Acuta talked about where our old ones came from. Bad gods are everywhere, making people hurt and kill other people!"*

Suddenly his eyes exploded wide open and fear hit as he remembered what the chief told him what the gods of their ancestors needed—human hearts. A picture flashed in his mind of Shana being held down on a large rock by these warriors that took her, screaming his name, helplessly struggling to get away. Then a priest mystically appeared in his mind, hovering over her cutting her chest open—"No!" Toca shouted aloud to stop the picture, putting his hands to his face, attempting to hide from it. Horror was running through him as his stomach wanted to be sick. He began to sweat as he still panted, trying to grasp enough air to calm him down, but it was actually causing him to hyperventilate.

As that picture dissipated like morning mist, the vision of John lying in the tent, dying, formed. John turned his head and looked at Toca as tears poured out of his sky-blue colored eyes like Shana's, sadly crying, softly asked, "Why didn't you take care of my daughter as I asked? You were supposed to protect her?"

"No, stop it, stop it!" Toca gritted aloud into his hands as they were still covering his face with his eyes squinted shut. Illusions were haunting him; this was something he had never experienced. He sat there for a while, motionless, feeling alone, weak, and childlike. The man that was growing inside had slipped away as guilt and clouded thought was taking its place.

The tree branch he was sitting on gently moved. Toca felt for the wind that swayed the tree but it wasn't there. Again the branch stirred with no air movement and the old child became more frightened, knowing the answer—something or someone was in the tree with him.

Hands still up to his face, he barely spread his fingers apart, ever so slowly so he could peek through to see but not have his eyes seen. Only moving his eyes around in the minimal space, nothing was there. Then a shadow came and went. His heart began to beat hard, there was definitely something just in front of him. The sunlight again was blocked then reappeared as the shadow vanished. Thinking protection, Toca decided he would move as fast as he could while retrieving his knife and leap straight up to the branch above his. He would at least have height advantage to defend himself from what was sneaking in on him.

Shooting straight up, grasping the branch, he swung himself onto his feet with his knife at the ready, looking down. There wasn't anything there; quickly he moved his head all around, looking for something to jump up or out at him—but nothing. Finally he caught movement below within the patch of large leaves nearing the end of the branch on which he had been sitting.

Slowly separating the leaves, something was stealthily coming out and Toca braced himself for the attack.

Then jolting back sideways, something beside him, out at the end of the branch he was on, moved in the thick leaves, catching him by surprise. Slightly losing his balance, he put his back against the tree trunk and watched on as a long arm slowly reached out. The brownish hairy arm had long curled nails dangling down to the lower branch where he saw the first leaves separating. To his surprise, a small arm, looking the same as the one going down, grabbed ahold of the big one and the long arm pulled up slowly and gently.

Toca relaxed as he realized what was happening. The little one from below blocked the sunlight with its body as it held on being airborne momentarily until it reached the upper hiding place. A mother sloth was retrieving her baby to safety away from the one that interrupted their daily routine of eating up in the trees.

The movements of the animals were so smooth and serene that a calming peace flushed through Toca. Once the baby sloth was with its mother, they disappeared into the camouflage foliage as though nothing ever happened.

They shadow just like we do, he thought to himself. The peace quickly stirred into excitement. Then the excitement turned into clarity of thought, re-energizing the man he was becoming.

He turned his face into the direction where he last saw Shana and said in a firm confident tone, "I'm coming for you, Shana."

*****

The men wrapped up Mundi's arm with palm leaves and tightly tied thin tree vines around it to stop the bleeding.

"We need to get you to the shaman, he will fix you, Mundi," one of the men exclaimed.

Ignoring what was said, he asked, "Is Donta's body ready for travel?"

The men all answered back yes as they finished tying his body to a long strong bamboo pole.

This whole time, being attended to, Mundi was frantically looking out for his attacker to come back and save his woman and kill him and all the men. Peering into the deep forest and up around in the trees, he kept watching nervously.

Anxious, he blurted out, "Good, we need to go now!" He was desperate to leave, he had never seen such speed come out of a man, let alone a younger one, only from fierce predators. But this predator had a weapon and knew how to use it.

Attempting to help the men with the tragedy of losing a friend, but more over to distract him from his own fears, he exclaimed, "Let's get the young female to the headmaster, we're going to get a lot for her!" Then he added, "Take that useless body covering off, why would she want to wear such a thing?"

Ripping off her dad's sleeveless shirt, buttons popped everywhere. Her eyes went wide as she screamed loud through the gag and struggled to hide herself from their view. The men laughed at her reaction, not understanding why she would disapprove. No Indian, man or woman, wore upper body coverings, only the foreigners.

With one man at each end of the bamboo pole, several others helped lift up Donta's body so the poles rested on the two's shoulders. "We're ready," they exclaimed to Mundi.

They traveled the rest of the day and, by nightfall, finally made it to the Vaz Dias plantation main house. It was just inside the city with other buildings around it some distance away from the actual plantation itself. The men gave the young woman to the headmaster and told him what happened and how the young man killed Donta and injured Mundi.

He wasn't happy. Donta was his best and most trusted of all his Indian workers. Quickly turning to his new prize standing next to him, still tied up and gagged, he backhanded her across the face, sending her sprawled onto the ground. Then he yelled in Portuguese down at her for what was done, unloading his frustration. He was getting tired of the games and the hassles dealing with these Indians all the time.

Now the one person who did more for him than all these men standing in front of him combined was dead. The headmaster drew his knife from its sheath on his hip, turned back to the men, gritting his teeth, and narrowing his eyes as they cowardly took a step back. Stabbing the knife in the air in the direction of the forest, he growled out, "Go back out there and get the one that did this to Donta. I want to kill him myself." Flipping the knife in the air, catching it by the end of the blade, he twisted his body back around to the female and threw the knife, impaling it into the dirt next to her head.

Still recovering on the ground from the hard blow to the side of her face, her eyes went wide and caught her breath as the knife whipped by, stabbing the ground, only a finger length away in front of her face.

This was the last thing Mundi wanted to do, feeling what this unnatural predator did to him, gently rubbing the area of his wound.

His stomach was getting upset; he didn't know if it was from the throbbing pain in his arm or the thought of going back into the forest.

Grabbing the young Indian woman by the hair and lifting her up to her feet, the headmaster marched her to the guest house that was at the back of the main mansion. Before opening the door, he looked back at the men just standing there and yelled out, "Go get him, now!" They all turned and disappeared into the darkness.

Opening the door, he shoved her to the center of the room as she stumbled to the floor. Making his way in the dark to the table off to the side of the room near a window, he felt around for the box of matches. Striking a match, it lit up the area enough that he could see the oil lamp on the table. Taking off the glass top, he touched the match to the wick and it immediately flamed up. Putting the glass cover back on, the room instantly came to life with color and furniture appearing.

Turning around, he looked down at his fresh new woman, now sitting up, staring at him in fear.

"So what tribe are you and that mysterious young man from?" He was speaking in Portuguese then repeated in the basic language of the natives in this area of the Amazon. She sat there, gazing.

"You are a pretty young girl for an Indian, let me get a closer look at you." Bending down, he gave a deep unspoken laugh as he picked her up by the arm still tied to the other behind her back, walking her over to the side of the bed.

The young Indian woman was only wearing a small waist wrap with monkey skin flaps covering her front and backside; she saw the bed and began squirming, trying to get away, yelling through the gag. He pushed her down on it and said, "So you do know what's going to happen?" smirking, he said out loud this time.

Standing in front of her, he reached out for the gag in her mouth and said, "Now I'm going to take this thing out of your mouth and from around your head. If you start screaming, I'm going to hit you again and maybe again and again." He brought his other hand back across his body as if he was going to hit her and she flinched back, closing her eyes, waiting for another backhanded slap.

"Just because I'm already mad." Giving her the reason why, he then brought his hand down.

He untied the gag from behind her head and took it out of her mouth. She squinted her eyes open to see what was actually going on. Realizing he wasn't going to hit her, she relaxed a bit, blinking her eyes open.

"I'm going to ask you again, what tribe are you from?" he asked in the native language.

Not verbally replying, she did tilt her head slightly and gradually rolled her eyes to the side as if she was thinking. She didn't understand what he was saying but she could tell he had been speaking two different languages.

"What's your name?" he said, harsher in Portuguese. Staring closer at her face, he got out of the way of the light from the oil lamp across the room.

He was the one cocking his head to the side this time, peering closer as he grasped ahold of her face, squeezing her cheeks together with his big hand. "You look different than the rest of these Indians. Your skin is lighter and your eyes, your eyes are bigger and rounder." Then his head bobbed back as though something stung the end of his nose.

"What in the world?" He questioned aloud as he got up and went to get the lamp, bringing it back, setting it on the nightstand to brighten the area up around the bed.

Looking at her intently, for a moment in disbelief, then he questioned her. "How is this possible? Why are your eyes blue and not dark brown?"

Still staring at her face, he slowly looked down and back up her body. "She looks Indian, wearing almost nothing." Then his eyes stopped at the old small rock carving hanging from the necklace around her neck. He reached up to the small piece of whitish rock carved in some type of squared-off shapes.

Holding the necklace in his fingers, his eyes went to hers, not moving his head, and asked, "Where are you from?" Then he grasped the rock with his whole hand as to break the necklace from her body.

"No, don't take that from me!" she blurted out in her own native Indian language, knowing his intentions.

Surprised at her sudden outburst, he flinched, then with a big smile, he said, "So you do talk." He gently tugged on the cord around her neck to get another reaction, but this time, she stated in English, "Stop! Don't take it from me!"

This time, he dropped the necklace and instantly stood up, staring at her in shock. He recognized that language, even though he didn't understand it. Now she had his attention from his reaction.

When she and her father traveled to South American and into the Amazon, it was her father that did all the talking because he knew Spanish. Working slowly through the different dialects, he was able to communicate. Very few people in South America spoke English, especially inside the belly of the giant Amazon forest.

The headmaster asked in Portuguese with surprise, "You know English? How does an Indian know English?" She didn't understand a word he said except the word *English*.

Her reply was, "I speak English."

He stepped back, holding one of his hands to his face. He had no idea what to do. *There is no one I knew in Manaus that speaks English. So what is this dirty Amazon Indian woman doing speaking English? And why does she have blue eyes*? he asked himself.

This was very disturbing to him as his physical intentions with her left him. His mind was replaced with one very specific important thing to him. The only reason he was living in this forsaken rain forest and not in his own homeland was to get rich off the rubber tree trade.

The only people he ever saw with blue eyes were white Europeans. His mind went wild with illusions for the reason this Indian woman had rounded blue eyes and could speak English.

Then it came to him, blurting out in Portuguese, "You are a half-breed! Where did you come from? Is your father British? Are his people traveling upriver to take over this land?" The more he talked, the madder he got and the deeper he began to believe what he was making up. Paranoia was consuming him. The last thing he wanted was for the British or Americans coming up the Amazon and taking his treasure away from him. He had left his whole life behind; family, friends, country, everything to be wealthy and wealthy he was.

She sat there, looking up, listening to this big well-fed man with long black hair and a mustache that went around his mouth, forming a beard on his chin. It hung down the length of a finger to a point. He was fully clothed in nice attire and his boots went up to his knees. Every time he took a step, they made a clucking sound on the wooden floor. It had been a long time since she heard sounds like that. Every movement and sound was loud to her inside the house. But moreover was the sight and smell of everything in the room, the soft bed she was sitting on, the light coming from a lantern, chairs to sit on, and a table to use.

For a moment, her mind was at ease, seeing these conveniences, but her heart drew the thought away and became very uneasy. Looking around the room, she began to feel closed in and the smell was not natural and somewhat repulsive.

Over the past seven moons, she didn't realize how she had adapted to the forest. Her senses had become very sharp and the appreciation of the freedom and living in the openness struck her as she looked around the small house. Everything had almost the same specific shape—square with straight lines all over the place. The walls, floor planks, kitchen counter, tables, chairs, windows, everything now looked out of place, very unnatural, manmade, and closed in.

Focusing back to the man, she was afraid of him and what he would be doing to her. But what had her attention the most was the smells. They were making her nauseous as the closed-in feeling was giving her thoughts of a walled-in tomb shrinking in on her.

"Come on, were going to the main house." He grabbed her by the arm, lifting her off the bed, then leaned over and blew the flame out of the lamp. Briskly walking her out of the backhouse into the large well-lit-up plantation mansion from oil lanterns positioned all over the place, he told her, knowing she didn't understand, "I'm calling a meeting with the other plantation owners. I'll send my servants out tonight right away. We are going to get to the bottom of this."

*****

Leaping down to the ground, Toca stood up straight, closing his eyes. Slowly taking in a deep breath, proudly pushing his chest out, he began to clear his mind and reveal what secretly had been slowly slipping away—keen senses and awareness of his surroundings.

Being on the river so long, sitting in a canoe, he didn't realize how much he stopped using the things that will keep him alive inside the deadly forest.

Toca flashed back to Chief Acuta and him during training in the hidden valley. He envisioned the chief telling him, pointing into the dark unknown forest, "Do not look at the trees but peer through them. Watch for the smallest things with eagle eyes." Then the chief demonstrated by going through the motions himself, lifting his nose, smelling deeply. "Smell for the faintest odors with a nose of an ant-eater." Putting a hand to his ear, he said, "Listen for the quietest of sounds like ears of the deer and taste the flavors of the air as the snake does with its tongue." Visioning the chief turning to him, adding, "Toca, not only use your senses, live them in every step you take and breath you breathe in your life. But what you must trust the most, you cannot see, smell, hear, taste, or touch." Chief Acuta reached out and put his hand gently on Toca's chest. "Trust this in here. You might not understand what I'm talking about now but there will come many times, more than you can count, when the only answers to your troubles or situations will only come from in here. Trust what this tells you and you will live a long life."

Toca quieted his thoughts, with his eyes still closed, and inhaled slowly through his nose. He let the odors from near and far drift deeply within him, identifying and separating each one out. His ears warmed as he listened to the sounds whispering through the forest, positioning them in his mind. He was beginning to feel grounded and a part of the family of everything that grew in the forest.

"Home, I am back home," he said to himself as he slowly opened his eyes, allowing them to adjust to the light and the multitude of colors that flowed through the vegetation. His vision once again was clear. He was seeing far and wide in the thick forest. The smallest of things were catching his eyes: ants a distance away on their daily march, specks of pollen drifting through the air, floating in and out of the sunlight beaming through the high treetops. Camouflaged hidden creatures he neglected to see earlier were now very apparent. They were all around, watching him.

Up in the tree, next to the one he was in, a thin twig on a branch slowly wavered. *A brown stick bug*, Toca thought to himself. Moving his head straight up to the branch he had jumped down from earlier, he gazed into the clump of foliage. Focusing into the dark, looking through leaves, he saw several sets of eyes watching him.

"Thank you, mother sloth, for bringing me back to who I am," he said aloud.

Looking away, he visually searched for something specific. Spotting it, he walked over and reached down to the bottom of the vine of the laminia tree. Their vines grow from larger upper limbs down into the ground. Cutting it with his knife at the forest floor, he lifted the vine up, plugging the center with his thumb so the precious liquid inside would not pour out. When he got it to his mouth, he drank deeply, several swallows, then he let the vine drain its essence over his hair, face, and the rest of his body.

Drenched with the sticky milky fluid, he knelt to the ground and scooped up a handful of brown dirt filled with fallen greenish-tan leaves and twigs. Then showered himself repeatedly with it until he was completely covered. He stood still for a few moments, with his arms out and legs spread wide, to let the tree syrup dry firmly, holding all the forest debris to his body. Not only sensing the forest, he now looked like it from head to toe with the foliage breaking up the outline of his body as leaves and twigs stuck out all over the place. This was the ultimate camouflage for shadowing with his people.

He closed his eyes again while he dried and let his senses and mind loose to search for what they needed. He saw Shana when they first met come into full view, wading in the water, spearfishing, then the caiman attack. Next she was running to him in the water, hugging him the first time.

The scene moved to her kneeling at her father's side with her head on his chest, crying then falling asleep. Again jumping ahead, she was hugging him just outside the clearing when she thought he left her.

A new image appeared with her screaming at him not to throw the spear at the others in the canoes coming after them. Only to end up Shana hugging him once more the following day in the canoe, thanking him for saving them.

Still standing with his eyes closed, drying, he took another deep breath. Toca felt as though he inhaled something foreign because his chest was beginning to flutter and stir inside. *What is that?* he thought to himself. Then the fluttering of emotion moved up his throat to his mouth, watering it up, swallowing hard several times. His face flushed and felt like he wanted to cry. Swallowing again, he shook his head and thought, *Why am I suddenly feeling this way?*

Shana appeared this time to him on the beach where he found his Ado shell. He was holding up his prize, walking out of the water, and she came running to him with her big smile, once again hugging him. The emotion swung to happiness as the scene in his head put a smile on his face.

Killing that picture was one he saw earlier, Shana now screaming and squirming on the ground, being tied up by others. They picked her up and put her on a large flat rock as a priest-looking man walked out of the forest with a knife in his hand. The Indians held her down as the priest raised his knife high above her. Shana twisted her head, looking directly at Toca with tears flowing down her cheeks, screaming over and over, "Save me, Black Ghost!"

Exploding open, the white of his eyes, through the natural camouflage, were the only things human-looking about him. An eruption broke apart in Toca, spewing out everything he saw and felt, except for complete hard and angry determination to save Shana from these others.

Toca looked up to the sky, as Shana would do many times, but he shouted out loud, "You, god of Shana, prove yourself to me you exist! If you are really a good god, you will protect her and me from these others!" Instantly he turned in the direction of where they were attacked. With stealth and power, the Black Ghost disappeared from sight of the sloths.

CHAPTER 11

Toca quickly shadowed close to where the others attacked them. Watching and waiting from a distance, there were no humans around the area. Moving in with extreme caution, he took down the hammocks, folded them into packs, and gathered up everything belonging in them.

Looking around to make sure he didn't miss anything, he noticed something unnatural in a bush the direction of where the others and Shana's footprints went. Focusing in as he got closer, he realized what it was.

Taken aback, he thought to himself, *Why would they do this to her? She wants to be covered up*! He picked it out of the bush and noticed the small round things that held it together in front were missing. Finding them scattered around on the ground, he picked them up one at a time, getting angrier with each one, saying under his breath, "Shana wants to be covered! It's very important to her!"

Putting her top covering and the small round things into her pack, he took both bags to the canoe. Hesitating for a moment, looking at the canoe, he decided to relocate it and got in, slowly paddling out to the edge of the overhanging bushes. Using all his senses this time, he made sure there was no one in the area. Confident he moved out to the open water, keeping close to the edge. Swiftly, Toca paddled upstream until he got as close to the big village as he felt comfortable yet still a distance away. Turning into a very narrow well-hidden entrance in the foliage, he stopped the canoe before it hit the muddy bank. He didn't want to make any marks on the shore to give away his hiding spot. Stepping out into the ankle-deep water, he tangled it up sideways in the bushes, still floating but not able to move. Reaching over to long thin tree limbs, he hacked them off with the long knife and set them around the sides of the canoe to hide its outline.

Making sure everything was set, he put the long knife back into Shana's pack. Starring at it for a moment, thinking he might need it, he decided it would slow him down.

Without hesitating, Toca switched his train of thought and climbed straight up through the thick twinned branches, leaving the water without a trace. Slithering his way through the tree, going from one to another purposely in a straight line away from the river into the forest, he sharply peered down to the ground, looking for his target.

Only the white of his eyes were visible from the dirt and old vegetation that covered his whole body, making him invisible to someone looking for a man. Finally they fixed on what he was looking for—a smearing on the ground floor, dotted here and there of partial footprints. Toca found the trail of the others taking Shana toward the large village.

Listening and watching the world around him, the birds were singing their evening songs, telling the sun goodbye as it disappeared behind the trees. In the distance, a family of monkeys were whooping to greet the darkness entering the forest as they were going to their beds for the night.

Not sensing any signs of other human activity, along with the birds and animals at peace, told him it was safe to go to the ground and follow the trail closer as it got dark. Softly landing on the forest floor, staying in a crouched position, Toca peered all around him, confirming everything was all right. Then examining the footprints closer, he made out distinct individual prints. Finally with a whispered breath of excitement, "Here you are, Shana!" He found her prints among the others. Suddenly his joyous mood switched as he spotted something very small, dark, and periodically spotted along the markings in the dirt.

"Blood," whispering to himself. "This man has seen me, a Nashua." Remembering back to what Chief Acuta said, "The others cannot see you and they must not know we exist. You must protect our people."

Squatted down on the trail, staring at the drops of blood, Toca looked up through the darkening forest in the direction where the trail of prints were heading and stated without facial expression, "I cannot allow you to live since your eyes know I exist."

Slowly standing, he took his knife out and, at shoulder-height, carved out four vertical pointed lines the length of his fingers on the tree he just dropped from. This spot was now marked with the claws of a black ghost for him to find later.

With determination and purpose, he began to shadow without a sound along the side of the path the others left behind.

The moon never showed itself this night and the forest floor was soon thick with darkness. Slowing his tracking through the twisted vegetation, following a faint trail, Toca was beginning to get frustrated. He needed to get to Shana as fast as he could. His mind kept racing with visual horrors of her being hurt and killed for bad gods. But not knowing anything about these others or the village and where she was, this was the only way to get to her.

His ears were hit first. Something a short distance ahead of him was moving. Not able to see through the darkness, coupled with the thick forest, he inhaled deeply several times. Soon the night air brought to his nose the news identifying what it was—*Others!* he stated in thought.

Whiffs of smoke from something burning and old musty human sweat was smelled, but most of all, the smell of fear. It overwhelmed the other odors to the point he was not only smelling it but feeling it. Someone was coming his way and they were very afraid.

Without thinking, Toca stepped back less than an arm's length away from the trail of footprints, disappearing up against a tree trunk, facing what was coming his way. Slowly removing his knife, he firmly held it pointed down, tight and ready.

Very soon, through the wall of night, a faint echoing of light glowed, bouncing off everything near it. Coming closer toward him, popping flickers of a small flame made itself known as the source of the glow and the smell of something burning. As it moved behind trees and large fern leaves, it flashed on and off from full view. Floating at man's shoulder height above the forest floor, it had the illusion of being by itself. But as it got closer, Toca could see the flame guiding the outline of human bodies walking.

Hunkered together under the protection of the small fire that was at the end of a stick held up by one of the others in front, they were unknowingly almost to him.

He slowed his breathing and closed his eyes to the point he only could see through the squinted lines of his eye lashes.

One of them whispered something and the group stopped right where Toca shadowed against the tree, facing him.

Do they see me? he thought. The one who spoke stepped away from the group to the side of the Black Ghost and began relieving himself as his water poured onto the ground.

Perfectly still, Toca watched on, ever so slowly moving his squinted eyes, looking at each man standing a breath away.

His heart instantly throbbed hard, thinking its movement was going to give him away as he realized the one directly in front of him had a wounded arm wrapped up in a banana leaf. The same arm in the same place he used his knife to get away.

As the group waited for the one off the trail, the wounded man began staring directly at Toca. Not seeing Toca, but as the small flame flickered, lighting the immediate area up, it bounced around odd shadows and this shadow on the tree looked slightly out of place. Not sure what he was looking at, he stepped forward, leaning closer to examine the growth on the tree.

Only a couple of nose lengths from Toca's camouflaged face, the man lifted his good hand to feel and identify what he was looking at.

Toca, rigid in place, understood from the man's movements, he was perfectly shadowed; but something caught his interest.

The injured man slowly poked the growth on the tree. His finger pushed in slightly then smeared some dirt and parts of leaves. He looked at his finger then looked closer to the spot he touched.

Toca thought, *This other cannot get any closer, it is time for him to die*!

He exploded his eyes wide open, looking like two white flames as they reflected the light off the fire stick a few arm lengths away.

The man jolted with fear beyond anything he had ever seen but couldn't scream out or move. Standing in place, with eyes locked onto the eyes, glaring at him from the tree, he realized it wasn't his fear that jolted him or held him in place. But as he felt a warm liquid flowing down the front of his neck onto his chest his vision was getting clouded as he quickly felt weak throughout his body. Slowly reaching up to his upper neck and jaw area, he understood the tree had an arm holding a knife stabbed deep upward into his throat and skull.

The eyes of the tree closed and its arm went back down, hidden to the side of its trunk, as the man dropped to the forest floor, dead.

"Mundi, what are you doing on the ground?" asked the man, stepping back to the group from relieving himself.

Then the man holding the fire stick moved it over Mundi's body and asked, "What is he doing lying there?" They huddled around, looking down at him, when suddenly, the tree Mundi's body was crumbled up against flew out its branches, opening glowing eyes from its trunk, and came alive, screaming with scowling bright teeth.

Surprised and horrified by something they had never seen or expected, they all began screaming themselves. Looking at the live tree then at each other, back to the nightmare, all turned fumbling away as fast as they could. Bumping into each other, trying to stay in the safety of the light of the fire, ran back through the forest where they came, stumbling and yelling at each other to go faster.

The growth on the tree looked down to the man lying at his feet, gritted its teeth, and said, "I am Black Ghost of the Nashua, your life had to end because of what your eyes saw."

Toca looked up to the others fleeing in the distance through the dark night and took off after them.

*****

Several of the other plantation owners had arrived at the Vas Dias mansion and were being greeted at the front door as Shana was sitting in the great room. She was still tied up and guarded by a couple of Indian servants. The arriving men were dressed in their more formal attire, colorful long-sleeve shirts puffed out around the shoulders with ruffles of material in the middle of their chest. They wore dark pants, hidden by leather boots from the knees down, folded over at the tops. All the men had long dark wavy hair, adorning beards or goatees on their faces, hiding their lips.

As they entered the mansion, they all handed the greeting servant their large hats, drawing their swords off their hips and placing them in the sword cabinet which was at the side of the front door.

The great room had a vaulted ceiling with a large crystal candle chandelier hanging down, helping the fireplace light up the room. In the middle of the room were two multicolored full large couches facing each other with a sizable low table separating them. The top of the table was made from smooth imported marble, supported by finely finished carved wooden pillars. The giant rock fireplace was on the back wall facing the furniture and its dancing flames glistened their reflection off the top of the table. Above the fireplace mantel were two swords crossing each other, anchored to a metal chest body armor hanging on the wall.

Shana was staring at all the fancy things in the room. She had never seen so many shiny items with the beautiful colored drapes, rugs, and paintings hanging on the walls. She was very uncomfortable, not only from being tied up but being out of place. Most of all, everyone else was fully clothed except the male Indian servants guarding her. They were wearing colorfully decorated skirt-like pants, covering them from the waist to their knees. Around their arms, up at the biceps, were multicolored leather bands with feathers hanging from them, giving their brown skin flavor. Similar straps crossed their chests and backs attached to their pants. Both guards had fancy knife handles sticking out of sheaths anchored at their hips.

Shana's gaze around the room ended up at the front entry where the men showing up were talking loudly. The man that brought her into the house and that hit her earlier came out from another room and greeted the arriving men. He was dressed similarly as the others except his back and shoulders were wrapped with a soft black cape tied around his neck where lightly colored ruffles plumed out on top. On the back of the cape, a bright shielded symbol was embroidered.

He turned her direction and pointed as all the men stared at her. Shana was overwhelmed with embarrassment from not being covered. Trying her best to move out of their view was useless with her hands tied behind her and the two guards holding her seated down by the shoulders in a chair next to the couches.

Mr. Dias and the men came into the great room and stopped in front of her. He gestured toward her and began talking in Portuguese. "Can you see a difference in this young Indian woman?"

"Yes, she is a beautiful one, what do you want for her?" One of the other plantation owners asked with a big smile and a deep chuckle.

"She's not for sale, take this seriously. Look at her, do you see anything different about her?"

"Her skin is a little lighter than the other Indians, her eyes are roun—oh, look at that!"

"Her eyes are blue!" another plantation owner exclaimed, butting in, pointing at her face.

Mr. Dias answered back, "Yes, they are and that's not all." He bent down and firmly grabbed ahold of the necklace piece around Shana's neck, knowing the reaction he was going to get.

Grimacing back, not expecting him to do that, she said in English, "No, please don't take that."

All the men stopped talking and looked at one another, then exploded in aggressive conversation. Shana looked up surprisingly at all the men in an uproar about something. Their arms were being used to express themselves, flailing all over the place as they spoke, almost yelling at each other. Mr. Dias shouted out for everyone to calm down and invited them to sit down on the couches as he pointed to a servant to get them all something to drink.

Sitting, he gestured to the guards to bring the female to them and sit her down in front of them at the end of the low marble table.

Shana had stopped trying to resist being pushed around and was quietly focusing on ways she could get away. But so far, nothing looked hopeful.

Her thoughts went to Toca as she sat there listening to the garble of talking going on. Reflecting back when Toca and she first met and mysteriously they began understanding each other, she thought to herself, *How did we know what the other was saying? Why did we have such similar languages in the middle of nowhere, but here in civilization, I can't understand a single word these men say?*

Interrupting everyone in a deep discussion, a loud knocking came at the front door. A servant answered and a handful of Indian men, frantically talking loud, wanted to speak with Mr. Dias. Overhearing his name, he left the great room to speak with the Indians.

"What, he's dead now?" Mr. Dias yelled. Everyone in the great room were now standing, peering at the front door to all the commotion. The Indians were very skittish and kept looking back out into the night from the large lit-up porch.

"You go back out there and get me that ghost Indian!" he yelled, pointing toward the forest. They all shook their heads, not wanting to go, but he persisted in telling them what to do and slammed the door in their faces.

One of the men in the great room asked as he walked back, "What was that about?"

"When my hunting party was out and found this one"—glaring down at Shana then looked back to the men—"there was a young male with her. He killed Donta, my best Indian, then ran away. I sent the party back out to find him and now they are saying the forest came alive and killed another one of my hunters, Mundi. They're very scared and kept saying something Mundi was telling them about this ghost Indian. He moves fast and powerfully killed Donta with ease then disappeared like a jaguar or a spirit. Now they're saying the spirits of the forest has turned on them and will kill all of us." He shook his head. "Bunch of fools."

The men were silent as they listened. Some looked toward the windows of the mansion, trying to see these illusions in the night. One thought he heard something snap outside one of the windows but only saw a tree branch slowly waving in the night breeze.

Breaking up the atmosphere, one of them began to laugh, mentally brushing off the naive weakness of the Indians. They all began to laugh except Mr. Dias; he walked up to the fireplace and took down one of the swords, grasping the handle firmly, marched back to Shana, kicking her in the chest, lying her back flat on the marble table, and he put the sword to her throat.

Another one of his men is dead and he had enough. "Who are you? Where did you come from and who is out there killing my men?" he yelled in the local Indian language. The Indian guards backed away, getting nervous.

Shana looked into his eyes, trying to understand what he was saying, having no idea what was going on, replied in her native language as she began to cry, "I don't understand what you are saying. I don't know what you want from me."

Tears began to flow and she turned her head sideways, looking away in the direction of one of the windows. She peered past the small tree branch outside and into the darkness, asking in English aloud, "God where are you? Why have you left me to die?"

Abruptly she stopped crying, holding her breath and blinked her eyes rapidly to clear them. Shana thought she saw the tree branch slightly move unnaturally. Waiting for it to move again, she tried to adjust her head without stabbing herself with the tip of the sword that was still at her neck and began to smile.

Now it seemed the leaves on the branch were looking back at her. She had been here before, looking toward a tree, thinking something was looking at her, later finding out something was!

"Toca! Toca, help me!" Shana screamed. All the men flinched, catching them off guard with her instant burst of words.

Everyone thought she was going crazy. Shana tried to squirm out of her hands being tied, talking the whole time, explaining to them they better let her go.

*****

Following the retreating bunch of others to the large village, Toca never took his eyes off them through the forest. Once out of cover of the dense forest, he had a harder time following them; darkness was mainly his only refuge. But he was also distracted by all the new things around him, things he saw from a distance when they were at the endless water. Big solid huts Shana called buildings, open areas between the buildings, where no plants grow and people walked and used animals to pull and carry things, she called streets. At night, the buildings had light coming out through windows with small fire sticks hanging outside on the walls of each hut entrance.

Trying to stay focused, knowing he was taking a huge risk being out in the open, Toca had no other choice of finding Shana. She talked about these villages all the time so he tried to remember the things she taught him about them.

The men were moving fast as he shadowed them from a distance, hiding behind whatever hid his body—a rock fence, a tree or bush that was spotted here and there. Even a low depression in the ground, lying flat, blending into the dirt.

Finally the group got to one of the large solid buildings and had to climb rock steps up a short distance to get to the landing of the entrance door. Toca was hidden back a ways, watching and examining the whole building, and noticed it was larger than most and was brightly lit up all the way around with many fire sticks. Peering up to the roof, he saw, from the glow of the fire sticks, a long skinny rock formation sticking out of the top as a consistent flow of clouds were coming out of it, appearing odd. Then his nose alerted him what it really was—smoke!

Panic struck him, realizing where these men brought him. Toca saw in his mind Chief Acuta telling him, "In rock structures reaching high above the trees is where the priests cut out the hearts of people, giving them to the gods as gifts. Then the bodies are thrown into a continuous burning rock firepit to please the gods."

Toca was emotional seeing the smoke and thinking Shana could be dead already. He looked back down toward the others speaking frantically to someone at the open door. Movement caught his eye through a window on the side of the building. The light from the fire inside slightly wavered as though something was moving back and forth in front of it. Peering around, making sure no one was looking his direction in the dark, he moved quickly to the window, staying very low to the ground.

Once at the building, blending into a small bush below the window, he looked up and realized it was two body lengths high up. Trying to figure out how to see in, he noticed a tall tree with long branches at the back corner of the building. Moving to the tree, he quickly slithered up it without a sound, going to the higher branches that were angled straight up. At the base of one of the fatter branches, Toca looked out and down toward the window, then up to the top of the branch and back to the window.

Having seen this many times, watching monkeys, he nodded his head as though saying, *"This would work."* He carefully moved like a snail up the flimsy branch on the side facing the window. As he got higher, the branch began a slow long descent, bowing down along the building wall toward the window. Putting one of his feet against the wall, he controlled the speed of the branch as it lowered. Finally at the top of the window, he was able to let go with one hand holding onto the frame of the window.

Slowly wavering like a giant praying mantis, he moved into position to see inside, upside down, through the window. But first, Toca's attention was diverted, hearing yelling then a bang outside on the other side of the rock building. It came from the entrance area where the others were. Looking down that direction, the group of Indians skittishly walked away back down the street, huddled together, going from where they came.

Once out of sight, he peered through the window into another world taking his breath away. It was very bright inside with many strange things everywhere. In a state of disbelief, everything Chief Acuta told him was right in front of him. Priests dressed in bold colorful body coverings and appeared to have black paint on their faces, around their mouths, looking like hair growing in different shapes. Guarding them were two warriors with knives hanging on the sides of their hips.

The human firepit was there inside, confirming it was the building of sacrifices. It had a large rock opening big enough to hold several bodies as the flames reached high.

A large person walked into the room wearing some type of ceremony blanket on his back. *That must be the head chief or priest,* Toca thought to himself.

The man said a few words to the other people when he arrived into the big room and they all quickly looked around and some in Toca's direction, taking him off guard as he slightly wavered his head back out of sight. When he did that, a small branch off the main beam he was on broke, making a soft snapping sound.

Waiting for a moment to make sure no one was reacting to the noise, Toca moved his head back as slow as a sloth to see inside undetected. No one was looking his way now as all watched the man reach up above the firepit, grabbing a very long knife off the wall. He turned around, kicking something lower to the ground. Toca could barely see what it was because the men were standing around, blocking his view. As it fell back, he was finally able to see what it was among the people as they moved around, getting out of the way.

It was unreal but the story was true about the old ones. And it was being performed right in front of him.

The person kicked backward, hit his head hard as his body laid flat on a large rock with the flames of the firepit in the background, reflecting its fingertips of death all around.

The head priest leaned over and pointed the long knife to the throat of the black-haired one, lying there, and began yelling.

The priest is going to cut the heart out of the person just as Chief Acuta said! Toca thought, instantly getting sick to his stomach.

When the head priest stopped talking, the one lying on the rock said some words then slowly rolled his head in his direction and Toca went breathless. His nightmare vision from earlier was coming alive.

She said some words in his direction, with tears in her eyes, then awkwardly stopped and stared. A smile slowly came to her face, then she started screaming his name.

There was no thought or plan in Toca's reaction to Shana's death cry calling for him.

Without caution, he dropped down through the window, landing without a sound in a crouched attack position, then burst like lightning across the room. Just before he got to the group standing around the killing rock, he leaped up high above everyone, grasping ahold of the large shining branch coming down from the ceiling holding fire sticks all around it.

Toca swung over the people across the large stone Shana was lying on and, with both feet, kicked the head priest in the face, knocking him back hard. The priest stumbled backward, falling into the giant human firepit as Toca let go of the shiny branch and dropped to the center of the death rock, straddling Shana.

Completely shocked and in doubt, the other men stood there, speechless with gaping mouths and wide eyes. It looked human but had dirt, leaves, and twigs coming out of its body. What they heard earlier about the forest spirits coming to kill everyone was crouched in front of them, loudly screeching words and baring its teeth, growling.

The head priest was now crying for help, trying to get out of the firepit as his hands were being burned and his body coverings were catching on fire. Getting their attention, they all frenziedly went to help him get out, except for one that reached up above the mantel, grabbing the other sword and turned to guard off the intruder.

Toca lifted Shana to her feet and swiftly took his knife out, cutting her hands free. Grabbing one, they ran to the window, then he let go without hesitating and continued running and jumping out, flying to the ground. She stopped, looking down then back to the men, staring in disbelief. Swinging her legs over the window seal to a seated position, she hesitated then jumped down. Toca somewhat caught her, breaking Shana's fall as they both collapsed to the ground. Looking at each other for a moment to see if each was okay, both smiled, signaling all was well.

Screaming of pain could still be heard, coming out of the sacrificing building as the two old children ran from the large village into the protection of the forest.

CHAPTER 12

Slowly and quietly, the two maneuvered their way through the moonless night. Toca's senses were reaching new strengths of sensitivity. He might as well have had his eyes closed because he was listening and reacting to the slightest movements and sounds in the dark forest.

Before he touched anything, his fingertips already knew what they were going to feel. His nose was identifying specific odors the night air brought him—trees, bushes, insects, and animals. Many times, he stopped moving because he smelled something they needed to avoid then stepped to the side, going wide and around it.

Once again, his nose was the first to find what he was looking for—the heavy odor of the Indian that was lifeless on the ground from earlier in the night. Toca now knew exactly where he was. He never told Shana about the dead one they walked past as he gently held her hand, guiding her through the maze of vegetation. They didn't say much to each other, only things dealing with moving through the forest. On the path, he kept feeling each tree they went by until he finally felt the scratches he carved on it earlier. He turned them in the direction of the river and went straight to the canoe.

After a little time passing, Toca breathed out, heavy with relief, then let go of her hand and told her not to move.

He touched the water with the tip of his toes then reached out with a tree branch and pounded the top of the water several times. Not able to see or sense any danger, he was just making sure there wasn't any surprise out near the canoe waiting for them with large teeth.

Satisfied he retrieved the boat, but before he let Shana get in, Toca's mind and experience told him there was something in the canoe. Waiting, trying to pinpoint where and what it was, he slowly reached in to feel around. Underneath the rolled-up caiman skin, he ever so gently felt something cool and smooth. Slowly gliding his hand, he found the narrow end of his suspicion.

Once he was comfortable where his hand was, he whispered for Shana to move and step to the side. After she moved, he simultaneously gripped hard, pulling it quickly out, throwing it into the forest.

Shana turned to the noise in the vegetation behind her. "Toca, something is coming!" Shana whispered as she tried to see into the darkness of the forest.

"It's just a snake."

"I didn't think snakes made noises?"

Toca softly laughed, knowing she had no idea what he had done. "They don't unless you throw them into the bushes from the canoe."

Searching again in the boat, this time looking for Shana's pack, he took out her body covering. Walking out of the water, he grabbed one of the thin vines he had used to disguise the boat then told her to lift her arms out. Extending her arms, he touched her fingers, then slid them into an armhole. Stepping to her other hand from the back, he did the same, then brought the shirt together, wrapping the vine around her stomach to hold the upper covering closed.

Shana, realizing he had dressed her, grasped his hands, still wrapped around her waist from her backside and held them up to her face, bringing their bodies together. Holding this position, she began to cry. Emotionally and physically drained, she didn't say anything at first; she didn't have to.

Then softly, she asked, "Toca, why did they treat me that way? People are always mean to me. What did we do to them?"

Replying in the same gentle tone, he said, "All I know is what Chief Acuta told me. Out from the hidden valley, there are bad gods that make people do bad things. It's my fault, Shana, I am sorry they attacked us and hurt you and I didn't protect you." She felt his shoulders droop with shame.

Dropping his hands, she turned around and stated in a strong whisper, "You saved me!" she replied, looking up in the darkness at his face.

Still emotionally and mentally beaten, Toca said, "This never should have happened. I tell you all the time to be aware and I wasn't aware. I didn't use my senses to protect us. I have been using them less and less the more we journeyed on the river. But it will never happen again, I will be aware all the time." He raised his shoulders back up and drew her in tight, wrapping his arms around her, letting her know he was going to do just that.

*****

They had paddled their way past the big village of Manaus, using its night lights to give direction and distance, but not too much, to get close to the other side of the river where they had the other encounter seven moons earlier.

They expended themselves physically, getting away as fast and far as they could upriver for many days. Tired and out of food, they foraged along the way. Toca tried to encourage Shana, telling her when they get to the clearing, there was plenty of meat waiting for them. But it really wasn't helping with the mental state she was in. Not only tired and hungry, she was scared and traumatized.

She was having a hard time falling asleep whenever they rested. When she did fall asleep, she would wake up screaming from dreams of others coming after her.

Toca did his best to comfort her but he didn't know how to stop the nightmares. Taking chances, he would keep a small fire going for her through the nights, staying awake, watching for others. He hugged her frequently, knowing it was something she liked doing, but it never seemed to have the same feel or effect.

She never wanted him to leave her sight like when he was finding food and juja leaves. She would go with him and hold his hand all the time as a child would to its mother, never leaving his side.

Finally late on the ninth day from the big village, they arrived at the beach where Toca had killed the caiman.

He examined the sand, looking for something out of place—others footprints or prints of a caiman—but nothing was there. They pulled the canoe far up into the forest, where Shana had originally hid it, then covered it with tree limbs and vines. Toca smoothed out their tracks in the sand then they put their packs on and headed to the clearing.

Semishadowing their way through the forest, both were anxious and feeling lighthearted. It felt good to be somewhere they both had been before. But if they were honest with each other, it was a special moment because this was where they began their friendship.

Almost to the clearing, both stopped, crouching low, peering into the open area. As Toca did his routine senses patrol, Shana was fully understanding this behavior of his and was routinely doing it herself.

Nothing was there to discourage them so they continued around the clearing opposite from where Shana's father was buried. Cautiously reaching the other side, they went directly to where the caiman meat was hidden back in a ways from the clearing, in the ground under a log.

Not until the package of life-giving nourishment was dug up did they realize how hungry they truly were. It had been almost a full moon since their last big meal of meat. The dried caiman they took with them ran out several moons earlier and were always eating on the move.

Toca continually pushed them to get back to his people, reminding Shana they had a long way to go and there was very little time to rest or hunt. They would eat roots and other plants, easily accessible but never filling. Toca found grubs or other big insects to snack on but Shana, for the most part, still couldn't bring herself to eat them unless she was desperate.

He taught her how to fish, which she got fairly good at, and how to identify eatable frogs and other creatures around the river. But still, eating and sleeping was not priority to him, almost like he didn't care. The drive and importance of getting back with the shell from the endless water was mental food for him and he was always full.

Shana tried to understand what he would tell her repeatedly of this ritual manhood journey and becoming chief by doing this Katata Ado and why it was so important to get back before his thirteenth full moon rose. I didn't completely make sense to her so it was hard for her to have the same drive.

But for her, living in the Amazon forest, her father dying, being friends with an Indian boy, wanting to hide all the time seemed so unreal. She was caught in the middle of hanging on to who she was and where she came from to being here in the moment, fully letting go of the past. Accepting this was going to be her life until she died.

Sitting around the packages of dried meat they uncovered, they ate until they were full. A sensation both were enjoying, rejuvenating them physically but energized them mentally as well. It was a moment they didn't need to share with words to express how much this was needed. Not only feeling like they could possibly make it but was encouragement they could really do it.

Toca calmly broke the silence as he finished his last bite, saying out of nowhere, "I talked to your God before I saved you back at the big village."

Anything Shana was feeling or thinking instantly disappeared as she stopped in midchew and stared at him. It was silent, she was lost for words, frantically struggling to reply. Not knowing what to say, she thought to herself, *He talked to God? You haven't talked to him in a while. You're the Christian, here to be a missionary. Speak words of wisdom to him, quote Scripture...do something*!

Shana opened her mouth and all that came out was "good." She began chewing again, looking to the side, and thought, *Good! Is that all you can come up with? You have been talking about God, praying with Toca aloud, trying to get him to believe you have a good God, and all you can say is good? How pathetic!*

Toca interrupted her internal argument as he stood, saying, "Will you hang the hammocks? I'm going to look around and make sure it's safe here for the *whole night*"—emphasizing *whole night* with a smile—"and get some juja leaves and laminia tree vine full of milk. Eating that much meat"—putting his hand on his stomach—"we are going to need the milk to help our stomachs."

Shana looked up, smiling, hearing they will be sleeping all night long, and replied, "I'll have the hammocks up went you get back."

Toca turned to their folded hammock packs and placed them against the same trees they hung from before. Taking out the long knife from her pack, he poked the sharp end in the ground next to Shana, smiled, saying, "You will be all right by yourself." It was a statement but a question as well as if he was asking permission to leave her here alone.

Still smiling, she then nodded her head, letting him know she would be okay. He turned and vanished through the tangles of undergrowth on the forest floor.

Shadowing far from the clearing, Toca's mind wasn't only on gathering but more of having the experience he had the last time he was in this area. This time, he was the dark shadow coming and going in and out of the bushes and from behind tree trunks, sneaking and seeking.

It was quiet and had a hollow feeling as he searched the area back and forth for his shadow image. There were no prints or any other signs of the black jaguar. Disappointed he went back toward Shana, collecting the items he said he went to look for.

*****

It wasn't birds or monkeys that woke the old children up in the morning but drops of rain that slid their way off leaves from limbs above. As the water dotted their faces, they both came alive from a long and deep night's sleep, fully rested for the first time in a while. No nightmares, no fire burning all night, just deep refreshing sleep.

The rain didn't bother Shana as much anymore. She was getting used to it, understanding it was a major part of the life in the forest.

Toca was quickly on the forest floor, folding his hammock together and packing in as much wrapped meat as he could. Shana did the same, then filling their mouths full of dried caiman, headed back to the river.

Shana touched Toca on the shoulder as they started around the clearing the way they came and asked if they could go the other way to say goodbye to her father for the last time.

Giving her a grin of agreement, he changed his direction, carefully staying inside the forest, going around the other way. Getting close, Toca noticed the area of the ground where he dug the hole for John didn't look right. Squatting down, both looking in that direction, Shana whispered, "I don't see the cross we put on his grave."

"You mean the tree branches you put together and stabbed on top?"

She nodded. "Yes."

He didn't see it either but that wasn't all he wasn't seeing. The mounded dirt was gone. *Maybe the rains washed it away*? he thought.

"Stay here, I'll take a closer look," Toca told Shana, never taking his eyes off the site, pressing gently down on her shoulder.

Shadowing around to the other side of the grave in the foliage, there were no signs of others or animals. Cautiously he moved to the burial spot, kneeling down, looking at the details. Everything seemed old and the grave was sunken in like it was empty. Empty of dirt but also empty of a body. He slowly put a hand down into the rain-drenched grave and started to dig the mud out when something suddenly bumped up against him, taking him off guard. Toca pulled his hand out as though something just bit him in the grave and said, "What are you doing?" He was looking up at Shana.

Shana had run up to Toca, shocked at what he was going to do. "Why are you digging my father's grave up?" She bumped him hard enough when he pulled his hand out, he lost his balance, falling hands first into the grave.

Recovering from the sudden shock that it was only Shana, he said, "I told you to stay."

"I'm not going to stay watching you dig up my father?"

With his hands still embedded deep in the mud, he said, "Look at the grave, Shana. Your father's body is missing and I'm not feeling any of his bones. Your father's body isn't there."

In disbelief, she investigated the dirt then began digging herself. After a few moments of frantically throwing mud everywhere, she sat back on her heels, asking, "Where is he, Toca?"

"I don't know but we need to leave, this is not good."

Both stood, covered with mud. Shana felt like she was going to be sick then turned to the tree behind them to throw up. Instead she froze at what was staring at her face-to-face, then stumbled back a step, gasping for air, squeaking out Toca's name. Reaching beside her to get his attention, she finally touched him, gulping in air, screaming with all she had.

Toca quickly twisted around, slightly crouched, drawing his knife. Glancing back and forth, he didn't see anything until looking up to the side of the tree. There it was impaled on a short stub, sticking out of the trunk at eye-level.

Shana kept screaming until Toca tightly wrapped his arms around her, shielding her, walking away back into the cover of the forest.

Quieting down, looking back, she asked, "What is that, it...it looks like a small human head?"

"I don't know what it is, you stay here!" He let go of her, pointing hard to the ground, staring her in the eyes to obey him this time. Then he withdrew the long knife out of her pack and put it in her hands, saying, "Look at you, you are shadowed with mud, you must be Nashua," he said, smiling, trying to distract and lighten her up from this very disturbing moment with her father's body missing.

Turning cautiously, Toca crept to examine what frightened Shana. Looking at it close, he said to himself, "It's a head the size of a small monkey but looks like a man." The skin was leathery and tannish brown. The eyes and mouth were sewn shut as the thinning hair on top was dangling down like skinny legs of a large spider. As he looked around one cheek, near the ear, Toca suddenly stopped. He found out what and who it was. "John's head," he whispered in disbelief.

Now he was starting to feel sick, looking at the large black mole that was next to his ear. It was in the same spot and the same shape but smaller, matching the rest of his head.

They cut their heads off and use them for play, kicking it around fields. Then they put them up high on sticks for the gods as decoration. Chief Acuta's voice was echoing in Toca's mind as he turned around, looking at the clearing, envisioning John's head being kicked around by others.

He moved his eyes to the forest, looking through it, smelling deep and tilting his head, searching with his ears for anything. Nothing was coming to him, only the same hollow dark feeling he felt yesterday evening. Looking back at the grave, now knowing what happened to his body, he turned to John's shrunken head. Reaching up, he quickly pulled it off the stub and dropped it into the hole Shana dug. He pushed as much mud on it as he could, then whipped his face with the mud on his hands. Stepping over to Shana, hidden in the bushes, he grasped her empty hand, saying, "We have to go now!"

"Why did you shadow your face?" she questioned just as he put his other hand to hers, smearing mud. "What are you doing?"

"Others have been here."

He started to walk away as Shana asked with confusion in her eyes, "What was that on the tree?"

"I will tell you later, we must go now."

"Toca, stop, what about my father?" She stood still, holding her ground.

Something inside him erupted as he stared back. "You will do as I say, female, we have to leave!" Whispering loud, squeezing her hand, he then turned, forcefully tugging her arm, almost dragging her along. His strength had grown immensely since he was at the clearing last and didn't realize he was hurting her.

"Let go, you're hurting me?"

Looking back, seeing the expression on her face only loosened his grip as he kept moving forward to the river; getting away from here was his priority.

Once at the river, Toca quickly unrolled the caiman skin and put together the bamboo skeleton inside it, stretching out the life-size monster, then anchored it up high on the canoe as the roof. They've done this endless number of times to keep the rain out of the boat. Once in the boat and out on the river, he lowered it to the sides of the canoe which was only a hand-length up out of the water, giving it that live effect to scare people away.

Shana knew there was something wrong for Toca to be behaving this way. Whatever it was hanging on the tree scared him as well. She stayed quiet the whole time, understanding there was some urgency; and Toca always did things for a purpose so there was a good reason why they were doing this.

Awkwardly paddling upstream under their protection, Shana asked again what was back there which he responded, "Not now, Shana, we need to get far away from here." Wanting to change the hostile atmosphere and get her mind off what she saw as well as knowing what was effective on Toca, she began to hum. Soon she softly started singing. Under the caiman cover, she only had to whisper her voice for him to hear as it gently echoed inside with her singing and the soft raindrops.

It was doing the job of calming him down. His strokes of the paddle slowed and she could hear him breathing deeply with sighs of relief.

Later in the day, it stopped raining and they decided to go to shore to take a break and have some more of the meat.

This part of the river was new territory for Toca because he had journeyed by land through this area, keeping parallel with the river while keeping his distance. He began drawing what looked like a map to Shana in the dirt as they sat next to each other against a tree. He had three squiggly lines, separated, going one way and a larger line going across the other way at the bottom of the other three lines. At the top end of the first thin line, he drew what appeared to be mountains and, at the far end of the big line touching the three, drew a circle. A short way from the circle on the big line, he drew a canoe.

"What is this?"

"It is a drawing of where we are and where we need to go," he said as he looked it over. "This is the hidden valley where my people are"—pointing at the mountains—"this is the clearing where I found you and here is where we are now." He pointed to the canoe.

"So these lines are rivers?" Shana asked.

"Yes, when I left, I followed this river that flows out of the valley to this river here." He gestured out with his head to the water in front of them. "As I followed the black river, I decided to get away from it and follow along it from a distance because the trees and bushes are so thick near the water, slowing me down. Also Chief Acuta said others live next to the big rivers and I wanted to stay away from them. I had to swim across these other two rives, the next one we are going to come to in less than a moon's time away and the water is white. I mentioned it to you when we got to the milky-brown river."

"How far is it to get back to your tribe from where we are?" Shana asked, pointing at the drawing of the canoe.

Next to the map, he drew thirteen small circles in a row. Then looking down at his knife on his forearm, counted the cut lines on the handle which represent each moon that has passed. Then he explained, "The circles are moons." Scratching a line through two, he said, "It took me two moons to get to the clearing from my valley."

Scratching out two more, he said, "We traveled two moons to get to the endless water." Looking back at the handle of his knife to confirm the number, he marked out with his finger five circles.

"It took us five moons to travel from the endless water back upriver, back to the clearing." Counting the circles left, he added, "I don't know how far it is to my people but I know we only have less than four moons to get there."

"Four more moons?" Shana questioned painfully, wrinkling her face as her voice went a pitch higher.

Calmly replying as he stared at the drawing, deep in thought, he said, "Yes."

"Well, if it took you two moons walking to get to the clearing, we can easily get you back before the thirteenth moon going by water," Shana said in an encouraging tone.

Looking up, she had unknowingly poked at his pride and demonstrated how still naive she was about the journey. "I *didn't* walk." He emphasized to her. "I *ran* the whole time. It will be harder going up the river to the hidden valley for you." He stopped in midthought, looking back down at the marks, then continued,

"That river is smaller and flows fast because our valley is higher in the sky than down here where we are."

"How hard can it be? We've been canoeing for seven moons now, we're really good at it."

"Yes, we are but we've only been on slow-moving water with no rocks in the way, shallow spots, or waterfalls to go around. Many times we'll have to get out and carry the canoe through the forest. And with the fast-moving water, we'll have to paddle twice as much to move the same distance we do now. It's going to be very tiring the whole way."

He remembered being warned constantly in his young training with the chief. "It will physically take all you have to finish the Ado but your worst enemy will be what's in your head. It will be against you all the time and will be the hardest fight you will ever have in your life."

Changing his thought, *Maybe it will be easier on her if we go by land? No, Shana doesn't move fast through the forest and we have these carrying packs.*

Looking at Shana, he said, "You must prepare your mind before we get to the last river, it is going to be harder than anything we've done. Your body will fight you but what's in your head will fight against you even more," he said, pointing to his head.

Now her pride was being challenged as she looked at him sarcastically. "Toca, I have gone through a lot in my life. I left my people, moving away from my home, journeyed halfway around the world, both of my parents are dead, and people have hurt me all my life. Then I have spent almost a sun season in this place"—defiantly looking up and around the forest—"and you're telling me I need to prepare myself?"

"Yes," he said, calmly standing his ground.

"Well, you're not so strong, you were the one that ran away from whatever that was in the clearing this morning, I only screamed because it took me by surprise."

Toca hesitated with his response, knowing she had no idea what she was talking about and he understood the answer would hurt her deeply. He stood, putting his hand out for her to take his to stand as well.

"What?" she asked. "You're being nice now?"

Toca held out his hand with a slight frown on his face then told her, "You want to know what was in the clearing, fine. But I want you to hug me while I tell you."

"What, are you afraid—" She stopped midsentence. The look he had in his eyes were the softest and most sorrowful she ever seen from him. There was something he needed to tell her and she was realizing it wasn't good.

Shana reached for his hand as he helped her up, then he drew her to him, wrapping their arms around each other. "What is it, Toca?" she whispered.

"I wasn't running away from the clearing. I was protecting you." Hesitating, he then whispered in her ear, "What you saw was the head of…your father."

She flinched her head back. "No…it couldn't be! You don't know what you're talking about! It was so small, discolored, and old-looking." Seeing the image in her mind, she helplessly attempted to separate herself from him. But Toca held tight as her body began trembling and soft tears began to flow.

"I can't explain why it was small. I thought it was the head of a small monkey, but then I saw the growth on the side. The same shaped growth your father had next to his ear."

Shana was trying not to get too emotional. "I don't understand, why would anyone do that to him, he was dead. What did they do with his body?"

"All I know about others is what I've told you many times before, is what Chief Acuta told me. So far, everything he said I have seen. Bad gods making people do bad things. I have not seen a good god anywhere."

She laid her head down on his shoulder, feeling defeated, and said, "I don't know why God hasn't shown himself or talked to you or even me since we left the clearing the first time. But I do know there are at least two good people…" She looked up into his eyes. "You and me."

Toca's only reply was a gentle smile.

"Why did you talk to my God?" she asked.

"What?"

"You said yesterday that you talked to my God."

He hesitated, thinking about his reason, then answered, "Because I want to believe as much as you do that there is a good God."

His explanation struck her deep. She was so weak in her faith in God at this moment that she didn't want to acknowledge or accept the compliment. The only thing that went through her mind was, *If only I was believing there was one too.*

CHAPTER 13

Painstakingly the old children have struggled the past two moons of the last four after fleeing the clearing. They're now far up the final river, getting close to the hidden valley, and the mode of traveling has changed.

A little more than a moon ago, it began raining hard continuously for days. Besides fighting the rushing water and all the obstacles in the smaller river, it was getting very difficult, carrying the heavy canoe through the thick wet forest.

One night, completely exhausted, they didn't pay attention to how close they put the canoe next to the river's edge. The water level rose from the rain, reaching the canoe, lifting it up, and washing it downriver, never to be seen again. Fortunately everything was out of it. The hammock packs were hanging up in the trees and the caiman skin, now in different pieces, were spread out hanging over them, keeping them dry.

Losing the canoe made them adjust what they could carry in their packs, only taking the essentials. Shana kept her Bible which was now wrapped up in the chuacha waterproof tree bark. The machete, the remaining strips of cloth for her female times of bleeding, her sewing pouch, and her fire-starting rocks remained.

Toca held onto the Katata Ado shell and two sizable square pieces from the back of the caiman hide he cut up. As well as its teeth and claws, all for a gift for Chief Acuta to make a new waist wrap. Timely at this point, they had already finished the remaining dried caiman meat they had picked up at the clearing so they weren't carrying food on themselves any longer.

Their bodies continued to grow significantly at their age. Shana no longer has the body of a young growing female when Toca first saw her but that of a full-grown woman. Toca was taller than when they were in the big village and has largely filled out, showing firm muscles over his whole body compared to the skinny boy that left his home to become a man.

New lower body coverings had to be made to adjust for their growth. Keeping the same original style of male-member cover Chief Acuta made for Toca, Shana had him add medium-size flaps to the front and back like hers. She told him she wanted to match but truthfully wanted him to hide his private areas better. He agreed, thinking it was a great idea because it was what the chief wore except Toca's was made from monkey fur.

Shana was still wearing the weathered shirt of her father which she had cut the sleeves off and shortened the lower part up to her belly button early on in their journey. She had reattached the buttons that popped off when the shirt was ripped off her when she was captured. Sinew was used from the same monkey Toca killed to make their waist flaps when they first started up the new river.

Shana also added a new look with their hair. She stopped wearing her bonnet when she cut off the upper part of her dress along with the undergarments and boots early in the journey because it was too hot and uncomfortable. Now her hair was woven in two long braids, one on each side of the back of her head which draped forward over her shoulders. She also talked Toca into pulling his scraggly hair together back in a ponytail like the men did in her tribe back home. Using thin strips of hide from the monkey's tail was used to hold the new looks tightly together.

Following alongside the smaller river on foot, making their way through the thick forest was the most exerting experience Shana ever had. Already worn out from the long journey, the continuous weaving, ducking under and climbing through ferns, trees, bamboo grooves, day in and day out, was a draining task that seemed to never end.

Shana couldn't have imagined when Toca told her to prepare herself that she would actually be this physically depleted and mentally defeated. At first, he was helping her with encouraging words; but the closer they were getting, the more aggressive and demanding to go faster and keep up he became. He seemed to be gaining energy as hers was disappearing.

Toca was doing well physically but emotionally, anxiety and worry was consuming him. Getting back to the ceremony hut on time was priority but what was bothering him the most was he has yet to see this God to save his people that Shana says is with them.

He was doubting more and more it existed and that her father and she made this story up of this God so Toca would care for her and take her to his people.

They had been trudging along for most of the day when abruptly, Shana stopped and plopped to the ground, exhausted.

Toca turned around and said with a raised voice, "Shana, we can't stop now! We're really close, the thirteenth full moon is going to rise soon."

Totally fatigued, she fumbled out words. "I can't go any further, I'm so tired and hungry."

"I know you are but we have no choice, we have to keep going. I must finish my Ado on time to be the next chief. I've told you that many times!" he urgently responded in a loud tone.

Shana looked up at him with tears flowing and her lips quivering as her body rocked back and forth, starting to cry, as she spoke, "Toca…we keep walking but we never get anywhere. Are you sure you know where you are going?"

He was becoming outraged as her comment hit his pride hard, and he replied, "You question my ability to get us to the hidden valley?"

"No, no, I didn't mean it that way. We keep going and going as if this journey has no end. I can barely lift my legs and arms anymore. I feel like I'm going to die right here and I don't know where here is?" She looked around the forest, throwing her hands in the air, appearing lost.

Shana had slowed the journey and was holding Toca back. Often he thought to himself, he made a bad decision agreeing to her father before he died to take care of her. Even though her endurance and strength were gone, Shana was getting used to the Amazon and doing well moving through the thick undergrowth. Toca had done a great job teaching her to survive, making shelter, finding food, knowing what was poisonous and dangerous. But she still was missing the strong purposeful drive he had to get to his people on time.

Toca was glaring down at her as this unusual rage was overtaking his mind like a quiet black fog, stealthily moving in, beginning to control his emotions. Unexpectedly he wanted to slap her and force her off the ground, pulling her up by her hair, and yell, "*Do what I say and stop crying like a baby. You're wasting my time!*"

Like a shrieking alarm from a monkey warning its troop of danger, the voice he heard screaming those words wasn't his but Jucawa's. Realizing his hands were clenched to hit her and his teeth gnashing out anger, Toca could not believe what he was thinking of doing. This was not him, not him at all.

He was going to be sick and his chest became so heavy, his legs were giving out, and he hit the ground hard with his knees in front of Shana. The person he hated the most almost came out of him. To hurt the one that has become his closest friend and would protect with his life.

He leaned over and put his arms around her, not knowing what to say except gently apologize for pushing her hard and demanding so much from her.

Appreciating what he said, she returned the hug, finding themselves again in the position which, over their short relationship, was always comforting. She cried for a moment longer on his shoulder, then slowly pushed herself away.

As they were kneeling, facing each other, she desperately needed strength and understanding. Completely on her knees, physically, mentally, and spiritually, she went to the only thing she had left, except this young Indian man in the middle of the Amazon—her faith.

Closing her eyes, she bowed her head.

Toca instantly thought to himself, *She is going to talk to her God again*! A dark fog swirled in as his patience with her and this invisible God was fading fast daily.

He closed his eyes, trying to calm himself down. He didn't like this feeling but it was consuming him. As she prayed on, Toca began listening to what she was saying.

"Please, God, help me, give me strength and understanding to continue this long journey. Thank you for helping us get this far and keeping us safe..."

He stopped listening, shaken by what she said. *Why did she say that? I've done all the work to get us this far and I'm the one that has kept us safe. Why would she thank this God that has never shown itself?* he thought sarcastically.

He listened in again as she finished. "Sorry for being weak in my faith, letting go of your hand and not trusting in you like I know I can, amen."

When Shana opened her eyes, she was shocked. Toca lifted his head, opening his eyes, glaring at her. A giant smile came over her face then quickly leaned over joyfully as she wrapped her arms around him again then leaned back, glowing with excitement.

What is wrong with this girl? thinking to himself, still glaring. *She is always sad and crying, then happily smiling? Can't she ever make up her mind how she's going to feel?*

Giddy with joy sweeping through her for the first time in many moons, she said, "God finally just talked to me! Giving me encouragement, reminding me he is here with us and what my purpose is." Taking his eyes off her, he looked around the area, listening for this God talking.

"God inspired me from what you were doing with me."

Confused, he asked, "What did I do?"

"You were praying with me!"

"I was?"

"Yes, you were, for the first time on this journey, you had your eyes closed and your head bowed."

Knowing he did have his eyes closed, he asked, "Is that when you see your God, when your eyes are closed? I didn't see him," he said somewhat sarcastically.

"Yes...no, it's hard to explain." She thought for a moment, shaking her head back and forth, then continued, excited, "I have always told you, God is everywhere but he is especially in here." She put her hands to her chest, meaning her heart. "But only if you give him your heart—"

His eyes went wide and moved slightly back defensively away from her.

Surprised at his reaction, she asked, "What's wrong, Toca?"

"You said give him your heart."

"Yes, for you to have a relationship with God, he needs you to give him your heart."

Toca was beside himself, he didn't know what to do. Panic was overwhelming him as his eyes went back and forth, looking around, then back to Shana, trying to understand what was going on. He had begun to believe he wasn't bringing a god to his people because he's never seen it. But just now, it became worse. He was bringing a bad god to his people! Chief Acuta's early comment echoed in his ears, "Better a quiet death than have your heart cut out."

Toca stated loudly in mass confusion, "Where is your God, I have never seen him and you say he is everywhere? This has all been lies, you…you and the white man you call your father did not tell the truth! You and he made all this up so I would take care of you when he died."

Yes, Toca, she is lying to you. His anger and doubt now had a voice of its own in the dark fog of his mind and it was powerful.

"Toca, what's happening, what's wrong?" she asked in total disbelief. "Where is this coming from?"

His heart was in pain from frustration, then he drew his knife, quickly standing up in a crouched-attack position and said, "Bad gods want the hearts of people to live, your God will not take my heart!"

Shocked and speechless at his reaction, it was slowly coming to her when they first met. He asked her if her god kills people and he's always saying, "Bad gods make people do bad things." Which she always thought to herself, they can't make you, man chooses to be bad.

Shana relaxed a little, sitting back on her heels, putting on a soft smile at him for being naive. She was also realizing she had done a terrible job of explaining God to him.

Knowing she had to fully get his attention, she looked up at him, saying gently and respectfully, "Toca, Black Ghost of the Nashua, my friend and protector, soon to be chief…" Pausing, she shook her head as she gestured with her hands outwardly away from her chest, saying slowly, "My God, our God doesn't want your heart"—then gestured toward her chest—"he wants to live in it."

Still rigidly on guard, Toca listened as she explained. For Shana, it was a revealing moment. Her eyes were just uncovered and she could clearly see what was hidden from her this whole trip which she should have easily known. He was looking for a physical tangible god and she was always talking about a God in the spiritual sense. *How could I have been so stupid*? asking herself, she then continued.

"We don't cut out anyone's heart, that means you would die. God wants your heart to beat strong in you so he can live in it, so we have life with a purpose. We can't see or feel God," she said, gesturing with her hands in the air like she was touching something. "We see him in everything he has created and what he does, experiencing him by complete faith with his spirit living in our hearts. Do you know what faith is?"

Toca just stared at her.

"Faith is believing in something you cannot see. We cannot see God but he is everywhere, like I have told you many times."

Sternly he peered at her, slowly saying, "Why would you believe in something you cannot see?" He was infuriated, believing he's been tricked and lied to, then began yelling at her, "You have played me for a child long enough, Shana! We are only days from my people and I have no god to bring them! My people are going to die and it's my fault. I have failed them!" He was falling deeper in anger, sorrow, and self-pity.

She saw his pain and was understanding his confusion but something was still missing, *Why is he suddenly thinking this way*? She stood up and attempted to hug him but he stepped back and said, almost yelling, with his head now turned away from her, "Don't touch me, I saved your life many times and have taken care of you and you did this to me and my people. I trusted you!"

Trying to stay calm and speaking with a gentle voice, Shana said, reaching out, attempting to touch his arm, "Toca, where is this anger coming from, I am telling you the truth."

"The truth! The truth is, I have taken care of you and kept you safe. I am the one you should be thanking, not something you made up! You stop this…this act of closing your eyes and talking to nothing. You and it are all lies!"

The dark raspy voice speaking slithery to him in his mind was trying to give him a satisfying answer. *Toca, you are finally seeing what I know. There are no good gods except yourself.*

Like a tall tree falling over, hitting the forest floor, violently vibrating the ground, Shana's inner emotions were awakened. Now a woman, her soft gentle look on her face suddenly vanished and her eyes narrowed in on his.

Toca watched closely with his knife ready. She stepped forward boldly to where the knife was almost touching her stomach, then leaned her face into his and said in a low monotone voice, gritting her teeth, "How dare you accuse me of lying. Everything I have said to you is the truth!" Her fearless intimidation instantly began to deflate him as well as the thought of his statements being false.

Still boldly glaring, raising her voice, she said, "Everything you have seen and heard from my father and me is true! And I will give God all the glory for everything because he provided all this"—motioning toward all the things around them—"so we can have life! He's the one that gives you"—Shana poked her finger into his chest—"the knowledge and strength to take care of me. He's the one that knows what we need and when we need it because he is all-knowing.

"And you"—poking him again—"have proven you don't know everything because you're always asking questions."

Toca was in a blur with no words to back up anything. She hesitated, stepping back, calming herself down, and continued, "I trust God with my life more than I trust you with it. I have gone through many things I don't understand that have given me pain. But at the end of every day, God is still with me, are you?" She paused, waiting for an answer.

Toca, still beside himself, attempted to answer, "I guess I…yes, yes, I'm with you."

"Good!" she stated loud as he flinched. "Because God is here with you and me, and I'm with you and you're not going to get rid of us this easily." Her blowup instantly blew away. Settling down, Shana asked with an expected expression, "Now can I finish what I was telling you about God living in us and faith?"

He was now foolishly standing in his attack position as she sat down to continue the conversation. Contemplating how he was going to recover from this, he lowered the knife, putting it away, then embarrassingly sat down like a child.

"Okay, then…" Pausing to remember where she left off, she then continued, "As I said, to have a relationship with God, he must live in your heart, he doesn't want your heart cut out. I don't understand where you would get an idea like that?" She shook her head. "We live by faith that he created us and everything here." She was pointing to the world around them again. "He is living everywhere with us, but the greatest thing of all, he's a God that loves us, he's a *good God*," she said, emphasizing the last two words to wipe away any of Toca's false illusions.

"Toca, God will only come live inside you if you ask him. Our God gives you a choice if you want him in your life or not. He doesn't force you to do anything. God allows things to happen in our lives that can direct our steps so we understand him to grow closer to him. It's a relationship we can't have if we're dead with no heart."

Shana stopped talking for a moment, giving him time to process what she said as she herself was surprised with what came out of her mouth. It was the first time she shared God deeply like that with anyone. *Where did all those thoughts and words come from*? she asked herself, then smiled inside, knowing from memory it was one of those moments her father talked about when the Spirit of God would speak through her.

"I didn't hear your God talking to you?" Toca broke her concentrated thoughts.

"What?"

"Earlier before you yelled at me, you said God told you something about your journey. If I was praying with you, how come I didn't hear him?"

Taken off guard, she had to think about it, then answered, "God talks to us many different ways." She gestured with her hands as if she was holding her Bible. "Through the Bible, which are his words written down for us to read. Remember me telling you that and you would put it to your ear to hear him?" She smiled, trying to have a livelier atmosphere but little reaction came from him as she continued, "He will talk to us in our heads"—pointing to hers—"hearing or seeing God in here. Like when we are asleep, dreaming, or awake and we think someone is talking to us but there is no one there." Toca raised his eyebrows at that explanation as she went on.

"Finally how he talked to me this time was when I saw you praying with me. Through daily situations, he speaks to us. God allows things to happen, arranges or lays things out for us, purposely directing our steps through life which speaks to us, letting us know he is God, inspiring us to rely on him which gives us purpose."

Seeing he had calmed down and had his complete attention, Shana was suddenly mentally and physically feeling great relief. Having her eyes reopened of her purpose and finally the door opening for her to share God thoroughly and plainly with him was exciting and uplifting. But taking time to sit and rest was extremely rejuvenating.

Toca was taking this conversation so serious it was distracting him from being the bully he's been lately, pushing her through the maze of the forest.

She continued, "That's how I heard God talking to me. Seeing you with your eyes closed and head bowed, God inspired me of my purpose. To bring the knowledge of him to you and your people so you will have a good God to live in your hearts."

Also feeling the relief from the tense moments, Toca smiled as he mumbled, "A good God to inspire our people."

"Yes, I am bringing a good God to inspire your people is what I'm trying to say."

This time, he was giddy as he was hearing familiar words, giving him encouragement in this conversation. "No, that is what Chief Acuta told me to do or our people will die. Bring back a good God to inspire our people." Toca hesitated for a moment.

The secret of the Nashua people he has held onto tightly needed to come out. He was feeling and going through what Chief Acuta said during his ceremony. Debating to tell the whole truth about his people and their past. But he knew now he had to do and say something to save the Nashua from the path of death they are on before it was too late.

Uneasy, he got comfortable where he was sitting, looked around like Chief Acuta did that night of his ceremony as to keep what he was about say to Shana a secret from whomever could be listening. Which was one other as Shana looked around, trying to see what Toca was looking out and about for, then Toca opened with, "I have only told you a small part of my people and their past. You need to have the knowledge that was given to me before I left on my Katata Ado so you understand why I need a good God and why I need to get back before the thirteenth full moon."

Shana slightly leaned back with questionable eyes, saying to herself through them, *Who's the one that's been lying?*

Taking a deep breath, preparing to let out what he's been hiding, Toca began, "Chief Acuta believes gods inspire people to do things and the only gods our old forefathers knew were bad gods that made priests cut the hearts out of people and cut their heads off then burn their bodies."

Stunned, she suddenly was feeling nauseous at these horrifying thoughts, realizing she was about to be informed of the vital information she had been missing the whole journey.

"The first ones that started the Nashua tribe ran away, leaving their people and these terrible gods, journeying more than a full sun season from a faraway place north many, many generations ago. They found the safety of the hidden valley where these gods have never found us. Then they named our new tribe Nashua, which means new beginnings, and decided to never let the younger generations know there is such a thing as a god. They did this to protect them from the evil they experienced for all generations to come."

Toca paused as Shana sat wide-eyed, listening. "He said our people are slowly dying because we have no purpose for living. So he told me that on my Katata Ado, I must find a good god, if there is such a thing, and bring it back to inspire our people so we will have purpose to grow strong and not die off, never to be seen again."

Shana was trying to put his unbelievable story together and asked, "So, Toca, are you telling me your people never has had a god?"

"None of my people except the chief and I know of our tribe's full history and knows there is such a thing as a god. I still don't understand what a god is. You see this in me now." He pointed to himself with questionable eyes toward her.

"Why didn't you tell me this before?"

"It is a secret that only when one completes the Ado and takes over as chief is the story told to the new chief. Jucawa is the only one that has completed the Ado in our tribe and is next in line to be chief. But Chief Acuta doesn't want him to take his place, he believes he'll do bad things to our people. And I accepted his burden to find a good god and complete the Ado. He will make me the next chief instead of Jucawa to take his place when my time comes."

Shana was still in awe how Toca has kept his story from her this whole time. Finally she was beginning to understand what was driving him so hard to complete his manhood journey. And how important it was why he needed to get to the hidden valley before the thirteenth full moon rose in the sky.

She heard a name she didn't recognize and asked, "Who is Jocwa?"

Pausing, trying to stay calm, he answered, "He is the one I told you when we first meet that we will never talk about. But you do need to know who he is. His name is *Jucawa*," he said, pronouncing it correctly for her. "He is my father but not my real father. He died when I was a baby and Chief Acuta gave my mother and me to Jucawa when he completed his Katata Ado. My whole life, he has been very mean to us. He yells and says hateful things to my mother and me and hurts us all the time. Chief Acuta said he doesn't understand why he treats us that way. The people in our tribe highly respect him for his great Ado journey but they fear him. My chief said when one accomplishes the Ado, that man has learned to be honorable, wise, and treats everyone kindly with peace."

"So Chief Acuta told me I must complete the Katata Ado. If I don't finish the Ado, Jucawa is the only man that can be chief. Chief Acuta said when I finish the Ado, he will make me chief instead of that horrible man."

With eyes of compassion, Shana said, "Toca, I am so sorry for the burden you have been carrying for your people. Now I see clearly why you must get back in time and I'm sorry that I've not tried to fully understand before. Most of all, I have slowed your journeying down and you have been very patient with me for the heavy pressure that is on you."

Her sorrowful expression, heartfelt concern and understanding, and apology was a huge relief to him. It was like he just pushed off a giant rock from his shoulders and was able to sit up straighter as his lungs suddenly were able to breathe easier and deeper. His mind seemed to have cleared from the dark fog of anger and frustration as he now relaxed for the first time in a long time.

"I'm sorry, Shana, that I have been pushing you so hard. I trained all my child sun seasons for this so I'm prepared and then expected you to prepare in a very short time. I didn't mean to pull my knife out on you, you scared me because I didn't understand what you were saying." He smiled, shrugging his shoulders, and added, "I still don't."

Shana laughed. "You can be so funny and you don't even know it, Toca. You're always trying to make me feel better."

Both mature old children were relieved from their first major confrontation. The harsh and scary moments with climaxed emotions, they both wanted to quickly forget as something new was unveiling within them. Looking deep into each other's eyes, they were seeing the other from a different perspective.

Shana put her hand gently on top of his that was resting on his thigh and slightly squeezed, holding on. It wasn't the same way she used to hold his hand the many days after they fled from the big village for security, this was different. Her eyes were peering right through him, telling him there was a secret behind them.

Her fingertips began to slowly and softly maneuver under to his palm and between his fingers, spreading them out, then interlocking them, bringing their palms together. Their eyes had worked their way to their hands, watching the slow dance, intertwining themselves perfectly.

An incredible tingling sensation went through their bodies. Toca's breath was sucked out of his lungs as his heart began to pound in his chest. Shana was getting lightheaded and her stomach fluttered with the essences of butterflies' wings.

Even though it was only a few moments of sharing and experiencing each other with a simple touch and gaze of warmth, it was a new imprinted flash of something big to come. Something they knew without speaking was finally showing its face, changing their relationship forever.

Lingering a little longer, they both simultaneously let go of the other's hand as the moment began to feel awkward. Not sure what to do or say next, they fumbled with words and clumsily stood up with each needing space.

Toca turned around and started to look for something in the area for them to eat. A little ways away, he spotted an old fallen log. Getting to it, he looked back to Shana as she was wandering around, looking up into the trees, doing the same thing. Looking back at the log, he leaned over and began peeling off the old bark, finding one of his favorite snacks—fat white grubs.

Shana was searching for a laminia tree to get its precious milk from one of its vines. Not only for something nourishing to drink but also to rub in her hair. Her female instincts were suddenly heightened to look good for Toca and the first thing she needed to do was get her hair shiny and soft.

Calling back to Shana, telling her of his find put one in his mouth. Not hearing her respond, knowing she really didn't like these bugs, asked again to tease her as he dug another one out. "Shana, I didn't hear you, don't you want one of these juicy grubs?" He picked it up and turned around, dangling in the air for her to see.

Dropping the bug, his eyes couldn't believe what they were seeing. It took a couple of blinks to react as his ears finally heard his name whispered to him as they were being squeezed out of her. "Toca...help!"

Instantly like a crack of a whip, he was physically hit from behind his feet with such swift force, it thrust his legs into the air and came down hard on his back, taking his breath away.

Jumping back to his feet, he looked for Shana but she wasn't there. Out the corner of his eye, on the ground, through thick ground foliage, he saw the thrashing movement.

Catching his breath, he yelled, "Shana!"

He could barely see her hidden by coils of the body of a giant anaconda squeezing the life out of her. The black and dark-green snake was as long as the trees of the forest and just as wide. It was the most feared creature in the forest, even a jaguar is no match for such a beast.

It was the long solid tail of the snake that hit him, fighting to strangle its next meal which had stealthily come up, swiftly attacking Shana.

Again a groggily murmured, "Toca..."

Without hesitation, he drew his knife and jumped at the snake. Straddling one of the coils around Shana, he stabbed deep with both hands holding the knife. Pulling the knife out, he went to stab again; but as both his hands were grasping the knife in the air, his arms were instantly blocked from coming down because the head of the snake had the whole center of his body in its huge jaws.

He screamed in pain as many of its small teeth embedded themselves into his flesh. Toca looked down and all he saw was the snake staring at him with one of its giant eyes. The long narrow pupil thinned itself, telling him it was thinking. The next moment, he found himself flying through the air as the snake threw Toca off its back.

A tree promptly stopped his body, hitting hard with his back and head then dropped down to the ground. Jumping up, gasping for air he went to grasp his hand tightly around his knife for another attack, only to realize it wasn't there. It had fallen out of his hands when his body hit the tree. Desperately searching the forest floor, he couldn't find it. All that was there were old leaves and broken branches from the tall trees above. Quickly he had to find something, taking one of the long-dried branches, he broke it in two, snapping it down on his knee. Now he had two exposed sharp jagged ends in his hands and, without any more delay, ran after Shana.

Swiftly the young strong Nashua was back on the snake where his woman was held captive. With one stick, he stabbed the sharp broken end into the snake as deep as he could. Instinctively knowing what was going to happen next, he already had reached back with the other stick, then with all his strength, thrust it in the direction of where the snake's head was going to come from and it hit its mark. The snake, with its mouth wide open, came at Toca but the stick sank deep inside into the soft tissue, penetrating a vital area, doing extreme damage. Its mouth was slightly propped open by the stick as it flogged the forest floor, releasing Shana, bouncing Toca off.

Squealing and hissing sounds of pain came from within the beast as it violently thrashed the vegetation, hitting tree trunks around it so hard it was causing them to sway high above.

Toca scooped up Shana's lifeless body up into his arms, off the ground, and ran a safe distance from the wounded snake. One hard hit with its tail could break bones or even kill one of them. He laid her down on the ground and looked into her eyes but they were closed.

He put his hands around her face, telling her to wake up, but she didn't move. Panic started to build deep within him as he looked back for the snake. Not seeing it anymore, he looked to his female friend and began gently shaking her by the shoulders.

"Shana, Shana, wake up!" he yelled over and over again. "Don't leave me, don't die! Come back to me!"

CHAPTER 14

"Please, Shana, come back to me!" Toca begged her lifeless body as he stopped shaking her, laying her back down. Closely he hovered over the body, looking back and forth, trying to figure out what to do.

Desperation was setting in and he couldn't think straight. He never felt this type of fear before as he was getting scared. Then as fast as the snake had struck him earlier, his emotions switched and got mad as he looked at Shana, just lying there.

"Wake up! We need to go, you keep slowing us down again and again!" Shouting at her, deliriously saying what was on his mind, "You're going to be my…my mate and you're supposed to be bringing your good God to our tribe to save us!"

Toca hesitated for a moment as it was coming to him in a dark sarcastic voice, slithering through his emotions. *Now what are you going to do, Toca? How did you expect this God to save your people if it couldn't save Shana's father and now her? The one you love.* Changing its demeanor, it asked helplessly, *But why, why, Black Ghost, would a God, she said loved her, allow this? Or…*pausing to be dramatic, *did it to her?*

Toca became outraged. "Your God! You, you did this to her!" he yelled as he stood up, peering and pointing around, trying to see him.

"She trusted you! She thanked you for always protecting her and you let this happen? What kind of God are you? You're no different than the gods of my ancestors! All you gods are alike, all you want is death. First you killed her father, then you take her! If this is what gods do, then I don't want a god. I don't want any of your kind! My ancestors were right to leave their gods and hide, never to be found by one of you again!"

A roaring fire of fury within him was getting out of control as if a mighty internal wind was fueling it with every word.

It was a standoff. "Come on, you want to kill someone else, come and get me, I'm here!" he was shouting boldly, strutting the forest floor around Shana's body, looking up and around with an invitation of open arms.

"I'm Toca, *Black Ghost.*" He pounded his chest several times with his fist. "Killer of all great beasts. The giant caiman died with one strike of my knife. Others are dead with no effort at all. Now the fiercest of all animals—the anaconda—is hurting and fleeing me because what I did with my own hands." He swayed his arms out, wide open, to show this God he had nothing to hide.

"What do you have for me? You don't scare me, show yourself, come on and get me!" screaming, he beat his chest again, then took a fighting stance.

Standing there in silence with all his senses sharp and ready to defend or attack, a calm cool and gentle breeze swept through the hot humid forest. The leaves on the trees began to softly clap, rustling together as if they were applauding an arrival. Any noise made by birds or animals stopped as though giving honor to what was approaching. The sun repeatedly came and went, slowly through the high canopy with each motion of the long limbs as they swayed back and forth, rejoicing from the soft movement of air.

As gentle but swift as the breeze came, Toca instantly was mesmerized by the serenity of the moment. Still standing motionless, his senses were the only things getting any attention. The smell of the forest was fresh, fresh as an early morning rain. The colors of the trees, ferns, and the sky were brilliant, almost glowing, glowing to a point he felt the need to squint his eyes.

But instead of squinting, he closed them, taking in the incredible peace that had consumed his mind, body, and spirit instantly. For a moment, Toca felt he was nowhere in time and place, then his ears heard a voice. One that was made up from all the life in the forest combined, speaking as one, softly and clearly saying, "Love her as you love yourself and you will find out how much I love you."

Opening his eyes, wanting to look around for the person talking, knew the voice didn't come from the outside of his body but within his head. He wasn't scared or alarmed but was filled with a warm comforting peace.

He looked straight up to the sky to see if it was the sun's rays, warming his body, but it wasn't. Not in direct line of sight of the light coming through the small opening in the canopy, he took a step backward to step in it. To step in that healing light, he saw come down more than a half-sun season ago, giving more life to Shana's father when he watched on in the clearing from the forest.

With the step back not watching, Toca tripped on Shana's body, accidently sitting down hard on her chest. Pulling himself off her, he quickly went to his knees at her side. Gently taking her by the head to tell her lifeless body he was sorry, he noticed the beam of sunlight was acutely shining directly on her.

Suddenly with a loud gasp, she opened her mouth, taking in a deep breath, surprising him so much he dropped her head down on the ground, jumping back. She coughed and gasped for more air, then her eyes began to open as she blinked repeatedly, trying to focus and understand what happened. Shana turned her head on the ground as her gaze landed on Toca. She attempted to sit up and take deep breaths while clutching at her ribs. The painful squint on her face told the story.

When Toca sat on her chest, it compressed her lungs and heart hard enough it started them working again, but it was the light of the sun, shining high in the sky, Toca believed gave her a new beginning. "Shana...," Toca softly said her name with relief, kneeling next to her, gently lifting her head and shoulders up enough to put his arms around her as she laid her head on his chest. "I thought I lost you."

Silently and with gentle movement, Toca began rocking her in his arms. They stayed in this position for the longest time, overwhelmed of what just happened and grateful she was alive. But moreover was the hypnotic sensation that moved between them of excitement combined with serenity in this new phase in their relationship.

Shana was the one to break the silence of their oneness. "Toca, I'm hurting really bad, are we going to be okay?"

It took him a moment to answer, then slowly leaned back as she tilted her head, looking up into his eyes tenderly, he answered, "Yes, my Shana, we are going to be okay."

She peacefully held back the pain and smiled, then laid her head back against his chest, closed her eyes and fell asleep.

*****

It was getting very late in the day as he held her there on the forest floor. Before it got too dark, Toca needed to get their hammocks hung up. Slowly laying her on the ground, he went to look for the carrying packs. After finding them, he found the best trees to spend the night, wanting to hang the hammocks higher than normal, just in case the giant anaconda was still around.

The cluster of trees had many strong branches, extending out higher than he could reach, he climbed one of them with the packs. Once at a long branch, he tied one end of each hammock to it side by side. Then he leaped over to another tree's branch of the same height and tied the other ends of the beds to it. Leaping to the ground, Toca looked up to see his work. He had tied the hammocks closer to each other than normal, then an idea came to mind.

Quickly looking around, he found a thin strong vine, hanging from one of the trees, and grabbed for his knife. Realizing again he had lost it when his body hit the tree from the snake throwing him, he retrieved Shana's long knife, wasting no time, cutting the vine off high. Then put the knife blade between his teeth and went back up to the hammocks.

Crawling into his bed, he leaned over and pulled Shana's to him. Then he began to poke small holes in the thick canvas, along the edges where the hammocks touched, with the tip of the shiny knife, finger-lengths apart. Then weaving the vine in the holes from one hammock to another, he then tied a knot at the ends where the holes finished. Now having one big bed, he rolled back and forth between the two hammocks to see if it worked.

Perfect, he thought.

Jumping down, Toca gathered their items that were in the packs and threw them up into the air, landing on the large bed. Then spotting a juja plant nearby, he pulled a handful of leaves off, rolled them into its oily ball, and tossed it up in the hammock as well.

Looking toward Shana sleeping, then back up in the trees, he said to himself, "Now if it was only that easy to get her up there."

"Shana," Toca whispered, waking her as he gently shoveled his arms underneath her, bringing her to a seated position.

"Shana, I need you to wake up." She slowly opened her eyes, giving him a quick smile which immediately went to a hard grimace of pain. She gave out a faint cough and tried to take a deep breath but groaned in agony instead.

"I need your help to get you up into the hammock," he said, looking into her half-opened eyes.

Hesitating, she slowly answered with a groggy voice, "I can't, I hurt too much when I move."

"I know but you have no choice, I need to get you up and away from the night dangers on the ground." Standing her up on her feet, still in his arms, lifting most her weight, she gave out a loud moan, leaning over to one side.

"I'm going to put you on my back. I need you to wrap your arms around my neck and hold on as I climb the tree."

"No, Toca, please. Just lay me on the ground, I'll be okay."

"I will not, you will hold on tight until I get you into our bed," he said firmly.

"I'm in a lot of pain. I think I have some broken ribs," she said, standing in his arms as she gently touched the midsection of her body.

"I know you are. I'll get medicine in the morning for the pain. But right now, we must get you up into the tree. You know it's too dangerous on the ground at night."

She reluctantly agreed.

Toca turned his back to her and she pressed the front of her body to his back and slowly lifted her arms, wrapping them around his neck.

"No matter what, don't let go. Act like a baby monkey on its mother's back. Hold on and I will get you to safety up high."

Reaching up around the trunk of the tree and with all his strength, he pulled both of them up. At the same time, he gripped the sides of the tree with his feet and immediately pushed up with his legs and repeated several more times until they got to the branch that held one end of the hammocks. Crawling out on the limb, Shana's hands slipped apart and they both lost their balance. Quickly Toca bounced up on the side of his back and shoulder, where most of her weight went, and it bumped her in the air slightly to the center of his back to balance them again. She screamed out in pain as she landed down on her side.

"Shana, hang on we're almost there."

She adjusted herself, gingerly grasping around his neck again as he continued into the hammock. He rested her down off his back slowly and helped her get as comfortable as she could be.

The items tossed up, he moved to one end of the hanging bed, then wiped the juja oil ball all over the ends of the hammock where they attached to the trees and on the trees' branches themselves. Once done, he peeled apart the ball of leaves and spread them down below where they will be sleeping.

He lay next to her, giving as much comfort as he could, then realized, for the first time, they were falling asleep for the night in each other's arms.

*****

It was a rough night sleep for the both of them. Shana battled with pain throughout the night as well as trying to take deep breaths. Toca on the other hand wrestled with mental torment of almost losing Shana again.

Peering into the emptiness of the night, he was upset with himself. *I'm to blame again, I was to protect her from getting hurt and failed. I wasn't being aware of everything, only thinking about myself finishing my Katata Ado and saving my people.*

With Shana in his arms, he rolled his head, leaning it against hers, thinking, *She lost her father, and her mother died a sun season before that. She has no family and she's never going to be able to go back to her home. How has she been able to keep going and why does she? Is this God of hers really inspiring her?*

Maybe Chief Acuta was right. We do need a god to give us purpose to grow and... adding in his own words, *even give meaning to our life. I think that's what Shana is saying through all her words about her God and this relationship with it.*

Questions were running through his mind as he closed his eyes, trying to fall asleep and clear the confusion, but the race of ideas kept coming at him. *Wonder if I never found Shana, would my journey have been different? Would I already be with Chief Acuta, celebrating my Katata Ado?*

I have taken many different paths I didn't plan on but the journey is still the same. Go to the endless water and back to the hidden valley. Shana was a dramatic change in my plans, it's been harder. I did many things I wouldn't have done or experienced if I was by myself. Maybe it's been harder but I am stronger, wiser, and more experienced with life journeying the unplanned paths. Giving her one last gentle hug of affection and security, he whispered aloud, "You are making me a greater chief for my people, Shana."

Finally satisfied, his mind, emotions, and his body drifted away with the calmness of the night.

*****

"Whoop, whoop, whoop!" The screaming alarm of monkeys a short distance away startled both the old children awake sleeping next to each other.

Toca whispered into Shana's ear, "Be still and don't get out of the hammock. I'll find out why they're upset." He slowly sat up, looking down and around the forest floor as he stretched his muscles, trying not to attract attention.

"Be careful, Toca," she said, softly adding, "Can you find me some medicine as well? I want to get going so we can get you to your tribe before the thirteenth full moon shows itself."

He looked at her in amazement and thought to himself, *She wants to keep going even though she's hurting and should rest for several days. She's thinking about me, not about herself.*

He responded, "I will find medicine and food. You go back to sleep, don't move and be very quiet."

Still sitting up in the hammock next to her, he watched her as she closed her eyes. Toca gently touched her face with the outside of his hand softly stroking her cheek.

She's so beautiful, he thought to himself.

He grabbed the long knife from its protective sheath Shana had made then looked away in the direction of where the monkeys were wildly sounding off.

He swiftly rolled out of the hammock, not to disturb her, and lightly jumped to the ground, staying crouched, not making a sound as he landed. *I've got to find my knife, this thing is too big and heavy to carry around in my hands.*

The sun was just rising as its warm rays were penetrating through the trees here and there, wherever it could find its way under the canopy. Toca disappeared into the shadows, avoiding any contact with it, and slowly drifted toward the troop of monkeys bothered by something.

The closer he got, the more distinctly he could recognize individual monkeys and their positions high in the trees. Finally he saw them. They were rapidly swaying back and forth on the limbs, shouting as they stared at something on the ground. Toca knew this body language always meant danger and it was their attempt to scare and intimidate.

He stood motionless, peering around a tree, working his eyes back and forth in the direction they were looking. He couldn't see clearly through the thick ground cover or movement of anything catching his eyes so he lowered his body and cautiously crept forward.

Toca held the long knife, pointing it out in front of his face as he slowly moved one of the leaves to the side so he could get a glimpse of what the monkeys were looking at.

Looking hard at every detail of the area, he still couldn't understand what they were screaming about.

Wait! he told himself as he stopped all body motion, including his breathing, to focus on something out of place.

There it is, I see it, he said to himself. Lying still, half of it out in the open but camouflaged among the fallen leaves and branches and the young brush hardly up off the floor of the forest.

"The anaconda," Toca whispered under his breath so silently he could barely hear himself. Patiently staring at it for the longest time, he never saw it move. It was the second half of the body that was out in the open and he could see the areas where he had stabbed it with his knife and stick close to its midsection. There was a large patch of dark dried blood on the body and a small drying puddle on the ground where it had oozed out of the wounds.

The head and the first half of the body were hidden away in a think bushy area. It looked odd for a moment because it appeared that the body completely ended at the vegetation, like it had been cut off right at that point.

Toca needed to stay hidden from everything, including the monkeys, but he wanted them to stay focused on the snake to be his eyes from above. If anything changed down on the ground, their voices and body language would tell him what to do.

Retreating a safe distance to a small stagnant puddle of muddy water, he shadowed himself with the ritual striped bands from the dark mud around the water. Then he thoroughly covered the long knife on each side to hide its shine.

He crouched back low to the ground and looked in the direction of the snake. His heart began to beat faster as his breathing quickened as well.

Out of nowhere, his thoughts went to Shana, like he was being prompted, and said to himself, *I hope you're okay and not in too much pain. I'll get medicine for you soon.*

The strong, gentle, and peaceful voice from yesterday softly answered, *Shana is fine, Toca.*

Thinking to himself, Toca replied, *Yes, because of what I've done.*

With a firm tone the voice said, *I've allowed all this to happen because I'm showing you the truth.*

What truth? Toca shook his head as if he was shaking something off, like a bug.

The monkeys were still upset but had quieted down. He decided to go around them on their backside and come in on the snake head-on. If it was to attack, at least he would be away from its deadly tail.

I will finish you and have you for our morning meal! Toca stated in thought.

Taking a deep breath, then looking around the whole area one last time, with the long knife gripped tight in his hand, he shadowed himself into the forest. With each step barely touching the ground, he left no print. His body was in motion but couldn't be seen. Sounds he made mirrored those of leaves falling from the treetops—total silence.

Moving through the plants of the forest as if he was air, he went way out and around the animals in the trees, making sure not to be seen or smelled by stragglers lurking a short distance away from the main group. Toca had no problems until he was most of the way to the other side of the troop, getting close to where the head of the snake should be.

The terrain quickly sloped up, finding himself higher in elevation with the vegetation depleting on a rocky outcropping. With hardly any brush or trees to hide behind, he was going to be exposed if he stepped out any farther so he crouched down to think. The hilltop was about two times his height, higher off the ground where the snake was, and it appeared to quickly end at a ledge with a short drop-off. It did give him the advantage of being above the snake's head.

Then it came to him. *I'll quickly step to the ledge of the rocks and get the attention of the monkeys. They'll get excited and start jumping around and screaming loudly again. That will distract the snake, then I will jump down off the ledge on top of it and stab the long knife deep into its head just as I did with the giant caiman.*

Still crouched behind cover, he felt hesitation.

What's wrong with you, are you scared? he said to himself, *You're Toca, killer of all beasts of the forest, soon be chief of the Nashua.* Motionless, his breathing began to quicken and heart started to pound again.

If I'm going to be chief, I cannot be scarred of anything! I've already fought with this snake once, why would I hesitate to fight it again? I've got the long knife and it's already wounded and has lost blood. It should be weaker now, telling himself, attempting to build up courage.

You have nothing to fear, Toca, I'm here with you, the gentle voice encouraged him.

I'm not afraid, he replied unconvincingly.

Fear only discourages my children. And fear is the weapon the darkness uses to distract from the truth, and this is what I am doing with the snake. I am showing you the truth. The statement echoed softly in his head as he absorbed the strange statement.

He sat there for a moment, looking up at the small rocky slope, envisioning where he would quickly place his feet in order not to stumble. Looking at the ground before him, he deeply inhaled as if he was taking in power from the air. He went to close his eyes to clear his head but movement caught Toca's attention. He saw a row of ants orderly marching along on a mission. One of them was carrying a huge insect ten times its size in its pincers. Then a thought came to him.

Okay, you want to help me, give me the strength of that ant. By the way, I'm not afraid! he stated sarcastically, rebelling to the gentle voice.

Still crouched, he stayed there for a moment, there was no response in his head. "That's what I thought," he said under his breath as he lifted his head and narrowed his focus to the ledge he was going to run to, then jump off.

Gripping the long knife tightly in his strong hand, with stealth and agility, he ran across the rock outcropping to the ledge. He looked out toward the monkeys and his eyes opened wide as an empty panic ran down his spine as he didn't see a single one. They had left while he hesitated and didn't know it.

Alone, just me and the snake, Toca said to himself.

You're never alone, go! The voice in his head urged him as he peered down, focusing what looked like the last part of the neck that attaches to the head but he couldn't see the head itself. Leaning over farther to see where the head was, it appeared to go into a dark opening at the base of the short cliff drop-off.

It hasn't seen me! Toca thought to himself as panic left and encouragement took its place.

"Straight down and stab the long knife deep behind the head," he said to himself with teeth clenched and his eyes sternly focused on a spot then jumped.

Briefly airborne, he was on the anaconda before he could blink an eye. All at the same time, he straddled it with his feet touching the ground as the knife went deep all the way down to the handle as he held it with both hands. Toca tightly squeezed the snake with his knees, holding on as if it was going to violently try to whip him off as he held firm onto the long knife to keep it in the snake and to help balance him through the fight.

Sitting there with his eyes squinted and all muscles flexed, nothing happened. Slowly opening his eyes, Toca carefully twisted his head around to see the head of the snake. It wasn't moving but he couldn't get a clear view of it because it was in a small cave that was very dark. Looking back around, Toca let go of the knife and felt the snake's body with his hand. There was no movement and it wasn't breathing.

This thing is dead! thinking to himself. Still uneasy, he slowly got off the back and, with both hands, wiggled the side of the snake as if to wake it up.

He whispered, "The snake is dead." Then aloud, he stated, "The giant anaconda is dead!"

He patted it a few times, then slowly stroked the body, feeling the large scales that armored the snake. An emotion of greatness was swelling through his veins as he thought deeper and deeper about the moment.

Just then, *pssss*, the snake broke the silence. Toca jumped back and started to run as all courage instantly disappeared, reminding him he was still scared of the beast. Then another sound came from it that wasn't as intimidating, *gurgle, gurgle*. Toca hesitantly stepped back toward the body because it wasn't moving. He looked for where the sounds were coming from and it was at the handle of the knife. The inside air and gases of the snake were seeping out from the large gash that was put in it. Then with embarrassingly weak confidence, he laughed at himself for being so skittish.

He shoved the snake one more time just to make sure he wasn't imagining this and nothing happened, "You're dead!" he told the lifeless beast.

Turning, Toca gingerly peered into the entrance of the small cave where the head of the snake was laying in. Taking a moment for his eyes to adjust, he began to see deeper inside the tunneled entrance with a few small rocks scattered around, then whispered out loud, "Shana is going to want to see this." Pausing for a moment, then realized, frantically stating, "Shana…I forgot about her!"

Thinking this through, he quickly came up with a plan and said to himself, *I'll find medicine to stop her pain, then bring her here and we will cook a lot of the snake, finally having our stomachs full again.*

Reaching over and grasping the long knife, he started to wonder when and how the snake actually died.

Was it by the stabs on the side of the body or the stick I jabbed into its mouth? Or was it an instant death as I stabbed the long knife into its neck just now? Whichever it is, it's dead and what matters most of all. Then stating aloud the last three words, jerking the knife out of the snake, "I killed it!"

Toca tried to look down the snake to the end of its tail, in the direction toward where he first spotted it, but the bushes and ferns were thick where the snake's body had come through.

Good thing the monkeys spotted it when they did, if it had made it all the way into the cave, I would have never found it hiding behind all this, he said to himself, looking back into the dark cave entrance.

Slowly heading back toward Shana, Toca was carefully looking on the ground for yatowa flowers. His tribe used the small yellow petals of the flower to stop pain and the roots had a very special effect to them. Finding a couple of the plants, he dug up their roots and all. Now he needed some of the oily mud from under the magosu tree where the base roots grow up off the ground along the river's edge. This oily substance leaks from the roots and drops its precious oil onto the ground, making the mud rich with healing properties.

Before getting the mud, he needed something to carry it in. Finding a large bamboo stem, Toca cut off two hollow sections in the middle of the long beam, now having two long cups. One for mud and one for water. Retrieving the mud and water from the river's edge, he headed back to Shana.

As he approached the new large hammock, Toca could see she was still in it. He laid everything on the ground and quietly went up the tree, hesitating before crawling in.

She's so beautiful, thinking to himself. He was mesmerized with watching her sleep, then she moved to adjust her position and she grimaced in pain. She slowly opened her eyes, squinting, trying to focus on things around her. Looking right at him, momentarily not seeing him, she suddenly jerked back with wide eyes and gave out a quiet scream.

"Shana, it's me, Toca, you are okay," he said as he reached out and softly touched her arm.

Instantly relaxing, fully coming aware, she said, "You scared me, why are you shadowed? I couldn't see you for a moment, then I didn't know what I was looking at until I saw you smile and your eyes moved."

"Sorry, I didn't mean to scare you. I was watching…"—hesitating, searching for the appropriate words—"my beautiful woman."

Surprised at his new bold choice of words for her, she quickly replied, "So where have you been, my Black Ghost?"

Hearing he was someone's man swelled his pride, lifting his head a little higher. Then instantly switching his thoughts, the actions of excitement from an old child came out.

"Shana, I have great news. I had to shadow myself because I found the anaconda!" Changing his tone and facial expression, attempting to suppress his excitement. "Actually the monkeys found it, that's what they were whooping about. But I killed it!" he stated boldly as he crawled into the hammock and got close to her.

"You did what? You could have been hurt or killed!" She stressed.

"I had your long knife and I shadowed myself so it couldn't see me."

"But what if you got hurt and both of us are hurt, what would we do?"

"Be hurt together?" Toca answered honestly.

"Why would you do something like that, you should have run away!"

Confused she wasn't sharing his excitement, he responded, "It needed to be killed." Toca patted his chest with his fist, then said, "I'm Toca, the Black Ghost, killer of all that try to hurt me or my people." He changed his tone to be livelier. "We also needed meat and we have a lot of it now!" He smiled big, knowing that would please her.

She grabbed his arm firmly, not meaning to slap it, and said, "Toca, don't take chances like that, do you hear me? You have to take care of me, I lost my father I don't want to lose you too."

He didn't fully hear what she said after she aggressively grabbed his arm. The last person that touched him like that, he killed back at the big village, then Jucawa came to his mind. He silently vowed that one of these days, Jucawa would regret ever touching him and his mother that way. Many past hurtful things came rushing back to his mind. Jucawa was his enemy, even though he was his father.

"Toca, do you hear me?" Shana shook his arm and looked closer into his face.

It jarred his thoughts back to the hammock. "Yes, Shana, I hear you." Pausing to calm down inside, he said, "Don't ever hit me like that again!" He looked back into her eyes with anger, then looked down at her hand on his arm.

She let go of his arm and her face turned soft with surprise, not knowing if she hurt him or if he was mad.

It instantly broke Toca's heart when he looked back up into her face and knew he needed to explain, "Shana, I'm sorry, memories came back to me when Jucawa would grab or hit my mother and me like that. I know you didn't mean to hurt me and you didn't." He straightened up and lifted his arm, showing her it didn't bother him. His pride was at stake here, just like his status as a hunter by killing the snake and she wasn't recognizing it.

"Shana, you need to remember, I am of the Nashua tribe and all the old children that have accomplished the Katata Ado are men who are great hunters and that's who I am. A great hunter."

She leaned forward, closer to him, grimacing, trying to hold back the pain from her ribs, and said, "You have saved my life many times, Toca. I know you are a good hunter—if not the greatest—you don't have to convince me of that. What I want to convince you of is how much you mean to me. So if I show concern for your safety, that's me telling you my heart doesn't want to beat alone." She slowly and gently took his hand and placed it on her chest over her heart. Then she placed her hand on his chest where his heart beats. Looking deep into his eyes, Shana said, "I never want our hearts to beat as two, only as one." Then she leaned to his face and gently touched her lips to his.

CHAPTER 15

Toca sat there with his eyes open as her lips were touching his. *They are so soft*, he thought. He never touched lips with anyone before. He saw her eyes were closed so he closed his. His body started to tremble faintly and was getting lightheaded as the hammock and everything around him was starting to spin. Before he knew it, she slowly backed away and they opened their eyes. She had a glowing smile on her face, saying, "Toca, great hunter of the Nashua tribe, I'm sorry, I didn't mean to slap your arm. Will you forgive me?" Shana asked with the sweetest sounding voice.

He couldn't speak, the most unexpected moment just happened to him and his mind stopped working, staring at her in awe.

"Toca, are you okay?"

"I, um, I don't know what…I mean, I never have done that before."

"Me neither, except on my mother and father's cheeks."

"Why did you do that?" he said, coming back to reality.

She answered, still smiling, "Because we love each other."

"We love each other?"

She answered, slightly embarrassed, "Yes, silly, we love each other."

Toca put a puzzled look on his face, telling Shana, "That's what the voice told me to do to you."

"What?" She frowned

"A pure calm voice of the forest spoke to me yesterday in my head and said, 'Love her…'" He paused, trying to remember all the words, then started over. "Love her as you love yourself and you will find out how much I love you."

Shana's heart jumped for joy, trying to contain herself from bursting out in praise to God. She bowed her head, closed her eyes, and began giving thanks aloud.

Again? Toca said to himself as he imitated her.

"Father in heaven, thank you for protecting Toca as he killed the giant snake. Thank you for keeping me alive. Please heal me so I can be a strong woman for him. Most of all, thank you for speaking to Toca so he knows you are real, amen."

They opened their eyes together with Toca frowning, asking a question, "How do you know that voice was your God?"

"Easy, that's him, he's all about love!" So excited about this long-lost moment of God showing up, she almost forgot how much pain she is in. "I told you he loves everyone because he is love and wants us all to have more of it...or him, I mean!"

Not completely taking all that to mind, Toca had another question. "You called your God Father?"

"Yes, he is our heavenly Father."

"What do you mean?"

"He is the father of all things. He created everything you see and know," she said, looking around, pointing to everything around them. "Even the first man and woman."

Toca put on the same stare he always has, trying to understand new important information. She kept going. "He made Adam and Eve. They were the first people, and all people of the earth came from them. So God is the first father of all of us."

Toca was quick to ask, "Who was his father?"

Shana giggled as Toca looked on expectantly. "That question we have no answer. All he told us is that he is the beginning and the end. And since our faith is trusting what he tells us in his Holy Bible..." She pointed to hers, wrapped up. "That's as far as we need to seek and believe."

Toca sat there in deep thought, staring past Shana's face into the forest, trying to understand all she was saying. It was hard for him but things did sound right. He refocused back to her and realized she was holding her side as the pain was beginning to speak loudly, grimacing her face.

"Oh, I am sorry, Shana. I brought you medicine, it's on the ground."

After they both slowly and painfully made it down to the forest floor, Toca took one of the yellow flowers and pulled away the individual petals from its stem and rolled them up in a tight small ball.

"Put this in your mouth under your tongue and suck on it." Holding it up to her, she stared at it, then hesitantly opened her mouth and rolled her tongue back as he placed in under her tongue.

"Now the root of this flower…" He was washing several strands clean with water from the bamboo cup. "I need you to chew and shallow all of it." He handed it to her.

"Are you sure this is going to work?"

"It will work, just give it a short time," Toca said, laughing to himself as he looked down at the mud he was preparing.

While eating the root, she asked, "What are you laughing at?"

"You're going to feel really good, then feel nothing." Looking back up at her, he said, "Then you're going to be funny."

"What do you mean funny?"

"You will not be yourself. You're not going to talk and walk like you do."

"Huh?"

"You'll see, now lie down on your good side and lift up your body covering so I can see where you are in pain."

Shana did what he asked, then Toca leaned over her and started to gently rub the mud over her whole side. He could see where her skin was bruising in a large area with a darker color. She moaned in pain the more he rubbed.

"I'm sorry, I'm almost done."

"It hurth so mush." Her words started to jumble from the medicine.

He looked at her face and her eyes were beginning to slowly roll around.

"Good, it's starting to work. You're going to feel no pain soon." At that moment, he pressed firmer along her side to feel her ribs and his fingers found what they were searching for. *A couple of them are broken,* he thought to himself, not to alarm her that she was going to be hurting for a long time and she will not be able to move fast through the forest.

Toca remembered back a couple sun seasons ago when one of the men in the tribe fell out of a tree and broke his ribs. It took many moons for them to stop hurting and be able to climb trees again.

"Tocaa…I'm a feeelin' ggood naww, we goow naaww?" He couldn't control himself and started to laugh aloud. Her arm was swaying back and forth, trying to point in a direction for them to start walking.

"Whyee yooo laaaghin?"

"The medicine is working. You'll be fine for a while. Just lie down while I gather up our hammock packs."

After he quickly got the big hammock down, he had to cut the vines holding the two together and turned them into individual packs again. He went to Shana's side and said, "Let's get up, we're ready to go and start heading to the snake. We need to get some food into us before we get too weak."

"Thnnake?" She tried her best to open her eyes wide but the combination of the flower petals and roots were working really well.

"Yes, snake, the one I told you I killed, and now we have enough meat to get us to the hidden valley."

He pulled her up to her feet and put her carrying pack over her shoulders and the other over his. Then he draped the arm from her good side over his shoulder and wrapped his arm around her waist then started walking.

It was very slow going. Shana was doing the best she could but she had very little muscle control. With each step, she sluggishly dragged her legs, barely holding onto him. Toca had to make many stops to rest, thinking each time, *There has to be a better way to move her through the forest or just not give her any root to relax her. At this pace, we will not make it back in time before the thirteenth full moon."*

Finally arriving at the snake, he pushed their way through the thick vegetation, getting to the small open area at the head of the snake.

"Here we are, Shana," he said as he set her on the ground, leaning her against the outside rock wall.

"Yaaaa, Toocaaaa, thnake!" She groggily opened her eyes and was staring a couple of arm lengths away from the large snake, surprising her.

"It's okay, it's dead." Kneeling next to her, he leaned over and patted the dead animal to show her she didn't need to be afraid.

Calming down a little, she kept her eyes opened as wide as she could, breathing heavily.

"There is nothing to be afraid of." Toca still had his hand on the snake as he looked back and forth from it to her.

"Itth reellee biiggg, Toocaaa!" she said, looking at the beast with her head swaying back and forth.

"It is, now we have plenty of meat!" he stated, smiling while patting it again.

He looked at her and asked if she still had the yellow flower roll under her tongue and she nodded yes. He told her she could spit it out, that the pain medicine in it is probably gone by now.

After laying her back to sleep, he started cutting up pieces of the snake in long thin strips to dry over a fire.

Toca still couldn't believe how long the anaconda was. *No one from the village will believe me when I tell them how big it is,* he said to himself. Then he had an idea. *"I'm going to skin the snake from its head to the end of the tail and show it to them, then they'll believe me.* But after reexamining the idea, there was no way it would fit into his pack, plus it would be too heavy. He thought back to the caiman hide and how difficult it was just to put in and out of the canoe being so heavy.

Changing plans, he decided to only take a long thin strip of it, from the mouth to the end of the tail to show the length. Pulling the head out of the cave entrance, he took up the long knife and started at the mouth, going between the nostrils and eyes, around the stabbed area, past the center of its back to the end of the tail.

Once done, he laid it upside down in the clearing, next to the body, for the sun to dry it out. Walking down the length of the thin strip, Toca guessed it was eight of his body length.

Next he began slicing many thin slabs of meat, laying them out on the snake's back next to where he wasn't cutting. When he figured he had cut up more than they could carry, Toca dug a small fire pit in their little hideout.

He filled the pit with an old termite nest he found close by and started it on fire with Shana's two fire rocks, hitting them together, making big sparks. After he had the fire going, he gathered many long thin sticks to make a strong long-lasting fire and a smoke drying rack just like he made to dry the caiman meat at the beginning of his journey.

While laying the meat across the rack, Toca decide they would stay the night on the ground at this spot. Having the fire going all night to dry a large amount of meat would help keep night dangers away. Plus nothing could sneak up behind them and they would hear anything coming through the extremely thick undergrowth the snake's body was still in.

It was already getting late in the day and the sun stopped showing itself, except for its soft warm orange-and-yellow glow of evening light, telling the world it will see it again tomorrow.

The fire was burning strong as the smoke rose up and filtered its way through the meat, stealing any moisture it had, leaving a smooth flavor in its place. As the night quietly came through the forest, Toca sat there next to the fire, mesmerized by the dancing flames that started to give a show of its reflection off the surrounding rock wall and vegetation that enclosed their small hideaway.

"That smells good," a soft voice beside Toca spoke up.

"You're finally awake," he said, turning to her.

"Is it night already? How long have I been sleeping?" she asked as she straightened up, readjusting herself.

"Your body went to sleep this morning after you took the medicine, and your mind went with it when we got here about midday."

Bursting out in panic, she said, "We lost a whole day of journeying?"

"It's all right, it was a day for healing and getting food," he said with a smile.

The light from the fire was glowing off her face as he stared at her beauty with her gazing back. She slowly put on a smile and said, "You are an amazing man. Thank you for all that you do for me, Toca."

When she called him a man, something inside him dramatically transformed. He didn't quite know what it was, but it felt good, it felt right. It was like he had been walking through a thick dark part of the forest, and without warning, he walked out into an unexpected clear bright meadow. Instantly expanding his vision and everything about himself—older and wiser like his childish ways had disappeared and Toca the man was born.

He thought to himself, *I am a man now. I am doing everything that a man in my village does, even taking care of a woman.*

Still looking at his Shana, he leaned over to her face and touched his lips to hers. He closed his eyes and a rush of energy flowed through his body. He wanted to grasp her up in his arms and hold her tight. But instead, he slowly backed away and stared into her eyes without saying anything.

The fire crackled and drew his attention. Looking back closely at the meat, he decided it was time to turn this batch of thin slices over.

"How are you feeling?" he asked while working on the meat.

"I feel weak and very sore." She gently touched her side and said, "It's sore but doesn't hurt like it did."

Turning to her, Toca said, "Good, we'll eat soon then I'll redo the mud on your side and give you some more yellow petals of the flower and a very small piece of the root this time, then you need to go back to sleep until morning."

"What's that?" Shana asked as she looked behind them at the dark hole on the rock wall.

"It's where the snake's head stopped and died. It's a small entrance to a cave."

"How big is it inside?"

"I don't know, I haven't gone into it yet. I've been busy working on this snake ever since we got here."

"Let's go see...," she said, feeling a bit adventuresome and needing to move from sleeping so much. "You have many sticks in the fire, we can use them as light."

It sounded like a good idea so he grasped one of the longer sticks sticking out the side of the firepit and lifted the burning end into the air, brightening up the small hiding place. With his other hand, he clenched the handle of the long knife lying next to him on the ground then twisted around toward the cave entrance and said anxiously, "Let's go!"

Shana slowly gathered herself up on all fours, slightly stretching out as best as she could without upsetting her wounded side, turned, and followed her man.

Crawling on their hands and knees, dipping their heads as they started into the cave, Toca held the stick of fire in front of him to light the way as they entered. It was only a short distance until it opened into a larger area where they could stand up.

"Wow, this is bigger inside than what it looks from the outside," Shana commented while grimacing with pain as she stood up.

They both were focusing and refocusing their gaze as the light from the small flame danced inside the small cavern that was very dry, having a stale odor. There were rocks piled up along the walls of the oval-shaped room as though they fell off the walls, neatly piling themselves up. The center area of the floor was a soft dirt that had many imprints of lines of a giant snake slithering around.

Shana whispered slowly, "Tooccaa," as she grabbed his arm. Understanding the frightened tone, he turned, looking in the direction she was facing, and saw what she was seeing, oddly coiled up along the wall on top of a batch of rocks.

Its mate! he thought to himself, slowly stepping in front of her, lifting the fire and long knife toward the beast.

"Back up slowly," Toca told her as they both stepped backward, just a couple of short steps, in unison toward the entrance, still staring at the snake. The lighting changed from the fire, bouncing off the cavern walls; and being pointed at the snake, he noticed something different as a clearer view of it came to him.

"Shana, stop, stay here. I have the advantage."

He started to step forward as she clutched his arm again, saying, "What are you doing? Let's get out of here while we can."

"Trust me, I know what I'm doing." Before she could stop him, he pulled from her grasp and instantly lunged at the snake and swung the long knife down into the middle of it. The blade sliced deep, cutting through the body in several places all the way down to the rocks piled up on the floor. He let go of the knife and raised the fire stick high in the air in victory.

"No, Toca!" Shana screamed inside the small cave. It was very loud, echoing a few times. Her scream scared him more than the snake did and he jumped back from it when he heard the unanticipated loud shriek.

Quickly he turned to her now, knowing what he did wasn't very smart, remembering her slapping his arm earlier in the day. At first, it seemed funny but now she's panicking.

"Shana, it's okay, I was just having fun," he said, reaching back to her. "It's not a snake but an old empty skin of a snake, probably from the one I killed."

She moved her eyes from the snakeskin to him. He kept his distance, hoping she wasn't going to hit him.

She narrowed her eyes and, with gritted teeth, holding her side, said, "You scared me to death, don't you ever do something like that again!"

Toca couldn't help it and started to laugh, saying, "Sorry, my love, but that was funny."

"What did you say?"

Still giggling, he said, "That was funny."

"No, before that."

"Sorry?"

"After that."

He stopped, amusing himself, and had to think about what he said then it dawned on him. "My love."

Her eyes softened as her head slightly tilted to the side, putting on a gentle smile. "I love you too, Toca."

They stood there, staring, absorbing through each other's eyes a true man-and-woman moment.

Without warning, the flame on the stick started to flicker out. Toca glanced up at it then said, "Let's get out of here while we can still see."

They turned and knelt down to go through the short entrance, then he remembered, "Oh wait, I left the long knife on the rocks on the snakeskin." Turning with a couple of quick steps to the knife, he bent down to pick it up but his body jolted back then froze from what his eyes were looking at. Next to the handle of the knife, poking out of the pile of rocks, he saw something, something so unexpected that it made him jump back as though he was just bit by something deadly.

"Toca, hurry, the flame is almost gone."

He didn't respond.

"Toca, what are you doing, let's go."

Everything in him told him to run but he couldn't believe what he was looking at. He had to see more of it. Turning around, he quickly got them through the entrance, almost dragging her.

"Ouch..." She twisted in pain. "What are you doing, what's wrong?"

"I saw something in the rocks, we've got to go back in!" he said, excitedly moving around. He took the cooked meat off the rack and put on more raw meat. Then collected several long sticks and tied them together with a small piece of tree vine he had chopped down earlier when gathering wood. He stuck one end in the fire to get it going, then stabbed the other end into the ground. Reaching over to the pile of cooked meat, Toca took up two small pieces, giving one to Shana. She started eating as he put the other in his mouth and chewed it down quickly.

"What did you see?"

"I think I know but not totally sure, that's why we need to go back. Hurry and eat this too." He had gotten out several of the flower petals and rolled them up then handed it to her. At the same time, he was preparing some of the mud and told her to lift her covering up so he could rub some more on her side.

"What about the roots?"

"Later, I need your mind clear to see what I saw, the roots relax your body too much. Are you done eating?"

"You're going too fast, slow down, Toca. Whatever you saw, is it going to move or go somewhere?"

"Oh no! It's going nowhere."

"Then what's the hurry?"

"You'll see, come on."

He bent down, snatching up the new fire sticks, and quickly headed into the cave.

Once inside, as they approached the snakeskin and pile of rocks, Toca told Shana, "Don't let this scare you with what you're about to see." He slowly stepped next to the knife and lowered the flame to bring light to that area.

"Ahh." She caught her breath. "Oh no, no, no, Toca…is that what I think it is?" She hid behind him, peering around his shoulder.

"It looks like it to me."

"What would it be doing in here?"

"Maybe it's the leftover from a meal of the snake?"

"Oh, that's horrible to think."

"What do you think you would have looked like if that snake got away with you and swallowed you whole, then later on came out the other end?"

"That's going to make me sick, stop it," she said, gently pushing on his shoulder.

"It looks like it's still connected to the rest of it under the rock pile."

They were staring at bones and not just any bones but white thin bones of a human hand. Most of the bony finger pieces were still connected, sticking out of the rock as though reaching out, asking for help.

Toca handed the bundle of fire sticks to Shana, then moved the large pile of snakeskin to the other side of the cave.

Kneeling back at the incredible find, he slowly lifted off rock by rock to what ended up being a complete full human skeleton, lying contorted sideways with the front facing their direction. Toca stood up, staring down at it.

"How did it or, I should say, how did the person get here? Are there any other people in this part of the forest than yours, Toca?"

"No, the only others Chief Acuta told me about were the ones near the white, black, and brown rivers and at the endless water. No one else deep inside our forest."

Shana burst out, "Look at that, it's just like yours." She quickly pointed to the bottom of one leg bone near the foot. Again stunned, Toca couldn't believe what he was looking at—an anklet with three talismans on it. Bending down with hesitation, as if it was going to come alive, he reached out and touched it. Then quickly stood up, taking a step back with a look of unbelief on his face.

"What is it? What's wrong?"

Sluggishly with thoughts going through his head, trying to make sense of it, he said, "This man is Nashua."

"Are you sure? How do you know it was a man?"

"Our tribe symbol is the sun. And that one"—leaning over, pointing—"is a yellow round sun and only men wear their talisman at the ankles."

"Who are you?" Toca said softly, staring at the skeleton as he relaxed, kneeling again. A kinship was quickly forming in his spirit with this dead one. He reached out and laid a hand on top of the skull. Closing his eyes, he went through memories, trying to think of anyone or of stories of people they lost outside of the hidden valley but no one came to mind.

"What is all that?" Shana said as she pointed to one of the walls, looking around. Toca stood back up and turned to where she was pointing. With the brighter light, everything in the cave was clearer. Taking a couple steps toward the center of the cave, his eyes began adjusting to what he was really seeing. Slowly turning around, gazing at all the walls, the dark spots and cracks were a continuous picture that had been drawn.

Making a complete circle, getting back to the spot Shana had pointed to, he realized it was the shape of a moon. Next to it were twelve straight marks.

"What does that mean, Toca?"

"It's how we count the passing of moons, that means twelve moons passed for whoever was here in this cave."

"It makes sense how the rocks are piled against the walls, he must have lived in here. But how did all those rocks neatly get on top of him?" Shana questioned.

Stepping back to the dead one, he knelt down and asked, "What happened to you, Nashua?"

Very faintly, he heard a response. *I am showing you the truth.*

His eyes opened wide, looking right into the empty two dark pits of the skull peering at him.

"Did you hear that?" He looked back at Shana.

"Hear what?"

"He said something."

She frowned, saying, "No, he didn't."

"I heard him say, 'I am showing you the truth.'"

"Toca, I didn't hear anything, it must have been in your head."

"My head? My head! That's right, I heard those words this morning in my head." He stood up and looked at Shana as she still held the fire stick up in the air.

"You did?"

"Your God talks to me, at least, I think its him."

She looked at Toca, perplexed, as he continued, "I was hunting down the snake and he spoke in my head and said, with a lot of other things, 'I am showing you the truth.' The same exact words, what does that mean?"

"Well, my father always told me when God talks, we must listen and wait, keeping our eyes open and mouths shut because a great thing is going to happen."

"Like what?"

"I don't know but we will see soon."

"How do we know it happened?"

"When it happens, there will be no question it was God. He's always that way, he likes to show how wonderful of a Father he is and how great a God he is."

"But I don't understand, we're not looking for anything. Why does he need to show us something?"

"God knows everything from the past and everything that is going to happen in the future. He is able to use all situations—even bad ones—for his purpose for people that call him their God and love him and ask him into their heart to live."

Once again, Toca was trying to understand the things she was teaching him about her God.

"There's so much," he said to himself.

Toca looked back at the skeleton. "Do you think we should cover him back up with rocks?"

"Yes, he's here for a reason and this is a really good spot to be buried."

"Okay, but I'm taking the anklet to show Chief Acuta, he might know who he is." Reaching for the anklet, it easily came off from being dry and old.

"Let's cover him better so you can't see any bones this time," Shana said as she knelt next to him and picked up a rock.

"First we should straighten him out flat on the dirt and fold his arms to cross his chest like we did with your father." He didn't get a response and looked at her as she had a sad expression on her face, realizing he said something stupid. She was still hurting over her father dying. "I'm sorry, Shana, I wasn't thinking—"

"It's fine, I get those rush of emotions when I see my father in my head and it takes a few moments to get over them."

Looking back to the dead one, Toca moved more rocks out of the way to be able to lay the skeleton flat on the dirt floor. Once the dirt bed was ready, he began slowly adjusting it into a straighter position, as bones were coming apart, then gently folded the arms across the rib cage.

"That looks better, Toca, but there must be a rock or something under the back, making the chest stick up too much."

"I thought I got everything cleared on the ground?" He slid his hand under the backside of the rib cage and felt the problem. Grasping it, then pulling, the whole skeleton came with it.

"What are you doing? You're messing it up," Shana said.

"There's something attached to the bones on the back. Let me roll him over a bit..." The bones clanked together as more fell apart, lifting it up. "So I can see what it is. Can you lower the fire down, please?" She lowered the light as he rolled the skeleton over and he saw the obstacle. It was embedded deep between the backbones.

He quickly let go of the skeleton, sitting back on his feet, staring again back at the dark eyes, now looking sad and in pain from what was in him. "This is a bad thing, a very bad thing!"

"Toca, what is it, what's under him?"

"A knife…it's stuck all the way to the handle in him."

"Oh, my Lord, that means—"

He finished her sentence. "Someone killed him and buried him here, never to be found."

CHAPTER 16

Toca rolled the lifeless bones completely over, exposing what caused his death. In a very solemn tone, he said, "Shana, bring the flame closer."

She knelt next to the body, holding the fire out over the bones. The excitement of the moment had vanished. What appeared to be a simple passing away of a person, buried in a quiet peaceful place, turned into a tomb of death. Now they were in a dark hole in the ground meant to hide a horrible thing.

"Nashua," Toca said slowly, with no emotion.

"Nashua, Nashua what?"

He sat there, staring at the knife handle.

Then she persisted. "I know he's Nashua, you already said that."

"Not him, the knife. It's Nashua," he stated, pointing at it.

Shana leaned back, saying, "This is really bad, isn't it, Toca?"

"We killed one of our own people, how did this happen?" His heart was sinking quickly while his mind was mystified, trying to make sense of it all. The only time he heard about someone killing another was when Chief Acuta told him about their old ancient ones.

Toca grasped the skeleton and gently rolled it over again to see the front rib cage.

"Good, the ribs aren't broken and the heart wasn't cut out."

Shana was taken aback for a moment. "What? What are you talking about his heart being cut out…oh, that's right…" She paused for a second, thinking about the recent conversation then continued, "Your tribe came from a people that cut out the hearts as sacrifices to their gods."

He nodded his head in confirmation then said, "I'm taking the knife as well." He rolled the clanking old bones over onto its front side and grabbed the knife and tried to remove it. It was stuck between the ribs and the backbones. Working the handle back and forth, loosening it, the bones kept rattling and several more came apart as Shana cringed. "Ahh, that's not right."

Finally the knife came out and Toca looked at it closely. Not recognizing the talisman image on the knife handle but it matched something. Quickly looking on the ground where he sat the anklet down next to the long knife, he took it up and examined the talismans together.

"The same, Shana, look, they're the same!"

"What does that mean?"

"He died by his own knife!" Toca stated, confused.

"Oh, this is getting worse or more interesting, I can't tell—ouch!" Shana yelped in pain as the fire got too close to her fingers. She quickly moved her hand down to the end of the shortened fire sticks. "We need to hurry, there's not much left."

Without saying anything, Toca sat the new items down next to the long knife and readjusted the skeleton out straight then folded the arm bones across its chest. Quickly he restacked the full pile of rocks over the whole area until they couldn't see any more of the Nashua's bones. Staring at the pile, thinking he should be doing something else, but nothing came to mind. Toca reached down and took up the knives and anklet, then turned, telling Shana, "Let's go."

"Wait, we can't leave without praying."

"Again? Always praying to your God." For the first time, Toca stated it aloud.

"Yes, I do and we'll never stop," she replied, giving him a disgruntled look, then closed her eyes, saying, "Heavenly Father, we don't know what happened here and we don't know why you allowed us to find this man but you have your reasons. Please protect us and help us to stay focused on looking for you in all things around us and the things you do with us. Help Toca to see you clearer and understand you more every day as we journey…" Hesitating, she took Toca's free hand, then said slowly, squeezing it. "Together for the rest of our lives, amen."

"Amen," Toca replied. Then he thought to himself, *Why would I say that? I don't even know what it means.*

They crawled outside just in time as the flame went out on the stick and the flames from the firepit took over lighting their way. Toca put the dead Nashua's knife and anklet in his pack then sat next to the fire, stabbing the long knife in the ground, then went back to working the meat. His mind started to wander deep in thought, staring at the fire.

"Toca, I'm not feeling good again. Maybe I can have some more medicine?"

He didn't respond.

"Toca, did you hear me?" she said calmly with no answer. "Toca!" she sharply stated this time.

Her louder voice jerked him back to the moment. "What?"

"I'm hurting."

Emotionless, he replied, "I'll get you more of the flower. Are you hungry? Do you need more meat?"

"I am hungry and do you still have water in the bamboo cup?"

"Yes, sit down and get comfortable." Motioning her to lean against the rock wall, he continued, "I'll get everything for you."

He was in a dreary mood and it saturated their enclosure. Shana, sensing the cold atmosphere and, being a woman, needed to talk it out, asked, "Are you doing all right?"

"Yes, why?"

"So many things happened yesterday and today, I'm getting worried about you."

"I'm strong, don't worry about me," he stated confidently.

"I know you're strong but everyone gets overwhelmed with things sometimes."

"What do you mean?"

"When too much or too many things come at you at one time, it's hard to control it all or understand them like these mosquitoes," Shana said as she swatted at the air, trying to get rid of the bugs swarming the area.

"Mmm...," he grunted. "I understand, my body is strong." He clenched a fist and slowly beat his chest once. "But you're right, there are many moments running in my head"—holding his hands up to each side of his head and moved them in a circular motion—"many things are happening and I'm getting confused."

"Talk to me about them."

Toca handed her a small rolled ball of flower petals to put under her tongue then several strands of roots to eat. Picking up the bamboo cup of water, he gave it to her, along with a slice of dried meat, then sat back down next to the fire.

After gathering his thoughts, he said, "Your God is always talking in my head, at least, I think it's your God from what you tell me and I don't understand what he means." Pausing, he then pointed back and forth between them and continued, "Then you and I...we feel deep inside for each other, it's new to me. I didn't expect this to happen on my Katata Ado." Moving his hand, pointing toward the cave entrance, he said, "And then all the things in there with the dead Nashua."

Toca took another moment to think then finished. "We are only about two, maybe three days from the hidden valley, but with you hurt, it will take longer and the thirteenth full moon is going to shine in the night's sky soon." He buried his face into his hands.

Wanting to ease his pain and clear his head, she spoke as her mother would speak to her. "It's normal to be confused and overwhelmed when many things are happening, especially when we are young."

"I am not young, I am a man, you called me that today," he quickly responded back.

"You are a man, Toca, a young man. But thaath doessn't..." She paused, trying to work her mouth freely as the roots were starting to take effect. "That doessn't meeen you caann hhanndle it allll. Thiss iss wwwhy I praaay allll thaa tiimme fffoorr Goddd'ss helpp." Shana's muscles were relaxing so much she was falling asleep.

Toca looked at her swaying head and body, as she tried her best to stay sitting up, then told her, "You need to sleep now, you'll feel better in the morning." He laid her down flat on the ground and put her pack under her head. Bending over, Toca kissed her forehead and she sluggishly opened her eyes, trying to give him a smile of thanks.

Shuffling back to the fire, he put more sticks on it to light up the area and to help finish another batch of meat that needed to be dried. Looking up to the sky, checking for rain, all he saw this night were bright tiny dots peering through the treetops high above.

Standing, he made his way through the thick vegetation that camouflaged their home. Stepping into the small clearing where the back end of the anaconda stretched out, Toca closed his eyes and let his senses take over in the darkness. Quieting his mind, he listened for anything that would make a sound but nothing responded. He breathed deeply, separating out the smell of the snake and smoke that invaded the air but nothing out of the ordinary passed through his nostrils, alerting him of danger. All was well, calming his mind and body.

As the night went on, sitting back against the rock wall next to the fire, Toca was hypnotized from watching the flames dancing freely in the pit. Their movements were smooth and the warmth was so soothing that he couldn't resist closing his eyes, drifting peacefully into emptiness.

Asleep in the dark emptiness of his mind, he heard someone but he couldn't make out what they were saying. Faintly in the distance, he started to see a glimpse of light flickering through the trees in the forest. Even though it was far away, shadows were starting to dance and he began to hear more people. The closer he was getting to the light, the more Toca realized he was stepping upward like climbing a mountain. Peering down with each step, he could see his feet were on smooth cutout rocks stacked on top of each other, stairstepping their way higher and higher. The higher he went, the clearer the voices became and brighter was the light. Instantly with the next step, Toca was at the top of what he was climbing.

Looking around, there were many people, with their backs to him, gathered in a circle, dancing and chanting around something next to the fire. They were wearing large headdresses, brightly colored with feathers and strange dark markings covered their bodies. The words they were chanting, he didn't understand. Soon they stopped dancing and everyone went silent as a beat of a deep drum thumped three times. Someone on the other side of the circle, which he couldn't fully see except for a hand raising with something in it, quickly disappeared back into the center of the crowd.

A bloodcurdling scream shot out from the middle of the people, making him flinch back and cringe. Then it turned to a cry for help, calling his name, "Tocaaa!"

"No!" Toca yelled back, recognizing the voice as he ran to him. Getting to the crowd of people, he pushed his way through, only to see Chief Acuta lying on a large flat rock, looking at him, holding his hand out in his direction. The chief's chest was cut open and blood was everywhere. Looking into his face, Toca watched as he pushed out his last words. "Black Ghost, bring me the songbird before it's too late!"

Laughter echoed all around Toca as the crowd began to dance, and chanting again, except for the one standing straight across Chief Acuta's body and the slab of rock. He looked up and gasped for air, shocked to see Jucawa. He was standing large and tall with eyes glowing wide and his mouth open, baring sharp animal-like teeth, hissing as the light from the fire reflected off his face. Jucawa's hand was raised high, holding the heart of Chief Acuta with blood dripping and draining down his arm.

Then screeching out words to Toca, Jucawa said, "Now the Nashua are dead and I rule the valley! Burn the old one's body so all memory of him is gone!" Then he began laughing in a devious and hateful tone and said, "He's gone, now we will make a new tribe, a powerful tribe!" Jucawa lifted his head back, peering into to the sky as he held Chief Acuta's heart high, boastfully laughing as cheering came from all that was around the area

"No, Jucawa, no!" Toca screamed as the others behind him grabbed ahold of his body, drawing him back into the crowd. He watched as they threw Chief Acuta's body into the fire and it began to smoke. The smoke got so thick, he started choking as it billowed into his face and his eyes were blinded.

Toca started coughing uncontrollably. Jerking his head back up for air, he hit something hard with his head.

He opened his eyes, blinking and glancing around to see where he was, and realized he had been dreaming and was sitting at the same spot he fell asleep, drying meat. The fire in front of him was smoldering and the smoke was drifting directly in his face. That's when it woke him up, leaning back for air, hitting his head on the rock wall. Toca stood, taking a couple of steps away, coughing and started deeply inhaling fresh air.

Exhaling several times, Toca's body was clear but definitely not in his mind. He was sick to his stomach from the nightmare. Just the thought of everything about it was wrong. Wanting to forget it, he said to himself, *We need to leave this place of death.*

Understanding he was only dreaming didn't help with feeling horrible inside.

He asked himself, *What did this mean? Why would I think such bad thoughts*? Bending down, Toca picked up the bamboo cup of water and sipped down one swallow.

It was getting light and the birds were beginning to sing.

After gathering the dried meat, Toca neatly filled his hammock pack with as much meat as it would carry. Then gently, he took Shana's from under her head, only putting in the lightweight items they had with them and included the new knife and anklet they took from the skeleton. This still left room for the thin strip of snakeskin, more yellow flowers, and the bamboo cups.

This is going to be heavy, he thought, putting his pack on. Then carrying Shana's in one hand, grasping the long knife in the other, Toca decide to get through the thick wall of bushes to give her a good start in the open.

Before completely stepping out, Toca waited and let his eyes, ears, and nose work for a moment. In the far distance, he heard monkeys beginning their day as many birds were singing, waking the forest up so all would know the sun's fresh light is coming their way. *Good*, he thought, *the sounds of peace.*

Then the picture came to his mind of Chief Acuta telling him he needs to bring him the songbird. *Why does the chief need a songbird? He's told me that twice now, the first time was at my Katata ceremony*? Trying his best not to relive the nightmare, he shook his head then stepped out, setting down the packs next to the long thin strip of drying snakeskin. Rolling it up tight, he put it in Shana's pack.

"Toca, where are you…Toca?" A trembling loud voice broke out.

"Shana, I'm in the clearing on the other side of the bushes, I'll be right there." He weaseled through to the other side of the wall of vegetation as she spoke up again. "You scared me?"

"What did I do?"

"I woke up, you and all our things were gone. For a moment, I thought you left me?"

Kneeling next to her, he wrapped his arms around her, knowing this is what comforts her the most, saying, "Shana…" Then slightly leaning back so he could see her face, he smiled, saying, "I will never leave you. My heart feels more for you every day we're together. You have become a part of me."

As she looked into his eyes, tears welled up in hers. He didn't know if it was the relief he hadn't left her, the words he just said, or maybe she was in more pain. Then he asked, "Why are you crying?"

"I don't know why, I'm just happy and filled with joy."

Toca frowned, confused, and said, "You cry about everything. Yesterday you were crying because you were tired and upset. Now you're crying because you're happy?"

"I'm a woman, we get emotional," she said, smiling, drawing him back into her, hugging him.

He whispered in her ear, "Maybe I'll figure you out one of these days. But right now, we need to go. The sun has woken the forest and it's starting to smell bad in here." Letting go of her, he pinched his nose.

Toca helped Shana slowly stand, and when she rose up, her necklace swung out from inside her shirt. The pendent caught his eye and he bobbed his head back, thinking to himself, *That's always been an odd-looking talisman.*

Shana stepped to the side, out of sight of Toca, to relieve herself as he turned, picking up a couple pieces of the remaining dried meat to eat for breakfast, then went back to the packs.

When Shana slowly appeared through the wall of foliage, she said, holding her rib cage area, "My side really hurts, but if I don't breathe deep and lift my arm, keeping it close to my side, I think I'll be okay."

"Can you wait a while before I give you more medicine? I need to find more yatowa flower and get more tunga mud from the river."

"I think so, let's go and see how it is." Nodding in agreement, Toca put her lightweight pack over her good shoulder then put his on. He handed her a strip of meat then took a big bite of his. Taking up the long knife, they headed out slowly in the direction where they first encountered the snake. He wanted to find his knife he lost when he hit the tree with his body from the anaconda throwing him.

Slowly getting into the area where the attack was, he recreated the battle not only in his mind but did hand and body motions as well. Looking for the exact spot he jumped on the anaconda then tried to pretend the snake biting him and throwing him off.

Confused with what he was doing, Shana asked, "Did you eat some of the flower root?" Trying not to laugh, she held her side.

"No."

"Then what are you doing, jerking around like that, walking backward with your arms swimming in the air?"

"I'm going through the fight with the snake in my mind," he answered, pointing. "Over there is where I jumped on it next to you and stabbed it. Then he threw me into the air over here where I hit this tree up about that high." He was now pointing up a little higher than his head.

"How did it throw you?"

Motioning with his arms, he said, "It grabbed me all the way across the center of my body back and front in its mouth, bit down, and tossed me in the air to here."

"You were in its mouth?"

"Yes, didn't you see me? I was right next to you."

"I was being crushed to death, Toca, I couldn't see anything," she said with a slight giggle.

"What are you laughing at?"

"Do you hear yourself? A giant anoocona?"

"Anaconda," he said, correcting her.

"A giant anaconda, I had no idea a snake could grow so big"—spreading her arms wide then twitched with pain—"then sneak in and attack me. And you, you are like a…like an ant to a frog jumping on its back. Stabbing that big thing with your small knife. It must have felt like a little splinter to it. Then it takes you into its mouth and throws you a tree-length away and you don't find that funny. It's something that only a person would dream about or have nightmares?"

"No, Shana, I don't see anything funny about it," he said firmly without hesitation. "This is life here." Toca motioned around the forest. "Any moment, anything can and will kill you in the forest. I don't know what your forest or land is like, but here, everything eats you. The animals, fish, bugs, water, and ground, all things eat you in our forest. You should have been eaten many times by now." He lifted a hand, counting the number. "The first, giant caiman, more caiman downriver, poisonous frogs I stopped you from touching, all the scorpions, centipedes, poisonous spiders, and snakes that I killed or stopped from getting to you because of the juja oil. Then this…the most powerful beast in the forest, the black-and-green anaconda, what's next, Shana…"He paused, staring with a blank face. "We don't know. But we must always be ready to kill or die, do you understand?"

"Yes, I understand," she replied, rolling her eyes slightly irritated from his speech she's heard many times during their journey, then asked, "But how did I get away from the snake?"

"I jumped back on it and stabbed it with a stick, and when it came to bite me again, I stabbed it deep in its mouth with another stick in my other hand. When I did that, it screamed and let go of you, thrashing as it went away."

"Wow! This is an amazing story…you are amazing, Toca. You aren't scared of anything. You are like the warriors or hunters of my people many years ago. They would fight and kill anything to—"

He jumped in, finishing her sentence for her. "To protect their people and live?"

"Yes…Yes, that's exactly right."

"I would have never stopped fighting the snake until you were safe or it killed me. And yes, I am an ant to a frog, a man-ant!" he said proudly, commenting on her frog-ant comparison.

Now she was really about to burst out in laughter but held back, asking, "A man-ant, what's that?"

"Have you ever watched ants? They have great strength and are not scared of anything!" he said with enthusiasm while puffing his body up and out. "Ants are very strong, they can carry in their jaws great weight, and when they fight, it's fierce and don't stop until they have killed what they're after. Also they don't stop fighting if they're hurt. You can cut their heads off and they will still bite you."

She slowly replied with sarcasm, "*So*…do you want to change your name to Man-Ant instead of Black Ghost?"

Staring at her twitching wrinkled smile, he finally saw what she wanted to laugh at. "I'll stay with Black Ghost, ants are irritating and we can easily crush them." He gave her an approving smile so she could laugh aloud.

She giggled as much as her side would let her and said, "Oh, Toca, you have many talents and being funny is one of them."

A little embarrassed, he said, "Okay, enough of this, we need to find my knife, let's look around this area." In a circular motion, he gestured near the tree with his hand.

After a while, he finally found it inside a bush a short way from the tree. "This is a good find, I feel whole again." He said, putting the long knife in Shana's pack where she could reach it with her good side, then slid his own knife in its sheath on his forearm. "Now let's find some medicine and get to the river for the mud."

Finding several full clumps of flowers, enough to last several days, he only gave her a few petals for under her tongue to stop the pain. He decided to hold off her eating some roots to see if she would do all right, not relaxing her muscles.

Stretching out the plants so its roots didn't touch the flower petals, Toca rolled them up in a large leaf from a bush, and carefully packed it in Shana's hammock pack.

Shortly when they got to the river, Toca said, "Shana, you need to wash your body clean of the dried mud I put on you yesterday."

"What about you?" She wrinkled up her nose. "You smell like a dead snake and smoke and your shadowing from yesterday is a big mess." He looked down, realizing she was right, and answered back, smiling, "Looks like when the little children of our tribe pretend to shadow like their fathers and smear mud all over themselves."

They both took off their packs and, at the water's edge, went through their routine safety check for predators hiding and waiting for its next meal. Convinced it was all right, Toca helped Shana into a pool, up to their shoulders, in slow-moving water so she didn't have to fight the current. After a few moments of enjoying a refreshing soak in the cool water, they both began to rub their bodies, face, and hair to clean off the dirt.

"How are you feeling?" Toca asked.

"The flower is starting to work but I'm still very sore."

"Good—*aaahh*!" Toca bellowed out in agony. "What was—yaaa!" He yelled out, looking down in the water, seeing fresh blood floating to the surface as he shoved his hand hard into the water to stop what was attacking him. "Get out of the water, someth—aaa!" shrieking in pain, he yelled to Shana, grabbing her arm, quickly getting them on shore.

"Aaw…not so hard, Toca, my side." Now she expressed her pain.

Looking down Toca's body, it was dripping blood in several areas, she asked, "What happened, what attacked you?"

He looked closer, easily identifying what bit him, then wondering why, bent his head over closer, examining his midsection then spun around, trying to see his front and back. Realizing the answer to the question, he said, "Look at all these small teeth marks around my body." He was twisting around, showing Shana.

"Yes…oh!" It just came to her. "Those are teeth marks from the snake, they're so many of them and in straight rows, look at that." She was amazed, peering close, walking around him, pointing to the pattern of the multitude of miniature puncture wounds which many were faintly beginning to bleed again. "But what attacked you and why didn't we see these holes earlier?"

Thinking it through, Toca said, "It was piranhas, the small ones we catch once in a while with all the teeth?"

Acknowledging him, she nodded her head, seeing the damage those things could do.

"I was probably bleeding slowly from the teeth marks because they're not too deep. During and after the fight, you and I were on the ground and the blood must have picked up dirt, absorbing it, then dried. Later when I shadowed to kill the snake, I didn't think about the dirt already on me. The water washed off the dirt, exposing and loosening the dried blood, attracting the piranhas. They started biting me right at the reopened dotted holes from me rubbing the dirt off, see..." Toca pointed at the small areas of skin and muscle that were shredded by the fish bites that were directly on teeth punctures from the snake. "I guess we won't be swimming anymore today," he said, breaking a smile, attempting to hide the pain.

"We need to stop the bleeding! It's dripping all over," Shana stated, getting excited.

He looked down at the areas the piranhas shredded off him. They were bleeding fairly well down his stomach and back. At first glance, it was alarming but the spirit of being a man slowly came out as he stood straight up, pulling his shoulders back, saying, "I'll be all right, it's only a few wounds I can fix." Inside he wanted to cringe in pain but he wasn't about to let Shana see that.

Taking out the long knife from her pack, he handed it to her and said as he unrolled the large leaf, pulling off a few petals from one of the flowers, "Sit down against this tree and rest, I need to look for a different flower to stop the bleeding and heal these open gashes. I might be gone a little while because it's hard to find."

Without waiting for a response, he quickly rolled up the petals then put the ball under his tongue and headed into the forest.

It did take a while to find a specific batch of trees, then looking up high, Toca spotted what he was looking for. Not only was this flower hard to find but very difficult to get to. It's part of the tree itself which grows out at the ends of the younger branches near the top of the trees.

After the long climb, it took some time to cut off several branches that had blooming flowers at the ends, then he said to himself, "I should have brought the long knife and gave her my knife, I could have chopped these off quickly with it."

Hearing a large eagle screeching high above, Toca peered up through tree limbs, trying to get a look at it. Moving himself higher to the top of the canopy, he was able to poke his head out into the open sky and see the magnificent giant bird soaring effortlessly as it peered down at him. In awe of the moment, it was very rare to be so high off the ground to where he felt he was part of the blue sky itself.

It filled him with fresh air, rejuvenating his mind as the pure unfiltered sunlight energized his body. Not expecting this situation and the effect of its sensation, he realized it was something he desperately needed. Clearing his mind while settling his spirit, everything that seemed overwhelming, confusing, and important clouding up his thoughts suddenly appeared small and insignificant.

Looking down on the canopy of trees, as far as he could see, gave the illusion the ground was an endless flow of green waves. Living on the ground, hidden by the towering trees, and crowded in by all the thick vegetation with a brown forest floor at his feet, this view instantly gave Toca a picture of a larger greater world. His view was endless as his ears tuned into the powerful and invisible flow of air that orchestrated through the treetops, rustling their leaves as they slowly swayed back and forth.

The sun was so bright he had to squint as its warmth permeated everything, pulling moisture from the ground and all living things to rise, forming billowing clouds, adding color as they create a symphony of rolling shapes. All for the grandeur of the openness that is the world above where only eagles can go.

The time of inspiration was short-lived as Toca was feeling pain again which was making him weaker as blood still slowly oozed from his body. He closed his eyes, inhaling deeply, attempting to absorb the moment and take it with him. Then he opened them, looking up for the eagle to thank it for calling him to the top of the world. Not seeing the smooth gliding bird anywhere, he turned his gaze downward and made his way back to where he lived on the ground, then made quick time getting back to Shana as he ran.

He smoothly came in, finding her asleep. Not wanting to frighten her, he stood a couple of steps away and softly said her name. She opened her eyes, looking up at him, and asked. "Are you okay, did you find what you needed?" Her eyes left his and looked down his body, seeing that it was covered with fresh and dried blood even down his legs.

Before he could respond, she blurted out, "You're still bleeding, it's all over you!"

"I'm going to be okay. I know you are hurting but I need your help with this."

"Of course, what is it?"

"Since I've got blood on me and I'm still bleeding, I need you to go back into the river where we were and grab a couple handfuls of the long leafy strands of red moss that grows around the rocks at the bottom."

She didn't move and had a blank look on her face.

"Shana?" He tried to get her attention.

She slowly responded, "Are you crazy?"

"Crazy?"

"Yes, crazy. Out of your mind. You want me to go back into the river where those fish are?" she said, stunned by his request.

"Yes, I need the moss for the holes in my skin. The piranhas won't hurt you, they only attack when they smell blood. That's why they attacked me and not you."

Relaxing her body, settling her emotions, she thought about it and said, "That makes sense, but still, look what those things did to you?"

"This, this is nothing," he said, looking back down at the small open areas missing skin and pieces of shredded muscle dangling out. "You should see what the bite of the wadgada fish can do. Its mouth is big, full of long sharp teeth that can take your arm off with one bite." He finished his comment, looking back to Shana, impressing her with this new information.

Sitting there with her mouth agape, shocked, and without moving her lips, she asked, "There are fish in there like that?"

Excitedly Toca said, "Yes, and many, many more. These rivers are full of different fish and many other things we've never seen before!"

It slowly got there in his brain she wasn't excited like he was but completely frightened again.

She spoke up slowly, erupting, "This whole journey on these rivers we've been in a little canoe and there are fish like that?" Growing in anger, pointing to the river, she kept going, "Why didn't you tell me? Why did you have me get in there all the time to cool off and bathe?"

"I did tell you. I've always said we need to be aware all the time and everything wants to kill you. I just said that earlier when we were looking for my knife," he reminded her defensively as he now pointed in the direction where they came from.

"You never said anything about fish with big teeth in the water biting your arms off or being able to kill you! Even when you taught me how to fish, you should have said something!"

"Why, I taught you how to fish for the ones we like to eat."

"That's not the point!"

"I don't understand why you are so upset, scared, and afraid?"

"Because I would have paid more attention or never got into the water if it's this dangerous!"

"Why wouldn't you have gone into the water? Nothing ever happened to you, even when I killed the giant caiman, you didn't get hurt. You enjoy being in the water, besides it's part of the forest and we need it to live." Toca said, confused why she was being this way.

But this wasn't new, he thought to himself. *She was always fearful and frightened of most anything.*

Shana lashed back. "Because I knew about the dangerous animals or fish you told me about and that I could see. Not the dangerous ones I couldn't see or didn't know about! We need to see and know what's going on in our lives to be safe."

With a confused and disturbed look on his face, Toca hesitated before replying, then questioned her, "Isn't every day of our life journey full of dangers? We will never always know what's in or behind the trees in the forest or what's in the rivers. If we worry or are afraid of what might happen to us, how can we ever walk forward on land or paddle a canoe on water? We would never get anywhere. That's *not living, that's dying*. Being afraid and hiding does *nothing* for us!"

He paused without a reply from her, and in the back of his mind, what he just said sounded so familiar. Quickly thinking about his own people, they have been hiding in the hidden valley for generations yet they were dying. And from what the chief told him, his statement he said to her was true.

Shaking the dreadful thought away, he continued, "Shana, you have talked with your God more times than I can count. You constantly ask it to help and protect you; even thank it for protecting you. But that makes no sense if you are so afraid in your daily journey through life. Why talk to your God or even have one if you don't *trust* it?

"To me, Shana, your God must be *weak* and not care for you for you to be so afraid of everything. To me, that's a bad god, even if it doesn't want to cut your heart out. I don't see how a God like that inspires you and gives you purpose. That's not a god Chief Acuta wanted me to bring back to save our people."

Toca stopped talking, knowing he said enough or maybe too much. But what was said needed to come out, even if it did hurt her. He was tired of her being fearful all the time like a young child and was finished holding back what he thought about her God.

The hollow disappointment began to swell within him again, similar to the other day when they got to this area and the dark fog began to cloud his mind.

Without saying anything else, Toca turned and walked a little ways downriver and cautiously looked for danger; not finding anything, he kneeled at its edge and began splashing water up onto his body, washing the blood off, staying out of the water.

Shana was speechless as his words struck her hard, knowing he was right. Even though God had refreshed her mind of the purpose of being here with Toca, she was still feeling lost and inadequate in who she was as for most of the journey. The truth had come out of her own mouth, her words and actions completely told her side of the story. She believed in God but, truly in her heart, did she trust him? Shana was getting confused and unsure about herself and her relationship with God.

Then an unfamiliar voice began to slither into her mind, consuming her in a way she never felt before, causing her stomach to begin to churn into a knot as it said, *Do you really believe this God of yours really cares for you? If he is a good God, why would he let all the bad things happen to you like your mother and father dying. And now, you're badly hurt, then you've just lost the trust of the only friend you have? When are you going to grow up and stop trying to hold this invisible hand your father told you to never let go of? It didn't do him any good.*

Sitting there, Shana could barely control her body; she wanted to throw up as she began to squirm and her head became dizzy. She was being consumed with something foreign, then instantly, as though coming to her rescue, a cool breeze came off the river, causing her to close her eyes as its peace washed through her, calming her down. Suddenly she found herself in a dreamlike state, visioning herself with her father when he was lying down in the tent and just had given her life instructions about her relationship with God. In her mind, she felt John's hand up against her face, gently stroking her cheek as they shared a loving moment between a father and daughter. Shana deeply inhaled, soaking in the moment of warm serenity, wanting it to last forever.

My hands are always open to you, Shana, hold on tight, I am always with you, my child. A strong, calm, and gentle voice took Shana by surprise as she opened her eyes, looking side to side for who was talking to her, only to find her hand was up to her cheek as if she was really holding the hand of her father.

The cleansing peace settled her down as she knew God showed up at the perfect time, regaining his reign in her. The refreshing picture of her father caused her to reflect on him and things he would do and say all the time. *One who follows Jesus must live by faith, trusting him no matter what we see or do not see. What we understand or not understand, believing no matter what is in front of us in our life journey that everything will work for the good because he loves his children so much. And his will and purpose for us is greater and more wonderful than we can imagine.*

Her father's last words were echoing louder than ever. *Follow in the footsteps of Jesus then you will never have anything to be afraid of.*

Through all this mental and spiritual commotion, she hadn't moved from sitting against the tree. Her eyes found Toca down the river, cleaning himself from all the blood and now was walking back up. To her surprise, being fearless and showing confidence, he walked directly into the river where they were before, up to his chest, and went underwater for a few moments, coming up with both hands full of the long wide strips of red leafy moss.

Without speaking to each other, Toca dropped the moss next to Shana where he had left the large blossoms of the tree. Then he bent down, taking out one of the bamboo cups from her pack and retrieved oily mud from under a nearby tunga tree.

Once back to Shana, there was an awkward silence between them as he gently coated her side with the fresh mud. Not mad at each other but it was a confusing and a troubling moment for them both.

Having her eyes opened about her true shallow and young walk with God was good and bad at the same time, but losing the respect and trust of Toca was terrible. Looking at his face, she could tell her faith in God—to him—was weak and any credibility about God Toca had faded and may no longer exist.

Toca, on the other hand, struggled that he didn't do a better job teaching her the ways of the Nashua. Living with confidence, not being afraid of the mysterious things everywhere. But he too was stressed, bringing this invisible God of Shana's to Chief Acuta as well as regretting he didn't look harder for another god.

How was he to believe in her God and what would Chief Acuta say about it? He had never seen it but maybe heard it or was it just his own mind talking to him. But still, how could or why would he want to believe in Shana's God if she herself didn't trust it?

The deadly dark spiritual fog had been waiting patiently to move in on the old children throughout their journey to destroy and blind them of their purpose. Not until the snake attack, it had no reason to interfere because its enemy, the true light of this world, had not spoken until then. Now the forces of dark and light were in full battle within the struggles of the old children.

Stealthily, it was reaching out with tentacles of defeat, sadness, self-pity, and regret. Whispering with power of a taunting smooth voice, telling them both differently and separately but at the same time, *You have failed in bringing a god to the Nashua people. Foolish child, you are not worthy of the responsibility that was given to you for a dying people.*

CHAPTER 17

Toca finished putting mud on Shana's side as she sat up against the tree and began working on his own medicine. Taking the tree flowers, he shredded them whole, putting all the pieces in the empty bamboo cup. Adding a little water, he stirred and crushed them up, turning them into a grayish paste with an end of a stick. Then taking the wet long strips of the broad leafy red moss, he gently stretched them out flat.

With portions of the grayish paste, he smeared it thick on each open wound, flinching every time as the medicine stung. Kneeling next to Shana, he had her help with the one on his back he couldn't reach. After applying the pasty medicine, he wrapped the wide red moss strips over the pasted areas and around, wrapping his body.

Shana asked, "What does the red moss do?"

Standing up, Toca answered, "It's going to get sticky soon, then as it dries, it shrinks, tightening itself to my skin, staying on for a very long time, keeping the medicine in place where the piranhas bit me."

Again she was astonished with his knowledge at his age of everything in the forest and complimented him. "You continue to surprise me with what you know, Toca," she said, smiling to bring warmth to a cold atmosphere between them.

He smiled back somewhat, then bent over with his hand out to help her up and said, "We must go, we can still make it a little ways upriver today."

Shaking her head sideways, not taking his hand, she replied, "No, Toca, I'm not going any farther right now."

Keeping his hand out, he said, "Come on, Shana, I know you're hurting. So am I. But we must push ourselves."

She looked at him with a face of sorrow but with an encouraging smile. "No…I am not going any further with you…you are going *alone*."

"What?"

"I made this decision when you went into the forest looking for your medicine. I have slowed you down and I could not live with myself or even live with you knowing it was my fault you never became chief."

"Don't talk like that, we'll make it!"

"No, we won't and you know it. It has to be done this way." Her chin quivered as her eyes began to tear up. "I will stay here and you… you run like you have never ran before, Toca, and get to Chief Acuta before it's too late."

Toca was standing, dazed at what she was telling him to do without her. She slowly and painfully stood by herself, a breath away from his face, with tears flowing down her cheeks. "Toca, the man that has my heart." She lifted his hand to her chest and placed hers to his. "I will be in here with you the whole way, thinking, dreaming, and praying for you with every breath I take that we are apart."

He grabbed her hand, pulling it down between them and stated, "I will not leave you alone, Shana. I must protect you!" Still shocked at the thought of leaving her by herself, it never crossed his mind.

"But not right now, Toca, you have a responsibility first to your people." Shana worked her hand loose from his grasp, laying it back on his chest. "Chief Acuta gave you the burden to finish the Ado or *Jucawa* will be chief," she said, emphasizing Jucawa to get him motivated to leave. She looked down at her side hip strap where she had something wedged next to her skin. Pulling it out, she handed it to him, saying, "When you show him this shell from the endless water, you will save your people from Jucawa and what he would do to them." She had gotten the shell out of his bag when he was getting his medicine.

Thinking about what she was saying as he looked at the shell in his hand, she told him, "I will be all right, you have taught me more about surviving than you realize. I will be aware at all times," she stated, letting him know she understood what was most important in the forest, then continued, "I will slowly follow the river up, and when you have finished your Katata Ado ceremony, you come back for me."

This was making sense to him, but still, the guardian in him couldn't fully release her or was it his heart? Thinking about her being alone, unprotected, was strong; but looking closer inside, he thought, *I will be alone without her.* He found out at that moment how much he really felt for Shana and how much she was a part of his life, no matter their differences with her having a God or not. It was instantly weakening his insides and hurting his heart.

Now looking into each other's eyes, she added, "I have everything I need—food, medicine, hammock, the long knife, and most of all, God."

Giving her a quick questionable grin to the last word, she spoke before he did. "I have growing up to do, learning more about God and our relationship. I am still an old child on my womanhood journey with him. Just like you, now understanding more and more what Chief Acuta taught you as a small child, now having to use that knowledge to survive." She thought he would understand this explanation which he did, turning the grin into a faint smile.

"But as I do this, you must do the same if you are to bring a good God to your people to save them from the death Chief Acuta told you about, even when you do become chief. God will be here with you too." Patting his chest again, she said, "You have talked to God and you say that he has talked to you too which means God wants to have a relationship with you. But for you to have an everlasting relationship with him, giving you and all the Nashua people purpose to live, you must ask him to come and live in your heart.

"Chief Acuta said to bring back a good God to your people and you are, Toca!" she stated it very confidently. "But it has to start with you, Black Ghost, their future chief. If they are to have any new beginning of knowledge and relationship with God, the God of all things."

She looked away, lowering her hand, saying, dejected, "I would understand if you do not ask God to come into your heart and take him to your people. Because I haven't been a good example for you."

Pausing, then looking back up, she finished, saying with more of a poised and assured expression, "But it was God that knew you were going to look for him and when you were going on your Katata Ado. God knew it a sun season before you did. That's when he told my father to go and journey deep into the Amazon forest and tell the Indians about him. Then with perfect timing, you found us in the middle of nowhere a day before my father died." Shana pointed to herself. "Me being here with you isn't by chance or accident. When someone is looking for God, as Chief Acuta told you to do, God will find a way for us to find him."

This was an amazing and mysterious thought which made complete sense. And at the same time, a larger and broader picture of this God was showing itself for Toca. Similar to the same perspective he saw earlier on top of the tree, looking down at the vast green canopy with the never-ending blue sky above.

He was now definitely visualizing more of a God he thought came to him through the forest when he believed Shana was dead and the forest came alive in a way he never experienced.

Toca had no words; he stood in front of her, listening and thinking.

"Are you understanding what I'm telling you?" she asked.

He hesitated then answered slightly, only nodding his head.

"Good, now you must go." She reached up and slowly stroked his face. His eyes wanted to water up but he held back with a painful cringe. Lifting his hand to hers, holding it close, tilting his head.

Looking into each other's eyes, Shana said, "Don't worry, I will be safe. Because starting right now…I will not fear anything and trust my God with my whole heart to protect me, not you."

He widened his eyes at her statement, as it almost came across as a challenge, but he understood what she meant and what she was doing.

"I will miss you so much these next days," she said as she gingerly removed her hand and hugged him as he softly wrapped his arms around her, not squeezing too hard. They leaned back and kissed each other, standing next to the river, as the sun shone bright with colorful birds singing and darting here and there. Almost in a playful manner, celebrating this fresh innocent union of the two old children, only days away from becoming true young adults.

They separated their lips, holding onto each other, deeply gazing into the eyes of the other.

Toca broke the silence. "Thank you, Shana, for doing this for my people and doing this for me. But I need you to do one more thing." Through the cringing face, trying not to get emotional, he said, "I don't know the medicine for the pain I feel right now in my heart leaving you. But I know you have a gift that helps calm me and gives me peace, taking my mind somewhere else to forget the pain."

Shana attempted to smile brightly with her quivering chin as tears were still flowing. She knew exactly what he wanted and needed, feeling the same pain. They released each other, slowly stepping back as Shana began taking deep breaths, trying to blow out the sadness filling her insides.

He looked around the area, confirming the items she needed, then said, "I must run very fast so I will only take the shell." Tucking it deep inside next to his knife in the sheath on his arm, he told her, "You will need to bring your pack filled with all the items we've brought and found and as much meat as you can carry. I will come back for you as soon as I can."

Then peering upriver, thinking his way to the hidden valley, he was about to give this old female child the key to his protective home. She would be the first other to enter the hidden valley since his ancestors first found it. Hesitating as he looked back at her, he didn't know if Chief Acuta would actually approve; it never crossed his mind before.

"What is it, Toca? What are you waiting for?"

He said directly, "You understand, Shana, you will be the first other to ever enter the hidden valley since my people started living there more sun seasons than I know?"

She thought about it then said, "Yes, I do."

Looking back upriver, he knew this had to be done and gave her these instructions. "The entrance to the hidden valley is the secret that guards it. The river suddenly appears to come out of the cliffside of the mountain. You must get into the river and swim up under the protective overhanging rocks and plants reaching low, almost touching the water. The valley is hidden and protected by high cliff walls, all the way around the outside of its mountains with thick vegetation growing out of it."

With the secret revealed, it was time to leave; he slowly started walking backward, keeping his eyes on his woman, standing in the open next to the river, alone. With each step away, their breathing quickened and hearts began to leap in their chests as anxiety and panic was sweeping through them.

"Sing to me, Shana, sing!" he shouted out to her.

She shook her head awake, blinking rapidly while clearing her throat. Thinking quickly what to sing, nothing came to her mind except for a childhood song and she opened her mouth and did the best she could, being emotional. "Jesus...loves me this I know...for the Bible tells me so..."

Shana kept singing as she watched him fade away into the forest, disappearing as though he was only a vision in her head. Emptiness and loneliness had her full attention. She didn't know exactly how long she stood there, singing over and over, waiting for him to quickly come back running into her arms but it never happened.

*****

Toca was nearing the end of his second day since he left Shana behind. He stayed on the ground, running hard and fast, weaving through the forest plants all the time now. After several times using the trees to swing over obstacles, it became too painful, stretching out his arms from branch to branch, reopening his wounds as small strands of blood streamed down his body.

But the pain and blood were always quickly forgotten as the familiar rhythm of swishing through the thick green life of the Amazon felt wonderful and freeing.

Clouds had come in dark and thick as it began raining earlier in the day, making it harder to run in the mud. The small river had been rising from the rain which got him to think how more difficult it will be to get through the river into the valley through the secret entrance.

Suddenly he found himself up against an impenetrable rocky wall covered thick with vegetation. Bending over heavily, panting, trying to catch his breath, worn out, relieved, and excited at the same time, he said aloud, "I made it." He had pushed himself harder than he ever did before because last night, he worked his way up to the top of a tall tree to see how full the moon truly was. It confirmed he only had one more day to make it until it rose full for the thirteenth time since he left.

Closing his eyes, still bent over from exhaustion as the rain continued, he blew out all the anxiety and worry that had been building, to get back in time. Without thinking, he spoke these words aloud, "Thank you."

Opening his eyes, he became conscious of what he said and asked himself, *Who am I thanking*? Shana came to mind. *Without her telling me to go ahead without her, I wouldn't have made it.* Then a vision of her thanking her God in her prayers for helping them on their journey was seen. Shaking his head to get rid of the thought, he brought his hands up to his face and wiped off the rain and sweat thinking, *What has this unseen God done*? Toca looked around the rain-drenched forest then, with an unexpected burst of frustration, yelled out, "Who are you? Where are you? Show yourself to me and I will believe in you!" He looked in every direction, waiting for the voice to answer but there was no immediate response.

Toca lowered his head, taking in a big sigh, thinking, *It's all been in my head.* Just then, with perfect timing, a bright flash exploded across the sky as spider webs of lightning shot in every direction, followed by a loud *boom* echoing out into the forest.

Toca flinched from the startling scene of clouds illuminating their fierce power. Silence was left behind as he cowardly waited, looking up, moving his eyes back and forth, expecting something else to follow to respond to his aggressive challenge. But nothing else happened as the raindrops kept falling, hitting leaves and the ground splashing back up, miniature shouts of themselves all over the place. In the background was the rush of water flowing from the entrance where he needed to go up.

Looking toward the muddy brown water, hurrying its way out of the valley as though trying to escape from something, Toca began to contemplate how he was going to make his way up through it. The water had risen so high it was touching in spots where the rock ceiling was infested with thick vines, branches, and foliage reaching out and dangling down, bobbing in the fast-moving water.

Do not be afraid, Toca, I am with you. Finally the familiar voice spoke peacefully and calmly, encouraging him again.

Are you? Toca responded back in thought.

I have never left you. Believe in me and you will know and see the Truth.

Wiping his face again, he said out loud, "Shana said I need to ask you in my heart for you to be my God and the God for my people?"

Trust me and I will show you wonders and a relationship you have only dreamed about for you and all the Nashua people.

Physically weak while trying to recuperate, Toca was in a dilemma. Was this truly a god, a good god, a mystical unseen god he was about to show the hidden valley? The place of sanctuary for many, many generations where the knowledge of a god didn't exist. Safely shadowed deep in the forest where a god has never found them. And he, an old child for at least another day, is about to break the only sacred decree of his ancestors by bringing this god to them which Shana said it had to be through his heart.

Not wasting any more time, he had to fulfill Chief Acuta's request and believe Shana truly had a good god for his people, a god that has only whispered to him so far. Closing his eyes, bowing his head like Shana said, "God of Shana, I don't know your name or your shadow image. If it is true that I must ask you to go into my heart to be my God and a God for my people, then I will do this and allow you to live in my heart." Not knowing how to get this God into his heart, the only thing he's seen Shana do that worked was looking into the sky, talking to it as rays of sunlight shone through, touching her and her father.

Having this picture in his head, Toca opened his arms wide, exposing his chest upward, lifting his head to the sky, eyes still closed, he shouted over the noise of the rain and river, "I ask you, God of Shana and her tribe..." He hesitated from the unknown then boldly finished. "Come and live in my heart...*now*!" He stated the final word in anticipation of the possible painful penetrating moment.

Not exactly sure what he was truly expecting, he stood exposed and vulnerable in the pouring rain, naked except for his small waist flaps and manhood wrap underneath as the withering red moss bandage was wrapped around his midsection. Toca thought that maybe his chest would instantly swell up with a hot sensation or even a heaviness of wisdom and power would flood his insides, he didn't know, Shana didn't tell him.

Not feeling anything, he waited a little longer then slowly opened his eyes, thinking maybe his surroundings might have changed. Peering around the area, then at his body, he asked out loud with great expectation, "Are you in my heart?"

There was no response, then he asked, looking around then down at his chest, "Shana's God, are you in there now to help the Nashua live?"

Waiting patiently for the bright peaceful voice to speak to him again, Toca began to get uneasy.

Did you really believe anything was going to happen? The dark harsh fog appeared, gloating as it filtered his thoughts.

Toca's insides were getting twisted up as his anticipation and open invitation to this God was fading, turning again into doubt and frustration.

In a boastful hard tone, the darkness said, *I told you already, there are no good gods except for yourself. Why waste any more time? Go and save your people all by yourself, Black Ghost.*

Toca stood, firming up his body, breathing deep as his teeth began to clench. Regret mixed with anger and self-determination was building inside. He pulled the shell from the endless water out from the sheath on his forearm and stared at it. Then shoving it deeply back into its safe hiding place and, without any more delay, boldly, without caution, went into the torrent of brown water and battled his way up. Toca had to swim fiercely into the current, then underwater, holding his breath for long periods of time while trying to not get trapped and tangled up in the dangling vegetation. After what seemed to be forever, he finally made it through the invisible gate leading into the hidden valley.

Once on the other side of the entrance, Toca desperately hung on to a large limb hanging out over the water from the shore and struggled to pull himself up and out, collapsing on land. He had strained himself running the past two days and eating very little, then this fight up the flooded river completely depleted him. Trying to stay awake, his body went lifeless as his eyes slowly closed, surrendering to sleep.

Later after the sun disappeared above the dark clouds, night settled and the rain stopped. Darkness filled the valley as a thick humid fog rose from the drenched ground.

Toca gasped, jerking his head up, looking around, trying to focus and remember where he was. It took a few moments because it was so dark, he kept thinking his eyes were closed or he was blind. With the sound of the river and normal night echoes of frogs and bugs singing their mating calls, it was coming to him. "I'm back home in the valley." He sighed with relief.

Knowing every part of his home, he tried to figure out where he was from the village. Sitting up, his mind cleared from sleeping deeply as his eyes finally were able to faintly adjust to the night and was able to see slight patterns of trees and low-growing plants. Slowly getting up, he rearranged his waist wrap and manhood cover which had slid a little to the side and checked on his knife and shell still firmly in the sheath on his arm. Bending over, he grabbed a handful of mud filled with debris and shadowed his body.

Knowing the direction of the village from where he was at, Toca began to slowly work his way through the dense dark forest. The little rest he got rejuvenated him as the excitement built with every step for this long-awaited moment he envisioned over and over in his head. It took a good part of the night after letting his senses take control to guide him slowly and safely to his final destination at the center of the large valley.

Quietly squatting down, shadowed behind a bush just outside the village, Toca peered through the misty night air at the faded shapes of all the huts spread out in the open clearing. It was very difficult to see anything and he wished the heavy clouds were gone, blocking the light of the stars and moon.

It didn't seem to have the same life he remembered, but it was dark, late into the night, and everyone was asleep. He thought of Chief Acuta sleeping and how excited he would be when he wakes up and goes to the tribal hut, only to find an anklet waiting from him on the ceremony mat, letting him know the Black Ghost had returned. Then he saw his mother's face in his mind, smiling, filled with joy from hearing her old child returned as a man.

Slowly weaving his head side to side, he tried to focus in on the tribal hut. Spotting it, Toca decided to go around the village in the cover of the forest and enter the hut slowly from behind. But before he took a step away from his shadowed spot, a sensation came across him as though someone or something was looking at him. Observing every detail in the darkness, he couldn't see anything to confirm he was being watched so he cautiously moved forward.

Once there, finally touching the back of the hut, all the pressure that had been heavy on him, since he left here thirteen moons ago, seemed to have vanished. He slowly took his knife out of the sheath, leaving the shell in, and bent over, cutting his anklet off. Putting the knife back, he let his senses reach out, but surprisingly, nothing came back except black empty silence with a stale musty odor. He hesitated to move forward because it didn't feel right so he waited for a few more moments. No other warning came to him, so cautiously, he slithered along the wall as he went around to the entrance, peering up into the dark room. Then swiftly and silently as a black ghost, he went in, feeling for the mat and softly laid his anklet down in the center of it. In a blink of an eye, he was gone.

Toca left the village stepping as his spirit image would, proudly without a trace, vanishing through the dense wet forest. He decided to go a far distance away from the village where the mountains start towering upward around the valley. There was a particular spot Toca wanted to go that was very rocky and had hot steamy water streaming out of the mountain, pooling up in different areas. His people used this special water for rejuvenation and healing—both he desperately needed.

He knew he was getting close as the air was beginning to have the taste and smell of sulfur and other minerals that were in the hot water. Still having a good part of the night to go, he decided to feel around for a good-size tree trunk, go up it, and lay his tired sore body across a couple fat limbs. Once up and secure to where he wouldn't accidently fall out, he laid his head down and was quickly asleep.

*****

The sun was out but couldn't be seen, still hiding behind a thick blanket of clouds, holding on to its water. Only the sun's glow was being released from the sky, letting everything alive know it had a new beginning.

Toca hadn't moved since he fell asleep. As usual, the beautiful birds of the Amazon were fluttering around, singing to everything that would listen. As Toca lay there, motionless, still shadowed with stripes of dark dry mud from last night, one of the smaller birds landed in one of his open hands that was stretched out. The gentle touch of the bird's small talons on his skin was just enough to wake his mind but not his body. It was almost like a dream, not frightening him but gave a sensation of being tickled in the palm of his hand. The bird twitched around and began chirping its song from the tree branch it thought it was on. The singing was close enough to Toca's sensitive ears it brought him from what he believed to be a dream, realizing it was actually happening. He didn't open his eyes or move, not wanting to scare the bird; then as fast as a strike of a snake, he collapsed his fingers, caging the colorful feathered creature.

"Got you!" Toca said as he straightened up in the tree. He peered between his fingers at the bird, telling it, "You're going to Chief Acuta. I almost forgot to bring him a songbird. Your timing was perfect for me to bring you tonight." He thought about what he said, hearing the words, *timing was perfect*, the same words Shana used to explain her God. Not thinking much of it but the idea of her God possibly doing this did give this God some merit.

With the bird in his hand, he was trying to figure out how he was going to keep the little one, for all he had on him was his waist flaps. With his other hand, he untied it, taking it off and sat on one of the flaps. Quickly and hard, he pulled on the strap itself breaking the thin strips of sinew that weaved their way through the edges of the flaps without damaging the rest of the waist wrap or main strap. Laying out the monkey skin flat on his lap, he brought the bird close to his mouth and quickly blew into its face, momentarily paralyzing it by sucking the breath out of it. He then laid his hand out on the flap, rolling the bird up gently to hold it but still be able to breathe.

Up in the tree, he sat for a while with no pressure to journey any longer, just taking in the moment. He was back home from his long Katata Ado, reminiscing over the incredible things he did. Satisfied his Ado was a great one with exciting and respectable stories for his people, his mind wandered to the person he had become. Realizing the Katata Ado truly did change his life. Not only was he physically a lot taller and much stronger but mentally and emotionally had grown up and was a wiser person. With experience and knowledge gained from all that he has gone through, he told himself, *Chief Acuta was right, the Ado teaches one to be a great leader, to be chief of the Nashua.*

Then out of nowhere, Shana's face appeared in his head. Except for the first two moons passing on his journey, he has spent the rest of his moons traveling with this other. Protecting her and learning about new things and about faraway lands beyond the endless water. Thinking of her, he gave a slight internal laugh as he gazed through the trees around him. He did learn from her that he understands females less now than ever before. Every day and night he was with her, it seemed he would get more confused the longer they were together. She was up and down with her emotions; the ups were higher than the treetops then fell lower than the ground they walk on, then back up again.

He leaned back against the tree with the bird in his hand, looking down at it as it looked back, rapidly blinking its small black eyes while moving its head side to side. Watching this innocent, soft, gentle bird, his heart started to reflect deeper on how he felt about Shana. Even though this was a very new man-and-woman type of relationship between them, it seemed they've been in this moment for a long time.

He slowly and deeply inhaled then exhaled, drooping his shoulders, finding himself lonely without her. No matter about her emotions or that they were having a difficult time with trust or the understanding of her God, he still envisioned her by his side day and night. Shana was truly a part of him physically, mentally, and emotionally.

Through the day, he stayed in this area, far enough from the village not to be accidently seen. He took several long baths in the hot steaming pools on the mountain, refreshing and invigorating his muscles. He had taken the red moss wraps off and decided not to replace them for the wounds had scabbed over well, healing and weren't bleeding anymore.

Finding a laminia tree, he cut off one of its vines, taking several filling swallows of its milk then poured the rest on his head. Letting it set for a while, he washed it out then drew back his long black hair into his new look Shana made up for him in a tight ponytail.

He foraged around, finding plenty of plants and some fruit to eat along with many fattened grubs, then napped the day away until the sun, still hidden on the other side of dark clouds, fell behind the high mountains, slowly shading the valley until darkness filled the air again. With the arrival of night, the clouds decided it was time to release its abundance of water and fell to the ground in large droplets, pounding everything in their path.

At the onset of night, Toca was becoming more anxious the darker it got. The time away from his people, especially his new father, Chief Acuta, had worn itself out and he couldn't wait to get to him. Through the rain, he made his way stealthily to the village. Once at the edge of the open area, still hidden, he stopped and let the senses of the Black Ghost work. Just like last night, it was dark and silent, except for the annoying rain, hindering his eyes, ears, and nose to work at their best.

"Why did it have to rain tonight, the night of my great return?" he said to himself, almost pouting. Looking down at his body, the rain had washed off the shadowing lines he put on earlier. He scooped up a big handful of mud and as much small debris he could and slid lines of it all over himself, hoping it would stay on long enough to get inside the tribal hut.

Not seeing any movement or anything out of place was good but he was sensing inside the same thing he felt last night, as if there were eyes peering at him. He looked deep and hard everywhere around him but couldn't find the eyes he was looking for; so he shadowed to the back of the hut, just like last night, and around to the entrance. In the dark rainy night, with his head back up against the bamboo wall, he closed his eyes, thinking, *This is it, my life is about to change. I'm going to be a man and be the chief of the Nashua people when it's my time.*

Chief Toca? The words crossed his mind, standing there as a moment of apprehension appeared. Then a splash of panic hit him as he thought it through. *How can I be chief? Even though I accomplished the Katata Ado, am I really ready? I am only a young man.*

*Only a young man...*Thinking back, he remembered Shana stating those same words to him at the cave when things were getting mixed up in his mind and he was becoming overwhelmed with everything happening.

With calming peace and smooth refreshing strength, the awaiting voice whispered to Toca in this perfect moment of unexpected hesitation and anxiety, *"I was with you when you met your spirit image, the black jaguar, and it turned you around to go back to Shana to find me. I was with you when the giant caiman gave you great courage, purpose, food, and shelter. I was with you when the moonlight showed you the target, protecting Shana from the others in the canoes. I was with you when the mother sloth calmed you and reminded you of who you are as a Nashua. I was with you when you fought the giant snake, giving you another great victory, having it show you the truth and giving you food. I was with you when the cool soft breeze flowed through the forest, demonstrating how compassionate I am, as you stumbled and fell on Shana to help her breathe again. I was with you when the eagle called for you to show you my wondrous splendor, giving you a small glance of how big I truly am. I was with you when the lightning and thunder unveiled my strength from only a whisper, and I never have to answer a challenge because I am God, your Creator. I know all things that have happened, is happening, and is going to happen to you, Toca. Fear nothing, my child, for I am always with you.*

A full sun season swept through his mind in a blink of an eye. The unfolding of this revelation of his experiences was awe-inspiring. Everything was making sense and was getting clear for the first time, beginning his true understanding of who and what this God of Shana's is that might be living in his heart. Relief and fulfillment were blissfully consuming him as fear, worry, and regret were falling off him like the raindrops flowing down his body to the ground. Only to be trampled and soon to evaporate and disappear.

Toca opened his eyes, knowing the words spoken to him were true because he personally experienced every one of the sensations from the different situations. Then looking down at his hand, with the small songbird safely wrapped up in the monkey skin, it suddenly gave out a couple of chirps as if to say, "Go inside, Toca, you are a man and I am with you."

Moving his head, peering up into complete darkness toward where the mat was last night, he repeated his steps. Silently and softly, his feet floated on the bamboo floor of the tribal hut then sat down, without a whisper, exactly where he was thirteen moons ago.

Silence and darkness illuminated the special hut. Toca looked straight ahead, trying to get a glimpse of Chief Acuta or at least a shape of his body sitting in front of him. For a few moments, it appeared he wasn't there, then he heard what sounded like the chief standing up. It was unsettling how things were or were not going, he wasn't sure. His internal senses were screaming out alarming echoes that something was wrong.

How could anything be wrong, why isn't he talking to me? Maybe I need to start the ceremony? So Toca thought what should be said and it came to him.

"Chief Acuta, father of Toca, the Black Ghost of the Nashua has returned." He stopped talking, realizing he was speaking in the new enhanced dialect he and Shana came up with and repeated what he said in his normal tongue, then continued, "I returned before the thirteenth moon rose full in the sky and I have"—getting it out of the sheath on his arm, he continued boldly and proudly raising his voice—"returned with a shell from the endless water!"

He placed the shell on the mat in front of him, anxiously waiting for the response he's been envisioning for a long time.

Silence still echoed in the room. *What is he waiting for?* he thought then the other things came to him.

Grasping the rolled-up bird beside him, he added, "I have also brought you a songbird"—placing it next to the shell then finished hesitantly, leaning forward in a faint whisper—"and returned with a...good God for our people."

Finally he heard the chief taking a breath to speak. Toca's body was nervously squirming, being so eager to hear the words he dreamed of and journeyed so far for.

In a soft whispered response, Toca had to stretch his ear up to hear these words, "You have brought back a shell..." Pausing, then exactly at that moment, as if planned, a crackling explosion from the dark clouds outside permeated the night over the village as lightning flashed its tentacles across the sky several times.

Toca flinched, looking back outside through the thin spaces between the bamboo making up the walls and the open door of the hut. Turning back around, his eyes went wide in shock as he jumped, leaning back off the mat. He was horrified looking up at a black jaguar standing up on two legs. The shock strangled his breath, killing his insides. Looking down, towering over him was not what Toca ever thought he would see as he cried out in disbelief, "*Jucawa*!"

Jucawa, wearing his jaguar hide with the cat's mask over his face and the rest of the pelt draped down the back of his body, repeated himself quietly with teeth gritted, "You have brought back a shell that my people will never see, and they will never know you were here!"

As the lightning continued to pierce the darkness, illuminating the room, Jucawa lifted a long spear in his hand and slammed the butt of it down hard on Toca's shell shattering it to pieces.

Toca screamed out, “No!” Then he looked up just in time to see the shaft of the spear swing around, hitting him on the side of his head, feeling nothing as emptiness filled his head and his eyes slowly closed before his body thumped, lifeless, to the floor, unconscious.

CHAPTER 18

The past four days Shana has been making her way slowly up along the river toward the hidden valley. Her broken ribs were still hurting but she had made a sling for her arm out of the material from Toca's hammock pack to relieve the painful pressure.

It started raining again last night, then stopped early morning before the sun's glow started warming the new day. She missed the large caiman hide Toca used to protect them from the heavenly downpour that seemed to never end. Now she's been cutting down large fanned-out leaves, blanketing them over her body to keep dry while sleeping.

The birds seemed to be singing louder than normal this morning, Shana thought to herself. *Probably because it's the first time the sun's been out in several days.* She moved into a spot where its beams of golden light were able to peek through the trees, saturating her. Besides warming her body, it was helping raise her spiraling spirits because of her pain, the dreary rain, but most of all, from missing Toca. She reflected on how true it was when he told her about the Nashua's spirit image was the sun and its meaning was new beginnings. Mornings like this felt fresh, new, and alive.

As she began journeying again, her energy level was high, moving faster along the small river this morning than all the other days, and by late afternoon, she couldn't go any further.

He was right, she thought, amazed at the impenetrable high rock wall covered with thick foliage. Not able to see past or above the treetops, there was no way in advance she could see these mountains that shot up high out of nowhere. Looking at the small river, it appeared to be coming out of solid rocks with dense vegetation, hovering over the now-calmer and clearer running water, camouflaging the actual source of where it was coming from.

"It's a good thing he told me about the hidden entrance to the valley and how to get in. I would have never found it or known what to do," Shana stated, looking all around the area, then asked herself, *I wonder why Toca hasn't come back for me already*? Looking downriver, she thought, *I hope we didn't accidently pass each other and he's far downriver looking for me.*

Turning back up, looking to the secret door of the valley, she said to herself, "Maybe his people are still celebrating and it's lasting longer than he thought?" She smiled, thinking of how excited everybody would be, especially Chief Acuta and his mother. Then she imagined Toca himself, grown-up, full of pride, sharing his great stories, then it struck her. *How is he going to introduce me to his people and the chief? They've never seen an outsider or even know others exist from what Toca told me.*

She contemplated if she should wait for Toca to show up or try to go into the river and up through it to get inside the valley herself. Concluding to stay put and wait for him, Shana reminded herself to be aware and sat quietly for a while, watching, listening, and smelling the air before making a camp. Not sensing any dangers with the birds singing as they darted here and there, then a troop of monkeys far across the smooth-running small river making playful noises put her at ease that everything was fine. After taking a short rest and putting a few more yellow flower petals under her tongue for pain, she unloaded her pack and found a couple of trees to hang the hammock. Looking through her supplies, seeing what was needed, Shana went looking for a juja plant and yatowa flowers to replenish her needed medicine.

Quietly strolling through the forest, she was finding everything she was looking for and more. There was an abundance of different fruits she picked to eat later and even found a laminia tree, getting excited about it as she felt her dirty hair. She took off the sling holding her arm up and put the fruits, juja leaves, and yatowa flowers and roots in it, draping it in a different direction around her neck. Then she cut down the vine hanging from the tree as high as she could reach from the ground, clogging the center hole with her finger. Next she cut it close to the ground, quickly clogging the open hole with a finger from her other hand.

Before getting back to her makeshift camp, she stopped short and listened intently; she thought she heard something. And she did—there was something quietly moving around in her things.

Her heart started to beat faster and her breathing got heavier as she quietly kneeled behind a wide bush. Setting the vine down carefully so the ends stood up, leaning against the branches of the bush, she then took the sling off around her neck. Sliding the machete out from the sheath, which she had positioned between her skin and her waist wrap, holding it in place, she readied herself.

Listening and smelling deeply, all she could sense was the sound of something quietly eating. Slowly peering through the bush with the long knife pointed out in front of her, she was taken aback at what she saw. Smoothly swaying back and forth was the most colorful snake she has ever seen. It had an orange and white base color with small paw prints like black rings dotted all over. But this snake was different, it seemed to be furry all over. As she was being hypnotized, watching the smooth back and forth motion, suddenly behind the snake, a huge head lifted and turned around. It had the same coloration as two large beady eyes were staring straight at her. The body of the snake disappeared, as the head came around forward a step, Shana suddenly realized the snake was actually the tail of a very large cat much bigger than herself. Sticking out the side of its mouth was a piece of the dried anaconda meat it found to eat from her stash.

Shana instantly knew she was its next meal. There was no time to think, only react with it a couple body lengths away. All she could do is keep the machete pointed at the cat as she stood up as tall as she could to possibly intimidate it.

A deep vibrating growl came from the jaguar as it began flinching its upper lip, exposing large sharp fangs with its tail whipping back and forth.

"Jesus, please, please help me," Shana begged under her breath. Then less than a blink of an eye, the cat leaped at her over the bush with its wide paws in front and claws extended. She screamed as loud as she could, "Toca!" following the body of the jaguar up in the air with the end of the long knife.

She was hit hard with both paws, one on each of her shoulders, feeling the claws dig in as her body went back, hitting the ground, and the weight of the animal knocked the air out of her. Her eyes squinted close, anticipating to be ripped to pieces; but all she was feeling was the full weight of the cat on her. Her hands were stuck between them as she was still holding the handle of the knife.

It was getting harder to breathe but nothing was moving so she slowly opened her eyes, only to see her face being smothered with jaguar fur. Beginning to believe the impossible just happened, Shana tried to get out from under the dead weight of the large cat. Her heart was still racing and her body began to shake as adrenaline was pumping fast throughout her. She let go of the handle of the machete as the rest of it was impaled at the base of the neck, sticking out on the other side. It cut perfectly through the throat and up, severing the spinal cord, killing the cat instantly.

Squeezing herself away and rolling the heavy body off her, she thought she heard her name. Sitting up, filling her lungs full of air, she heard it again. This time, she knew it wasn't in her head. Carefully Shana stood, watching the cat's limp body, then looked away in the direction she heard the distant voice.

"It's coming from the hidden entrance," she said out loud. Then she yelled, "Toca!"

A moment passed, then she got her reply but it was weak and sounded painful. "Shana, Shana."

Swelling with excitement, she looked back at the dead jaguar, making sure it was dead but also clarifying this wasn't a dream, she turned back to the voice and burst out, "Toca, I'm here, come through the entrance, I'm here!"

Again soft, weak, and lifeless. "Shana, help me..."

She stood still, listening, not believing what she heard was correct, then heard them again faintly, "Shana, help."

Everything within her was instantly refreshed and energized. She totally forgot about the dead jaguar and her broken ribs, her man was needing her help. For Toca to be calling out for help, something was very wrong and she was not going to let anything get in her way from saving him.

Quickly she went and rolled the cat over, pulling the long knife out, and put it in the sheath on her hip. Looking out to the river, she realized she needed to secure it better so she looked around and spotted leftover rope that she had taken out of her pack when she unloaded it. Measuring out and cutting a piece the length of her torso, she tied one end to the top of the sheath and the other end at the bottom. Lifting it over one shoulder, it draped across her body with the knife and sheath flat against her back.

"Toca, I'm coming!" she yelled as she walked out into the river. Going up the current, Shana attemped to swim by bouncing off the bottom with her toes barely touching. Getting to the vegetation, there were vines snaking their way all over the place and leaves of many kind poking out everywhere. It got dark and hard to see as she went under the wall of rock covered with green and brown foliage, tangling herself up here and there. She had to go underwater in spots, holding her breath, bobbing up only to hit her head on limbs above the water. Finally making her way through the passage, it was getting brighter and she started to yell out again for Toca, when suddenly, something grabbed her arm from within the tangles of the vines and branches. She screamed out as instantly, all her fears showed themselves in her mind—a snake, maybe a killer fish, or even a caiman.

"Shana...," a frail voice whispered.

It took her a moment to come to her senses that her name was spoken as she replied, "Toca?"

"Shana, I can't move...I'm trapped...too weak...I can't..."

"Toca." She was blinking hard and stretching her head forward to see him in the shadowed strands of branches and leaves.

She reached out for him as he stopped talking. Touching his body through the vegetation, she got no response—he was lifeless.

"Toca, hold on." Not panicking but focused, she was able to find a foothold at the bottom of the river to hold her place in the current. She took out the long knife and started frantically cutting him free of the tangles of vines and limbs that were holding him captive. Finally free, she turned his body, facing up, and put her arm around his neck and started swimming quickly with the current, dodging obstacles out of the valley's hidden entrance.

Once they were out of the tunnel and into the open, Shana slowed down and drifted to shore. Getting her footing in the mud, she got out of the water and took Toca's hands, dragging his body fully out of the river. She plopped down on her knees, exhausted at his head and could hardly believe what she was looking at. His body was limp but he was still breathing. He was slowly bleeding from many large swollen bruised bumps on his head and face, down his arms, back, chest, and legs that were welted up, black and blue. Then more blood caught her eyes, slowly oozing out of a gash in his lower stomach area to the side. "He's been stabbed!" she exclaimed.

"Toca, what happened to you?" Shana became emotional as she looked him over, lying there, unconscious, helpless, and appeared to be dying.

"No, no, God, don't let this happen. Please don't let him die too, please no," she begged as she began crying gently while laying her head on his chest.

Shana quickly pushed away her emotions and took action. She knew it was up to her now to be the one to be the caretaker and protector. She stood and looked toward where she had her things and at the dead jaguar, deciding it wasn't a good hidden area. Looking down at Toca, she decided to move him to a good hiding spot, then come back for their things. Leaning over, grabbing both his hands, she started dragging him away from the river. After a while and taking several breaks, she finally found a spot she was satisfied with. Before leaving to get their stuff, she leaned him up against a tree, checking his breathing and bleeding. Both had slowed down. She didn't know if it was a good sign about the bleeding; was he running out of blood or it was stopping on its own? But the breathing was scaring her, she had been in this exact spot before with both her parents. The breathing would get slower and slower until they both died.

She ran back to the area next to the river and packed up all the stuff as well as the remaining dried meat the cat didn't eat. Before leaving, she stared at the dead jaguar, still in awe of what happened. Then she remembered Toca telling her his real father was killed by a black jaguar. Then thought, *I should be dead too, I only held onto the knife pointing it forward and closed my eyes. The cat was the one that stabbed itself.*

Getting back to Toca, she hung a hammock much lower to the ground, guessing how high she could lift him. Then with all she had, clumsily raised him up, sliding him into it. With the adrenaline gone, she was now feeling her broken ribs and the pain was coming on strong with the pulling and lifting she's been doing.

Pulling off a few yellow petals from one of the flowers, she rolled them and put them under her tongue. Looking at Toca, she thought, *He's going to be in real pain again when he wakes up.* She pulled a few more petals, rolled them, and opened his mouth and placed them under his tongue, thinking, *Maybe I can stay ahead of the pain for him.*

Looking his body over, she picked off many leeches that had themselves suctioned to him. Thinking of what else she could do, she picked up the two bamboo cups and went back to the river to find mud from under a tunga tree.

Passing the dead jaguar again, Shana thought what would Toca do; and instantly, it came to mind what he said about every kill, "Don't waste anything."

"I'm not eating a cat," she said aloud, "But its beautiful fur is really nice." Staring at it a few more moments, she turned and went on her way along the river, cautiously finding what she was looking for.

Back to Toca, she gently rubbed the oily mud all over his wounds on his head, face, and the rest of his body, except where he had the deep cut near his stomach. She thought hard what the flower looked like that he got up in the trees for healing where the piranhas attacked him. Looking up, Shana tried to judge how much daylight was left to go look for these special flowers and noticed high up in the trees the hammock was hanging from, there were several branches with these flowers.

"Those are them!" she exclaimed. "Thank, thank you, Lord!"

But as she stared up high, the excitement left her and fear began to overtake her.

You're still afraid.

Shana looked down at Toca, as though he just made the statement, but he was still unconscious. She swung her head around as if someone else was there but didn't see anyone.

You'll always be afraid, Shana. The voice now was dark and sarcastic.

At first, she began to cave in, then she remembered what Toca scolded her about—her fears and trusting her God.

"Not anymore!" she exclaimed loudly. "Heavenly Father, I have to climb way up there to save Toca. Help me to have faith in you and not to be afraid."

You were not afraid to stand up to the jaguar or to go into the river entrance to the valley, why be afraid now? This voice was the voice of power, peace, and comfort she knew.

Without hesitating, she started up the tree and kept going and going. She struggled, lifting herself and stretching over to other branches, never stopping. She kept her eyes on the prize of the flowers and never looked down. While she was climbing, her mind wandered to the story of Peter in the Bible, getting out of the boat, walking on the water to Jesus until he looked down then began to sink. "I'm not looking down, I'm not looking down," she kept telling herself.

Finally she was at the base of the branches that had the flowers blooming way out at the ends. She was holding on with a death grip to the narrowing limbs that had begun gently swaying back and forth with her weight. She shakenly let go with her good hand and reached back, pulling the machete out of the sheath. Then swung down on the branches several times and both branches quickly fell far down to the ground. Slowly putting the knife back, she calmly slid her way down, and before she knew it, she was back on the ground.

Looking back up at her accomplishment, a smile came across her old child face. *I did it! No, we did it, thank you, Jesus.*

"Mmm…" Toca started to moan himself awake with his eyes still closed.

"Toca, you're awake," she said, surprised, kneeling at his side.

"Jucawa…no, no…Jucawa!" he grumbled out, not fully conscious.

"Toca, it's Shana, I'm taking care of you." She gently stroked his face.

He grimaced as his head slowly moved. "Why did you do that, Jucawa, why?"

"It's me, Shana. I'm here and you're going to be okay."

"Shannnaa?" His words stopped and his facial expressions relaxed as he went back to unconsciousness.

Shana bowed her head as she grasped ahold of his hand. *Oh, please, Jesus, help Toca, heal his body. Help me to know what to do, protect us tonight, and thank you again for protecting me from that big cat, amen.*

She let go of his hand and felt his forehead. *He's getting hot,* she thought to herself, then picked up the muddy bamboo cups and went back to the river. She washed them, then filled them with water, and went back to Toca. Examining the stabbed area, she gently pushed down on it and a lot of watery blood gushed out. Then she poured a little bit of water over it, washing it clean as blood still seeped out.

Searching around for her sling that was filled with fruit, juja leaves, and yatowa flowers she picked earlier, she dumped them out and used it as a temporary bandage. She wrapped it around his body, with the material sling over the wound, then tightened it, squeezing his stomach together to try to stop the bleeding.

Thinking intently for a moment, she remembered something she saw a white doctor back home do when someone cut themselves badly and the bleeding wouldn't stop. She looked to her small pile of things she's been carrying in the hammock pack and lifted her Bible that was wrapped up. Unraveling it from the waterproof tree bark, she opened it to her favorite verse and safely hidden between the pages was the thin sharp needle that used to be in her sewing bag. She had lost the needle holder and started putting it between the pages of the Bible so it wouldn't poke through anything.

Now she needed thread, the sewing thread she brought with her on the trip had been used up moons ago. Looking down at her waist flaps, at what she used before to sew them together, she said out loud, "I need fresh sinew." Then she quickly turned her head in the direction of the dead jaguar, then looked up to the sky to judge how much sunlight was left. *It's going to be dark soon,* she thought. *I need to make a fire first.* Putting the needle back between the pages of the Bible, closing it up and setting it to the side, she picked up the machete and went wandering around for wood and a termite's nest.

Once back with everything she needed, she made a small firepit and, with her fire-starting rocks, quickly had a fire going with the dried termite nest. Then she slowly piled twigs and leaves and larger branches until she had a strong fire going. Deciding to make another trip for wood because she knew it will probably be along night, she was soon back and ready to go to work on the jaguar for its strong tendons. Taking several long-dried branches that had caught fire at the ends, along with the machete, she went to the dead animal and made another firepit and gathered wood in the area to last for a while.

Looking at the colorful animal, she admired its beauty and its size as the light from the fire began to dance, bringing life to a quiet and calm evening.

Remembering how her people, so many times, would cut up deer, coyotes, and other animals, as well as watching Toca skillfully work on animals of the forest, she began imitating movements of the pictures she had in her head. Working hard and intently, she had taken the colorful coat off the cat and spread it out on the ground with the fur down. Then looking closely and cutting down the leg areas, she found what she was looking for. Cutting and peeling away tendons, she stretched many long strands out, laying them on to the cape.

Taking a short break, she realized that she was in pain again and thought Toca would be too. Getting back to him, still unconscious, she looked at the sling bandage closely, lifting a stick still slowly burning and saw that the deep cut was still bleeding. Peering up at his face, she stroked it and said, "You're going to be fine, Toca, your woman is taking care of you." She smiled at the thought of them as adults and her taking care of her man.

Picking up a flower, she pulled six petals off it and rolled three up, putting them under her tongue, then did the same for him, taking out the old ball she left in from earlier. Then she thought through what she was going to do next and wondered if Toca would wake up because it was going to get very painful for him.

Still with the whole flower on her lap, she remembered how the root affected her, making her fall asleep. *How am I going to get him to eat some root*? she asked herself. The only idea that came to mind was she was going to have to chew the root up finely then put it in his mouth, hoping he would swallow it. So she did just that, careful not to swallow the juices squishing out of it as she chewed. Then she opened his mouth and spit everything she had in her mouth into his as he lay there, motionless. *I need to wash it down*, she thought. Taking up the cup she used to wash the wound earlier, she lifted his head up, opened his mouth, and slowly poured some water in.

Toca's body naturally gagged and choked a little but the natural swallowing process happened to clear his throat as she tightly held his mouth shut then he relaxed again. She laid his head down, opened his mouth, and everything was gone. "Yes!" Shana got excited that it worked, then moved over to his stomach area and removed the sling tied around him.

Closing her eyes, she was picturing the steps in her head what the doctor did. Opening her eyes, she looked at the now-smaller fire, put a few more pieces of wood on, and watched the flames get higher. Picking up the machete, she poured a little water at the end of the blade and washed it clean from using it on the jaguar. Then Shana pointed the end of the long knife into the flame until it started to turn color, getting really hot, then turned to Toca. Her hand started to shake, looking at what she was about to do, then she said out loud, "Oh, God, please make this work, I'm going to hurt him really bad. Toca, I'm sorry—" Then Shana slid the hot pointed end of the machete into the cut until it wouldn't go in any farther without cutting him more. At the touch of the hot blade to his skin, it hissed as it burned and slightly smoked. Toca's lifeless body jerked at the pain and his eyes quickly opened, then he went limp again unconscious.

His reaction scared her, and she jerked the knife tip out, then watched for what was going to happen next but nothing did. She looked close to a now-charred wound and it appeared the bleeding stopped, cringing her nose at the smell of burnt skin. Putting the machete down, she got the needle out from the Bible and slowly poked it in and out of the flame, thinking, *Why did the doctors always put things in the fire before touching wounds on the body*? Then she took a long strip of the sinew and, holding it at each end, weaved it back and forth in a tip of a flame.

Satisfied it heated up enough, Shana tied a little knot at one end, then picked up the needle which had a small notch, carved opposite to the point that would hold the end of the thread. After setting it into the cradle of the notch, she looked at the burnt opening again, then hesitantly pinched the skin just outside the cut and looked at Toca's face to see if he reacted. Not moving, she proceeded to thread the needle with the sinew over and over through the skin, tightly, until she had sewn the whole length of the cut together and tied it off.

She gave out a big sigh of relief, not realizing she was holding her breath most of the time. Then she lifted a burning end of a stick out of the fire to lighten up where she was doctoring Toca's wound to see the details. A bit surprised and pleased that everything was looking good, she started working on one of the flowers she chopped down from the top of the tree. Tearing it into little pieces like Toca did, she dropped the pieces in the cup that was empty, and started grinding it over and over with a small stick, adding a little water from the other cup, until it was a smooth grayish paste.

Turning to Toca, she swiped up a couple of fingers full of the paste and softly coated the area she just sewed up. Then she took the sling she used before and rewrapped it around his stomach and gently secured it.

Looking up to his face and head where there were a couple of spots the skin had been broken, she smeared the paste on along with the tunga mud, rubbing it in.

Sitting back on her feet, breathing deeply with relief, she was finally finished with what she could do for him at the moment. Emotions that were suppressed since the attack of the jaguar started to wedge their way out as she turned around toward the small depleting fire, trying its best to stay alive. Pulling her knees up to her chest and wrapping her arms around her legs, Shana slowly leaned her forehead on her knees and began to cry.

CHAPTER 19

It was a terrible night's sleep for Toca and Shana. Toca was restless, never completely waking up but mumbling and jerking around in his sleep. For the first time, Shana slept in a tree. There wasn't enough room for her in the one hammock with Toca, and with his squirming around, she wouldn't have been able to sleep anyways.

The morning couldn't have come any sooner. At the slightest light, Shana was down from the tree, checking on Toca's sewn-up wound, then decided to work on the jaguar skin. Once again imitating Toca, she dragged the pelt next to the river and scrubbed the inside with sand, mud, and water, then washed it out. When she laid it out in a spot for the sun to dry it, the front of both of her shoulders began to hurt and her skin was soon stinging in pain. She looked down and realized, for the first time, her top cover was ripped on both sides and there was dried blood, soaked down her top and the top of her arms. Looking back in the direction where Toca was, she decided it was safe to take her top off and see what was going on and why she was hurting.

Stunned at the bruising that began to show was the least of her concern. Realizing when the big cat jumped at her and both of its paws hit her shoulders, and driving her to the ground, its sharp claws had put fairly deep scratches perfectly down her front shoulders and upper arms. It obviously was overlooked because of the other excitement—saving Toca—and not to mention she was premedicated with the flower petals for her painful broken ribs. She hadn't put any under her tongue since last evening so it had worn off through the night.

Carefully looking for danger in the river, she decided it was okay to take a bath and wash off all the mud and blood, then wash her hair with the tree milk in the vine she cut down yesterday that she brought with her to work on the jaguar hide.

Feeling refreshed and clean, Shana then washed the ripped and well-worn piece of a shirt that was the only original clothing she had left. Once it was fairly clean from the dried blood and dirt, she put it on and quickly went back to check on Toca, also to take more of the yatowa flower because now, the deep scratches were screaming with stinging pain. They began to slightly bleed again from her rubbing the dirt and dried blood off.

As she passed the jaguar carcass, she looked at the skinless head with the large fangs exposed, protruding from its jaws, she thought back to her people. *The dried skulls were always a big prize with bears and mountain lions. Maybe I'll cut its skull off and clean it up for a gift to Toca…no, Chief Acuta*! Thinking of the excitement it could bring the chief from an unexpected outsider and an old child female.

She stared at it for another moment then, without thinking any more, swung the machete down, severing the head perfectly from the neck. Picking it up, she was amazed how big and heavy it was and went back to their camp, holding it in both arms. Once there, she put fresh pain-killing petals under both their tongues, got the fire going again, and ate some of the fruit she gathered yesterday.

Sitting next to the fire, she picked up the bamboo cup with left-over drying gray healing paste, added some water and stirred it up. Then with her back to Toca, she took her shirt off again and smeared it on some of the claw marks. Running short, she took the second flower from the other branch she cut down and repeated the whole process until all her open cuts on her shoulders and down the front of her arms were covered, having some leftover again.

Sitting there with her legs crossed, letting the paste dry before putting her shirt back on, she watched the small flames bounce around. A breeze wisped around and she heard the soft ruffling of pages from her Bible lying next to her. Looking at it, she realized she hadn't rewrapped it back up for protection. The moving air was acting like invisible fingers, flipping through the pages, then instantly stopped—both the air and pages. The Bible sat there, open, as Shana reflected back to when she read it last. Since she had it safely wrapped up in the rubbery waterproof bark, it had been out of sight, out of mind for quite a while. Picking it up, the breeze stopped flipping the pages to the book of Judges in the Old Testament, chapter seven. She remembered her dad reading this story to her about Gideon and how God proved his greatness and power by having Gideon reduce his army of about 32,000 to 300 to defeat an army of about 135,000. The second verse got her attention which is the whole point of the story, "*The Lord said to Gideon, 'You have too many warriors with you. If I let all of you fight the Midianites, the Israelites will boast to me that they saved themselves by their own strength.'*"

Shana. She heard the voice but didn't look around; she knew who it was and peacefully closed her eyes.

Shana, I brought you here and I have shown you things you needed to see and allowed things to happen to you and Toca to have full experiences; all so I will be worshiped and glorified. Hold my hand tightly like a child and don't let go. For only then, through me, will you have the strength, knowledge, and wisdom to do what you have to do, bringing the knowledge of me so I can work through you for the Nashua and to protect Toca from himself.

"Shana." The voice was instantly different with a groggy breathless tone. "Shana." There it was again, then she realized it was actually coming from behind her. Her eyes shot open and swung her body around.

"Toca? Are you awake?" she asked with excitement.

He slowly opened and closed his eyes, trying to focus and adjust to the light. Breathing deeper and attempting to move, he quickly gave into weakness and pain.

"Don't move, you're badly hurt," Shana said, kneeling up next to him.

"How did you…" He tried to speak, then paused to swallow, wetting his dry throat. "Get to the village so soon?"

"We're not in your village, we are outside the valley, near the hidden entrance."

"What…but I was in the tribal hut, where is Chief Acuta…" Then his eyes opened wide as a surprising surge of energy came out of his voice, lifting his head up as high as he could to look around eagerly. "*Where's Jucawa*?" He tried to get out of the hammock but Shana held him down by his shoulders.

"Stop moving, Toca, you're hurt. You're going to rip the sewing I did on you!" she said, raising her voice.

"Where is he? Where's Jucawa? I'm going to…" Pausing again, he put his thoughts together. "I'm going to kill him!" he yelled out, trying to sloppily fight Shana to get up. Then it hit him as he crunched his stomach to sit up, instantly dropping back down in awful pain. "Aww…my stomach hurts." He gasped as he brought his hands to the painful spot, only to feel a strip of hammock material wrapped around him.

He tried to blink the pain away, looking at Shana and asked, "What's wrong with me?"

"You have been beaten or hit with something all over your head and body. Then it looks like you've been stabbed on the side of your stomach."

"What do you mean stabbed and hit?" Then he remembered. "He hit me!" Then he projected angrily. "He crushed my shell, then he hit me on the side of the head with his spear." Reaching for the area, he remembered being hit and flinched in pain when he touched the spot on the side of his head.

Shana sat there, confused and surprised at what he was saying. "What do you mean he hit you and crushed your shell?"

He looked around and attempted to understand where he was. Realizing he truly wasn't in the village and they were alone together, he calmed down. Laying his head back on the hammock and tilting it toward Shana, he explained, overtaken with pain, "I was in the tribal hut on the mat where I was supposed to be before the thirteenth full moon. I was waiting for Chief Acuta on the other side of the mat to start the ceremony. It was so dark I could barely see my hands in front of my face. After a few moments of silence, I thought maybe I was to start the ceremony so I told him I have returned with a shell, the songbird, and a good God. As I was talking, I heard him stand up, then lightning brightened the sky, lighting up the hut, and it was Jucawa, standing in front of me. He slammed down the end of his spear on the shell I had laid down on the mat, breaking it to pieces. Then before I knew it, he swung it around and hit me on the side of my head. That's all I remember."

"Why was Jucawa in the hut and not Chief Acuta?" she asked. "And how did you get all these bumps and bruises and get stabbed?"

"I don't know," he replied but had a good idea, then paused, trying to remember the exact words Jucawa said. Then it came to him. "Jucawa said just before he hit me, 'My people will never know you brought back a shell and they will never know you were here.'" Toca paused to think, then added, "Why did he say his people…unless, Chief Acuta made him chief while I was on my Katata Ado?" He was feeling anger and confusion at the same time. "But why would Chief Acuta do that when I was coming back with a shell?" His eyes got big with worry at his next thought, looking at Shana. "Maybe Chief Acuta died?" Toca suddenly was stricken with deep sadness, swelling up, as he mumbled out, "He was very old." Toca turned his head away from Shana as tears began to quietly flow.

Shana stepped into the conversation. "You don't know if Chief Acuta died."

"Then why was Jucawa there?" He fought back at her with words of confusion. "Chief Acuta made it very clear he did not want Jucawa to be the next chief. Wait…" Toca's eyes were moving back and forth as he now stared up to the treetops, lying in the hammock. "During my going-away ceremony, the chief did say Jucawa had been asking him to step down and let him be the new chief because he was getting too old and very weak. Maybe Jucawa forced him out of his position which means Chief Acuta could still be alive!" A sudden change of ideas and emotions invigorated him, giving him energy as he wanted to get out of the hammock.

"Help me out of the hammock, Shana, I can't lie down any longer."

Holding his arm out for her to grab, he looked at his forearm and asked, "Where's my knife?"

"I don't know. When I rescued you, you had nothing on you except your manhood cover. Even your front and back flaps were gone."

Noticing what she said was true, he looked back at her then was surprised he didn't notice it before and asked, "Where's your top cover?"

Quickly looking down, not realizing she hadn't put it back on, only her necklace with the white stone carving was there against her chest. Slapping her hands across her breasts, clutching each shoulder, she squealed out from some minor pain. "Ouch, aww…don't look, Toca, I need to put my shirt back on."

Concerned about her painful reaction, he asked, "Do your ribs still hurt that bad?"

She answered calmly, not wanting to alarm him, "Yes, but that's not why I cried out." She let go of her shoulders with her hands and draped them over her breasts.

"Why do you have gray medicine paste on your shoulders and down your arms?" His concern was heightened, not knowing what happened to her, he asked, gritting his teeth, "Did Jucawa hurt you too?"

"Everything's okay, Toca, and no, Jucawa did not hurt me. I never went into the hidden valley. I have not seen another person." Hesitating while wondering what his reaction was going to be, she slowly said, "I was attacked."

"Attacked? By what?" Toca raised his head and voice, staring hard at her.

"A…jaguar," she softly answered, leaning back a bit with apprehension, putting an uneasy grin on her face.

Taken by surprise, he was speechless for a moment, then blurted out, "What…how did you…when did this happen?"

Seeing how much it affected him, she got a little prideful for everything she did. "Well, yesterday—"

"Yesterday! Where!" he said, raising his voice.

She leaned over, picking up her shirt, then put it on and turned her head toward the river and pointed. "Over there, a little ways." Then she leaned over the other direction, grabbing the furless head that was set down where Toca couldn't see it and lifted it up between them.

"Waaa!" he squawked out with surprise, leaning away. Then he slowly came forward in awe. "You killed it!"

"Yes, I did!" She smiled then said, "Well, I held the long knife out as it jumped at me and it went through its neck when it landed on me, actually killing itself."

"No! You killed the jaguar!" Then he doubled back his excitement and asked, "Was it a black jaguar, a black ghost?" He was getting somber at the thought.

"No, it had a beautiful orange, yellow, and tan coat with black rings everywhere."

Toca sighed with relief, then asked, "So you skinned it, the whole thing?"

"Yes, I did, and I also scrubbed the inside like you do." She put on a big smile as their eyes finally connected, not just looking at each other but seeing into each other for the first time since Toca left her behind. It went silent between them as they just stared, sharing a moment of speechless love.

Toca was the one who broke the silence as he said quietly, "I missed you, Shana."

"I missed you too. I never want to be away from you that long ever again," she lovingly stated back as she lifted her hand up, grasping his.

"How long have we been away from each other?" He still had no idea how long he was unconscious and how much time had passed since he was hit by Jucawa.

She quickly thought and said, "I heard you yell my name after I screamed yours out when the cat attacked me yesterday. You weakly cried out for help from inside the entrance of the tunnel the river runs through. So I went in after you, almost all the way through to the other side, and you were tangled up in the vines and branches in the water. I cut you free and swam back out and brought you here. I spent the rest of the day and some of the night working on you." She pointed to the bandage around his stomach area. Then finally, she answered the question after counting the days prior when she was on her own. “We’ve been apart for five days.”

“Five days?” he responded, leaning back, looking up at the canopy of the forest, wondering where the days went. Then he slowly adjusted into a more comfortable position and asked to fill in the blanks. “How did I get into the river and far down from the village? I don’t remember anything, Shana.” Sounding worried and frustrated at the same time, he continued, “What are we going to do? I need to get to my people and find Chief Acuta and my mother!” The more Toca talked and thought, the more he was getting anxious and uneasy.

“You’re going nowhere!” she stated firmly. “You are badly injured. You could still die from that stab wound. I don’t know if you are badly cut inside or not.”

He looked down at his stomach. “I want to see it.”

“Okay, I need to check it and maybe put more gray paste on it anyways.”

As she slowly unwrapped the temporary bandage from Toca, he looked close at her shirt and said, “Your top cover is all torn up, you can’t wear that anymore.”

She looked down and around at the shredded shoulders and front part and replied, “It was getting worn out anyways, what am I going to do?” she asked, picking at the ripped areas.

“You know what I’ve been telling you,” Toca said firmly through his discomfort.

She replied sarcastically, “I know! The Nashua woman do not wear top coverings, it doesn’t serve any purpose.” They went silent for a few moments, thinking this dilemma through as she finished with looking at the wound and touched it up. She explained what she did to him before she sewed him up and he reacted surprisingly.

“You stabbed me with the long knife as it was fiery hot?” He couldn’t believe she did that.

“I had to, it stops bleeding,” she said, pointing to the area. “See? No more blood.” He could hardly believe it. He thought he would remember something so painful like that happening to him. Looking down and seeing his first real bad damage to his body that could have killed him, he complimented her.

"You are going to be a great Nashua woman, Shana, my woman. Thank you for saving me this time." He meant what he said but it was a major hit to his pride.

Shana leaned over and gently kissed him on the lips then said, "You're welcome, Black Ghost, man of the Nashua, my man." She leaned back with a loving smile on her face as they stared into each other's eyes, realizing again how much they mean to each other.

Breaking the moment as she's done many times before, an idea came to her. "I've got it, Toca!" she blurted out with excitement.

"You've got what?" he asked, oblivious to where her mind was at.

"I'll make a top out of the jaguar skin! It will be beautiful!"

He lay there, slowly trying to come out of a romantic moment to thinking about clothes again, then asked, "But maybe you want to keep it together like Jucawa did with his when he killed the black jaguar?"

"Why would I want to do that and what am I going to do with it? You said he wears it all the time? Why?"

Trying not to get mad at himself for bringing Jucawa into their conversation, he said sarcastically, "Yes, he does and he brags about it to everyone all the time."

"You didn't save the giant caiman or the great anaconda to wear, Toca?"

Her comment stumped him for a moment. "I…I guess you're right but I did bring back pieces of them to show my people what I did."

"There's nothing wrong with having things to show others what you accomplished as long as you don't flaunt it to everyone or make it your god."

"What do you mean make it your god?" Toca popped his head back on the hammock, putting on a wrinkled confused face.

She thought for an answer then said, "Anything can be a god to people such as Jucawa's black jaguar skin. It sounds like it's the most important thing in his life and what he thinks gives him purpose or meaning. Isn't that what your people respect or fear about him, not just the skin but that it means so much to him he makes it the most important thing in his life and what he did to get it?"

Toca nodded, beginning to understand what she was saying.

"It sounds to me like Jucawa worships the skin and what he did so much that he wears it to hide behind so the real Jucawa can't be seen. What does he have to hide from?"

Now Toca was lost. "He doesn't have anything to hide from, he did a great thing by killing the big cat as he got hurt doing it. Then he finished this long journey we did. But he ran the whole way, we canoed most of it. He is a great Nashua for everything he did." Toca found himself slightly defending Jucawa or was it the pride of his people? He wasn't sure then, backstepping, not to be on Jucawa's side. "But he is still a bad man."

"I understand what you're saying but isn't that why he's a bad man. Because he thinks so much about himself and his prize of killing the cat and his great Katata Ado that he doesn't care about anyone else but himself? Those things are the only things that give him his inspiration for purpose and his identity."

Toca slightly shrugged in agreement, still not fully sure he was understanding what she was completely saying. "Yes, I guess so."

"I know I'm right, that's why Chief Acuta is a great chief because he puts other people first compared to Jucawa who puts himself first. The chief's identity is his people and how he loves them. Jucawa's identity is his own accomplishments and what he does for himself."

Toca sat there, deeply pondering what she was saying. This was a new perspective and way of looking at things.

Sitting on the ground next to the hammock, Shana knew she was on a roll, explaining this power struggle going on within the Nashua. She had seen it before with her people and with the white people that came onto their reservation. With upbeat confidence, she continued, "Whatever is the focus and the most important relationship or thing in our lives, that is what becomes our god."

Her talking this way was strange but was beginning to make sense so he asked in a slight sarcastic manner, "Is your God the most important relationship in your life?"

"Yes, he is."

Taken aback because he thought she would say he was, he frowned at her.

"Toca, he has to be, not you. I worship God, not you. Once again, the most important relationship to you will be your god. I cannot ask you that I be the most important relationship because I, and our relationship, would become your god." She paused for a moment, remembering all the things they talked about over the past ten moons, then continued, "You talked about bad gods. Every relationship or things we put first in front of God is a bad god. Because whatever it is that takes our focus off God, who created us and made everything, will become more important to us than God himself." She swung her arms out to all that was around them, then grimaced as she put her arm back down against her side, crying out, "Ouch, that hurt." Then she continued, "Does that make sense?"

He nodded in agreement, still lying down on the hammock.

"Do you see better why Jucawa acts the way he does? He is selfish and he has become his own god and that is a bad god."

"Maybe you're right, Shana, he's always been mean and bad to everyone, only doing what is good for himself, not his family or the Nashua," Toca stated, then went silent with a blank look on his face. Now he was the one thinking about something completely different.

"I don't have a shell to show Chief Acuta and my people that I did the Katata Ado. What am I going to do Shana? Jucawa crushed it. I'm never going to be chief now." He started to worry and get upset.

"You were there at the endless water, I was with you almost the whole trip. I will tell everyone you did it."

"But what about Jucawa, why did he crush it and why did he hit me like that and why did you find me in the river at the entrance?" He was rehashing the scene repeatedly and couldn't understand it. Toca suddenly found himself being more emotional than he wanted Shana to see but it was becoming overwhelming. He had spent a full sun season working and fighting hard to accomplish something that Jucawa destroyed in a blink of an eye.

"Toca, stop worrying about it, there has to be a good explanation. I will go into your village and talk with Jucawa and find Chief

Acuta and your mother and bring them all here and we'll all talk about it."

"What, are you crazy?" He raised his voice, using the new word she used on him five days ago at the ridiculousness of what she said.

"What else are we going to do? You can't move for a while, not to mention swim upriver through the key to the valley until you heal up."

"No, I will not allow you to go to the village by yourself."

"Oh, you're not?" She bobbed her head back, surprised at his statement.

"No, I'm not!" he replied in a deeper harsh tone.

With a little bit of sarcasm, she asked, "So what's your plan? You don't have your anklet, knife, or shell. The thirteenth full moon has passed and you are weak and in pain and can hardly move." They both heard, coming out of her mouth, that Toca has been defeated with no way to succeed. Then attempting to get her way, she added, "You already told Jucawa that you brought me here so he would expect me to show up, wouldn't he?"

He scrunched his face as he replied with whatever pride he had left, "What are you talking about, I never told Jucawa you are with me."

"Yes, you did, you said you thought you were talking to Chief Acuta and told him you have returned with a shell, a songbird, and a good God."

Regaining verbal ground, he responded, "I did say that, I never said I brought Shana, an old female child."

"You said you brought the songbird. That's me!" She pointed both her hands to herself.

"What?" He was still confused. "I don't know what you're talking about, Chief Acuta said to bring him a songbird so I caught a small bird the day I went to the ceremony hut at night."

"Why did he ask you to bring him a songbird?"

"I don't know, he said something that he had a dream the night before I left the valley for my Katata Ado and it was very important for me to bring back the songbird." Just then, he remembered his dream, changing his tone of voice, and excitedly told her, "I also had a dream, back at the cave. Chief Acuta's heart was being cut out by Jucawa on a big rock and he reached out to me, saying, bring him the songbird." Pausing, he asked, "What does all this mean, Shana? Did Jucawa kill Chief Acuta?" He started panicking again with emotional thoughts whirling around in his head.

"I don't know what the dream meant, Toca." Then Shana began smiling big, then it turned into a joyful quiet laughter.

"That's not funny, Shana!"

"I know it's not, I'm laughing at something else." Shaking her head in disbelief, seeing a bigger picture of what was going on, she replied, "I just realized, this whole time we've been together, you never asked me what my name means or I guess you would call my spirit image." She sat there, calming down with a smiling grin across her face, putting her hand back on top of his.

It took Toca a moment, then he put it together as his mouth dropped open and asked, "Your spirit image is the songbird?"

She couldn't control her excitement any longer. Jumping to her feet, giddy, she slowly spread her arms out as far as the pain would allow and acted like she was flying around the firepit as she began to sing an upbeat song.

He couldn't believe it; how could he have completely missed this? She sang the whole way on their journey and he never thought when Chief Acuta meant the songbird, it was her.

"Why didn't you ever tell me that was your spirit image?"

Answering between words of her song, she said, "You never asked?"

He lay there, looking back up into the trees again, in relief and disbelief.

Shana stopped singing and dancing around next to the hammock and looked down at Toca, saying, "So you were to bring him a songbird, here I am!" she stated as if she was a prize. Then laughed again and started singing and dancing around the firepit.

Toca wasn't quite in the same happy mood as she. He was more concerned with what was going on in his village and was getting annoyed with her. "Shana, stop that, we need to figure out what has happened with my father, Chief Acuta."

She quickly stopped and said, "Sorry but don't you see how God has been involved this whole time? Even before you left, God was the one that planted the thought of a songbird in Chief Acuta's dream about me. God knew I was going to bring the knowledge of him to your people so you would know him. Isn't that great!" She was giddy again.

He stopped to think about it as the idea was unraveling itself to him. "You are right about your God. He is everywhere and he does speak to us in many different ways. He spoke to me in my head when I hesitated and started to worry just before I entered the tribal hut." He put on a slight grin, looking in her direction.

"He did? What did he say?"

Toca closed his eyes, trying to remember all the inspiring words that gave him more confidence in this God of Shana's. Keeping his eyes closed, he said, "Your God said to me, 'I was with you when you met your spirit image, the black jaguar, and it turned you around to go back to Shana to find me. I was with you when the giant caiman gave you great courage, purpose, food, and shelter. I was with you when the moonlight showed you the target, protecting Shana from the others in the canoes. I was with you when the mother sloth calmed you and reminded you of who you are as a Nashua. I was with you when you fought the giant snake, giving you another great victory and showing you the truth. I was with you when the cool soft breeze flowed through the forest, touching you, demonstrating how compassionate I am, stumbling you to fall on Shana to help her breathe again. I was with you when the eagle called for you to show you my wondrous splendor, giving you a small glance of how big I truly am. I was with you when the lightning and thunder unveiled my strength from only a whisper and that I never have to answer a challenge because I'm God, your Creator. I know all things that has happened, is happening, and is going to happen to you Toca. Fear nothing, my child, for I am always with you.'"

Shana looked at him, very impressed he remembered all that. Not knowing half the animals and when these situations happened but it did sound like God talking. "Wow, that's really inspiring, isn't it?"

"That's what I thought and felt so I didn't hesitate anymore and quickly shadowed into the hut. But if he is always with me, how come Jucawa was in there and why did your God let him do this to me?"

Shana knew exactly where this was going because she had been there many times. "We're not always going to know why God allows things to happen, even bad hurtful things like my mother and father dying or why the snake almost killed me and why you got hurt now. But I do know that God has always been here with me." She pointed to her heart. "When I least expect it, he comforts me and lets me know everything will be okay because he is always with me, just like he told you." She looked up into the sky and said, "My father always said, 'How would we know if something or someone was good if we never experienced the bad? How would we know it was daylight if we never experienced the dark night? And how would we know the wonders and greatness of God, being a loving heavenly Father, if he never allowed us to freely choose and experience for ourselves life with him, and without him living alone in this bad, dark, selfish, and evil world?'"

CHAPTER 20

Several days have come and gone as the two old children confined themselves to this spot to heal and think through what they should do to get themselves into the village. And find out what had happened to Chief Acuta and why Jucawa was in the chief position. Toca was very frustrated, being so badly hurt, and that he wasn't more aware at the tribal hut. Also realizing Chief Acuta wasn't inside and he himself wasn't ready to protect himself from Jucawa hitting him.

His mind continued to fester as the dark evil fog fought for position in Toca, trying to convince him he was never going to be chief without a shell to show his people anymore. Even then, if he did show up now, he would have failed both Katatas. And would never be given man status for getting back after the thirteenth moon, only to be an old child for the rest of his life. Jucawa was the only one that saw him on time as his words continued to haunt Toca, echoing in his head, *My people will never know you brought back a shell and they will never know you were here.*

Not only was Toca angry, he was getting depressed. Lying in his hammock, staring into the treetops, barely talking anymore, with only quiet groans of pain showing up here and there. The shady poisonous voice was relentless, whispering to him he was a failure and wasn't worthy of being a chief anyways, let alone a man. And the only Nashua deserving to be chief was mighty Jucawa.

Shana, on the other hand, was in fairly good spirits. Her relationship with God was being renewed and beginning to blossom. She was reading the Bible now all the time and was reflecting how God has been proving himself the whole journey through the Amazon forest.

Also it was a big boost for her that they were together, again making her world feel complete. She was feeling more and more like a grown woman taking care of the both of them—finding food, attending to their wounds, and finally being aware around the area, protecting them. They had completely traded roles for once since they met and she was enjoying it. But on the other hand with Toca, it was only adding to his depression.

She finished working the beautiful jaguar hide, softening it up with the milk from the laminia tree vine, then cut pieces of it off, making new body coverings for herself. With a wide strip of the multicolored fur, she made a top covering that went around her chest area going under her arms, coming together tied in the back. Her shoulders, arms, and lower half of her torso were exposed. Next she made front and back flaps that draped freely down from her hips to the middle of her thighs replacing the ones made out of monkey skin several moons ago. Finally she made a new machete sheath similar to the quick one she made when she went after Toca in the hidden entrance. The sheath hung tight across her back with the handle of the long knife sticking up perfectly behind her right shoulder for easy access but completely out of the way as the strap holding it together came across the front of her body.

Once she had her bright and colorful new clothes on, she danced around, showing Toca her fine work, asking him what he thought. "I finally finished my new clothes and long knife holder, Toca, what do you think?" she asked with a smile.

He slowly rolled his head over, lying in the hammock, not showing any emotion, and said smugly, "So that's what you cut up the jaguar hide for?"

Shana reflected back to him a hurt expression as she stopped moving around and replied, "I told you I was going to make things out of it and you didn't say anything."

"I am now. Why did you waste it on something you don't need? I told you Nashua women don't wear top body coverings." He rolled his head back away from her, continuing in a gloomy tone, "It doesn't matter, you'll never be Nashua and I…I am not going to be one either anymore. I'm never going back."

"What do you mean you're never going back?" she asked, raising her eyebrows confused.

With his head still turned away, he answered, "I can't go back, I will always be an old child, never a man to my people. They will never know I was there before the thirteenth full moon rose, Jucawa made that clear."

She knelt down next to the hammock and put her hand on his, saying gently, "Toca, you have always been a man to me. Not showing up on time or not having a shell doesn't mean you're not a man. It's who you are inside that makes you a man, they will understand."

"Not my people!" he snapped back, twisting his head in her direction, jerking his hand away from hers. "You must prove yourself, just like our first chief did and every old male child after him. How am I supposed to do that now? It's too late, it's over, I have failed!"

She stood up and looked down at him, upset he discarded her compassion and sympathy, and boldly stated, "So…Jucawa beat you up again and it appears he tried to kill you. So you're just going to run away and let your people live suffering like you and your mother have all your life? Is that what you want? You told me Chief Acuta wanted you to be chief, not him. Don't you want to honor his wishes? We don't know what happened. Maybe he did die, that doesn't mean you should run away. You are a man, Toca!" She raised her voice. "You have proven to me and to yourself you are worthy of man status and to be chief!" Shana paused, letting her words take their effect on him, then finished. "I didn't come all this way to give up. You and I both know it was God that brought us together and arranged all this for a purpose. To inspire you and your people to save them from certain death!" She raised a hand and started pointing at him. "You have a choice, act like a man and face Jucawa, telling your people the truth and letting God prove himself to you and them that he is all-knowing and powerful. Or act like a child and run away, knowing your people will certainly die!"

After finishing her last statement, she stood there with a stern look, with both hands now on her hips, staring at his bewildered beat-up face. Shana knew what was said was either going to make it worse on him or he was going to come out of this self-pity turtle shell and be hungry once again to be the future chief of his people, leading with courage, wisdom, and honor.

She turned around and started to walk away as he replied with a quick shout, "Shana, don't walk away from me, I am a man and you know I don't run from a fight!" She took another step as a smile came across her face, knowing which direction her challenge took him and it instantly gave her relief.

He clumsily and slowly sat up, trying to ignore the pain, then rose to his feet as he gradually straightened up, pulling back his broad shoulders as much as he could and stretched out the rest of his body. He was still very weak and off-balance from lying down for so long. As he stood tall, inhaling deeply, ready to verbally engage with Shana to regain his manhood, something fairly large caught the corner of his eye, faintly moving in the shadows of the growth of the forest, just outside the small hidden camp. Not reacting to draw attention and let whatever it is know he knew it was there, he took a couple of steps to Shana. With her back still to him, he slowly wrapped his arms around her placing his mouth close to her ear and quietly whispered, "Don't move or say anything, my love, there is something or someone hidden in the forest on the other side of the firepit."

Her body instantly stiffened, locking up at the unexpected words coming out of his mouth. "I don't know how long it has been there, I can't smell it or hear it, but I just saw it move. I'm going to let go of you and I want you to—" Toca paused, thinking he heard something. Intently listening, he wondered if he was just hearing things then faintly heard it again; something like a soft chirp from a cricket. Toca's eyes went wide, confirming and recognizing the sound. His body slightly began to tremble as Shana thought to herself, he is shaking from fear or weakness. Toca continued telling Shana, "I want you to climb up high in the tree the hammock is tied to and wait for me to come back. I'm going to pick up the knife we found in the dead one and shadow into the forest and come around to the back of what is stalking us."

Shana whispered, slowly twisting her head back, "No, Toca, I'll go with you with the long knife, you are weak and still badly hurt."

"I'll be fine, I will have enough strength, just do what I say." He slowly pressed her away from him toward the tree. He then walked naturally past the firepit, picking up a small piece of burnt wood, then took a step to the pile of items under the hammock, without stopping, grasping tightly the old knife. Before Shana was partially up the tree, he had disappeared into the dense green plants surrounding the small camp.

Toca quickly shadowed his body with lines of the charcoal piece of wood, grimacing off and on in pain as he stretched his body around, slithering his way in the opposite direction of the movement he saw. Excitement and adrenaline were building, giving him hidden energy and the strength he needed, moving as Black Ghost, swiftly turning and circling wide around to come in on to the backside of what was watching them. Without a sound, he snaked his way through the ferns and trees, staying in the darkest shadows, keeping focused with his eyes, ears, and nose. Not seeing what he was looking for, he could feel its presence as the hair on the back of his neck started to rise and a tingling sensation was spreading throughout his body. The closer he got to the spot he saw the movement, the harder his heart started to pound. With his knife ready, he stopped just a few steps short behind cover and waited for more information to come to his senses—hear it breathing, smell it, or see it move—but there was nothing.

Toca paused some more, then slowly moved his head to the left to see if it had moved but again, nothing. He then moved his body to the right like a praying mantis, imitating the movement of the leaves to blend in, and suddenly stopped all body functions.

Toca couldn't move; he found himself being the one hunted and he just lost. At his throat was the sharp tip of a spearhead that came out of the bush he was standing next to. It took a moment for him to think of what to do, then said in the dialect of the Nashua, "Father, will you ever let me win this game we play?"

A soft tired crackly voice came out of the bush and answered, "Only when you can win on your own, son." The spear withdrew itself back into the bush and the leaves slowly parted as the old and short shadowed Chief Acuta gradually appeared in front of Toca, looking up.

All Toca could do is just stare at him as emotions of joy, excitement, embarrassment, and relief let loose all at once and tears began to flow down his face as his chin uncontrollably quivered, swallowing deep. Chief Acuta leaned his long spear against the tree next to them and reached out and up, with both skinny arms wide open, as his hands gently and uncontrollably shook, saying, "I'm glad to see you alive, Toca, the Black Ghost." The chief's old graying eyes welled up with tears as he tried to show a smile through the ages of wrinkles.

Toca slowly stepped forward, bending over gently, touching his forehead to the chief's, then went into the unexpected arms, swallowing the chief up as he held them steadily balanced for a long time. Finally the chief patted Toca on the shoulders and said, "So you didn't forget our secret call."

Toca let go, stepping back, and replied, "I will never forget anything you and I have shared. I almost couldn't control myself when I heard it, I wanted to run to you."

Chief Acuta explained, "My eyesight has gotten bad and I couldn't clearly see if it was you or not in the hammock until you stood up. You've gotten so big and tall, then there was a female with you and you two were talking different. So I made our secret sound, and if it was you, you would be the only one that would know I was here and you would come looking for me."

Toca suddenly remembered Shana was still in the tree and told the chief, "Father, there is so much I want to tell you and show you, but first, I have someone you have to meet. Come, it will be all right." He hesitated, then Toca waved his hand for him to follow, shaking his head that it would be fine. They slowly made their way to the opening of the camp, stepping in view of Shana who was still waiting in the tree with the long knife out, ready to defend herself.

Lowering the machete, relieved to see Toca finally appear with his camouflage shadow markings, she suddenly tensed up again, pointing out with the long knife as the unexpected shadow behind him came to life. Shana leaped from the tree like a monkey to the ground, landing crouched as a jaguar, ready to jump at its prey, and yelled, “Watch out behind you, Toca!” Shana sprang up quickly toward him, moving faster than he had ever seen her. She began screaming with all she had as though she was a wild cat attacking, waving the long knife in the air, prepared to save her man.

Toca instantly stepped in front of Chief Acuta, moving one arm back and around to put him behind him again, lifting up the other in front of him to stop Shana, shouting out, “No, no, no, Shana, it’s okay, it’s okay!”

Shana instantly stopped midstride, a couple steps away from Toca, standing straight up with her head awkwardly held high, looking toward the sky on her tiptoes. Toca looked at her stance, not expecting the abrupt change of behavior, gazed down toward her exposed throat and saw the same spearhead that was at his throat moments earlier, now at hers. He followed the long shaft with his eyes as it went down under the arm he was holding Chief Acuta back with, then twisted his head back to see his father put on a slight smile as if to say, “I won again.”

Toca smiled back, giving him a deep laugh. It was moments like this he longed for repeatedly the past thirteen moons. Having his father with him, experiencing life together, and Chief Acuta always knowing and doing everything right. Demonstrating to him what it means to always be ready, aware, and what wisdom looked like all in one.

Toca looked back to Shana as he slowly moved his hand down onto the spear and pressed it down so the tip was pointing to the ground, saying, “Shana, don’t be afraid. The one behind me is Chief Acuta.”

Her expression completely changed as she was absorbing the unexpected information and relieved at the same time that she wasn’t going to have her throat cut open. Toca saw the look on her face as that big smile he was so familiar with started to show and he could see the excitement erupting inside her. He knew what was coming next and had to stop her before she really got hurt.

Toca stepped forward, firmly grasping her by the shoulders, stopping her from smothering the chief with hugs of affection.

"Shana, look at me...look at me." Trying to get her attention as she bobbed her head around his to get a look at the chief.

"Shana, remember, like me, he never in his long life has met an outsider or others." Toca was looking deep into her eyes as hers locked in on his, understanding what he was saying and knew she had to control herself. As their eyes were mirroring each other's, Toca's began swirling around and was getting lightheaded as his body started to weave back and forth.

Shana brought her hands up to his arms to balance him, knowing he had just overexerted himself, depleted of energy.

"Toca, lay back down. You're still very weak, everything will be all right. I will control myself." She smiled, knowing what he was thinking. He nodded as he breathed deeply, blinking his eyes, trying to get rid of the stars floating around in his head. Then the pain in his side shouted out, reminding him it was there as he bent over, holding the wound.

Toca turned around as Shana held on to him and said in Nashua tongue, "Father, this is Shana, an old child like me on her womanhood journey from a faraway place. She will be my mate, if you bless me with her. I'm badly hurt and extremely weak..." Toca's legs were giving out as they began wobbling.

"Toca, to the hammock now," Shana ordered as she let go of his arms and wrapped her arm around his body, stumbling him to the bed, laying him down. He squinted his eyes closed, trying to clear his head, then opened them, twisting his head sideways to look at Chief Acuta. But he was gone, disappearing as shadows do, with no sound, smell, and visibly without motion.

Extremely weak, in pain, and hardly eating anything for days, he looked around for the chief with his head on the hammock, then closed his eyes, passing out into a deep sleep as if this whole thing was just a dream.

As the day went on, Shana kept close watch over Toca as he slept. She was concerned he was getting worse because his body felt like it was getting hot.

The sudden disappearance of the short wiry and wrinkled old man with the long deadly spear caught Shana off guard but didn't surprise her. Toca would do the same thing all the time over the past ten moons. She looked for him for a while, but like Toca, he just vanished and she didn't even know which direction he went. Not wanting to leave her man alone, she went back to him and sat on the ground next to him lying in the hammock, holding his hand with one of hers and the machete in the other as she herself drifted off on a midday nap.

An unexpected peace had come over her, relaxing the anxiety of them not being alone anymore which helped her to fall asleep. Knowing there was someone else around was comforting, especially one that she knew she could trust.

Later in the evening, Shana still slept soundly, now with her head laid forward on Toca's chest as she sat on the ground with her legs stretched out under the hammock.

"Shana." Her name was so faintly said it didn't seem real. In her dreaming mind, she heard it again, but this time, it sounded like a woman's voice. "Shana." Her name was said a little louder as a vision of her mother came to mind. She could see her face smiling, calling her name, talking to her back in their house on the reservation.

Then she heard quiet whispering, not understanding a word; then once more, her name was kindly spoken. This time, it came with a soft touch on her shoulder, waking her to reality.

Flinching quickly around, facing the direction of where she was touched, letting go of Toca's hand, she stood, whirling the machete around out in front of her. Backing up to Toca's hammock to get her bearings and to protect him, she looked forward, blinking her eyes awake from the deep sleep. Standing in front of her in the shadows of the trees, two dark figures were cautiously peering at her. She thought for a moment, maybe this was still a dream until one of the shadows stepped forward and a long familiar spear stood upright as the butt of it softly touched the ground.

Gaining her composure, slowly understanding there wasn't immediate danger, she took a deep breath as she quickly looked back at Toca, still asleep, making sure he was fine. Then she looked back at the withering old man, wearing only a manhood cover, as she slowly lowered the machete and stood up straight, no longer in a crouched attack position.

They both absorbed each other, not truly knowing what to do, then the other figure gracefully came out from behind him. With the other person in clear view, Shana's eye's opened wide, dropping her jaw in shock as words slowly dribbled out of her mouth. "Mother?"

It was like her vision, she was seeing her mother but it wasn't her and she knew it, but how? *How was this possible*? she thought.

Shana didn't realize she said the word *mother* out loud in her native Indian language as the woman in front of her responded slowly in a different but familiar language, smiling with the gentlest of voices. "Yes, I am Toca's mother."

Now Shana really was in complete awe. Or was it confusion? She didn't know. All she wanted to do was hug this person tightly. The motherly presence was so strong and overwhelming, even if it wasn't her own mother, she couldn't help herself. Shana stepped forward, dropping the machete to the ground, she opened her arms and started crying. Wrapping her arms around this beautiful kind woman, she lay her head on her shoulder as though she was a baby. The tears of relief of someone coming to help them flowed. Tears of joy poured out to finally meet the people that meant everything to Toca. Tears of pain emptied out from missing her own mother. The weight of the world seemed to be breaking apart that Shana didn't realize had been building in her.

Toca's mother, Layana, lovingly returned with an embrace, letting Shana know she was well and that she was cared for. After a few moments of emotional release, a grunt came from the chief as he touched Layana's shoulder and pointed to Toca lying in the hammock. Both the females reacted slowly, letting go of each other as Layana lifted her hand to Shana's chin, lifting it up so their eyes would meet. She smiled then said softly, "Old child, everything will be all right."

Shana didn't totally understand what she said but knew what she was saying and it was comforting. Layana then looked past Shana to Toca lying down, then looked back with a head nod as if to ask her if she could approach him. Shana stepped to the side, pointing out to him as his mother methodically made her way to her son for the first time in a sun season, examining every detail of him and the surrounding area.

Kneeling next to his side, she watched him breathe and looked at the bruised and cut marks all over his body. When her eyes got to the wrap around his stomach, she looked at Shana in a questionable manner. Shana instantly knew she wanted to look at what was underneath so Shana gently lifted the wrap, not to disturb Toca sleeping.

Layana gave her first facial expression of concern at the sight of the deep cut area and the stitching but calmly went on with her visual exam. Back at Toca's head, she now touched her son, for the first time in a sun season, with the back of her hand softly and lovingly on his face and forehead. She nodded to herself, knowing what was wrong with him and where he was in the healing stages.

Leaning back to look at Chief Acuta standing at the edge of camp, Layana whispered a few words to him then gracefully stood, gingerly patting Shana on the shoulder, noticing the dried gray paste smeared down her shoulders and arms, then left the small camp, fading away into the forest. Shana couldn't take her eyes off Layana as she disappeared into the shadows. Shana shook her head awake as though she was hypnotized by the presence and movements of this new woman in her life.

With her head still turned away from Toca, she glanced over to Chief Acuta, standing in the shadows away from her. Not sure way he wouldn't come closer, she stayed seated at Toca's side, holding his hand. Looking back at Toca, it was getting awkward with the silence. Fortunately for the both of them, Layana was soon back, stealthily stepping into the small living area, going directly to Toca.

Earlier, seeing the bamboo cups sitting next to the hammock with water in them, she asked, nodding her head toward them if she could use them. Understanding Layana's intentions, she grabbed one, putting it in front of Layana as she knelt. Layana smiled at Shana as she set down a long thin hollow reed from the river on the ground then put several light-green leaves with yellow stripes, six purple round berries, and five fat squirming white grubs in the cup of water. Picking up a small stick lying next to the firepit, she started to stir and crush up everything in the cup. Stopping in midmotion, she looked at Shana, asking her if she would take over because she needed to get a yatowa flower. Shana got excited, recognizing the name and uncovered a part of her stash of all the items Toca and she had brought back.

Lifting one of the whole plants, roots and all, Shana handed it to her. At the same time, she opened her mouth, rolling back her tongue, and pulled out her last ball of the yellow flower that had lost its potency.

Layana, at first, smiled that they both were communicating but wondered why she had a piece of it in her mouth then asked, slowly pointing to Shana's shoulders and arms. "Do you have yatowa petals in your mouth for the same reason for the gray past on your shoulders and arms?"

Even though the words were sketchy, she understood, watching Layana's eyes looking at her body.

Shana replied slowly, "No, well, a little but mainly because of my broken ribs." She then took ahold of Layana's hand and gently placed it against her side. Slowly moving her hand around, Layana felt what Shana was trying to tell her as she gave out a shallow inhale and a painful look on her face.

Watching on from a short distance, Chief Acuta asked, not able to see exactly what they were feeling for, "Is she with baby?"

Layana quickly gave the chief a scowling look, knowing what he was thinking, and stated, "*No*!" Then she added, looking back at Shana with a comforting expression, "She has broken ribs."

"Ask the old female child about the dead jaguar," Chief Acuta told her.

Still looking into Shana's face, Layana asked, "Did the jaguar do this to you before Toca killed it?"

Shana didn't fully understand what she was asking but thought she heard something like, "Jaguar…Toca…killed."

Hesitating, Shana thought through how to respond as a voice behind them caught everyone off guard as he answered his mother in their language, "Shana's ribs were broken by a giant anaconda." He had quietly woken up, hearing Nashua words being spoken.

Layana spun her head around, with her breath taken away, hearing her son's voice, now deeper, more grown-up. At the same time, the chief responded, "Toca, you're awake!"

Toca and his mother locked eyes, instantly feeling emotions, telling each other stories through them. Silence captured the moment as they truly didn't know what to say or where to start. Toca smiled, still with his head lying down on the hammock, wanting to gather his mother up in his arms yet, at the same time, wanted to run away and hide. His mind began running rampant with embarrassment and humiliation, reflecting back to their last conversation about how he would protect her when he got older. Then her telling him to bring back a shell and he could change their lives and the lives of all the people in the tribe.

You failed, old child! the dark voice silently echoed in his head.

Layana slowly knelt near her son, wanting to hold him as she did as a child. To comfort him which always seem to take away his pains. She had to restrain herself as not to embarrass him in front of the chief as well as this new old female child. For in her mind, Toca was still her little boy; but now older, she understood how important pride and honor were.

Instead she stayed calm, putting on her beautiful smile, keeping her hands to herself, and gently said, "It is good to see you again, my son, you have grown more than I thought you would."

Toca was at a loss for words as his eyes went back and forth among the others staring back at him. His breathing quickened as panic was creeping in. Shana saw what was happening and knew what he was feeling and thinking, unlike the chief and his mother.

Understanding this, she had to come to his rescue to protect her man from losing what was sacred to him—honor and pride. Quickly stepping in front of his mother, kneeling to hide him from his family, she whispered in their own made-up dialect, "Black Ghost, focus on the truth." They looked deep into each other as Shana slowly nodded her head yes for him to agree and continued, "You were back before the thirteenth moon and you brought back a shell, a songbird, and a good God." Then she mouthed these next words, just in case the chief or Layana could hear and understand what she was saying. "I love you. You will be all right. God knows everything and is everywhere."

For reasons unknown, Toca instantly felt a shower of peace come over him. It was so strong he even looked toward the sky to see if it was raining but all that caught his eye was a huge beautiful light-blue butterfly with two big black dots, one in the center of each wide wing, appearing to be looking at him. As the incredible insect softly floated away, it gave the illusion of eyes winking at him as if to say, "I'm watching over you."

CHAPTER 21

Shana stood between Layana and Toca, waiting for him to have an emotional attitude change so he wouldn't be embarrassed and lose face in front of his two family members that showed up earlier today.

After the large light-blue butterfly calmed him, giving him clarity, and was out of sight, Toca's eyes drifted back to Shana. She had an encouraging smile, hoping he would quickly adapt to what she was doing, then mouthed a soft whisper to remind him what he told her moons ago. "The Katata Ado makes great men and leaders, prove it to them you are just that. You don't need to have a shell to see it in you, Toca."

Then she turned around to put pressure on him to follow her lead and said, with great confidence to Chief Acuta and his mother, very slowly, hoping they would understand the words, "Black Ghost of the Nashua has accomplished the greatest Katata Ado his people have ever known. He completed it before the thirteenth full moon rose but was almost killed during his return ceremony in the tribal hut."

Toca's eyes went wide, surprised she went that far, then put a firm strong look on his face as he lifted his head, trying to peer around Shana, staring at the chief and his mother with confidence.

The chief immediately took a step forward closer than he ever had, raising his spear, gently hitting the ground, making a deep thudding sound to get everyone's attention. He paused for a moment then, with a tone of wisdom, asked slowly, imitating how Shana talked, "What do you mean he was almost killed in the tribal hut?"

Shana looked directly at Chief Acuta, surprised he understood her as she completely understood him. She thought probably that Toca's and her version of their combined language had adapted to his more than they thought over the past ten moons. It was just harder to understand everything, talking fast. Stepping to the side so Toca could see the chief clearly, she asked, "Why were you not there?"

The chief stood, shocked, completely taken off guard that this old female child had this knowledge. Layana looked at him, surprised herself, then angrily mumbled these words to him, "You said he was hurt from killing the jaguar here."

Toca, in a firm controlled tone, said as he slowly tried to sit up as Shana helped him, "Shana killed the jaguar, that's how she got the scratches down her shoulders and arms."

Both chief and Layana looked at each other, then stared at Shana in disbelief. After a few moments of silence, the chief said, "Now I understand why she is wearing its skin. But I do not understand why she is wearing it around her chest?"

Completely taking a different path from the tense atmosphere, Toca started to laugh, then tried to stop as he grimaced, holding his stomach area, then lay back down.

Shana instantly blushed, comprehending what Chief Acuta asked. Not only because they were talking about her chest but that Toca had been telling the truth the whole time. Then she looked at Layana and truly, for the first time, realized she was only wearing lower flaps made out of deer hide, one in the front and one in the back, nothing on her upper body.

Still calmly laughing, Toca asked, "Why don't you answer him, Shana?" She looked around at him, giving him a silent glare as if to say, "Okay, you were right but don't push it."

Looking back to the chief she put on a smile and said, motioning with her hands, "Where I am from, my tribe wears upper and lower body coverings."

Layana turned to the chief, then to Toca and Shana, asking, "Where are you from? I did not know there were others."

Chief Acuta was quick to answer to be in control, speaking in Nashua, "Layana, there are things only the chief is to know and the old male children that go on their Katata Ados. This is to protect the Nashua."

"Why?" she asked abruptly. "Why keep things from your people?" She was not speaking in her normal controlled calm manner.

"There are many things out away from the hidden valley that we must stay hidden from. Many dangerous things that will hurt or even kill our people," the chief attempted to answer her without divulging the secrets of their tribe's past.

Looking and pointing at Shana, Layana stated, "This old female child is not from the hidden valley or Nashua. Does she look dangerous to you?" Something deep inside Layana was coming out that was needing answers.

She continued, "You and I are out of the valley, hiding from our own people because they want to hurt us and even kill you." Raising her voice, she said, "Now they tried to kill my son! What is so bad that we are hiding from on the outside of the valley?"

The chief stood his ground, not willing to share any more, staring at the ground. Then a grunting sound came from the hammock as Toca slowly stood, closing his eyes, swallowing down the pain and hoping to have enough strength to be involved in this important discussion.

Layana quickly went to his side as did Shana as both their eyes met at the same time, bumping into each other, going to his rescue. Shana physically and mentally held her ground with her position as his woman. For the first time, she was threatened by someone with her relationship with Toca. Then quick wittedly submitted, smiling, stepping to Toca's other side, knowing she was the new other.

Layana quietly understood what just happened and lovingly smiled at Shana, proud that Toca had a woman that cared for him this much. She bent over and picked up the bamboo cup filled with the items she brought back to camp and mixed together, along with the long hollow reed. Putting the straw-like reed in the cup, she held it up to Toca's mouth to drink as she slightly tilted her head up to tell him to drink what was in the cup through the reed.

He gave her that happy frown he always had when she would have him drink medicines that tasted bad through the straw. It always seems to taste better through the hollow water reed.

Sucking up the whole cup of mixed items, Toca gave a slight shudder and a squeamish facial expression at the bad-tasting leaves but unexpectedly tasted his favorite white grubs and sweet berries in it as well. With both women at his side and the chief in front of him with a distraught look, Toca knew he needed to take charge of the situation. Slowly pulling away from the women, he stepped in front of Chief Acuta, giving the respectful greeting of touching their foreheads together. Then he looked into the aging eyes of his chief and new father figure and asked, "Do you remember the three things you told me to bring back?"

The chief's eyes got wide as concern of secrets and privileged information might be said out loud, peered around Toca at the women a few steps away. Then looking back into the eyes of an older, bigger, much stronger and wiser old male child, he nodded.

Toca hesitated then responded with a whisper, "I brought them *all...* back with me."

The chief didn't know what to do or say for a moment then started to look around the forest as though something was watching them. Toca knew exactly what he was doing, he had done the same thing many times. Then he reached out, touching him by the shoulder, and said quietly, "Everything is all right, he is a good God."

Still with his weak eyes doing their best to see something, he began to smell deeply as he tilted his head side to side, attempting to hear and smell the unknown as his spear no longer was sitting on the ground. It was now pointing up and outward in a protective position with two hands holding it.

Toca moved himself in front of the spear to get the chief's attention, saying with a louder whisper, "Father, there is nothing to fear. This God knew you were looking for him two sun seasons ago. He told Shana's father, from a faraway place, to come to the hidden valley to inspire the Nashua, giving us purpose."

Regaining his composure, leaning on Toca's confidence that everything was all right, the chief's focus quickly went to Shana, saying to her, "Old female child, come here," as the butt of his spear pounded the ground again. Shana looked at Layana, asking with her eyes, "Did I do something wrong?" Both women started to walk forward, then Chief Acuta told Layana, pointing his finger at her, "No, Layana, you stay there."

Layana frowned at him, not understanding but obeyed anyways, stepping back next to the hammock.

Shana stepped forward as he stayed focused on her. When she got to him, he looked her up and down, then asked, "Where are you from, the endless water?"

Feeling uneasy and intimidated, she answered with a shaky voice, "No, from a land faraway north."

His eyes narrowed, crinkling his wrinkled face even more, asking, "What is your tribe's name and what is its tribal symbol?"

Shana loosened up her posture at the nonaggressive questions and answered, "The Manos tribe." Pausing, she never thought about what their symbol was but understood the importance for Chief Acuta. Knowing the Nashua's was the yellow round ball on Toca's anklet and the one they found on the dead person in the cave which represented the sun, meaning new beginnings.

The only thing that came to mind was around her neck. She pulled up on the string to bring out the miniature pyramid rock medallion that was hidden between her top covering and chest. When it was in the open, she grasped it. stepping closer to the chief so he could have a close look at it. As she did that, Chief Acuta squinted to focus on what she was holding in her hand.

Suddenly he started gasping for air, stumbling back, trying not to fall down from the explosive shock of what he recognized, bringing up his spear to stab Shana in the throat. With lightning speed, Toca grabbed the top of the spear shaft, just below the sharp narrow rock tip before it touched her. Then with his other hand, he ripped the weapon from the chief's hands, causing him to be flung to the ground.

Toca pivoted to face the chief lying on the ground, pointing his spear at him, and asked, "What are you doing? Shana will be my woman!"

Chief Acuta slowly crawled to his feet, trying to recover from two unexpected moments—recognizing Shana's tribe's talisman around her neck and that Toca easily put him to the ground. As he stood, he raised his voice, speaking loudly, pointing his crooked shaking finger at Shana. "You brought a bad god to our valley! You brought a bad god to our people! Our hearts will be ripped out of our chests! We will all die a horrible death, Toca, we will all die, just like our long-forgotten dead ancestors. I warned you at your going-away ceremony!"

Toca knew what the chief was saying and feeling. He had to quickly calm him down and gain his trust. He had never seen the chief this afraid; it was so strong of a feeling coming from him, Toca himself fought to keep a clear mind and not fall into the same trap of emotions he himself did when Shana told him her God wanted their hearts.

Letting the spear drop to the ground, he grasped the shoulders of the trembling body of the weathered old man, saying, "Father, I know what worries you but everything will be all right. I had the same fears with what this God of Shana's is and where he's at."

Still pointing his finger at Shana, he answered back, "No, no, Toca, listen to me, you have been fooled. You brought the bad god of our ancestors here to the hidden valley."

"What would make you say and believe this?" Toca calmly replied.

They were talking loudly and everyone could hear their conversation. Layana stayed her ground, away from the three, completely confused of what was being talked about. It was all foreign to her.

The chief stepped very close to Toca to whisper his secret. "Do you remember the small pouch I had you get for me that was hidden under the floor of the tribal hut?"

Toca nodded his head yes.

"And I told you the only thing left to show the secret of where our people came from was inside and until you became chief is only when I would show it to you?"

Again Toca nodded in agreement.

Still whispering, he said, "That talisman the old female child is wearing around her neck is the exact same one in the pouch!"

Toca dropped his hands from the chief's shoulder, stunned, instantly confused with many things racing through his mind; he glanced over to look at Shana, trying to remember all the conversations they had about where she was from and what the talisman represented. As he turned to face her directly, he bent over, picking up the spear then slightly pointed it in her direction, just in case, then spoke in their made-up dialect. "Where did you say you got that talisman again?"

Shana looked down at it hanging from her neck, laying it on the jaguar-skin top body covering, and answered, "My mother gave it to me when we she was dying."

"Where did she get it?"

"She said that her mother gave it to her like all the mothers before them had done for many generations."

Toca's curiosity was building as his defensive posture weakened. "Did your mother say where it came from?"

Thinking back to passed conversations with her mother, she replied, "She said their tribe long, long ago traveled north from a distant place before they lived where our people live now."

Toca was silent for a moment, thinking.

"Toca, what are you two talking about?" Chief Acuta asked anxiously, standing behind his much larger son.

Toca raised his hand to silence him, trying to put together a similar story he heard a sun season ago. Then he gasped in disbelief, quickly turning around to the chief, and asked in Nashua tongue, "The story you told me about our people escaping from their village. You said they split up, one going south and the other going north?"

This time, the chief nodded yes.

"I can't remember all that you said, what happened again?"

Whispering back to Toca, he answered, "This is a secret conversation we should not be talking in front of the females."

Toca got a bit frustrated and said, "Father, stop with the secrets. They are going to know everything sooner or later. What happened?"

The chief glanced over to both females, then looked back at Toca, still whispering, "Our people were being chased by the priest's warriors. When they got close, the group split up. One going north and the other going south to confuse the warriors. When the next full moon rose, they were to come back together at a meeting place then travel on together again. Our ancestors went south, and when they returned to meet with the other group, the other group never returned. So they thought that they had been killed by the warriors."

Toca put on a big smile as overwhelming clarity was uncovered. A deep laughter of excitement began building as the two stories came together, answering the chief's question, just like the one Shana and he had throughout their journey—why were they able to understand each other but couldn't understand others? Because they were from the same people that ran away from the bad gods.

Toca gave the spear back to the shorter withered chief as he turned to Shana, putting his arm around her, still smiling, trying his best not to laugh out loud, flinching at his side.

Everyone was looking at him as if he was delirious, then his mom spoke up, noticing his pain. "Toca, are you all right? Do you need more yatowa flower?"

Toca nodded his head yes, closing his eyes at the pain, then envisioned the responses of the chief and Shana with what he was about to tell him. Layana bent down, picking up the flower Shana gave her earlier, pulling off a few yellow petals, rolling them up. Stepping up to Toca, she said, "Open your mouth." He did so and she dropped the small ball under his rolled-back tongue. Still chuckling deep, letting the pain-killing ball get moistened up as he drew in its powerful medicine.

With his arm still around Shana, he stepped them forward close to the chief who was being as his father, being very apprehensive, kept his eyes on the talisman the old female child was wearing, taking on a protective posture.

Toca cleared his throat, attempting to be serious, and began an introduction. "Chief Acuta of the Nashua tribe, whose talisman is the monkey and is the adopted father of the Black Ghost. I present to you Shana, one of our own people from the original ancient ones that escaped from the tribe of the bad gods."

The chief flinched his head, tilting it to the side, narrowing his eyes at Toca, and said, "I don't understand."

Toca almost couldn't control himself from divulging the answer, stepping slightly away from Shana to look at her, and explained,

"Shana's ancient people were from the ones that went north that our forefathers thought were killed by the warriors."

Chief Acuta's expression completely changed as he calmed his body language and somehow had a look on his face that smoothed out some of the wrinkles.

Toca continued, "Like you, she has a small piece of our forefathers' history and they were able to find a good God. Now they are sharing this good God with their own people."

The story sounded like it could be true but he was not going to be easily fooled. Looking to Shana, he asked slowly so she could understand, "This God of yours, what does it want from us and where is it?"

Toca quickly twisted his head, giving her a glare she understood, and asked, "Do you understand what he asked?"

She nodded yes.

"Be careful how you answer!"

She thought it through for a moment, knowing it wouldn't be good to mention the word *heart*. Looking back at Layana, seeing Toca's mother, waiting patiently behind them, gave her an idea. She put her hand out to Layana to come over and hold her hand. Layana was glad to finally be involved with whatever was going on in this confusing conversation as she stepped forward, taking Shana's hand. Then Shana motioned the chief to take the other hand she held out.

He frowned at what she was asking him to do, then looked at Toca for an answer. Toca peered over to Shana with a questionable look, asking, *What are you doing*?

She just smiled back, mouthing silently, *It will be all right.* Then she said aloud, "Toca take your mother's hand and Chief Acuta's."

He paused, then said to himself, *I hope she knows what she's doing.* Then he took his mother's hand and held his hand out, like Shana, for the chief to take ahold of both of theirs.

With Toca involved, the chief didn't want to appear afraid so he boldly leaned his spear against the tree next to him then grasped ahold of the old children's hands. It was a very awkward moment as they were extremely close to one another and this new other was staring at them all. Especially for the chief, he didn't like being near other people anyways.

Shana began to speak slowly, looking at the old man so he hopefully could understand her. "Chief Acuta, you want to know about our good God?" He slowly nodded his head in agreement. "I will show you what God wants from us and where he is." She then looked at Layana, then back to him. "Layana, mother of Toca, and Chief Acuta, adopted father of Toca." Layana slightly crinkled her forehead, not understanding why the chief had been referred to now a couple of times as father to Toca, then just went along with it.

"You two are the parents of the Black Ghost, how do you feel about him?" They both looked at her as if she was crazy. She persisted for an answer, gently shaking their hands, repeating herself. "How do you *feel* about him?"

Layana answered first, being easy for her to answer an emotional question and said, "I love my son, he means everything to me." She turned, looking up at him with a smile. Then they all turned to the chief who was very uneasy to speak as an equal and to answer this strange question.

He hesitated, then boldly stated, holding his head high, "I am proud of my son. He is back from his long journey."

Toca looked to Shana who now had that expression on her face every time she gets excited and knew she wanted to hug each person until they couldn't breathe, slowly shook his head, telling her no. She responded with a giddy smile then asked the parents another question, "What would you *do* for Toca?"

Layana was beginning to enjoy this and didn't hesitate to answer, "I would do anything for him. He is my life," she said, looking at him with a big beautiful smile, making him feel uneasy. It was the same look he would get when he was a little boy.

Again they all turned to the chief for his answer. He paused for a few moments, then let go of their hands. He reached up, grabbing ahold of his shell that dangled down his chest and lifted it up over his head to release the string from around his neck. Looking down into his hands at what made him who he was, he slowly raised his head, staring deep into Toca, then said, "The Black Ghost said he has brought back everything I asked him to bring back to be chief and to save his people. I have always known Toca would be the next chief of the Nashua. I saw his strong heart as a child. It was always good and honest, just like his real father, Tundra." The Chief looked across to Layana, knowing this would affect her as he gave somewhat of a weak smile, then continued, "He has what most old male children don't have to be able to complete the Katata Ado—heart!" Then he slowly pounded his own chest with his free hand to represent what he was talking about.

He looked down again in his other hand at what he has been wearing for more sun seasons than he can remember. The one thing he cherished that has given him honor, respect, and power and said to Toca, "Kneel before me, Black Ghost of the Nashua!" Toca looked at the two women, then back to the old chief with a curious look, wondering what he was doing.

"Kneel!" He repeated, a little impatient, pointing to the ground.

Toca quickly responded, bending down to both his knees, gingerly wincing in pain, then looked up to Chief Acuta.

Without hesitating, the chief asked, "Black Ghost, did you journey to the endless water?"

Apprehensively Toca answered, "Yes."

"What was the color of the water?"

Toca thought it was a strange question but answered, "The color of the sky, blue."

"What did it taste like?"

"Like sweat, salty."

"Did you bring back a shell like this?" The chief opened his hand, showing Toca.

"Yes."

The chief hesitated, asking his final question, wanting Toca's full attention and the attention of both women, then continued, "If you were to be chief of the Nashua, what is your greatest responsibility?"

The women held their breath as they thought for the answer for themselves but Toca beat them to it as he boldly stated without hesitating, "As chief, I have the lives of the people and their future in my hands. The chief is not who makes the tribe, it is all the people that are Nashua that make the tribe. It will be my responsibility to be patient with my people, wise in making decisions, and strong, leading them with selfless courage."

Layana could not hold it in as she heard these incredible words come out of her son who now she knew was a true man. Giddy with excitement, she whispered under her breath, "Yes, you truly came back as a man and a chief."

Chief Acuta paused for a long time after Toca answered his question perfectly, then pondered with confirmation that the Katata Ado truly makes a great chief for the Nashua. Then a shuddering image of Jucawa came to his mind of what happened to him, asking himself, *How come he turned out the way he did*?

Shaking his head free of Jucawa, he looked to Shana, saying slowly for her to understand, "You asked me what I would do for my son. I will give him the one thing I almost died for, getting it on my own Katata Ado many, many sun seasons ago. The only thing that has given me meaning, respect, and power in my life. I am willing to give this to Toca to be a brother to the shell he brought back, giving him more patience, wisdom, strength, and selfless courage than I had being chief of the Nashua."

The chief took the necklace string in both hands, spreading it out, and put it around Toca's head, saying, "I am willing to be nothing so Toca will be everything to save his people."

The old man took a step back, grasping his spear leaning against the tree, then turned back to Toca, using the spear to help him slowly to the ground in front of Toca. Now kneeling, he placed the spear on the ground sideways before Toca, passing on everything he had that made him chief of the Nashua. Then he bowed his face to the ground in respect and honor as he handed the responsibility, burden, and position of chief to Toca.

There was silence among the four of them. Three of which couldn't believe what just happened. Toca was in shock as he looked back to Shana with wide eyes and an open mouth, in awe of seeing what he understood was a miracle, the first one in his life. Just earlier today, he was going to walk away from his people because there was not chance in his mind he could ever be a man, let alone the chief.

He looked to Chief Acuta, still with his head to the ground, and thought he should do something. Thinking quickly, he grabbed the spear, using it to help him up, grunting all the way. Holding the spear in his hand firmly, admiring the weight and balance, but most of all, that it was his now. Not only a weapon or a communication tool but a gift from his father that represented the highest status he could ever reach—Chief Toca of the Nashua.

Grasping it firmly, he hit the ground three times with the butt of the spear, making the loud deep sounds he used to hear to get everyone's attention to make an announcement. Pausing, he inhaled deeply, then said, "I, Toca, the Black Ghost, have accomplished the Katata Ado and I accept from my father, Chief Acuta, to be the new chief of the Nashua people."

CHAPTER 22

Shana was in disbelief of what just took place. She was supposed to be explaining God to them, not this. She looked to Layana, still holding her hand, who was smiling from ear to ear with tears running down her face. Not able to control herself, she joined the celebration and swung her other arm around Layana and hugged her tightly as they both softly cried tears of joy.

Toca turned around with a smile of his own, seeing his mother and Shana hugging. He stepped close to Shana's face and whispered, "Your God is a good God. We have just seen what could never happen. Something greater, beyond what I am or understand, made this happen. Thank you, Shana, for bringing your God to my people who will now be our God." Toca stamped the spear to the ground as though he just made a decree.

Chief Acuta slowly got up as everyone turned to him, his appearance was different. He too had a smile but his was a gaping dark hole with barely any teeth. A glow seemed to be beaming from his face, which hadn't been seen for a long time, as his stature appeared to be lighter, taller, and straighter, as though a very heavy burden had been taken off his shoulders.

As the chief regained his composure from his unexpected transformation, he gladly held out his hands for everyone to hold hands again as they obeyed his silent order, then said, "Old female child, you asked what I would do for my son. My answer is, I would die to myself for him." Proudly holding his head up, staring at his new chief, he continued, getting serious, glancing over to Shana, and said,

"I'll ask you again. What does this god of yours want from us and where is it?"

Surprisingly she was ready with the answers as she excitedly grasped his hand, looking across to Toca, and said, "Our good God loves us just like you both love Toca. The only thing he wants from us is"—she paused, looking around to the other three to make sure they would hear her clearly—"the same love you have for Toca." Pausing again to let that sink in, she then added, "God is everywhere like the air we breathe"—she inhaled deeply, looking around the forest and up into the canopy, still talking—"helping us on our life journey."

Toca interjected, giving credibility to his woman and this God he has struggled with for ten moons, "It is true, I have seen this God in many things during our journey. He is everywhere and has talked to me many times." Peering directly to the old chief, he said, "This good God knew you were going to send me to find him. But he was the one that actually found me!"

Looking at the chief for a response, he was thinking deeply at what was explained to him. A soft voice spoke up across from him, stealing his attention, asking everyone with her cheeks wet with tears, "Would someone tell me what is going on? What is a god?"

They looked at one another, knowing the answer but knew this wasn't the time to get into a deep conversation about it. Toca was the one to speak up in pure Nashua tongue. "Mother, we will explain soon what we are talking about, but for now, you need to trust me that we are doing what is best for the Nashua to change how we live so we do not die off."

Not understanding why he wouldn't answer her, she bobbed her head back with a new question and thought to herself, *What does he mean the Nashua are dying off?* Then submitted by only nodding her head, as she always did to Chief Acuta without words, saying, *She would wait.* But innocently, she asked aloud, "How are you going to be chief when Jucawa is the tribe's chief and our people are following him?"

Shana gasped out, putting a hand to her mouth, looking to Toca as he loudly responded, looking to Chief Acuta, "What?"

The atmosphere instantly changed as an invisible thick dark cloud swarmed in on the small camp. Silence came across everyone staring at Chief Acuta, as the forest evening noises took over.

Toca's legs became weak, not only from confirming what he thought might be true but was also physically spent. Shana saw Toca's face getting pale and his head slightly swaying; she broke the circle and put her arm around him, walking him to the hammock, whispering, "Black Ghost, my man, everything will be all right. Do not give up hope now. Chief Acuta wants you to be chief." Kneeling on the ground, reaching under the hammock, she uncovered their pile of things, taking out a strip of dried meat, saying, "You have barely eaten in days, quickly, eat a big piece of the smoked anaconda and get some rest."

Not wanting to say anything as his mind was angrily racing, he took the meat and bit off a big piece, quickly chewing it hard with frustration.

Looking back at the old man in respect, letting him hear what she was saying to Toca, she said loudly, "Chief Acuta has a good answer for you, but right, now you need to get your strength back." She finished with a smile to let the chief know everything will be fine and she trusted he had a good answer. Glancing back at Toca taking another bite, she stood, bending over him, and instead of kissing him, not knowing if they were allowed to do that in their relationship yet with his parents there, she slowly touched her forehead to his as she saw Toca do in respect of the chief's position.

Toca stopped midchew in disbelief. Then slowly started chewing again as she amazingly again touched him deep down, settling his emotions as everything else he was so upset about completely disappeared.

She turned to the two adults, staring at her with the same amazed expression, and said, "We need to let him rest." She gently swooped her hands as if to say, "He needs his space. Let's walk away."

She picked up the empty bamboo cups and said to Layana, "I'm going to get some water from the river. Do you want to come?"

Surprised at the invitation and anxious to be with another female, she answered, "Yes."

Before they left the small clearing, Shana stopped, letting her senses work the area. Her eyes saw everything as normal, looking through the forest for movement or something out of place. Her ears tilted, listening to the birds and distant monkeys talking to each other that the night is coming, but her nose is the one that got her complete attention. The odor of the area was getting strong from the dead jaguar carcass a short distance away. She crinkled her nose at the smell as Layana did the same thing in agreement, looking at each other.

Shana began to walk away as Layana turned to the chief, quietly saying as he was admiring Shana for being aware, "Keep watch over him." As she picked up the spear, handing it to him, pointing to Toca now drifting off to sleep.

When the women got to the carcass, Layana suggested they drag it into the river to stop the smell, sending it downriver, avoiding other predators coming in to eat on it, so they did just that.

While at the river, they both decide it would be good to do a cleansing bath. Taking off their body coverings, Layana complimented Shana on her new jaguar-skin coverings. Then Shana asked Layana, "Why do the women of your tribe not wear top coverings?"

Layana plainly answered with a question, "Why would we?"

"Well, you know…" Shana shyly blushed that she had to give details. "To hide your breasts."

"Why would we do that?"

"So the men don't see them."

"Why would we do that?"

Shana was getting a bit frustrated that she wasn't getting an answer. "Because it's part of the body that—oh, never mind, Layana. Maybe I'll understand when I see your people."

Shana looked down to wash off all the flaking gray paste on her arms and shoulders as Layana examined the four long scratches on each side with her fingertips, softly stroking the wounds. Layana gave her an approving smile that they were doing well, saying later, she would put something else on them to finish the healing. Then she looked closer at Shana's side where she had felt before for her broken ribs. The bruised area was fading away and told her what Toca said, "It will take a long time to heal and not have pain there."

Feeling refreshed and clean, they got out of the water and Layana applied more tunga mud on the side of Shana before they put their body coverings on. They both found it funny, just getting clean only to put back on the dark oily mud. When they were dressing, Shana swung the machete over her head that was in the jaguar sheath, strapping it around her shoulder. Layana asked what it was, only seeing the dark wooded handle sticking out.

Shana slowly pulled the shiny long knife out to show her; Layana, in awe, only saw something reflective, heavy, and thin. Understanding what she was thinking, Shana demonstrated what it was by swinging it across a branch of a broad-leaf tree, dropping it to the ground. Then she told Layana all the things they use it for and even showed her how she killed the jaguar with it.

Enjoying female conversation and getting to know each other, they noticed it was starting to get dark and needed to get back to the men.

The air was smelling better, walking back to camp with the cups full of water, as they collected food and medicine along the way, putting it all on the broad leaf Shana cut off. Back at camp, Shana didn't see the chief and asked Layana were he went. She made a faint two-tone whistle sound and the small bush near the head of Toca slowly moved as the head of a spear came out first, then the short aged man followed.

Shana noticed, for the first time, he wasn't wearing the weathered caiman front and back flaps Toca said he wore and asked quietly, "Chief Acuta, why are you not wearing your caiman flaps?"

Both he and Layana looked at her, wondering how she knew what he wore. There was another awkward pause, then Layana answered in a quiet voice, not to disturb Toca, "Jucawa cut it off to disgrace him in front of our people."

"No!" Shana exclaimed in disbelief, louder than she should have, covering her mouth with her hand.

Layana looked at the chief, now with his head lowered, not wanting to be seen in this shameful way, and said to him, waving her hand for him to come over to them, "Chief, come here, we will eat and talk with Shana."

As they sat down on the ground on the other side of the firepit, Shana was the one wincing in pain now as she crunched her ribs together, bending down. Layana quickly got up and retrieved the flower from earlier and rolled a few petals, handing the ball to her. Then sitting back down, she handed out some fruits and leaves she found on the way back as they ate silently for a few moments.

Realizing the fire was not going as darkness was starting to permeate the forest, Shana asked Layana if she could get some wood for the fire as she would get it going. Without hesitating, they both went different directions, Shana getting the fire rocks out as Layana quickly returned with things to burn for the evening. Arranging the items in the pit to start it, Chief Acuta and Layana watched on, not seeing rubbing sticks, wondering what this old female child was doing.

Shana kept her head down as not to make eye contact, knowing what she was about do would surprise them and didn't want to start giggling beforehand, giving it away. She stroked the rocks together several times as large flaming sparks flew into the pit, bouncing around in the kindling, starting it ablaze. Once she had it going, Shana put a few large pieces of wood into it to keep it going for a while.

Turning around, putting the rocks away in their pouch and back into the stash of things, she sat back down next to the others like nothing happened and took a bite of food. Looking up to the others, she couldn't help herself and put a large grin on her face. The Chief Acuta and Layana were in a moment of disbelief as they stared at this curious new other. Both of them now thinking, *There is much more to this old female child than we can see.*

Shana wanted to explain but was more interested with what they were talking about earlier and asked, "Why did Jucawa take the chief's flaps off, and why is Jucawa in the chief position?"

The two were still in awe of the mystical thing that just happened before their eyes and slowly refocused on what they were talking about. Layana knew she needed to explain because it was very embarrassing for the old chief so she started the story. "A full moon after Toca left, Jucawa secretly gathered all the men in the tribe without the Chief Acuta's approval. He convinced them Chief Acuta was too old to lead anymore and that they needed a new strong chief, one that had the greatest Katata Ado the Nashua ever knew. Not a weak old man with his mind missing him." Layana kindly smiled at Chief Acuta; with his head still lowered, she laid a hand on his shoulder and genuinely stated, "Which everyone knows is not the truth."

Looking back to Shana, she continued, "They all boldly approached him, then Jucawa told him, now was the time to honor him as the new chief of the Nashua. Chief Acuta said now was not the time, rather they needed to wait for Toca to return.

"This enraged Jucawa and he was the one that went out of his mind, like he was crazy in the head." She motioned with her hands, making circles around the side of her head. "He was screaming at everyone, jumping around, then got into the chief's face, saying these terrible things in a deep frightening voice no one had ever heard out of him before. It scared everyone—even me—but not our great Chief Acuta. He boldly stood his ground." Layana smiled proudly at him as he slowly raised his head, regaining some pride back as his eyes went back and forth between the women.

"Then Jucawa did something that shocked our people. He challenged the chief to fight for his position. Chief Acuta said that he would not, this was not the way of the Nashua. And since Jucawa would even think of such a thing, he told him he would never give the position to him. Then he stated that when Toca comes back from his Katata Ado, he would be giving the chief position to him when his time comes. Because Jucawa does not or ever has demonstrated what the Katata Ado teaches to be chief.

"Jucawa got so mad, he drew his knife and turned to all the men, telling them in this horrifying voice, if anyone is against him, he would kill them, just like he killed the black jaguar.

"Our people have respected Jucawa for his great Katata Ado, Shana, but what was happening took them off guard and they became completely afraid of him. Then he stepped up to Chief Acuta in the tribal hut, putting the knife to his throat, and told him, 'You will step down or I will kill you, Layana, and Toca if the old weak child even returns.'

"The chief calmly replied, 'You do not have to kill anyone, I will walk away.'

"Jucawa laughed at him, telling everyone he was right, that he was too weak to be chief. That's when he cut off his flaps and verbally disgraced him in front of everyone. Finally Jucawa told the chief since he was defiant and disrespectful to him, he could not live with the tribe anymore and had to leave the hidden valley." Layana paused, putting on a sad face, almost crying, thinking about one of the worst days of their lives.

She cleared her throat and blinked away the tears, continuing on, "So the chief left with only his spear and knife. I was not going to let him live by himself, so that night, as the tribe had a celebration for their new chief, I ran away, catching up with him, leaving everyone behind. For the past eleven moons, we have lived outside the hidden valley, in hiding, waiting for Toca to return.

"We have been living on the other side of the river. It had been raining hard for many days and the chief couldn't cross the river to warn Toca about Jucawa, knowing it was time for the thirteenth moon to rise. When the river stopped flowing high after the big rain, Chief Acuta came over to look for any sign that Toca had returned and that's when he found you two."

Layana was finished with her story, going silent and taking a drink while eating a few more bits as she peered into the fire that was lighting the area, flickering shadows around them.

Shana was drawn into the story so much she was slightly disappointed when Layana finished. Then an idea came to mind, looking over to the chief, still with only a manhood cover on, thinking the timing was perfect.

She went over to her things under the hammock and got out the two big pieces of caiman hide and the little pouch of its teeth and claws. Putting everything she didn't need back into a neat pile then covering it up, the old knife they found in the skeleton in the cave came to mind. Her female curiosity got to her and thought she would ask the chief if he would know anything about it. Leaning over, she gently took it from Toca's sheath on his arm as he slept.

Sitting back down in front of the adults, holding the big flaps of caiman in her arms, it took them a moment to clearly see what she brought over in the dim light as Shana began with a story of her own. "Toca and I met ten moons ago by him saving my life." This sparked the chief to life and had both their complete attention, staring in anticipation.

"My father and I were lost deep in the forest. He was very sick so I had to look for help. I wandered from our clearing where we were living to the beach of the Black River, looking for others."

Chief Acuta excitedly inhaled, knowing this river far away. Shana smiled at his enthusiasm and continued, "I decided to take a cleansing bath, then ended up wading in the water along the shore, trying to spear some fish to eat. As I got close to some flowering lily pads that surrounded a huge dead floating log, the log instantly came to life, bursting at me, opening its giant jaws full of large teeth."

"Ah, black caiman!" Chief Acuta quietly exclaimed as he was living the moment in his mind.

Seeing him in a different mood, she continued, motioning with her hands to build up the story, "I closed my eyes, putting my hands in front of my face. I knew I was dead, but then, I heard someone screaming from the sky coming down."

She paused, as the chief was so into the story he interjected, "Your God saved you!"

"No, no, well, yes. We will talk about God later. It was Toca. He had been shadowing me for two days, I never knew he was there. He was high up in a tree that was hanging over the river, watching everything." She pointed up into the bouncing shadows of the fire high up in the canopy to give some perspective, and without the adults seeing, she picked up the knife she brought over and, with energy in her voice, said, "When the caiman attacked, Toca jumped from high up, dropping down on its head, stabbing it with his knife, killing it instantly." She had reached back with the knife in her hand, slashing forward, stabbing the air in front of them, demonstrating the kill. Seeing the knife, Chief Acuta and his mother almost couldn't control themselves as they both quietly cheered, wanting to yell out, clapping for joy for the incredible kill and bravery of their son.

She sat the knife down next to her, then lifted up the two square pieces of caiman hide that were laying on her lap, and said, "Toca brought these back for you as a gift. He said the ones you were wearing were getting weathered and you deserved new ones."

The chief's mouth dropped open at what she was presenting to him. Layana began to cry as joy was filling them all.

He leaned forward, taking the hides, putting them on his lap. It took him a few moments to compose himself as for the first time in a long time, tears were slowly dropping from his face. He didn't care if the women saw him, he was so proud and grateful of his son. His fingers stroked the top hard side of the skin that had large armor bumps in square-like patterns.

His first words were, "This is a giant caiman, much bigger than the one I killed for my flaps. How long was it?" He looked up to Shana with the question. Thinking about how long their canoe was as they used the whole skin for cover from the rain, she said, lifting up fingers, "It was about five of me tall."

Both Layana and the chief gasped in awe, then he said, "Bigger than any caiman ever killed by a Nashua." He looked over to Layana and said in a strong tone, pushing his chest out, broadening his shoulders, "Your son is a great hunter and a true man, fully deserving to be chief!" Pausing and collecting his thoughts, he added, "He burned himself for ten moons to bring this back to me. He was thinking about his people, not himself." Shana smiled proudly for Toca. She knew Toca thought about them all the time and loved his people, especially his mother and his new father, Chief Acuta.

She decided not to say anything more about their journey. Understanding that she probably went too far already, giving the caiman hide to the chief, but the timing seemed to be right to lift up his spirits. Which it did in a great way for all of them.

Then the knife came to mind, picking it back up and reaching out to the chief with her hand opened, she asked, "Do you know anything about this knife we found?"

Completely changing the subject on him as he was still in a state of bliss over her story and gift, he leaned over to get a closer look in the dim light and squinted his eyes, peering at the handle, noticing familiar markings.

Taking the knife from her to examine it closer and in better light, it came to him whose it was. Then something deep inside him twisted around, churning his gut into knots. His chest began pounding like a drum as he started to rapidly breathe, swaying his body back and forth, bringing the knife flat to his chest, cradling it like a baby.

"Chief Acuta, are you all right?" Layana said, touching his shoulder, wanting to calm him down. "What is it, what's wrong with the knife?"

He couldn't speak as his mind was in a different time.

"Chief, what's wrong?" Both the females asked at the same time. Then Shana remembered the anklet that was on the dead one. She quickly retrieved it out of the pack, hoping this would help with whatever was going on with the him. Holding it out for him to see, saying without thinking in complete Nashua tongue, now able to understand most everything, "We found this where we found the knife. Does this help you?"

Still not himself, he stretched out his neck to see what she had, but this time, he stood up, giving the knife to Layana and backed away to the edge of the camp, mumbling to himself like he was a child trying to talk.

The women questionably looked at each other, then Layana looked down at what Shana had in her hand, recognizing an anklet, then looked at the knife in hers. She examined the carvings on the knife, then looked at the talisman on the anklet. She recognized the yellow round figure representing the sun but didn't know whose shadow image was on the knife or the two on the anklet.

"Chief," she said, standing up, getting next to him, grabbing his arm, trying to get his attention like she had to wake him up. "Chief, look at me." He didn't move so she repeated, shaking his arm harder. "Chief, look at me, whose shadow image is this?"

He slowly came back to reality, breathing slower, trying to control himself as he blinked away painful tears. He cleared his throat and went to speak but nothing came out. This time, he cleared his head and throat, trying again, speaking in Nashua, stumbling for words, and answered, "Um, on the knife is a shadow image of an old male child I sent away a long time ago on his Katata Ado."

Both the women gave a slight relieving sigh, now knowing what he was so upset with which didn't sound as bad as he was acting as Layana asked, "What is wrong with these to get you this way, this is a good find!"

He looked into Layana's eyes for a long time for her to see deeper at what he was saying.

"What, who is—" She stopped midsentence as she just understood what he was telling her through his eyes.

Shana turned to Layana and asked as she stood, "Layana, what is it, who are you thinking about?"

Layana crinkled her forehead, trying not to get emotional as past images came to her mind.

"Who is it, Chief?" Shana looked at him then back to Layana, now putting her hand on Layana's arm to get her attention and asked, "Layana, what's wrong, who is it?"

Layana looked at Shana and said, just before tears began to flow, handing her the knife, "The knife and anklet belonged to Tundra, Toca's real father. The one that was going to be my man."

CHAPTER 23

The three stood, surrounded by the dark forest, as the small fire next to them projected large human-like images, dancing around the tiny camp, disappearing into the trees. Smoke from the fire ghostly swirled up into the canopy as an eerie sensation could be felt moving among them. The two Nashua's hearts were weeping, thinking of the past painful horror Jucawa told them about Tundra's death.

Shana, on the other hand, was stone-cold. Her quick-witted mind put together the secret true story. She remembered Toca telling her, God said the giant snake would point them to the truth; and now she was stunned at its miraculous reality. Glancing over to Toca, still sleeping, she was glad he wasn't awake to hear this news right now.

Her stiff position started to break apart as her body functions began to mimic Chief Acuta's but with panic, not sorrow. Heavy breathing was beginning to leap from her chest as she looked back to the adults now in a state of mourning. An old emotional scar just reopened and it hurt them deeply. The chief had Layana in his skinny arms as she quietly cried on his shoulder.

Shana picked up the knife and anklet Layana dropped to the ground and looked at them, wishing she had never brought them out. Quickly she turned to put them back where she got them from, praying this nightmare would disappear.

"Shana," the old man said, getting her attention, "Don't put them away, I need to show and explain the shadow image of Tundra that I gave him during his and Jucawa's going-away ceremony. Layana never knew what it was because Tundra never had the chance to show her."

Shana froze, looking at him wide-eyed. Then unconsciously, she began shaking her head no.

"What do you mean no, old child?" He was stunned at her telling him that.

She kept shaking her head with a blank face. This time, Layana spoke up as she was calming down. "Shana, what's wrong with you, why won't you obey the chief?"

Her response was messy like her thoughts, "I can't, I shouldn't…I shouldn't have shown you these things."

The chief and Layana looked at each other, then back to her, seeing her as shaken up as they were.

Chief Acuta gently moved Layana to the side and stepped up to Shana with his hand out for her to take. His wisdom of many years came out as he softly spoke, "Shana, who will be Toca's mate when you both are pronounced young man and woman during your old child releasing ceremonies." He paused for a moment to let her think through what he was saying, then continued, "Don't let my reaction in seeing the shadow image of Tundra influence you. I'm sorry I didn't restrain myself and scared you but it completely took me by surprise. It was a very hard time for us and the whole tribe when we lost Tundra because everyone loved him so much, just like they love Toca." He looked back to Layana, smiling, and added, "They are so much alike."

Layana reflected his smile back, nodding her head in agreement.

Turning back to Shana, he said, "Come to me, child, and bring the knife and anklet. I will tell you about Toca's father."

Shana started shaking her head again and sputtered out, "No, no, you don't understand!"

"What do I not understand? Come here, it will be all right."

"No, Chief, you don't understand." She raised her voice slightly to get his attention as her chin started to quiver and tears silently began streaming down her face.

Chief Acuta pulled his head back, twisting it sideways as he saw the light of the fire glistening off the water coming from her eyes, and tried to figure out what was wrong with her. Then he turned to Layana, motioning with his hand to come up and take care of this female.

Layana stepped up, taking Shana back to where they were on the other side of the fire. As they sat next to each other, Layana asked, "Do you need more yatowa flower, are your ribs hurting?"

Shana quickly shook her head no, knowing they were going to keep pushing her until the unknown truth came out of her mouth. She brought her knees up together and laid her head on them, attempting to hide her face.

"What is it, Shana, why is this bothering you so much? Are you feeling Toca's pain for the loss of his father?"

Again saying no with her head still bowed and eyes closed.

Being a mother, she had her own ideas of how to get an old child to talk, she looked up with a smirk, saying, "Chief, let's give Shana space and time to feel better. Maybe we should go back to our hut across the river for the night and come back in the morning. Toca should be awake, feeling better, and maybe he will know what is wrong."

Shana spring to life, lifting her head and waving her hands back and forth. "No, don't leave me alone and don't ask Toca anything about the knife or anklet or even tell him I showed them to you." The last statement alarmed the adults—there was definitely more to the story of just finding the knife and anklet.

The chief stood, picking up the spear near him and thumped the butt of it on the ground. His posture cast a huge shadow behind him against the wall of vegetation as the flames from the fire looked his direction, revealing his stern facial expression that said he had had enough.

Layana crawled back a step respectfully, then stood, leaving Shana alone.

Getting Shana's attention, he stepped up to her as her whole body began trembling. It had nothing to do with him intimidating her but from the terrible information she had for them.

Looking down at her, keeping is voice low, he still was able to use it powerfully. "Shana, share what is in your mind. What have you not told us?"

She collected herself, knowing she wasn't getting out of this dreadful situation, and closed her eyes, whispering, "God, please help me but, most of all, help my new family for what is about to be revealed to them."

Slowly opening her eyes, she took in a deep breath, crossing her legs, sitting up straight. Then she asked Layana and the chief to sit down in front of her. The sudden change in her demonstrated she was willing to share what she was trying to hide so the two calmly sat down close, ready to hear this mysterious secret.

Shana began another story. "Toca and I were only about seven sunrises away, getting to the hidden valley. We were exhausted." Changing her tone, reflecting back, she smiled out the side of her mouth, pointing to her chest. "No, I was exhausted. Toca was so full of energy and excitement because we were so close to getting back before the thirteenth moon.

"I had collapsed from being so tired and Toca tried to encourage me to keep going. We had a bad argument. When that was over and everything was fine between us, we started looking for food. That's when it happened."

Pausing to adjust how she was sitting, the chief couldn't help himself and blurted out, "What happened, Shana?"

Seeing he was already deeply involved in her story, she quickly continued with more hand motions to help recreate a better picture and said, "I was not being aware like Toca always told me." She moved her gaze past him into the black night, using her senses to demonstrate; then with open piercing eyes, she looked back to the others and continued, "Toca and I walked a little ways from each other, searching, suddenly"—she jerked her body with hands up—"faster than I could see or think, I was coiled up by a giant black-and-green anaconda." She collapsed her arms to her side, imitating being squeezed.

The chief and Layana gave out sounds of awe as they listened intently.

Changing her demeanor and body language, she said with excitement, "Toca came to my rescue again! He fought the beast, jumping on it and stabbing it. Then the giant snake bit him as the whole middle area of his body was in the snake's jaws." The adults were in complete disbelief as their mouths dropped with nothing coming out. "The snake threw Toca into the forest, hitting a tree, he got back up, jumping on, stabbing it again. This time, he was ready for the bite and stabbed it deep into its open mouth, down its throat. The snake began screaming in pain, turning to get away from the Black Ghost."

She hesitated to let the two absorb this great victory, knowing the devastating secret was coming. They were escalated to new heights with pride for their son.

Calming her own excitement, she said, "Toca took very good care of me. I thought I was going to die because the pain was so bad and it was hard to breathe at first." She touched her side where Layana had applied tunga mud. "He gave me medicine and comforted me. As I slept safely, high up in a hammock, he went out into the forest for a long time. And when he got back, he said he had killed the giant anaconda and we had to go to it where it was and make a better camp."

The chief raised his head proudly to hear that Toca did kill the snake, giving out an approving grunt.

"Toca also said God, our good God, had spoken to him through the forest, telling him the snake had a purpose, it was leading him to the…" She peered up into the dark canopy, as though looking for God, and finished, "the truth." She gave them a confirming facial expression that she knew what the truth was.

"Toca and I didn't understand what God was saying until… right now." Shana lowered her head with sadness. Lifting it back up, she dreadfully continued, "When we got to the snake where it died, Toca made camp and began cutting some of it up to dry by fire and smoke as I went back to sleep with yatowa root in my stomach and petals under my tongue. When I woke up, it was dark and Toca was still working the snake. We ate some of it—" She popped her head up with that old female child smile, slightly changing the subject.

"We still have some." She got up and got out a few sizable pieces. The long thin coiled-up snakeskin caught her eye and she tried to resist but was too weak. She picked it up, taking it back with her.

Handing them each a piece of dry meat, she said, "Eat, this is the anaconda and here is a small narrow piece of its skin. Toca wanted to bring the whole skin back but…" She rolled out the skin across the small clearing as most of it stayed coiled bumping up to a tree trunk. She went to the coil and unrolled it back to where she started then tossed the rest back in the direction she first rolled it out, then finished her sentence. "But it was too big."

Chief Acuta stood with more energy in his old body than ever, looking back and forth at the dried skin. He walked up and down it as many times as it was long then looked to the women, saying, astonished, "This is the biggest animal any Nashua has ever seen. And the Black Ghost killed it!" He raised his skinny arms in victory, wanting to wake Toca up and dance around the fire with him. But instead, he contained himself, sitting back down, wanting the female to get to the point as he tore a piece of the victory meat apart, putting it in his mouth, and asked, "Shana where did you find the knife?"

Hesitating again, thinking how to gently bring the horrible news, she began, "Where the snake died, its head and the front part of its neck had slithered through very thick bushes. We would never have found the hiding spot without the snake's body pointing through the bushes, stopping dead on the other side. Behind the bushes was a small open area, smaller than this where we camped and Toca dried the meat." She gestured around the camp. "Then the ground behind us came up high, forming a rock wall." She pointed over to the high rock wall a short distance away from where they sat. "Similar to the rock wall hiding the Nashua's valley. The snake's head actually stopped at an entrance to a cave that was in the wall."

"You found the knife and anklet in the cave!" Layana spouted with excitement.

"Yes," Shana said with a sorrowful smile.

The chief spoke up in an agreeing confident manner. "Jucawa buried Tundra in the cave. A safe hidden place." He slowly nodded his head that Jucawa had done a good thing.

"Yes, but..." Shana paused, not wanting to continue as she still had the grief-stricken face, looking away from them.

"What is it, child?" Layana gently asked.

Shana reluctantly continued, "Toca and I went into the cave with a fire stick to see inside. After crawling in through the narrow entrance, there was a big open room inside with markings on the walls." Shana leaned over, picking up some sticks next to the fire, throwing some in and keeping one to draw on the ground what they saw as the light of the fire got brighter.

As she drew, Chief Acuta asked, "That is the moon?" Confirming what he interpreted was right as he sucked hard, gumming another bite of dried meat.

Shana nodded her head in agreement, finishing stroking twelve straight lines next to it.

"Twelve moons," he stated, looking up to her.

Again agreeing, she hesitated to finish as Layana asked, "What is this meaning?"

Shana cleared her throat, pushing herself to go on. "Well, the cave had rocks neatly stacked around the walls. Under one of the piles of rocks, we saw...bones of a hand reaching out from the rocks." Shana looked at the two as they were drawn in with curiosity. "Toca took the rocks off, uncovering a full skeleton of a man."

Layana inhaled deeply, bringing her hands to her mouth as an image of her young love—dead—was peacefully buried.

"That is when we found the anklet still around his ankle."

The chief and Layana both gave out a sigh, almost as a relief, picturing old child Tundra, peacefully buried in a safe hidden place.

"But we found the knife..." She stalled again, getting their attention, bringing them mentally back to this small camp, as little flames from the fire jumped around, bouncing living shadow figures off the trees and bushes, having the appearance of being surrounded.

They gazed with confusion, waiting for her to finish, wondering why she wasn't as happy as they were.

Looking down at her fidgeting hands, they began to sweat and her breathing again pounded from her chest. She felt like she was going to vomit as her eyes watered up and her head was spinning.

Layana saw how distraught Shana was, grabbed her arm, and asked, "Are you all right, are you going to be sick? Have you never seen dead people?"

Shana exhaled her lungs, full of the anxiety, and answered back, "No, no, that's not it." Taking a moment to collect her thoughts, she blinked rapidly, shaking her head, and finally finished, "We found the knife… deeply stabbed in the back of the skeleton. I mean, Tundra's body."

A deafening silence captured the small camp. Only the crackling of the fire echoed as the dark shadow figures behind them appeared to be closing in around them.

Layana looked at Chief Acuta with a confused frown, then back to Shana. The chief didn't move; his mind was running as fast as it could, putting pieces together from the past fourteen sun seasons since Jucawa returned with the dreadful news of Tundra. His eyes were working hard, going back and forth as though he was seeing real images in front of him of conversations with Jucawa and his answers to questions about his Katata Ado. Then it all clearly came to him as he spoke aloud, "Jucawa never did the Katata Ado. Tundra finished it alone because Jucawa was too injured from the black jaguar. He lived in the cave for twelve moons, healing. When Tundra returned to take Jucawa back to the hidden valley, Jucawa killed him for his shell and came back to his people as though he did a great Katata Ado." The chief slowly moved his gaze to Layana, then to Toca sleeping on the hammock, finishing his revelation, "Living this lie all these years."

Without emotion, he slowly stood, taking a step next to the fire, picking up a cooled piece of charred wood, then slowly striped his body, mumbling a different statement with each stroke, "I have been a fool all these years. I have allowed Jucawa to treat my people poorly. I should have known this, he could never answer my questions about the endless water. Like what color it was or what did it taste like. He's never acted in the way the Katata Ado transforms a boy not just into a man but a *chief*." Stepping to Toca, looking down on him with compassion, he whispered, "I'm sorry, my son, I never stopped Jucawa from treating you and your mother the way he did." He glanced back to Layana with regret but an angry expression came next, directed at himself. Looking back to his wounded son, peacefully resting, he stated loud enough for the females to hear him, "I will no longer be a fool. This good God you have brought to the hidden valley to save our people *has* shown us the truth. Now I must rescue them from Jucawa."

Dropping the charred wood with his body freshly shadowed, he bent down with his head softly touching Toca's forehead. Without saying another word, he stepped back, picking up his spear, then looked in the direction of the secret entrance; then mystically, as the smoke disappearing into the night air, Chief Acuta slowly vanished into the forest.

The two females awkwardly stood motionless for a long time, waiting for Chief Acuta to return, but with every breath, the night air was getting thicker and heavier. They didn't know what to do or say as their minds attempted to absorb the revelation of this living lie now exposed. Painful darkness appeared to come alive, strangling their emotions as the only thing they thought to do was to go to sleep for the night, hoping they would wake from this nightmare of truth.

Throwing a few more pieces of wood on the fire, Shana checked the placement of her machete strapped to her back, then pointed up into the trees, looking at Layana. Knowing what she was saying, she nodded in agreement and they both climbed the tree Shana had been using as they collapsed together on top of several large branches that came together, forming a small platform, padded thick with many palm leaves tied down with thin vines.

Morning came with them wide awake, listening to the birds singing to the forest, letting everything know it's a new beginning. Bugs began swarming them as Shana hadn't wiped juja oil on the tree when they went to sleep. Reaching over to one of the broken limbs of juja leaves she had brought up the tree a couple of days ago, stripped and rolled a ball of leaves, then smeared the oil on her arms and legs then handed the ball to Layana. She did the same thing, then finished the ball up by wiping down the tangle of branches they were sitting on for the next night.

Dropping the finished ball of repellant to the ground, Layana took Shana's hand in hers, looking kindly into the old child's eyes who appeared to have much wisdom and experience in her young years, and asked, "What do you think we should do now?"

Before Shana responded, a cool refreshing morning breeze washed its way through the forest, cleaning the drowsiness from their faces as it came directly at them, brushing their hair backward. Enjoying the gift of the forest, the tree slightly swayed back and forth as a soft yet powerful voice whispered to Shana through the moving air, *Awake Toca, he has not finished my purpose. He needs to go to his people quickly.* Her eyes closed, drawing in the nurturing morning air, sprang open at the words she heard. Knowing exactly who was speaking to her, everything suddenly became clear. The truth was not an end but a beginning of something more, more than she was aware of.

Quickly dropping from the tree, she picked up one of the bamboo cups of water and took a swallow, kneeling down next to Toca. Touching his shoulder, she softly spoke to him to wake up.

Layana was down from the tree next her, quickly asking, "What are you doing? He needs as much rest as he can get."

"I know but the breeze spoke—I mean God spoke to me through the breeze that Toca needs to wake up to quickly go to his people."

Layana looked up and around the forest then back to Shana, as though she was crazy, and said, "I didn't hear anyone speaking and what is this God you have been talking about?"

"Layana, we will explain who God is later, but now, Toca needs to get to the village. I don't know why, maybe they are in danger. Maybe it has to do with Chief Acuta?"

"Where is the chief?" A deep groggy voice spoke up in front of them as Toca lifted his head, looking around. He woke up to the females conversing, getting every other word, coming out of a deep sleep.

Shana urgently replied but, with passion, said, "Toca, my love, you're awake." She glanced to Layana, slightly embarrassed, realizing what she said in front of her, looked back to Toca, and asked, "How do you feel?"

He rubbed his eyes as he slowly stretched out his body and answered, "I feel good. Whatever mother had me drink and eating some meat helped." Gently he rotated his body, sitting up, trying not to use his stomach muscles, then took a few deep breaths, stretching out his torso, slowly stood, testing himself for balance and strength. Confidence was gripping him as he worked his neck and shoulder muscles, twisting his head back and forth, then expanded his muscular chest out, stopping when he felt a pinch of pain at his side. Standing tall, Shana didn't realize she was gleaming up at him as his mother beamed with pride, seeing her son as a grown man.

He looked back at the two females staring at him and asked again more directly, "Where is the chief?"

They looked at each other, then Layana nudged Shana to speak. Shana handed the cup of water to Toca which he drank, finishing to the last drop. As quickly as he was done with the water, Shana handed him some food left over from last night. Taking it from her and slowly chewing, he made eye contact with each of the females as their eyes quickly went to the side, avoiding his piercing glare. He knew they had something very important to tell him but they were scared.

He approached them from a different angle, having an idea where Chief Acuta went, and asked, "There is only one place the chief would go for you both to act this way and that place is?"

Layana was the one to give it away as his eyes slowly followed the slight movement of her head in the direction of the hidden entrance.

Toca responded, "So why did the chief go to the village?"

The females again looked at each other then back to him. This time, his glare had a hint of anger with it. Shana knew she had to tell him the truth.

As she spoke, her body shyly wiggled and twisted. "Chief Acuta did go back to the village."

"Why?"

"To confront Jucawa."

"Why?"

Hesitating, knowing Toca was going to erupt with anger, she unconsciously took a half-step away from him. Layana noticed what Shana did and did the same thing as she gazed up to her son, now much bigger, stronger, and intimidating.

Shana strung out her first word as she answered him, "Because we found out the truth."

"The truth about what?" Toca was getting impatient with this game as he stepped forward to both the females, stating, "Stop this! What is going on?"

Shana internally said a quick prayer, then lifted her hand, gently placing it on his chest, and told him, "Toca, remember when you told me God said the giant anaconda would point you to the truth?"

He nodded yes.

"Last night, we were talking while you slept and I got out a few of the things we brought back with us." She stopped, waiting for him to get mad, but he stood there, motionless.

She continued, a little more relaxed. "When I showed them the knife and anklet we found in the cave, I asked him if he knew whose they were."

Toca narrowed down his eyebrows, sensing the answer was not good. He asked, needing this conversation to be over and for the truth to finally come out, surprised her by his next words, "Shana, daughter of John from the Manos tribe, whose shadow image is the songbird, soon to be my woman, tell me *now*"—he forcibly pointed to the ground—"what is the truth the good God pointed to through the anaconda?"

Her eyes opened wide in fear, staring at Toca as she felt a heavy darkness strangle her throat, whispering pure evil. It had nothing to do with Toca but something completely foreign attacking her in her mind as she withered from the black doomed words, *The truth will only kill the Nashua tribe, you have failed*!

Toca saw Shana stricken with fear and instantly changed his demeanor, taking up her hand, putting it on his chest, believing he had scared her, and softly said, "Shana, it's all right, what is the truth?"

As though she had woken up from a bad dream, she openly blurted out, "The knife belongs to your real father!"

Toca let go of her hand, completely taken off guard, then attempted to make sense of this unexpected news. He looked down and around, thinking about all the conversations about his father and what happened to him. The females had seen the same facial expressions last night with the chief. Then Toca looked up to his mother, asking with his eyes only, *Is this true*?

Layana reluctantly, trying not to cry, nodded her head.

CHAPTER 24

The newly declared chief of the Nashua stood transfixed, with his mind running together with many thoughts. Moments of the past with Jucawa, his mother, and then finishing with Chief Acuta. Seeing clear pictures of pain and suffering Jucawa put on everyone, boasting about nothing that truly happened. There was no great Katata Ado for him; he lived in the cave, hiding as he healed from his wounds. Toca visualized his father returning to help him back home, only to be stabbed in the back for his shell. Buried alive in a pile of rocks, reaching out of his grave for help, taking his last breath, knowing he would never be seen again.

Toca looked to the ground next to the fire, noticing his father's knife and anklet. Focused on them for a moment, Shana softly but with some urgency put a hand on his shoulder to get his attention. "Toca, God just spoke to me in the wind before you woke up. He said you need to hurry to your people."

His thoughts were drawn from the past, forcibly directed to old Chief Acuta, weakly by himself with Jucawa. Then a familiar slithery dark voice infiltrated his thoughts, *You are weak, child. Jucawa has the strength of the tribe with him, you will never defeat him and become chief.* The evil one knew the closer Toca got to the village, the stronger the old male child would become and was grasping at any chance to keep the light of the world, the good God, out of the hidden valley.

Completely ignoring the irritating voice, Toca bent over, picking up the knife, looking carefully at the shadow image, then stroked it with his finger and said with intimidation, "I have killed men before, protecting my female and my people. I must do it again!"

Toca slowly slid his father's old knife in the sheath on his arm, then looked to his mother with a ferocious expression who was stunned at what she heard from her innocent son. Now talking directly to her, he said, "I will make Jucawa's death painful. With more pain than what he did to you, Father, and me." Giving Shana a glance, he told her, "Your good God has done a great thing for the Nashua by pointing out the truth."

It was like a repeating vision for the women as they now watched Toca do exactly what Chief Acuta did. He slowly shadowed his body with coals from the fire, mumbling under his breath with every stroke. Then without looking back to say goodbye, he mystically blended in with the morning fog, wisped his way through the forest, and disappeared without a sound.

The females were as silent and cold as the fire that went out in the night. Left alone in the vast forest as the men in their lives were gone, going in the direction of unknown danger and consequences. Shana slowly began to panic; she had felt this feeling before when her mother, then her father, passed away—empty. With Toca's last words going over and over in her head, it was making her sick to her stomach with the horrible thoughts of killing.

Whispering under her breath, "No, Toca, don't go." Saying it again and again, getting louder and louder until she was shouting. Layana firmly grabbed Shana's shoulder to calm her down and said, "Shana, stop, he's not coming back."

Shana turned to Layana, feeling like a child, and replied, "But, Mother, they are gone, they left us alone. There is going to be fighting and death and it could be him that dies." She gazed back in the direction Toca left into the forest for the longest time, wishing he would reappear, walking back to her. She ran through her mind what she would tell him. *You were right, my love, yesterday when you were thinking about leaving the hidden valley and forgetting about being a Nashua, let's just walk away.*

Layana, on the other hand, was surprised Shana called her mother and how good it felt. Thinking it over, she answered in a motherly fashion, leaning into her. "Shana, we will be all right and so will Chief Acuta and Toca. But didn't you say this God"—Layana looked around the area, trying to see this thing—"said Toca needed to quickly go to his people?" Being naive about God but hearing the things she heard from Chief Acuta, Shana, and Toca discussing about it, she added, "It was very important for you to follow what it said to tell Toca. This God must know what is going to happen. Would it tell you something knowing it would harm you or him?"

Shana popped her head back as the childlike fears of loneliness and worry fell off as Layana reminded her God had spoken, instantly correcting her thinking, providing hope, and giving her strength. Turning to Layana, she hugged her, then stepped back and said, "We need to go to the village after them." She stepped to the hammock, taking it down from the trees, putting all the items they brought into it, except for two pieces of dried meat, then turned it back into the carrying pouch. Next Shana climbed the tree, up to the branches she had been sleeping on, and rubbed more juja leaf oil all over the place and on the backpack, leaving it safely in the tree.

Back down on the ground, she handed Layana one of the pieces of meat, telling her, "We'll eat as we go." Checking the position of the machete on her back and adjusting her new jaguar-skin clothes, she turned, heading in the direction of the hidden entrance as Layana followed.

Suddenly a strange sensation happened under their feet as birds and animals of all kinds could be heard screeching with fear, flying, running, and jumping in all directions. The trees began to sway back and forth as Shana turned back to Layana, asking with her eyes, *What is going on?*

Layana replied with no verbal answer, shrugging her shoulders to say, *I don't know.* The ground shook harder, causing the two to lose their balance, falling into each other. They stood hugging in confusion, watching their surroundings move like they have never seen before. A short distance where the mountains' rock wall protruded high up, forming the camouflage around the hidden valley, began making loud explosive sounds. The solid wall of rock was cracking in places as rocks and boulders fell from high up, pounding the forest floor, making vibrating sounds, echoing through the dense forest. The females looked in all directions, still holding each other as the loud eerie movements and sounds seem to be coming at them from all directions. They dropped to the ground and huddled, peering all over the place, trying to understand what was happening.

*****

Chief Acuta traveled slowly through the night to get to the village. His eyesight slowed him down considerably, feeling his way in the dim moonlight as his stamina was not what it used to be. By morning, he finally got to the edge of the village. Hazily looking around at the scattered huts, the whole area appeared lifeless. The morning fog had lifted and he noticed, being aware, using all his senses, the birds of the forest were not even singing their normal new beginning songs; it was silent. The air, for some reason, had a musty odor.

Nevertheless, determined to expose Jucawa of his lies, he boldly made his way toward the center of the village where the tribe's large firepit was surrounded by long logs for seating. Out from huts, little by little, whispers could be heard as people slowly stepped into the open. Gawking at the short skinny wrinkled old chief, bare of all his normal body coverings and decorations, only adorned with the shadowing stripes and his manhood cover, holding tightly to his long spear. He kept focused on his destination, not paying any attention to anyone, only concentrating on his duty. Once at the side of the firepit, he paused, catching his breath, then lifted his spear, as he had all the years he was chief, and pounded the butt of it hard, three times, on the biggest log to make the loudest and deepest echoing alarm for every Nashua to come to him.

Everyone hesitated, looking at one another, trying to figure out what was going on. They haven't seen the old chief for almost a full sun season. But their apprehension was more for waiting instructions from Chief Jucawa on what they were to do.

Again Chief Acuta pounded his spear on the log, sending a message for everyone to come to him now. This time, he spoke as loud as he could with his tired voice, "Nashua, people of the hidden valley, come to me!"

Slowly people reluctantly and cautiously made their way, keeping an eye on the old man and the tribal hut at the same time, watching for the great Jucawa to step out.

"Listen to me, my people. I do not have hard feeling toward you for what was done to me. It was not your fault!" He looked confidently toward the faces he has known all their lives. Not a smile could be seen as he peered around, trying to see as well as he could.

Unexpectedly he was taken aback with surprise. All the men had their heads shaved, except for a brim of short hair going around the lower part of their skulls above the ears. From the bottom of their noses, going around their heads upward, half their faces and all of their scalps were painted black as night.

Looking harder to see clearly what he was seeing, when the men blinked, he bobbed his head back in disbelief as their eyelids were painted white with a black dot in the center, representing eyes. So when their eyes were open or closed, it gave the illusion you are always being watched.

The women, on the other hand, had their heads shaved completely opposite with the sides and back of their skull exposed with a tuft of hair adorning the top of their heads. Then a painted red-striped ring, the width of a finger, went across their eyes and all the way around their skull. At the back of their heads, two white eyes were painted over the red stripe as to appear they had eyes in the back of their heads.

Never seeing or dreaming of anything like this in his life, it was disturbing, slightly making him sick yet very intimidated. *What is the reason for this? What has happened to my people*? thinking to himself, *Something very bad is going on.*

There was an empty silence in the village, almost as if nothing was breathing. Nevertheless, he boldly continued with his speech. "Everyone, I have known you your whole lives and you have known me. I led you honorably with kindness, respect, always telling you the truth." He paused to moisten his dry throat to speak loud and clear. "I have come back so the truth about your new chief will be known. Toca, the son of Tundra, stepson of Jucawa, has returned successfully from his Katata Ado but with sad news.

"You older ones, with many sun seasons behind you, remember when Jucawa and Tundra went together as old male children on their Katata Ado and Jucawa returned, telling everyone Tundra died by the black jaguar. Then Jucawa proclaimed he did the Katata Ado while he was badly wounded, bringing back the jaguar's skin." Finally a stirring in the crowd of people, agreeing, they raised their hands not in victory but as though they were imitating paws of a big cat with extended claws, whooping and hollering, repeating the name of their great chief, "Jucawa, Jucawa, Jucawa—"

Chief Acuta hit the log again with his spear for everyone to be quiet and they instantly went silent. His back was turned to the tribal hut as he stared across the crowd, looking deep into the eyes of his people, completely captivated at what he had to say. Taking another breath, his confidence was building that he would be able to take control of his people again with the next part of his story. Before he exhaled, something hit him silently with a thump, very hard, in the lower back, shooting excruciating pain through his torso, poking out the front, completely taking his breath away without words.

At the same time, from the edge of the clearing where the chief entered the village, everyone heard a loud prolonged scream, "*No*!" The people turned, seeing a man running full force toward them, yelling so loud in their direction, the ground began to shake.

Back up in the tribal hut, Chief Jucawa stood in the open doorway, decorated with his black jaguar skin. The head of the big cat was draped over his head with his beady eyes peering through the eyeholes of the skin which looked just like the black painting the rest of the men had on their faces. Jucawa's expression dramatically changed as he looked out in disbelief at the man running at them, saying under his breath, "It can't be…you're dead!" Thinking his legs had become weak at what he saw, he grabbed ahold of the bamboo wall to brace himself, only to find out that it wasn't him but everything else was shaking. He heard trees breaking apart and falling to the ground. As distant rocks were crashing down the high mountains, the crowd below him was in complete disarray, wondering what was going on.

The Nashua people finally heard familiar shouting by their great chief, but this time, it was not in a boastful angry tone but more of a panicked scream. "Someone has entered our hidden valley to kill us! I warned everyone this would happen! Look what this old man did to all of us, he brought in danger from the outside to kill his own people!" Pointing out toward the man getting close, he yelled out, "Nashua, protect your chief!"

Instantly the black-headed men went in every direction, trying to keep their balance from the earthquake, collecting weapons, as the females screamed from the chaos, gathering the young children, hiding them in their huts.

*****

Once through the secret entrance and in the hidden valley, Toca ran through the forest toward his village as the Black Ghost, leaping over vegetation, weaving around trees and through bushes, gaining speed the closer he got. He no longer felt physical pain as images of Jucawa consumed him, numbing everything except for the vengeance building with every breath. Anger raged on like wildfire within him, blocking any logical or rational thinking.

As he got to the edge of the village, he stopped to bend over, catching his breath and to get a clear view of what was happening before he went in. Besides seeing a crowd of people around the fire-pit, which was normal first thing in the morning, his eyes went to the tribal hut behind them, standing bigger than the other huts. A figure suddenly stepped out from the shadows with something lifted in its hands. Then before Toca could do anything, an object was thrown into the crowd of people, hitting the back of the short one speaking to everyone.

Instantly recognizing the figure at the firepit now with a spear stuck in his back, Toca uncontrollably lost himself. Screaming out in horror, he ran with all he had to rescue his best friend and father. As he ran toward the crowd, he started losing his balance, thinking he was getting weak again. Determined to save Chief Acuta, he pressed on through the trembling. The crowd began scattering and screaming in a frightful manner; and before he knew it, strange-looking men with black faces and heads started running toward him, shouting with raised weapons. It reminded him of the others he had seen during his journey with painted faces and thought maybe his tribe had been found and overtaken in the hidden valley.

Spears began to be thrown his way as he dodged them, staying focused on the one standing in the entrance of the tribal hut. Thinking quickly, he turned to the side, running back into the forest as Black Ghost, shadowing into safety of the thick plant life. The men running after him kept pursuit, losing sight of him. The farther away from the village, the slower they ran, looking every direction for the one that disappeared in front of their eyes.

Toca jumped up to a tree branch, swinging to several other branches so his footprints couldn't be followed as though he vanished into thin air. He dropped down into a broad fern bush, turning back in the direction he came, waiting for the strange painted men following him. He grasped tightly, in his hand, his father's knife, ready for an attack.

It took a few moments for the men to catch up as they slowed to a walk, looking around, trying to determine where he went. Whispering to one another, they ended up going different paths in small groups to locate any sign of the intruder in their valley. Several men ran, less than an arm's length, past him as he invisibly stayed shadowed. When the last runner of that group went by, Toca slithered from his hiding spot quickly and quietly came up behind him, grabbing him around the face, covering his mouth, kneeing him in the back, causing him to fall backward to the ground. Toca spun around with all his weight on top of the man, keeping his hand over the man's mouth. Putting the knife blade firmly to his throat, he whispered, looking at the frightened man with piercing eyes, gritting his teeth as a wild animal, and asked, "What tribe are you?"

The painted-faced man tried to squirm away but Toca pressed the knife harder to his throat, cutting in on the skin, causing a little blood to start streaming down his neck.

"You will stop moving and be quiet or I will cut your throat open!" The man obeyed as he looked closer at Toca, thinking he knew the man behind the familiar shadow marking across his face and body. Stopping all fighting, the man attempted to talk under Toca's hand.

He whispered, "I'm going to let your mouth go to talk, but if you scream, your life ends here!" Toca narrowed his eyebrows, letting the man know he meant what he said, then slowly let off on the pressure. The man said quietly in Nashua tongue, glancing around to see if there was anyone else with them, "You look like someone I know."

"Who are you? Are you Nashua?" Toca demanded as he asked quietly as he pressed down on the man's mouth, blocking his nostrils as well to stop him from getting air.

The man mumbled, then squirmed again as fear suddenly took him from not breathing as Toca was overpowering him, and said, "I have no more time, you tell me who you are or I will kill you now!"

The man nodded his head in agreement with wide eyes then relaxed. Toca carefully removed his hand again as the man quickly responded, "Yes, I am Nashua or at least used to be."

"What do you mean used to be?" Toca questioned, very impatient.

"Chief Jucawa made us into new people, stronger people than what we were."

Taken by surprise by this crazy idea, Toca asked, "So if you aren't people of new beginnings, then what are you?"

The man frowned back with curiosity of how this person on him knew details of his people. Then as the shell dangled from Toca's neck, swinging in his face, he focused in on it. His eyes went wide, putting everything together, seeing the shell, he said excitedly and louder, "You are Toca, you have come back from your Katata Ado!"

Toca looked down at what caught the man's eyes then looked back at him, still holding the knife to his throat, and said boldly, "I am Toca, the Black Ghost!" He paused then said proudly for the first time, "Chief of the Nashua!"

There was silence between the two men on the ground as they each went through their minds what each other said. They didn't realize the shaking of the earth and swaying of trees stopped as they were still in grips of each other.

The painted-faced man said, "Chief Jucawa said you never returned from your Katata Ado and you were dead."

This sparked a new fury in Toca as he replied, putting back the pressure he had earlier with his knife, "I did return on time before the thirteenth moon with a shell but Jucawa was there, not Chief Acuta! In the dark, Jucawa hit me on the head and beat me while I was not awake anymore. Then he stabbed me with his spear in the side." Toca let off on the pressure, just enough for the man to peer up at Toca's side which slightly had ripped open and was bleeding again.

As the man peered at all the semihealed injuries all over Toca, he was coming to a new realization as Toca finished sarcastically, "Then Jucawa must have dragged me to the river during the night to die. Do I look dead to you?"

The man shook his head no, not knowing what else to say or do or even believe. Jucawa had control over the people, treating them harshly when they didn't do what he wanted them to. In turn, he brainwashed them to believe everything he said which caused the people to blindly follow him and not question him. But now, this young man on him, ready to kill him, has said so few but powerful words. Not only did they sound truthful but felt like it.

The painted-faced man relaxed, knowing deep inside Toca could be trusted, and said, "My name is Cumonta, I am your mother's brother. I am your relative, Toca."

Toca peered at the man, trying to look past the black paint and the strange painted eyes. Mentally putting long hair on the man, he began to see his facial structure he remembered from thirteen moons ago. Toca, convinced he was his relative, said, "Relative or not, if you follow Jucawa, I will not hesitate to kill you like I will be killing him!" He pressed the knife hard back on the man's throat, narrowing his eyes, putting his face a breath away, letting his relative know he could die right now.

The man attempted to retreat but there was no room to move as his eyes went back and forth, looking for help, then Toca asked, "What is your decision?"

His relative's insides were churning, then out of nowhere, emotions began to take over, controlling his behavior as Toca noticed a tear slowly form then stream down his face as the man slowly spoke with a trembling chin. "Please help us, Toca, Jucawa is a crazy man!"

Surprised at the instant change, he didn't believe how the man was acting and didn't loosen up the pressure of the knife as the man's words began to flood out. "He has power over us we can't stop."

Toca sarcastically replied, "Jucawa has no power, he lives a lie!"

"He is very powerful, Toca, you don't know, you have been gone a long time."

"I know Jucawa!" Toca yelled out, then he looked around, making sure no one was around to hear him, then continued, "He beat me and my mother all the time and treated us like no one else in the tribe and you or no one else came to help us!"

"He did the greatest Katata Ado and was going to be next chief, we couldn't do anything."

"Yes, you could have. You even let him dishonor Chief Acuta, then made him leave the hidden valley!" Toca was getting angrier the more he talked until he said Chief Acuta's name. This took his mind back, seeing the chief, his father, with a spear in his back.

With urgency, he got back into the man's face, saying, "Chief Acuta made me chief of the Nashua. He didn't make Jucawa chief, Jucawa took it from him! That's not the Nashua way! I am your true chief and you will do as I tell you, Cumonta. Do you understand?" The man, stumped by this, had no other option, then agreed with Toca, nodding his head.

"Good, I will let you go and you will tell the other Nashua men what I have said. If you try to harm me or Chief Acuta, your sister, or my woman…" Slowly, with the deepest of anger, gritting his teeth, Cumonta began to see a Black Ghost come out of the man on top of him as Toca growled out, "I will kill you and every Nashua that follows Jucawa. On my Katata Ado, I killed many men, much bigger and stronger than you!" He paused to let what he said soak in, then suddenly pressed himself off Cumonta; and before he could finally take a deep breath, the Black Ghost disappeared.

*****

Shana and Layana were finally making it to the village. In anticipation of the unknown, Shana had already taken the machete out of its sheath as she followed Layana. Once at its edge, they stopped to look for the men. The village seemed to be void of life as there was no one to be seen and the morning fire was not going. Layana, familiar with her home was able to closely see details, as Shana was trying to absorb the actual scene of the whole surroundings, making the adjustments in her mind of the true arrangement of Toca's home. Focusing on something odd-shaped slumped on the ground near the firepit, Layana pointed out to Shana that it looked like a person sitting down.

Layana began to step out into the open but Shana held her back because she was not done being aware. Nothing alarmed her except for the silent noise, a colorless sight, and a balmy odor. The area had a sensation of old death that everything needed to be burned to be able to start over with fresh life. Just when Shana was going to push Layana forward, her eyes caught movement in the sky up near the high rim of the mountains. Dark clouds were quickly clustering together, crashing into each other in an erratic angry manner as they slowly began to hover over the edges of the valley. This massive display had the appearance of a dark blanket of doom being draped over the valley to smother it.

Suddenly a smaller white soft cloud separated itself from its large dark rumbling relative, moving in front, transforming itself into a completely different beautiful shape. Before Shana knew it, a silhouette of a flying horse appeared with broad wings and a tail stretching back out to the thundering dark clouds, as though it was pulling the blanket of doom over the hidden valley. The sun, now rising higher, peered over the other side of the valley's rim, beaming its light on the mystical beast of clouds, soaring with magnificence. Now glowing as it ran across the sky, even Layana couldn't help seeing the incredible vision. Blinking several times, thinking she was imaging this, she looked at Shana in awe. Shana had her head up but her eyes were closed as though she was talking to herself. Shana quickly opened her eyes, looking at Layana, staring at her, and said,

"We must hurry and get everyone out of the valley! God is going to destroy it! That is what's happening with the ground shaking."

Layana didn't saying anything, trying to comprehend what was said, glaring into Shana's eyes. Then she looked back up at the spectacular scene as it was dissolving back into formless shapes, blending back with the dark rumbling clouds, slowly pressing forward toward destruction. She worked her mind around the earth shaking and the cloud forming into a flying animal, pulling a fierce storm behind it. Along with all the chaos with Chief Acuta, Jucawa, and Toca, her female intuition was screaming to her that Shana was right, something beyond her is about to happen, then without hesitating, she said, "Let's go!"

The women made their way to the huts, moving their eyes from place to place to see someone or something that would tell them what was going on. Layana couldn't help herself and began whispering into huts for her friends as she passed by, making their way to the firepit, "Is anyone here?"

"Chief Acuta!" Shana exclaimed, scaring Layana, being shoulder to shoulder as they tiptoed their way. Then she ran to the slumped pile next to the firepit, seeing it clearly now as the chief. She was struck with horror, seeing a spear stuck in his back, coming out in front as he was kneeling in a pool of blood with his torso sitting straight up. Slowly and cautiously, she walked up to him as she gently whispered his name, "Chief Acuta…" Kneeling in front of him, Shana dropped the machete to the side, glaring in disbelief. She heard a soft thump and rustling of dirt behind her, then looked around as Layana had dropped to the ground on her knees as well, stunned at what she saw. Turning her head back to the old man, she could hear raspy breathing, then a groan of pain. He forcefully opened his eyes to see who was in front of him, then gave a small smile, closing his eyes again. Shana moved close to his side, gently touching his shoulder.

Feeling her hand, he leaned sideways into her as she then wrapped her arm around him, staring at the spearhead protruding from his stomach area, and said as she softly touched her forehead to the side of his, "Oh, Father, Chief Acuta, what happened?"

He weakly opened his eyes, turning his head to look at her, and asked, "Shana…is your God a good God?"

She was trying to be strong, blinking away emotions, and nodded.

Barely moving his lips, he asked, "What is its name?"

Such a simple question but one that had the most powerful answer, she encouragingly said, "His name is…*Jesus*."

"Jesus…Jesus." he repeated, slowly nodding his head yes.

Shana hugged the dying chief in her arms, which seemed to be a norm for her in her young life, and said, "You will see him soon in a better place with no pain because your spirit lives on, if you want to."

"That"—he coughed while wincing his face in pain—"would be good."

She paused to let her thoughts be right, then continued, "Jesus is the good God you have been looking for and he is here with us right now." This sparked a little energy in him as he glanced around the village with his head wobbling, trying to finally see this God. He stopped moving his head as a deep chuckle came out of him as his eyes seemed to be looking at someone in the distance. Shana looked in the direction he was facing but didn't see anyone as the chief mumbled, "Jesus, your God, is like the bright morning sun." He turned his head back to Shana, finishing, "He is like a new beginning."

Shana couldn't control herself as tears began to follow. Tears of sorrow but mostly tears of joy that Jesus showed himself, caring, in full love for this old skinny wrinkled man deep in the Amazon forest. Finally the purpose of why she and her father started this journey two sun seasons ago and what Toca was sent out to find had come full circle.

Shana gently touched the side of the chief's face, as his breathing became shallower, and said, "Jesus is waiting for you to go home with him. Reach inside from your heart and tell him you believe in him as your God. He is the only one that can save you and your people from dying off."

There was a moment of silence, then Shana moved her head around to see if he was still alive. Then she saw a small smile forming from the toothless mouth, telling her something was different about him. Then she added, "Jesus loves you so much, Chief Acuta. You *are*"—she emphasized—"the greatest chief the Nashua will ever have. Because you followed your heart to send Toca to find God to save your people. Now your people will have a chance to have Jesus in their lives and live. They will live with purpose because he will always inspire us to live for him. Giving us a new beginning with him every day."

She tilted her head on his that was now laid on her shoulder. Peace was blanketing over them as the air suddenly felt warm and light, easy to breathe. This opened the door of her heart to do what God blessed her with. Eyes closed with the chief's, humming began to come out from her, turning into soft flowing sounds from her mouth. The beautiful gentle words of a song worshiping and praising Jesus was soon heard, making its way to every part of the village.

Chief Acuta slowly moved his head to face Shana, saying with a smile, as she quieted down to hear him, "You are the songbird your God told me about." He closed his eyes for the final time, collapsing his whole small fragile body against her as it released his spirit to grasp the hand of Jesus to walk him home.

There was complete silence as though everything was holding its breath in the valley. Shana raised her head to look at Layana, still kneeling on the ground. Surprised, she saw many women standing with a red painted stripe around their heads with children that had made their way cautiously to the firepit, surrounding Layana. Then to her right, at the edge of the clearing of the village, movement of men with painted black faces and heads stepped out into the open, staring at her and Chief Acuta, who had been watching and listening as they hid in the forest.

Layana was the first to cry out from the death of her friend. Soon little by little, sorrowful wailing could be heard from everyone as they all went to their knees in respect but in more disbelief. The death of a person was always hard but this was the first time anyone of the present Nashua tribe in the hidden valley had seen someone die at the hands of another person.

Shana joined these new people to her in mourning, softly crying, but hers was with joy. Joy of knowing Chief Acuta was in heaven, joining her mother and father, walking hand in hand with Jesus. Toca had talked about him so much over the past sun season, it seemed she had known him all her life.

Totally out of place, yelling suddenly could be heard behind her up in the tribal hut. There were two voices and one she recognized, spouting out furiously, was her man, Toca. The other, she assumed, was Jucawa as his words and tone were that of retreating.

The yelling turned into noise of thumps and thuds of body weight being thrown and tossed onto the floor and against the walls. Everyone could only see shadows darting here and there inside the dark large hut. Shana knew what was happening as urgency erupted out of her to help her man. Standing, lowering the chief's body to the ground, she turned, grasping the machete and started to run up to the fighting. But before actually taking a step, the scuffling instantly stopped as a man's voice squealed out in dying pain. Every Nashua, including Shana, inhaled deeply with despair, knowing someone was just killed—but who? Shana took a few steps toward the hut as she was grabbed by the arm. She turned to see Layana by her side, they looked with hopelessness into each other's eyes, not knowing who would walk out of the entrance. Hearing something from the tribal hut, they looked back up just in time to see a man slowly walk to the entrance, stopping, looking out to the village.

Shana began to scream in horror as everyone else cowardly looked away, whispering to each other. Layana's face went blank, losing all emotions, then grabbed the machete out of Shana's hand and started running, shrieking at Jucawa standing in the doorway with his black jaguar hood over his face. Just before she got to the steps, he suddenly leaped out in the air toward her. She stopped just in time as he missed her, hitting the ground flat on his face. She saw her opportunity, grasping the machete in both hands, raising it behind her head to take a full swing down on his neck. Hesitating for him to look up so he would see his death coming but nothing happened. He just laid there, lifeless. Hearing the sounds of footsteps walking on a bamboo floor, Layana looked up to see her son standing tall, boldly peering out to his people. He had given Jucawa the death blow with his father's knife. As Jucawa had stumbled to the doorway, grasping for life, Toca kicked him in the back, shooting him out of the hut, dead in front of his mother as a gift.

It went silent in the village, then joyous words could be heard as the Nashua pointed up at a new man, in awe of killing the powerful Jucawa. This time, there was no wailing of sadness, but soon, cheers of freedom were echoing throughout the village.

Toca stepped down from the hut and bent over, pulling the black jaguar skin off Jucawa's body. As he looked up to the spot where Chief Acuta lay, he took his father's knife, still in his hands, and began cutting and ripping the cat hide into pieces, tossing them on the corpse beside him.

When he finished, he walked over to the chief's body and slowly took the spear out, then cradled him up in his arms, standing. The Nashua had slowly gathered around the scene where death had occurred twice. With his arms firmly holding the chief, he shouted out, intently glaring at everyone, "I am Toca, the Black Ghost, son of Tundra, son of Layana, and"—he paused, making sure he had everyone's attention, then looked down in his arms—"son of Chief Acuta." Looking up, he continued, "I hold in my arms the greatest of all Nashua chiefs. He chose me to be the next chief of our people because I completed my Katata Ado." He turned, pointing with his head, looking at the ground. "Unlike that dead liar who stabbed my father, Tundra, in the back, who was a real Nashua man that completed the Katata Ado, not him." Pausing, he looked around as the men had gathered around their wives and children. Toca saw in their eyes, Cumonta had told them what he said to tell them. Then he gave a slight head nod to each man as they stared at their new chief, nodding back, agreeing with the change of events.

Taking a deep breath of relief, the atmosphere swiftly had become peaceful and calm. Toca looked next to him where his woman, dressed with a colorful jaguar skin, was proudly standing, admiring her man taking control. Thinking to herself, the Katata Ado truly does exactly as it was intended to do—create a strong, respectable, and wise man out of an old child who is able to be an honorable chief.

Toca looked away back to his people, eyeing him for instructions of what they were to do now. Completely changing the subject, Toca's first direction as their chief was, "Hiding in this valley is no longer a new beginning but has become an ending grave. We must leave now before it is too late and find a new home!" Shana and Layana quickly glanced at each other, then back to him in disbelief, thinking to themselves, *How does he know*?

Seeing their expression, he said with a smile, "I saw the cloud shaped like a flying animal as you did, pulling dark destruction over the valley as God said to me, 'It's time for the Nashua to stop hiding and start living a new beginning of purpose with their loving God. You must leave the valley now!'"

Hesitating for a moment, reflecting back to his Katata ceremony thirteen moons ago, looking down at the old withered dead chief in his arms, he said, "You inspired me with your love for your people by following your heart to save them." Looking at Shana, he added, "And this good God has inspired me, over thirteen moons, that no matter how impossible anything got for us, he made it all possible. Especially right now, a new beginning for the Nashua to come out of the shadows."

ABOUT THE AUTHOR

Everyday life is seen through the lens of circumstances, situations, or as a story. Very few people have the vision to see life as a story and fewer can tell the story. D. L. Crager is one of those few individuals that can tell a story and tell it with memorable grandeur and excitement that will take you into another world.

D. L. Crager continues to live an adventurous life with his wonderful wife, Shelly, their kids, and grandchildren in the northwest. He is a successful businessman, an avid outdoorsman, and is very involved with his church family. He has profound stories to tell that will powerfully move and excite everyone's ordinary world when they read his books filled with adventure, mystery, and relational growth. His goal is to be extraordinary in all that he does; his mission is his relationship with Jesus Christ.